Behind him,  picking up it

Ten yards was an uncanny silence which lasted for the smallest part of a second, followed by a heart-rending explosion which shattered the night. A heavy wave of concussed air blasted across the field, lifting Fitzgerald off his feet and hurling him to the ground. He wiped the dirt from his mouth as he picked himself up and continued walking. The sixty-thousand dollar fire raged behind him. Sixty thousand dollars and no insurance.

Chance Fitzgerald was wearing his customary smile when he said: 'Damned airplanes. Just like women . . . unreliable.'

THE FIFTH
FREEDOM

John Templeton Smith

SPHERE BOOKS LIMITED

For Michael Sissons

SPHERE BOOKS LTD

Published by the Penguin Group
27 Wrights Lane, London W8 5TZ, England
Viking Penguin Inc., 40 West 23rd Street, New York, New York 10010, USA
Penguin Books Australia Ltd, Ringwood, Victoria, Australia
Penguin Books Canada Ltd, 2801 John Street, Markham, Ontario, Canada L3R 1B4
Penguin Books (NZ) Ltd, 182–190 Wairau Road, Auckland 10, New Zealand

Penguin Books Ltd, Registered Offices: Harmondsworth, Middlesex, England

First published by Michael Joseph Ltd, 1988
Published by Sphere Books Ltd, 1989
1 3 5 7 9 10 8 6 4 2

Printed and bound in Great Britain by
Richard Clay Ltd, Bungay, Suffolk

Acknowledgements

My grateful thanks to the following people who greatly helped in the researching of this book.

To my friend Michael Collett, Coventry – who preserves history with his unique airline, Air Atlantique – for suggesting the title.

To Jack O'Sullivan, Jersey – the flying doctor – for his continuing help with medical details.

To Vincent Paver, Guernsey, for the fascinating insight on explosives.

To the management of the Hotel Metropole, Geneva, for the splendid service on my many visits.

To my friend and colleague of many years, Randy Plant, Oklahoma, who talked me through a float plane take-off.

To Master A. L. M. Andy Payne, 242 OCU, RAF Lyneham for the useful tips on the Hercules.

To Mike Willett, Civil Aviation Authority, London, who doubtless remembers our long-ago airline days, for defining the freedoms of the air as laid out at the Chicago Conference of 1944.

To Alan Herd, New Zealand, who unwittingly set the Khartoum scene more than a decade ago.

And finally to my many aviating friends around the globe who continually offer criticism, advice and support; for they are the ones who live the adventure.

Man's life so little worth,
do we fear to take or lose it?
No ill companion on a journey, Death
lays his purse on the table and opens the wine.

BASIL BUNTING
'The Spoils'

The Freedoms of the Air:
The *fifth freedom* is the right to fly into the
territory of the grantor state, and take on or
set down traffic to or from third states. This
right is, however, confined to services which
originate or terminate in the territory of the
carrier's flag state or which serve its flag
state as an intermediate stop . . .

International Civil Aviation Conference,
Part 1, Final Act and Appendices I–IV,
Chicago, 7 December 1944

PROLOGUE

28 November

Milan, Italy

FRIDAY 0540 HOURS

SEAN EUGENE FITZGERALD would have preferred to die in a high night sky. Stars twinkling like an inverted Broadway. Soft moonglow. Silent jet streams carrying him across an uncharted ocean. In that place he had always belonged. Down here, he had never possessed the same confidence. Now, however, it didn't seem to matter. The last battle had been fought. The woman had taken the holdall containing the eighteen million dollars and the dark shape of the man had raised his gun to the aim.

The aviator glanced skyward, searching for a break in the snow clouds. It was as though he was seeking one last glimpse of his own little corner of heaven.

8 October

Geneva, Switzerland

WEDNESDAY 1125 HOURS

THE TERRACE OF the Hotel Metropole breathed that calm serene beauty which lent moments of peace to the restless soul of Otto von Klaus. Tormented by the memory of a wretched childhood in early post-war Munich; of being clothed in threadbare rags; of body lice; of running sores which never seemed to heal; of too much watered-down potato soup; he now lived a life of excess in all things. All things but one. He retained his anonymity; wore it like some vast, impregnable suit of armour; his past locked away from those who may seek to pry.

His emotionless grey eyes panned unseeingly across the lake and the small white yachts searching for a gust of wind. They also failed to take in the splendid flowers and trees of the Jardin Anglais directly across the Quai Général-Guisan; or the impeccable waiters serving tea in delicate porcelain cups. The two veiled Arab women in black chadors sitting silently and still might also have existed on some other plane. For Otto von Klaus the unusually warm autumn day and the tranquil elegance of the Metropole was nothing more than a momentary escape from his offices in the Place Bel-Air, and the dozen telephone lines which burned up more air time in a day than the average Swiss family did in a year. It was also a few moments of blissful silence to ponder the wisdom of arms dealing with Iran. The facts, already assembled in his well-ordered mind, presented themselves one by one.

5

IRAN: A country that has not 'legally' received US weapons since the takeover by the Ayatollah Khomeini in 1979.

SULIMAN: The man from Iran. Description: cruel, dark, swarthy features. Hawklike nose. Right eye missing. Wears black eye-patch. Lean, hard physique. Age: difficult to assess; 35–40–50? Profession: probably ex-soldier. One who had done his fair share of fighting with Iraq! Now, buying agent for the Iranian government. Has shopping list for weapons, which includes procurement of one Lockheed Hercules C–130 transport plane. Financial: seems to have access to unlimited funds, a high percentage of which is in Europe. Marital status: according to Sudanese passport which he travels on he is single. The passport is of course a forgery. Hobbies: likes the nightclubs and gambling and alcohol, and the pretty young girls. General: an unknown quantity. Dark and dangerous. The type who may well put a knife in your back for no other reason than a rainy Tuesday (he had voiced a strong dislike of the European weather). Method of contact: directly to one of von Klaus's companies in Monaco. A company which supplied auto spares to Iran via various backdoors.

HARDWARE: Lockheed Hercules C–130 aircraft. Country of origin – USA. Extensively used by US military forces as well as other military establishments throughout the Western world. Therefore must be classified under 'weapons' status.

QUESTION: What did he – Otto von Klaus – know about aircraft?

ANSWER: Technically nothing. Financially – high capital cost moveable asset.

REQUIREMENT: One aviation expert. Must be discreet with no ties, family or otherwise. A shadowy figure to counter similar shadowy figures who may suddenly materialise when a large four-engined military aircraft of US manufacture is transferred to a foreign registry.

FINANCE: Could cause problems. Letters of credit against an Iranian bank were practically worthless. Cash would be the only way – black market dollars. And as any good dishonest businessman knows, vast amounts of black market money attracts the underworld. The crooks who deal in the stuff.

CONCLUSION: Dangerous. Too many risks. Too many chinks in the armour. Too far across the thin red line which divides honesty and dishonesty; legality and illegality. Shelve indefinitely.

With the seemingly easy decision made to drop the deal, von Klaus's eyes refocused on the present and the Kir Royale before him. The champagne was flat by now but he drank it anyway, then extracted an oval Turkish cigarette from a gold cigarette case and lit it. He coughed as the smoke caught in the back of his throat and made a mental note to cut down on his sixty cigarettes a day consumption. It was a resolve he made often. One he never kept. He sat a few minutes longer, enjoying the soothing qualities of nicotine on the nervous system before counting out the exact change for his drink on to the starched white table-cloth. With that done, he checked his blue silk Dior tie was in place, straightened the lapels of his lightweight grey suit, and easing his overweight frame out of the chair, walked with hurried little footsteps towards the roof door which led to the elevator.

By the time he had walked the short distance down the Rue du Rhône to his office in the Place Bel-Air, a plan was formulating in his mind. It was something he had never considered before, being too wrapped up in his work, too involved in the process of making money. Of putting a fortune between himself and the past. Now he realised he was there. Had been for years. He was worth millions. He would never have to beg, or clothe himself in rags, or eat wurst or potato soup again. No, a man with all the money he had acquired could live in luxury for the rest of his life. He went straight to his inner office and buzzed his secretary.

Lisa Wendell-Holmes was a total career person. Had been for the past three years; ever since the death of her husband. Then financial circumstances had forced her back to work, not that she minded having to pick up the threads of an old and almost forgotten life; in a way, it was a kind of therapy. A way to work off the hurt that came to her during the long and lonely nights. As for new relationships, she had avoided them like the plague. Losing her husband had caused more pain than she thought she could bear. She was not going to go through that again. Simple as that. There were no regrets however. Well, perhaps occasionally during the long winter nights; then it would be nice to have the company of a man. A voice to talk to. Someone to make supper for.

She was an extremely attractive forty-two years of age and possessed energy and elegance, as well as a vision of clean neatness which looked as if it had just arrived from a beauty parlour. Her blonde hair was pulled back and rolled in a chignon, a black velvet ribbon adding the final touch.

She had been with Otto von Klaus's company for three years and was, above all else, responsible for the German's present good fortune. Apart from the usual assets of any competent executive secretary, she was blessed with an unusually brilliant business sense. Her grasp of any new company project — from water boreholes in Nigeria to desalination technology in Dhoa — was in most ways superior to that of her employer. In fact, Otto von Klaus was typical of the majority of self-made men. He simply employed the brains, used their ideas — which he claimed were his own — and at the same time paid the lowest going rate. When the brains decided they had been exploited for long enough they moved on. Von Klaus then rehired; always using the same wordy inducements for future advancement and limitless earnings. The promises were as hollow as the man.

'And how was the Metropole?' Lisa enquired, sitting down on the opposite side of the vast mahogany desk.

'The Metropole!' he replied, lighting a cigarette and pausing to cough. 'The Metropole is still the same. Only in Switzerland could they take an empty fifth-floor roof, fill it with plants and tables and chairs and cheap imported waiters, and charge twice the amount for a mediocre champagne as they do in the ground-floor bar. You of course know what they are selling?' Lisa shook her head, even though she had heard it all before. 'They are selling silence. Or as near to silence as this city can offer . . . next I think it will be the air we breathe.'

He stopped talking and swivelled his chair towards the window. There was nothing to see, except the grey concrete walls and glinting windows of other offices. It was, he suddenly decided, very much like a prison. He had exchanged one kind of poverty for another. The urge to escape was as strong as it had been in those bleak, bitter days just after the war. He turned back to the desk and placed his cigarette in a glass ashtray at his right hand.

'I have been thinking of the companies,' he said, matter of factly. 'I am going to sell out . . . retire.'

'Retire?' the word echoed from Lisa's lips with disbelief. 'When? When will this be?'

Von Klaus picked up his cigarette and inspected it for a moment. 'Straightaway, I think. Once I have assessed the current worth. You need not worry over your job though, I will still need a private secretary . . . you will work for me of course!' It was more of a command than a request.

Lisa gave a small, frozen smile. 'Yes of course . . . however, I think your timing may be a little imprudent if you are thinking of selling the companies on the open market.'

Von Klaus looked up sharply. 'Imprudent! How do you mean imprudent?'

'The five town electrification project in Nigeria is still waiting government approval, and even then we will need to get the letter of credit cleared through the Standard Bank in Lagos. Other European companies have been waiting up to two years for payment.'

'One company, one contract,' von Klaus snapped. 'Our group has a great deal to offer to the right buyer.'

Lisa pressed on. 'Then there's the desalination contract in Dhoa. With the recent cutback in oil prices, the "desert greening" programme has already suffered a major setback. If oil drops much further we could end up losing quite heavily.'

Von Klaus stubbed out his cigarette and placed his fat white hands on the desk before him. He inspected the well-manicured nails for a moment, frowning at the dark brown nicotine stains on the first and second fingers of his right hand.

'Maybe so,' he said at length, 'but it is only swings and roundabouts as you English say. Long term we have a very saleable group of companies.'

'You intend to sell out the entire group! Why not just the poor performers?'

'No, Lisa. All, everything. It is over . . . today I decided against a deal which would make the company perhaps millions. Once I would not have thought twice about it. And I also said that once the gambling instinct goes it is time to get out.' He pulled himself out of his chair and paced thoughtfully across the room. 'So, what do you think the current worth of the group is?'

For a while she did not reply. She was thinking, wondering why the German race were so one-geared. Their harsh strident voices she didn't mind. Their automaton-like efficiency she admired. But there had been times she had wished for a moment or two of gentleness. After all, he was selling out her future as well. Three years of promises of a directorship in one of the companies; of salary increases which had never quite materialised. Promises of a company car; she still used her own for company business and paid the bills from her own inadequate pay cheque.

'Well?' von Klaus's voice lifted impatiently.

'Current worth!' Lisa said absently. 'Difficult to assess. N.L.T. in Paris would of course be interested in taking over the group; but you know Alain . . . the original Parisian Jew. I think he would offer as low as fifteen millions; based on the last set of audit figures, that is.'

'Dollars?'

'Swiss francs.'

The German's eyebrows shot up. 'Swiss francs! For everything . . . the Gibralter company as well?'

'And the fifty per cent holdings in London and Nigeria.'

'Not enough,' von Klaus snapped. 'You think I have worked day and night for thirty-five years ever since I was a boy for that. No, fifteen million is far from enough.'

Lisa felt like saying, 'Not enough for what?', but knew

that flippancy aggravated her employer. She would let him stew in his own juice for a while. He might even come back to her tomorrow and casually remark that the idea was, in his considered and expert opinion, a little irrational at this moment in time. She would nod agreement and say something about the wisdom of his decisions.

'I'll leave it with you for today then,' she said. 'After that I can call Henry in London and ask him to fly out for a meeting . . . should you decide to go ahead, that is.'

'Yes, yes,' von Klaus replied dismissively. 'I will think about it. Now leave me.'

Once Lisa had returned to the outer office, the German rubbed his face tiredly with both hands, then returned to his chair. Worn red leather edged with brass studs. One of his first possessions. Something which had followed him around Europe. From office to office, town to town, country to country. With any other man it might have represented a lucky omen. A nostalgic yesterday. To the overweight German it was just so much flotsam. A few Swiss francs at the end of numerous pages of inventory.

The remainder of the afternoon passed quickly, with von Klaus throwing himself into his work with a greater amount of zeal than usual. At five o'clock he considered his earlier discussion with Lisa. He was certain her figures were wrong. After all she was merely a woman, a secretary. He knew better. He was after all the brains behind the organisation. The man who had made it all possible. One hour later at precisely six o'clock he pushed the papers aside and made a few short entries in his pocket diary. It was a habit he had picked up over the years. It was an instant record. A log of his movements and more important business dealings. At the end of each year he would make a summary and transfer it, along with the new year's resolutions, to his new diary.

With that done he lit a cigarette and went across the room to the drinks cabinet. One Johnny Walker Red Label with lots of water. His six o'clock Englishness, Lisa had once called it. Not that he minded her sometimes mindless prattle; anyway he was not very nationalistic and Germany

11

belonged to another lifetime, the one he had locked away inside his head.

Sitting with the whisky in his hand he started thinking about all the free time he would have. He realised he had never taken a holiday in his life. Not that he resented the fact. Holidays had always been for ordinary people. The people with too little ambition. They spent the money they earned and that way never accumulated sufficient to become really wealthy. The German had realised from the outset that you had to make money work for you. Pfennigs made pfennigs if used wisely.

So, he thought, holidays! Where to go? He did not have an answer to that question, but consoled himself with the thought that Lisa would know.

He half smiled. Yes, she had been one of his better investments. Hard working. Uncomplaining. Her cool English image also produced loyalty; something which was hard to find these days. A pity about her aloof manner though. It had been three years since her husband Philip had been killed in the car crash, and it was only because the young man had worked hard for Otto that he even considered offering her a job. Well, perhaps there had been personal reasons. She was, after all, a beautiful woman; a little stern perhaps, but still beautiful. And she did have very shapely legs. Not that he had ever got any further than simply admiring them from a discreet distance. It seemed she had a heart of stone. He dismissed the thoughts from his mind. It was no use dwelling on something which was unobtainable. Anyway, wasn't today Wednesday? His night to visit Marie in the old town. A faint spark lit up his small grey eyes. Now, she had a heart that was anything but stone. He drew deeply on his cigarette and started coughing.

In Gloucestershire, England, it was night. Graveyard dark. A cold front lay down the western side of the British Isles, bringing gale force winds and driving rain. It was not a night for flying. Especially in light twin-engined airplanes. And especially not for over seven hours from Staverton to Iceland. However, for Sean Eugene Fitzgerald, Chance to his friends, it was simply work. Not his usual kind, but as his last job in Nicaragua had nearly ended in death at the hands of the country's Sandinista rulers, this was a welcome departure. An easy way to make money. Only the weather to think about. No guns, no missiles. Could catch on, he reasoned, as he taxied the aircraft on to the runway. Could have found the way to last the duration. He smiled at the thought. Not enough adrenalin in just flying, Chance; it's for the birds and those nice clean-cut career guys. Now you, you're an aerial gypsy. An outcast. You belonged to the twenties and thirties, the old barnstorming days. Flying the night mail with 'Lucky' Lindbergh. You're a silk-scarf-and-goggles jockey looking for new ground to break. Frontiers to open. Except you're about fifty years too late. Now they've taken all the romance away, handed it over to the computerised logic boards of the civil service, where grey little people invent grey little rules. Now they've built airplanes that are real safe. The risk, the element of danger, it's gone. Extinct! Just like you, Fitzgerald. You're a dodo. An obsolete aviator. An out of place, out of time, genealogical misnomer.

Fitzgerald smiled, a quick easy movement which shadowed the laughter lines around his eyes. Then he was running through the pre-take-off checks, his long elegant fingers caressing switches and levers as gently and lovingly as they would any beautiful woman. A final reassuring glance with the aid of a flashlight back into the cabin of the Navajo, at the two fifty-five-gallon tanks lashed securely to the floor – the extra fuel to enable him to reach Reykjavik in one hop – and it was time to go.

He opened the throttles smoothly, his eyes taking in the manifold pressures and r.p.m.s, and anything else that could be red-lined. All normal. Brakes off. The Navajo accelerated sluggishly down the black shining tarmac. Rain built up in wavy pressure patterns on the windshield, diffusing the runway lights into small exploding yellow flowers. At 100 m.p.h. and no more flowers, Fitzgerald hauled the aircraft off the ground into a slow lumbering climb.

'Was that enough adrenalin?' Fitzgerald asked himself. 'Never even broke sweat.'

'How about the high ground? Lot of it hereabouts.'

'Night separation!' he answered himself.

'Night separation . . . what's that?'

'Night! Dark! Therefore I cannot see the outside world. *Ergo* I am safe.'

'You're crazy.'

'That as well. Goes with the lifestyle.'

Fitzgerald's habit of talking to himself or the airplane was interrupted by the Staverton controller asking him to change frequencies to London and wishing him a safe flight. He thanked the man and selected the London frequency.

'London, good evening. Delta Foxtrot's on frequency, passing two thousand for eight zero.'

There was a moment's pause before an attractive female voice came back, 'Good evening, Delta Foxtrot, squawk ident and proceed direct Wallasey.'

Fitzgerald acknowledged. Nice voice. Blonde, brunette or redhead? Slim figure perhaps. Attractive? Sure to be with a voice like that. And therein lies the tragedy. You cannot have a love affair with a voice. Or can you? The aircraft hit the turbulence before he found the answer.

In pilot terminology there are three kinds of turbulence. 'Light' – when the coffee in the first-class section measures it as a slight ripple. 'Moderate' – when loose articles start their own flying lessons. 'Severe' – when the aircraft is out of control for fifty per cent of the time. It is also when the instrument panel vibrates with so much violence that the instruments become unreadable.

The turbulence that night was of the latter variety. Fitzgerald gritted his teeth and fought silently with the controls. No bullets, no missiles, eh, Chance . . . just weather . . . think wars are nicer! He managed a grim little smile before knocking on the wing inspection lights. Right on cue – ice! It was going to be that kind of night. Rough and uncomfortable. Maybe seven and a half hours of black friendless night; radio-warped voices; intense mental concentration; posture-related body cramps; adrenalin by the bucketful, and sometimes – just sometimes – heartache.

It was two minutes later, as Fitzgerald was fighting the

weather towards his cruising level of eight thousand feet, that the heartache sought him out. It was easier to pick out than the visual, for that you needed to be looking in the right direction. This was aromatic. The wrong kind of aromatic! Suddenly it filled his head, plummeting him to the roots of his being; his whole life verticalised by a fleeting sensation. Avgas! High octane petrol. The stuff that went into the tanks. It registered about one milli-second later. He swung round in his seat, the flashlight from his side pocket already in his hand. He snicked it on and shone it back into the cabin.

For a moment his heart stopped. Fuel was gushing from the side of one of the internal tanks. He couldn't tell if it was a seam which had fractured due to it being pounded against the steel restraining cables, or whether a connection had come adrift. Either way it didn't matter. What did was that highly inflammable petrol was swilling around the cabin floor. And all he could do was watch. He considered engaging the auto-pilot and going back to try and stem the flood, but auto-pilots could accidently disengage. There had been a story running around southern Texas a few years earlier of a pilot who went back into the cabin to play poker with three passengers in an airplane not dissimilar in size to this one. The autopilot had somehow tripped out, putting the aircraft into a gentle descent. The pilot was found in the wreckage, still in the back of the plane, clutching five court cards. It seemed he had the winning hand.

With a knot of fear growing inside his stomach, Fitzgerald turned back to the instruments and the more immediate job of keeping the aircraft right side up. The flashlight was still in his hand. His thumb moved to the switch to turn it off and stopped. Electrical switches can generate small sparks. And small sparks in a small airplane full of gasoline suddenly became a dangerous and unlovable combination. He placed the flashlight down between the pilots' seats and tried to fight off the nausea caused by inhaling toxic fumes.

The stopwatch said eight minutes. Eight minutes since leaving the Staverton runway. He turned the aircraft back on to a reciprocal heading. Now it was eight minutes to get back. Eight minutes! Four hundred and eighty seconds to sit inside a time bomb, surrounded by looms of electrical cable which at that very moment were charged with electrical current. Four hundred and eighty seconds to work out which switches and levers had to be activated for landing. Not normally a problem, except this time you had to visualise which one might produce the unwanted spark, the catalyst which would serve to scatter you and your airplane into a million incandescent pieces over the earth below.

Sweat began collecting on Fitzgerald's forehead, running down his cheeks in rivulets. He bit his lower lip in a moment's concentration and felt the blood run warm and faintly comforting in his mouth. His left thumb hovered over the radio transmit button, preparing for the first action. Press and hold, that's all you have to do, he told himself. Press and hold and talk. Press and hold and talk into the latest style of revolver. Russian roulette with a difference! Played high in a stormy night sky; locked inside a tiny capsule full of dancing instruments and sweat corroded switches. And the switches are the triggers. Push the wrong one and the bullet smashes into your skull. And even if you are lucky and avoid the killing switch, there is still a catch. Two engine-driven alternators pushing electricity all around you. And one wire shaken loose by the turbulence produces the bullet you didn't expect.

Fitzgerald closed his eyes and thumbed the transmit switch. Nothing happened. No Elysian fields, no whiter than white angels, no golden gate leading to Valhalla; nothing but the muted buzz of a carrier wave in his headset. 'Mayday, mayday, mayday . . . Delta Foxtrot . . . position sixteen miles north-west Staverton . . . descending through five zero . . . we have a slight fuel problem . . . returning Staverton. Be advised cannot transmit after this call . . . will listen out this frequency for landing instructions; ETA Staverton zero eight . . . this is Mayday Delta Foxtrot.'

Now the second action. Release the switch! The aircraft hit a particularly bad patch of rough air in that passing second and Fitzgerald's thumb was jarred away from the switch before he had realised it. The London controller

16

came back immediately, clearing him down to three thousand feet and asking him to stand by for further instructions. The attractive female voice had, however, been replaced. The voice was now cold and uninteresting. A fifty-year-old bald guy with a paunch and an ugly wife, not to mention the soul-destroying shift work and perhaps the beginning of an ulcer. Then again, he might have been an ex-pilot. They were the worst. Resentful and jealous of those guys who were still up there in the best place God made.

Sliding down the unfriendly sky Fitzgerald noticed, as if for the first time, the transponder. One of those sophisticated bits of equipment that sent radar pulses to the ground controller's radar screen. And every pulse was highlighted by an amber filament, a flashing bulb which meant short bursts of electrical energy. Dangerous. Bloody dangerous! To switch the equipment off meant moving a single switch through three positions. Three more bullets! Conversely, to leave it on would mean maybe another three hundred flashes before landing. Three bullets or three hundred? He reached forward and twisted the switch all the way to off. A quick teeth-gripping action. Three empty chambers clicking in his ear in a split second. He wiped the sweat from his eyes and slumped back in his seat, flying the aircraft by instinct and trying to recall what he had missed. It was always the way; he knew that from experience. It would be the simplest of things in the end. That one basic everyday action; the one he couldn't remember. The one which would kill him.

The avgas fumes were causing tears to run in a continuous stream down his cheeks. His vision was heavily impaired as he left the radio beacon to commence the final let-down. He still hadn't heard from London with the landing clearance. Perhaps he was too low to receive them now! It made no difference; one way or another he was going in.

'So how's it looking?' he asked himself.

'Fine, just fine. Eyes burning like hell. Another five minutes of this and I really will be regretting I never took up Braille.'

'Nice to hear you've still got your sense of humour.'

'Humour! Who said anything about humour? Insanity maybe.'

'Aviator's sickness you mean. So what's left?'

'Just the landing gear.'

'Any chance of a spark?'

'Hell I don't know . . . haven't flown one of these crates for ten or more years.'

'OK, how about the flaps?'

'We'll do without.'

'Landing lights?'

'I can hardly see the instruments, why should I worry about lighting up the outside world!'

'So it's just the wheels . . . one lever.'

'Check . . . one lever.'

'Best of luck.'

'No problem, I'm invincible . . . didn't I ever tell you?'

'Yeah, that's what I mean, best of luck.'

Fitzgerald made a conscious effort to relax as he eased the Navajo down through the black screaming night. The worst, it seemed, was over. Except for the foul-tasting bile climbing up his throat and the white-hot pokers driving into his eyes.

According to the stopwatch there was one minute to go. Two miles at approach speed. He reached forward to lower the landing gear, had, in fact, commenced the cycle of pulling the handle out before pushing it hard down, when he stopped. Four hidden bullets smiled innocently back at him. Four inert light bulbs. Inert until he moved the handle. The first, a red, indicating undercarriage unlocked and moving. The other three – greens – telling the pilot wheels were down and locked.

Fitzgerald hurriedly unscrewed them and dropped them on to the co-pilot's seat. Then, hand on lever . . . out . . . and down. No sparks, no explosion. The aircraft slipped out of the dark rain cloud, the runway one mile dead ahead. A blurred vision of dancing yellow runway lights. Nothing to it, Fitzgerald said to himself, just drop it in between the lights and pray to God the wheels are where they are supposed to be. The seconds unfolded in the usual night landing way. The illusion of being suspended in a lunatic rocking chair. Wind, rain and engine noise. The dropping down to the black void between the parallel rows of lights. Then, with no landing lights of your own to pick out segments of the runway, the slight checking back on the control column. Watching the line of lights down the left side suddenly rush into a continuous yellow line. That final acceleration of earth which told you you were only feet away from touchdown.

The wheels hit once, bounced and settled. Then Fitzgerald was standing on the brakes, bringing the machine to a juddering stop less than half-way down the runway; well away from any buildings. If there was going to be an explosion at this late stage of the proceedings he wanted to make sure there were no innocent bystanders caught up in the ensuing fireball.

He was reaching for the mixture controls to kill the engines when the one simple everyday action – the one he had been unable to remember – greeted him. Stopping engines would produce two more clicks of the chamber. Two more bullets. Two red lights. Alternator failure warning. He reached down and unscrewed the left one. The other, the right, was locked solid. Corroded, cross-threaded, it didn't matter, it wouldn't move. He pulled the left mixture to idle cut-off and waited until the engine had stopped. Then he unstrapped himself and went back into the cabin and lowered the rear door, throwing his holdall out at the same time. Still choking on the fumes he went back to the cockpit, reached down between the pilots' seats and placed the right engine fuel selector lever to off. He didn't know how much time he had before the fuel remaining in the line was consumed, but within seconds he was out of the plane, walking quickly across the grass.

The rain on his face felt good, like the clean night air which washed into his lungs. Away in the distance the lights of the small terminal building flickered a welcome. Behind him, the aircraft's engine missed a beat before picking up its former low burbling note.

Now in the distance blue flashing lights were swinging away from the buildings. Fire trucks. Ten yards further and the engine noise behind him died. There was an uncanny silence which lasted for the smallest part of a second, followed by a heart-rending explosion which shattered the night. A heavy wave of concussed air blasted across the field, lifting Fitzgerald off his feet and hurling him to the ground. He wiped the dirt from his mouth as he picked himself up and continued walking, his holdall slung across his right shoulder. The sixty-thousand dollar fire raged behind him. Sixty thousand dollars and no insurance.

Chance Fitzgerald was wearing his customary smile when he said: 'Damned airplanes. Just like women ... unreliable.'

In Geneva it was also night, an autumn chill in the air. A thin mist drifted silently off the lake, softening the sharp contours of buildings along the left bank, emptying the streets from the Quai Général-Guisan to the western end of the Rue du Stand. It was the same up the hill towards the old town, with the exception of two slow-moving figures thirty metres apart.

Joaquim Matos would have been a handsome young man had life dealt him a kinder hand. A bottle fight with a sailor in Lisbon had left him permanently disfigured; a long ugly scar ran from the corner of his left eye, down his cheek, to his lower jaw. His dark features were set in a deeply etched scowl as he followed the other figure up the hill.

Until seven days earlier Matos had been employed as a waiter in a small but select restaurant on the Route de Florissant. It had been a busy night, the chef shorthanded in the kitchen and two waiters absent due to illness. This had resulted in Matos working a double shift. It was therefore understandable, to him at least, that by the end of the day he would be on the verge of exhaustion. And exhaustion, like hunger, brought on irritability in the young Portuguese. So it was that when the fat German caused a scene over the 'langosta asada' – ignoring pleas that the lobster was fresh – Matos grew angry. Not that he actually hit the abusive fat man, although his clenched fists were never far from it. It was more the wild and dangerous gleam in the waiter's eyes that silenced the German. But only temporarily.

The German, it seemed, had influence in certain quarters, not least with the owners of the restaurant. Matos was fired the following morning. To Joaquim Matos, however, it was more than losing his job. It was losing a lifeline to survival. Survival for himself, his wife, and their three-year-old son. For the past six days the Portuguese had walked the Geneva streets from dawn to dusk seeking employment, but it was a bad time of year for work in the hotel and catering trade. Now with only twenty-four hours remaining before his Swiss landlord evicted him and his family from their rented rooms, his mind was fixed on a single purpose – revenge.

Otto von Klaus, unaware that he was being followed, coughed and wheezed his way up the Rue du Puit-Saint-Pierre. Eventually, having paused more than once to catch his breath, he moved past the darkened shape of the old armoury and its collection of antique cannons. The cadence of his footsteps increased as he turned right into the level Grande Rue. Even up here, it seemed the mist had followed him. He saw it now as a faint blue-grey smoke caught in the yellow lights of the many antique shops which twisted with the narrow cobbled streets. It was as he slipped into an alleyway a hundred metres further on that Joaquim Matos made his move.

'Stop!' Matos screamed. His voice, trapped in the narrow confines of grey concrete, seemed ten times louder than he had intended.

Von Klaus swung round, his face pale and taut. He backed hesitantly away as his eyes focused disbelievingly on the glinting knife blade extending from the man's hand. There was a long moment of surprise, of not comprehending the reality of the situation. The end of that long moment was given over to fear. To a weakening of the bladder. To a chill mask of perspiration. To an increased heart rate. Even the words in his throat seemed to be dying of fright. His fat white hands crept defensively forward in a vain attempt to guard his enormous stomach, while his feet shuffled inevitably backwards. His bladder weakened further and started to give way. Forcing his thighs together in an attempt to avoid disgracing himself seemed to have the effect of freeing his speech.

'What . . . what do you want? . . . money?'

'Money!' Matos spat. 'Money!' He inched forward, eyes wild with anger. 'You do not remember me, Mr von Klaus. The waiter from Le Catalan . . . one week ago.'

Von Klaus backed further away, deeper into the alleyway with the bare electric lightbulb which threw a harsh light on the two men. The door underneath that light led to Marie's house. If he could reach that he would be safe as she always left it open for him. A few more metres was all it would take. A few more footsteps and he could get away from this knife-wielding lunatic.

'Le Catalan . . . Le Catalan! What are you talking about?'

'I think you know, Mr von Klaus. You lost me my job at the restaurant. Last Wednesday night. You said the 'langosta' was not fresh, that it was bad. Now there is no more work for a waiter. Now I am forced on to the streets with my family.'

Slowly, imperceptibly, the events of the previous week filtered back into von Klaus's mind. He wiped the sweat from his forehead with a shaking hand. 'Ah yes, I remember. I had had a long day. I was tired you understand. Very tired . . . but I did not want you to lose your job. Listen . . . listen . . .' – the voice was pleading now; a high pitched whining sound – 'I can speak with the owner of the restaurant. I know the man. I can get you your job back . . . how does that sound?'

'It sounds like lies,' Matos said with a sneer. 'You people are all the same. Because you have money you think to rule people's lives. Yes, you are all the same . . . so I promised myself tonight that I would cut your heart out.' He laughed crazily at the thought. 'If you have a heart that is . . . do you have a heart, Mr von Klaus?'

Too frightened to answer, the German remained silent. He reached quickly into his inside pocket, grabbed his wallet and flung it at the madman's feet. 'There is money . . . take it. I can get you more as well. As much as you need.'

Matos ignored the pleading voice and the wallet, and

22

continued inching forwards, the knife blade making steady purposeful sweeps from side to side.

Von Klaus, in an attempt to buy time, said, 'So how did you know my name? How did you know I would be here tonight?'

'It is not difficult. I ask questions, then I follow you.'

Von Klaus attempted to soften his voice. 'Yes, yes, I see. That was clever of you. Extremely clever. Look, why can't we be sensible about this? What I am trying to say is that you are an intelligent man. You have just proved that. Half the Swiss police force would have got that simple little task wrong, I can assure you. But you, being discreet, being clever, found out who I was and then tracked me to a place that no one knows about. Intelligence! Yes, you have plenty of that . . . so why not let me help you . . . a better job than you had before! Perhaps I could even buy a small restaurant . . . You could run it for me. How does that sound?' There was a moment's silence before he added, 'I am a man of my word, believe me.'

Matos, feeling dizzy through lack of food and tiredness, paused. He felt his spirits lifting. Isabella his wife would smile again for him, would come back to his bed. They would find better rooms, better clothes. And food and wine . . . and happiness. The knife dropped slowly to his side.

'That is good,' von Klaus said in a shaky voice. 'Now just behind you, on the ground, is my wallet. Pick it up and take the money from it. That can be your first month's expenses . . . seven thousand francs. Is that enough?'

Mato's eyes widened in surprise. 'Seven thousand francs!'

'Expenses only. We will make a much better deal for your salary. Yes, I think we will do well in the restaurant business.'

Matos half turned and shuffled back to where the wallet lay on the damp cobblestones. As he stopped to pick it up, von Klaus seized his chance and ran for the door. It was locked. He wrenched the handle in disbelief. Locked! How? How could she do this? She knew he was coming. What was happening? He pounded the heavy oak door with both fists, screaming at the same time for the police.

Within seconds Matos was upon him, his dark eyes burning with an animal madness. The long blade swung down towards von Klaus's chest, but the German somehow twisted his huge frame and took the impact in his upper left arm. He knew instantly he had been wounded, but there was no pain. The shock somehow gave him courage, or perhaps it was fear that the next time the knife might find his heart. He grabbed the slightly built man by the knife arm, forcing the blade slowly away. The struggle continued; first one, then the other gaining the upper hand. Now Matos was screaming abuse at the fat man as the superior body weight began to overpower him. The long glinting blade turned inch by agonising inch towards the Portuguese.

It was then that the rear door to the house was flung open and Marie appeared. Her piercing scream frightened Matos more than the knife blade closing on his body. It would bring the police. In desperation he tried to turn and break free from von Klaus's grip. He might have succeeded if the knife had not taken that one final and fateful twist. It sank deep into his chest. Matos's eyes opened wide with a startled look that dying sometimes brings. The German's grip slackened and the young Portuguese, his eyes staring questioningly at the knife handle protruding from his chest, fell to the ground.

'Otto . . . Otto . . . what is happening? Who . . .' Marie's frightened voice faded to an open-mouthed silence as the German slumped back against the wall, his fingers clawing at his bloody shoulder. His face was ashen and contorted in pain.

'He stabbed me,' he whispered in disbelief. 'He . . . he tried to kill me.' Then he fainted.

9 October

Geneva, Switzerland

THURSDAY 0630 HOURS

OTTO VON KLAUS awoke clinging to the last slipping frames of a nightmare. A red street. A red sky. Red people with ugly faces mouthing silent screams. It was the antithesis of reality in more ways than one. Firstly, the more he had rejected the dream the more his inner being had wanted it to stay. Then there was the blood. The faster he had washed it from his hands the faster it had returned. He was bathed in sweat as he struggled to open his eyes. The pale lemon-coloured wall with the gilt-framed oil of Lake Lucerne was missing. It was there every morning at the foot of his bed. It was the first thing he saw! He blinked his heavy eyelids in panic. Someone had stolen the painting! Seventy thousand francs he had paid for it. And if that had been stolen, what else?

It took some moments for the sleep to leave his eyes, and a short while longer for his brain to comprehend the reality of the situation. A pink room, heavy with a woman's perfume. He struggled to lift his head and found an unbelievable pain instead. It coursed unchecked through his left side, bringing sickness to his throat.

Slowly it came back. Piece by unwanted piece. The man in the alleyway. The madman with the scarred face and the wild animal eyes. Then the struggle and the stabbing and the knife handle poking out of the man's chest.

After that, he remembered a doctor. A tall elegant man with neat black hair. He had been wearing a camel-coloured cashmere topcoat. The man had spoken no words, but silently and with a grim face stitched up the wound before administering a sedative. Von Klaus shivered. So it had not been a dream. It was real.

'Marie!' he called out. Then again and again. She came at the fourth call. Scrubbed clean of make-up, wrapped in a pink housecoat which matched the bedroom and puffing nervously on a cigarette, she looked more like a worried mother waiting for a long overdue child to return from her first date than a lady of the night.

'Good morning,' she said, moving across to the bed and kissing him lightly on the forehead. 'And how is the arm . . . it still hurts I think?'

'Damn the arm, damn the arm. Get my clothes . . . what time is it.'

She looked at her watch. 'Nearly seven.'

'Seven, damn. I must get to the office . . . I must call the police.'

She rested a hand on his forehead. 'There is no hurry, Otto. Besides, the doctor said you needed at least a few days' rest.'

'Doctor! Since when did I need the advice of a quack pill-pusher to tell me anything . . . now get my clothes.'

'You will have breakfast, though!'

Von Klaus thrust her hand away in anger. 'Breakfast, you stupid cow, what is this talk of breakfast? Last night I was attacked by a madman; what is more I stabbed him. The police will be asking questions. I need to see them, to explain it was self-defence . . . you will, of course, come with me to verify the facts!'

Marie, who had started at his sudden anger, now went across the room to the window and pulled the curtains open. The dawn sky, or at least what little of it could be seen over the irregular angles of rooftops, was leaden grey. Swollen with rain. She turned back to face Otto. Her dark hair, carefully dyed to hide the telltale traces of grey, fell in untidy waves on to her shoulders. Her face, becoming fleshy with age and without the flattering application of make-up, looked tired and old. The eyes, normally a deep soft brown, were puffy and bloodshot. The result of a sleepless night. She reached down and absently scratched her left thigh through the thin material of her housecoat.

'There is no reason for you to see the police,' she said casually. 'The man is dead.'

A curious numbness seemed to spread through Otto von Klaus, his mouth becoming so dry he could speak only with difficulty. 'Dead!' he croaked. 'Dead . . . but what of the police?'

'No police, I have taken care of it. The body is gone. It will be disposed of.'

'Disposed of . . .' von Klaus said in the same croaky voice.

'Disposed of,' she repeated. 'You seem to forget that my profession depends upon integrity. Once I have the police here, sniffing around asking questions, I have lost my clientele forever.' She reached down and pulled open her housecoat exposing her naked body. 'And at my age, and in this condition' – she motioned to her over-large breasts, cobwebbed with thin blue veins, and the thickening waist and hips, where white flesh creased in heavy folds – 'there is no way I could ever start up again in some other place . . . I am simply too old.'

She paused to stub out her cigarette in an antique china dish on the dressing-table before tugging her housecoat back around her ample body. 'So,' she continued, 'two of my young men have taken the body. It will be dropped in the lake, at the deepest point.'

Von Klaus, still white-faced from the knowledge that he had killed a man, was nevertheless regaining some of his composure. The woman standing before him seemed a total stranger. He realised he had never seen her by the light of day before. Always the night. Always the soft flattering lights complementing the carefully applied make-up and the slinky black gowns she wore. And always there was the mixture of whisky and Kir Royale to dull his senses. Now there was nothing. Nothing but cold morning reality. The woman, he decided, wasn't even beautiful. Once perhaps, but that would have been a long time ago.

'What about the knife?' he asked at length. 'Where is it? It could have my fingerprints on it. Have you or your "boys" thought of that?'

Marie moved closer to the bed. 'You worry too much, Otto. It is all taken care of. Now you rest quietly and I will make you breakfast ... I even have some freshly baked ramekins.'

'No breakfast,' he snapped back. 'Just bring my clothes. I have work to do.'

Marie let out a small sigh and went over to the wardrobe. 'But the doctor did insist you rested,' she remarked, taking his suit from amidst her dresses.

Von Klaus, half-way out of the bed, stopped. 'The doctor, yes. What of him? Surely he will report this to the police!'

Marie laid his suit neatly on the bed. 'No, it is not a problem. He is one of my clients. He will say nothing.'

'You are sure?'

'He is a well thought of medical man; a consultant at the Zurich Kantonspital, as well as here in Geneva. Consorting with common prostitutes could easily end his career ... yes, I am sure.'

For a moment von Klaus remained impassive, then his face twisted in a scowl and he swore with such venom that Marie started. His mind had suddenly recalled the reason.

'The door!' he growled. 'Why was the door locked last night?'

Marie moved over to the dressing-table and took a cigarette from a cloisonné box. 'A client was just leaving,' she said hesitantly. 'He was late. I was seeing him out through the door into the Grande Rue when I heard the banging and shouting in the alley.'

Von Klaus bent forward, his head sinking wearily into his hands. Why, in God's name, was he surrounded by fools? By incompetent idiots! How had he ever become involved with a prostitute! Suddenly, for the first time since childhood, he felt totally vulnerable. As though his fate rested exclusively in the hands of others. Marie most of all.

It took him more than half an hour to dress, the pain restricting his movements. Finally, covered in sweat and feeling quite wretched, he lit a cigarette. The inevitable coughing sent new waves of pain through his body and brought on a feeling of dizziness. He swore volubly, stubbed out the cigarette and made his way to the kitchen and the aroma of freshly ground coffee.

Marie looked up from the kitchen table as the ashen faced German entered the room. 'Sit here, Otto, I will pour you a cup of coffee before you go.' She stood up and moved towards the stove.

'My wallet,' he said, searching through his pockets one-handedly. 'You have seen it?'

She finished pouring the coffee. 'Your wallet? No. You are sure you had it with you?'

Von Klaus's lips twitched silently as his eyes grew wider with a kind of awareness. 'Last night,' he said, as if to himself, 'last night . . . in the alley . . .'

He stumbled out of the kitchen, down the narrow corridor to the back door. Unlocking it and flinging it open he went outside. The alley was deserted. No wallet. No sign of blood. Nothing. Had the man – his attacker – picked up the wallet and put it in his pocket? And if he had, had Marie's young men dropped the body in the lake without checking! And what if the body was picked up by a fisherman? He didn't need to pursue the sequence of events any further. He hurried back to the kitchen.

'You have found it?' Marie said hopefully.

'I have found nothing, damn you,' he snarled. 'But you will. You will go to those so-called friends of yours and tell them my wallet must have been on the body . . . unless, of course, these "friends" of yours are thieves!'

'Thieves!' she replied more sharply than she had intended. 'For your information they are good men. They would not steal.'

Von Klaus laughed sarcastically. 'Good men! Good men! They take a dead body in the middle of the night and throw it to the fishes, and you call them good men.'

There was contempt in Marie's voice when she said: 'At least, unlike you, they did not kill the man.'

Von Klaus grabbed her right wrist and twisted it cruelly. 'You will never,' he spat, tightening his grip, 'you will never say that again. I have killed no one, you understand?'

She nodded dumbly.

'Make sure you do or I will see to it that you have more

29

to worry about than an overweight body.' With that, he pushed her violently to the floor and stormed out, slamming the door so hard that flakes of chalk rained down from the whitewashed walls.

Marie, eyes full of hatred, massaged her bruised wrist, then dragged herself up from the floor. 'And I thought,' she murmured to herself, 'that high class clientele would be better. More gentle, more refined. No, Mariella, they are all the same . . . animals!'

The expression on her face suddenly changed to one of cunning as she pulled a container marked *Sucre* from the kitchen shelf. She took out the black leather wallet and emptied out its contents. Seven thousand Swiss francs and six credit cards. The remainder, driving licence, insurance, ID card and various club membership cards, could be destroyed. Putting the francs in her housecoat pocket she took the credit cards through to the bedroom. After a warm, perfumed bath, she would telephone Konrad Zwicky. His knowledge of the Swiss underworld was second to none. He would place the cards at a fair price.

13 October

London, England

MONDAY 0950 HOURS

BASE TO CHANCE FITZGERALD was a small part of crumbling red-brick Victoriana in Clapham, South London. It was a typical bachelor apartment – sparsely decorated and colourless, with framed pictures still waiting to be hung after nearly three years. Elsewhere, piles of battered books, from Dickens to Dostoevsky and Chaucer to Chekhov, stood in dusty piles. In one corner a large chess table with hand-carved Filipino figures was midway through an evenly matched game. In another, an Akai stacking hi-fi system was pushing out Rimsky-Korsakov's *Scheherazade*.

The apartment itself consisted of a lounge, kitchen-diner, bedroom, bathroom and a small boxroom, piled high with half-empty packing-crates. The whole had the atmosphere of a dusty left-luggage department at a railway station. To Chance Fitzgerald that is all it was. A place to rest his head between wars. A place for mail to collect on the welcome mat. A refuge from the big world where he would sometimes sit and think and recharge his batteries. The semi-permanence was in many ways reflective of his life.

Born in London of an Irish father and American mother in 1941, he had initially been educated at a Benedictine school run by monks from Ampleforth, England's leading Catholic school. His father – an air force pilot – had been killed over Germany in the latter stages of the war, and his mother had remarried an American musician in the early

31

1950s. They took the boy to St Louis, Missouri. Following further education at high school, he had briefly studied music at Indiana University. Following his Sophomore year, his mother and step-father were divorced. A young Sean Fitzgerald had quit college and joined the air force. Following serving in Vietnam and the trauma that war brought to thousands of young American warriors, he packed his valise and set out to find himself.

It was during a spell in West Africa that he met and married Maxine. The daughter of a wealthy businessman involved in multiple civil engineering projects in Lagos, the marriage had been doomed from the start. Maxine, an only child, was and always had been, spoilt. Even the inducements offered by her father to join the family business had failed to win him over. Too late he had realised he was a loner. Most vets blamed 'Nam, in the same way some pilots cited their love of the sky for their broken marriages. Fitzgerald, however, did not blame any specific thing, other than himself. He was a square peg in a round hole. A man seeking an identity. A life.

It was later, from his travels in the Far East, that he first came across the mystical thinkers. His reading of Tao Te Ching had resulted in a copperplate manuscript hanging above his bed. It read:

> Push on to the ultimate Emptiness,
> Guard unshakeable Calmness,
> All the ten thousand things are moving and working
> Yet we can see the void, whither they must return.
> All things, however they flourish,
> Turn and go home to the root from which they sprang.
> This reversion to the root is called Calmness,
> It is recognition of Necessity
> That which is called Unchanging.
> Now knowing the Unchanging means Enlightenment,
> Not knowing it means going blindly to disaster.

For Chance Fitzgerald those words amongst many others had changed him. Had given him an inner peace and tranquillity he could never have imagined. Above all, he would now know when it was time to return. To die. This knowledge, rather than weakening him with fear, had made him invincible. It also, in any war or conflict, made him a fearful adversary.

The pile of unpaid bills on the kitchen table looked reprovingly at him as he poured a glass of mineral water. Of course he should have paid them out of the sixty thousand dollars. But then there wouldn't have been an airplane, or a deal in New York to increase the sum by another thirty per cent . . . or a fire on an airfield in England! Not that he wanted or needed, or really cared for money. It was just that he had to prove something to Jack Audley, Maxine's father. Jack, the tough-talking Yorkshireman now lived in a mansion in Jersey. Jack the rough diamond, who had raised Chance's daughter Alice, while Maxine jet-setted around the world. From party to party and bed to bed. Jack, who on the rare occasions when Chance dropped in to see his daughter, would lecture him on parental responsibility. In his book that equated with money. And money equated with most things in Jack Audley's life. For that reason alone, Chance Fitzgerald wanted to show he could play the Yorkshireman's game and win. Once would be enough.

To most men pushing forty-six, losing their life savings in a fire with no insurance cover may well have been the final straw. The last energy-sapping blow which would leave them bitter and withdrawn. Unable or unwilling to go on. To Chance Fitzgerald, however, there was a reason. Enlightenment proved it, showed a new road ahead in a clear white light. The telephone call one hour later was something the Western world might refer to as a lucky break. To the Eastern way of thinking it was the continuation of a journey.

'Mr Fitzgerald?' The voice sounded slightly Germanic.

'This is he.'

'Ah good. Mr Fitzgerald, this is Otto von Klaus. I am calling you from Geneva; it is in connection with an aircraft purchase I wish to make.'

'Purchase, Mr von Klaus! Are you sure you've got the right man? I don't usually sell aircraft you see. I do fly them once in a while, however.'

There was a crackly pause on the line, reminiscent of storm static. 'You know Jacques Regourd in Paris, at Le Bourget airport. He mentioned your name to one of my employees ... he said you had advised him on aircraft purchases from time to time ... this is so?'

'Yes, I've surveyed planes for him once in a while, but that's slightly different ...'

'Not so, Mr Fitzgerald. Perhaps it is my poor English but that is what I want you to do for me.'

'What sort of plane do you have in mind?'

'I cannot say at this moment in time. Could you fly out to Geneva?'

'When?'

'Straightaway?'

'And how straightaway would that be, Mr von Klaus?'

'Sorry, I don't understand.'

'You mean now? Today?'

'Yes, today would be fine. I can have a ticket arranged for you. It will be waiting at the Swissair desk at Heathrow airport. This is satisfactory?'

'Yes, that sounds fine. Perhaps you could call me back and let me know the flight time.'

'My secretary will take care of that. I will tell her to pass you all the necessary details.'

Fitzgerald changed telephone hands. 'One thing before you go, Mr von Klaus. Money! I have to mention it because it's in rather short supply at the moment.'

Von Klaus said brusquely, 'Five thousand dollars for your advice, Mr Fitzgerald, plus all your expenses of course. After that, and if we can put the deal together there will be much more.'

Fitzgerald half-smiled. 'You sound like my kind of man, Mr von Klaus ... direct.'

'Until later then, Mr Fitzgerald.'

'Until later, Mr von Klaus.'

Fitzgerald replaced the receiver, increased the volume on the Akai system and went through to the bedroom. The haunting music from *Scheherazade* followed.

Hoisting his holdall on to the bed he began the seasoned traveller's ritual of laying out essential items only.

'A dollar for every time you've done this old son, and you'd be a rich man.'

It was raining heavily in Geneva as a worried Otto von Klaus nosed his Mercedes into the Avenue Louis Casai. He was driving one-handedly, his left hand hooked into the opening of his jacket. The pain killers he had taken earlier that afternoon were wearing off, causing him a great deal of discomfort. The dull throbbing ache down his left side was however of secondary importance as he listened to the rhythmical thud-thud-thud of the windshield wipers. The letter in his inside pocket was the reason for his concern.

It was typewritten and read:'I am writing to ask you for one million US dollars. A great deal of money perhaps, but as it will buy my silence over the incident in the Grande Rue on Thursday night, I think that you will agree it is worth every cent. It would, of course, be extremely inadvisable to speak with the police especially as you are on the wrong side of the fence now. The illegal side! And the police and the judiciary system have specific ways of dealing with people of our kind!

'Think over how you will get the money together – in used bills of small denominations, of course. I will be in contact before too long.'

That was all. A cryptic note which he had received at his home on the previous Saturday morning. He had sat trance-like for most of the day staring at the damning piece of paper, trying to evaluate the situation in a detached manner. But it was impossible. He was too involved. He had ended up late that evening writing out the exact sequence of events since the fateful killing. It resulted in the same four people being the prime suspects. In fact, to his way of thinking, there could be no one else. The four were Marie, the two young men who had disposed of the body and the tall elegant doctor who had tended his wounds. He had telephoned Marie's house later that night. The call had been unanswered. As had every call since.

In the meantime, the proposed sale of his companies had

received equally bad news from initial enquiries instigated by his secretary.

It seemed a London company was interested, but only if the price was in the region of ten million Swiss francs. That news, which had landed on his desk first thing that morning, coupled with the million-dollar blackmail threat, had caused him to reopen the Iranian file. After all, there was no reason he had to be seen to be involved. As he had earlier reasoned, employ a shadowy figure of an aviation expert to negotiate the entire deal. And if anything goes wrong, the aviation expert alone suffers the consequences. Also, and this lifted his sagging spirits briefly, if the man was the right type for such a job, he might also be able to assist in discovering the identity of the blackmailer. Some way, as yet unknown, he had to be rid of them. The person or persons who could very easily end up bleeding him dry. It would not stop at one million, of that he was sure. The nightmare of being plunged back into poverty was more than he could bear. He would rather be dead.

Geneva Cointrin airport was relatively quiet as von Klaus checked the arrivals board in the main concourse. His eyes had just settled on the landing time of Flight SR833 from London as being ten minutes earlier than scheduled, when a quiet voice said: 'Mr von Klaus?'

He turned to the voice, instantly aware of the white blond hair and the most vivid blue eyes he had ever seen. The man was dressed all in black. 'Yes . . . Mr Fitzgerald?'

Fitzgerald held out a hand, 'Chance will do.'

'Chance? Ah yes, and I am Otto.'

It was as they were walking through the exit that von Klaus said, 'So how did you know it was me?'

'Sixth sense. I seem to have the knack of putting the face to the voice.'

Von Klaus merely nodded before indicating the Mercedes parked in a no waiting bay.

It was as they were driving away from the terminal that Fitzgerald noticed the difficulty the German was having negotiating the winding airport roads.

'Hurt your arm, Otto?'

'Oh, it is nothing, a little sprain that is all.' Von Klaus eased the accelerator down then and the tyres whispered urgently out on to the dual carriageway. It was some moments before he added, 'I am not a man for preamble, if that is the correct word. I prefer to come straight to the point.'

'I'm listening.'

'Jacques Regourd in Paris mentioned that you were considered by some to be a mercenary.'

Fitzgerald smiled. 'The trouble with the French, Otto, no poetry in their souls. Now I would have said soldier of fortune . . . has a nicer ring, wouldn't you say?'

The German's face remained blank. 'Yes, I see. Anyway, the matter I mentioned on the telephone could be said to have' – he searched for the right words – 'political repercussions, I think you would say.'

'Go on.'

'The job I have in mind might not be thought patriotic by your fellow countrymen.'

Fitzgerald threw back his head and laughed. 'And which countrymen would they be, Otto? I am part Irish by a father who disagreed with Mr de Valera and went off to fight a war for the British; part English by default, being born there; and part American by a mother who hailed from St Louis, Missouri, and who took me back at the first opportunity.' He turned his head towards the back seat of the car. 'That tired-looking holdall is my country. Small and anonymous, but I like it.'

'But you have a passport?'

'Two. American and British. What they call a dual national, but I wouldn't worry about that; we all have to play the game to some degree or other.'

'Game! And what game would that be?'

'Obeying the rules, Otto! Obeying the rules.'

'A part of our heritage, our history. Yes?'

'History,' Fitzgerald said. 'I'll tell you a story about that; short, succinct, but very much to the point. "History is something that never happened; written by a man who wasn't there." '

Von Klaus looked mystified. 'I am afraid I do not follow.'

'Oh I shouldn't worry. Put it down to my Irishness, a subtle blend of irony mixed with a fine madness.'

The German steered the conversation back to the ground he understood. Plain facts. 'The aircraft,' he said. 'The one I mentioned on the telephone. What do you know about Lockheed Hercules. C-130s I think they are also called.'

Fitzgerald, his eyes holding the wet shining tarmac in the car's headlights, said, 'A little. Depends on what you need to know.'

'You could find one of these aircraft, to buy?'

'It's possible, but that is a very popular piece of machinery. Not many used models about. Pushes the premium up.'

'But you could still get one?'

'Let's say I could give it a try. What did you want, the civil or the military version?'

'There are two kinds?' von Klaus said with some surprise.

'C-130's the military one; the civil type is known as the L-100.'

'Ah,' von Klaus was thoughtful for a while. 'You can buy either type? Or do the military ones never get sold on the civil market?'

'Depends what you want them for. You didn't say.'

The German fumbled through his pockets with his left hand, wincing slightly as each movement brought a new pain. One-handedly, he extracted a cigarette from the gold case and lit it. His face had almost disappeared behind a thick cloud of smoke when he answered.

'Iran . . . that is where it is going.'

Fitzgerald's eyes opened fractionally wider. 'I see,' he said quietly, 'sounds even more expensive.'

'The money is not a problem. I think we can make a good profit if you can find the right aircraft.'

'What do you know about alchemy, Otto?'

'Alchemy? I do not understand.'

'In olden days it was thought you could turn base metal into gold. Many a so-called magician lost his head by promising his king he could do it; only to find that like the rainbow the dream receded the closer you got.'

Von Klaus frowned and puffed out another cloud of smoke. 'I still do not understand what you are saying.'

'You are thinking,' Fitzgerald said slowly, 'of supplying the Iranians with a C−130, which in anyone's book falls under the title of arms dealing. Nothing wrong with that, of course. Governments do it all the time. Only problem is we are not a government. Also, we are dealing with a volatile Arab people who put Christendom in the same category the European churches once put heretics. In short, aviation is a hard place to make a dollar.'

Von Klaus stubbed out his cigarette and concentrated on his driving for a while. 'So you think it is not possible,' he said eventually.

'Oh, it's possible all right, most things are in this life; it's just that we would be treading dangerous ground . . . did you ever walk through a minefield?'

'A minefield? . . . no.'

'Well, I have and I can assure you it heightens the perception beyond belief. Your Iranian proposal is that minefield. Very, very dangerous.'

'And what is the price of danger these days?'

Fitzgerald smiled at the solemnity in the German's voice. 'You lay out all the facts to date and perhaps we can agree the financial side when I've decided if it's going to work.'

Ten minutes later the Mercedes braked to a stop outside the Hotel Metropole.

'And that is all I can tell you,' von Klaus concluded, switching off the engine.

For a moment there was only the noise of rain as it cascaded off the car into the gutter.

Fitzgerald replied, 'Well that's something at least.' He turned his head and looked out at the grand façade of the hotel. 'Looks a nice place.'

'I think you will like it,' von Klaus answered, opening his door. 'One of the best we have.'

Fitzgerald climbed out and closed the door. Somewhere, from out of the dark wet night, church bells tolled vespers. 'Would you listen to that now,' he said softly to himself. 'They never give up trying to get you back, do they?' His face was bleak for a fleeting second as he made his 'way through the rain and up the steps into the hotel.

The Metropole is a massive structure of concrete and stone looking out over the English garden which adorns the banks of Lac Genève as it nears the Mont-Blanc bridge. No sooner across the threshold there is something to admire in the world-famous fresco by Dominique Appia. It sets the tone of the hotel, which is one of calm, refined elegance. Along the far side of the lobby is the alcoved reception area. Opposite that, a beautifully furnished lounge of low tables and chairs leads to the main bar, a little masterpiece in the style of the twenties. It was to that bar that von Klaus and Fitzgerald now went.

'Please.' Von Klaus indicated a low black leather chair. He waited until his guest was seated before easing his substantial weight into a seat opposite, raising a hand to a red-jacketed waiter at the same time. 'You will of course have a drink.'

'Just mineral water, Otto, thank you.'

Von Klaus muttered something in German to the waiter, then turned back to the table. 'My secretary will be along shortly. I hope you do not mind, but she will need to work with you on this matter.'

The smile slipped from Fitzgerald's face. 'Now that sounds difficult.' His voice had taken on a sombre note.

'Difficult?'

Fitzgerald leaned forward across the table, looking casually left and right before he spoke. 'Yes, Otto, difficult. What we have here is a highly sensitive operation. From what you have so far outlined I think I can improve on the overall plan of action. That, however, takes people. People I will need to recruit; people I already know would stand up to a military-style screening.' He checked once more for eavesdroppers before continuing in the same low voice. 'A few rules of this particular game are as follows. We adopt a code, thereby avoiding the use of plain English in spoken or transmitted information. That also means we do not mention the country we are dealing with again — militarily sensitive. Quite simply we do not divulge any information unless it is on a need-to-know basis. Normally, all of that would be easy except when you introduce the unexpected, i.e. a non-screened person. Now you've increased the risk element by as much as a thousand per cent.'

The German frowned. 'A thousand! I think this is perhaps too big a figure.'

'Don't count on it. One careless word is all it takes; all it ever takes come to that. And I'm thinking there'll be a lot of words before this business is through.'

Von Klaus lit a Turkish cigarette and lapsed into a bout of coughing as the waiter placed the drinks on the table, made an elegant bow and hurried away to another beckoning customer.

'Not good for your health, Otto,' Fitzgerald remarked, indicating the cigarette.

Von Klaus wiped a smoke tear from his eye and lifted the crystal flute of Kir Royale. 'You are right I think, always the coughing. Perhaps now is the time to cut down... Anyway, a toast.' He raised his glass. 'To our business venture in the belief that we will succeed where your alchemists failed.'

Fitzgerald smiled and drank a little of the mineral water. 'Going back to the other problem,' he said. 'How well do you know your secretary?'

'She has worked for me for three years.'

'Doesn't mean a thing to me, Otto. The CIA like the KGB have been known to plant agents for thirty years or more; sleepers they're called. It's after those thirty years, about the time you think you know the person as well as your own mother, that their master's voice beckons and they do whatever unsavoury little act they've been conditioned to do.'

Von Klaus was unmoved. 'But you are talking of spies. Political scandal. This is simply a small sales transaction.'

'Wrong! Not simple. And you'd better believe that when I start making enquiries to buy up the machinery in question, that the odd CIA guy will creep out of the woodwork. They'll stay at a distance, of course, watching and waiting... they're very good at that.'

Von Klaus's face showed concern. 'Whatever,' he whispered urgently, 'it must not be traced back to me. My business is too... too established. You understand this?'

'Respectable was the word you were looking for, Otto, and of course I understand; but that is where your secretary being involved could implicate you by her very presence.'

The German's eyes registered understanding. 'Yes, I see. Thank you for that, but somehow she will still need to work with you. She knows my company network better than anyone, and the financial transactions we have to activate are not easy. Also, as you will have a great deal to do on the technical side of the operation I doubt you will have time to be of much assistance in this area.'

'Not if you want the deal wrapped up before Christmas.'

'So, still the problem with Lisa!'

'I'm sorry.'

'Lisa, my secretary. Still we have the problem.'

Fitzgerald was thoughtful for a matter of minutes, weighing the situation carefully in his mind. 'What if she left your employment!' he said at length.

'Left . . .'

'And worked with me outside Geneva; then when the deal is concluded and the coast is clear she comes back.'

'Yes, perhaps this is good.'

'Would she be willing to do that?'

Von Klaus started rising from his chair. 'We will ask her, she is coming now through the lobby.'

Lisa Wendell-Holmes' first impression of Chance Fitzgerald was of a lithe fit body, longish blond hair, and striking blue eyes set in a handsome tanned face. His smile made something rise within her body, an intangible sensation leaping from behind the carefully built barricade of years. It came upon her like a swell rolling in from the ocean and she barely had time to recognise it before Otto was saying, 'Lisa let me introduce you to Mr Fitzgerald.'

He took her hand. 'Chance. I'm pleased to meet you, Lisa.'

He was not particularly tall, she noticed, but there was power. Something other than muscular strength. And the eyes, apart from their vivid colouring, were frank and entirely unafraid. He was smiling now as he talked, the soft almost disguised Irishness commanding attention. She steeled herself then. Philip was gone; she would not become involved again.

A new round of drinks was ordered, following which Otto outlined the meeting thus far.

'So, Lisa,' he concluded, 'what do you think?'

Fitzgerald turned to her and added, 'We should be able to complete the transaction by early December.'

Their eyes met and she forced herself to look away. What was there about this man, she thought, which made her feel giddy and unnatural? As though she was being lifted right out of reality. Even the sound of her own voice seemed as though it belonged to someone else.

'Yes, it seems a sensible approach.' She took a sip of Kir Royale. 'You said outside Geneva. Where exactly?'

Fitzgerald said, 'I leave tomorrow. I'll give Otto the outline of the operation first thing in the morning then I'll fly to Zurich.'

Von Klaus looked up. 'Zurich?'

'I'm on holiday. People checking back might find I visited Geneva only once and then flew straight back into London. This way if I spend a little time moving around Switzerland it should make it more difficult should someone start digging.'

'And Lisa?' the German added.

'Lisa can join me in London on Friday; that can be the termination date of her employment with you . . . I'd put a back-dated letter of resignation on file as well. You can never be too thorough.' He turned to Lisa. 'Is that all right with you?'

She nodded. 'Whatever Otto says.'

Von Klaus nodded approval and finished his drink. 'When will you have some news on the availability of the . . . er . . . machinery?'

'Allow me ten days.'

'That is too long. The customer is only in Europe for the rest of the week, then he returns to his country . . . It is much more difficult for me to contact him there, you understand?'

'OK, five days. Say Friday. It could add to the bill, however . . . trying to get information in a hurry.'

The German afforded himself a rare smile. It was not so much the mixture of Crème de Cassis and champagne, but the knowledge that Chance Fitzgerald certainly seemed the right man for the job.

'Let me have a breakdown of costings in the morning before you leave. I will see you have the money.' He glanced at his watch. 'Now if you will excuse me; I have other pressing matters to attend to.'

Fitzgerald drew up the basic plan of action that night in his comfortable room on the third floor and presented it to von Klaus at his office early the following morning.

The German studied it carefully before making any comment. 'This is good, Chance, very good. Especially the company named Relief Air. Where did you get the idea for that?'

'I was wondering how we would deliver the machine without causing heads to turn. We needed a front for the operation. A legitimate means of moving the aircraft around without creating suspicion. The Sudan seemed the obvious answer. We offer our services to the Red Cross to carry out airlifts to the starving millions . . . in fact we can thank a guy named Bob Geldof for the idea.'

'Ah yes, I have seen him on the television news. A long-haired rock and roll singer, I think.'

'Something like that. Anyway, as outlined, the famine relief programme for that part of Africa is very close to the public's heart, so it should give us no problems in our first move to Khartoum.

'From there it is simply a case of departing on a regular supply drop mission and conveniently vanishing. By the time the search parties have set out to find the "crashed" plane, we have disappeared into a low-level sunset on course for the country in question.'

Von Klaus intervened, 'And the part about the re-appearance of the crew! You think this is possible?'

'I'll think about it some more, but for the time being we can safely assume that the Sudan is quite big enough to lose our piece of machinery in. Lots of swamp land to the south, you see. So after the delivery flight is complete we smuggle the crew back to the southern Sudan and get them to lie low for a week or so. Then they appear in Juba one fine sunny morning, telling of the horrendous crash and how they have struggled through the horrors of equatorial Sudan, fighting off man-eating crocodiles and millions of swarming insects, not forgetting the fierce heat and quicksands. That they have forgotten the exact position they went down will not really matter . . . they will be heroes.'

'You will have no problem finding the right people to do the job then? It sounds very dangerous.'

Fitzgerald gathered up the money which the German had counted on to the desk earlier. 'This is what it is all about, Otto. You'd be amazed what you can buy with money.'

Von Klaus nodded knowingly. He wanted to say 'And will money help to find and silence a blackmailer for me?', but decided to approach that problem from a different angle. He took an oval cigarette from the silver box on his desk and pushed it absently towards Fitzgerald. 'You would care for one of these?'

Fitzgerald shook his head. 'Good soldiers reckon they have three lives in a war. One is down to luck; the other two alcohol and nicotine – which both have the nasty habit of killing off brain cells thereby reducing reaction time. And in a war you need as much of that as you can find.'

'But this is not a war!'

Fitzgerald laughed. 'Perhaps not, let's just put it down to a weakness of mine. Always thinking ill of the world. Anyway, looking on the brighter side, this particular little skirmish of ours should be pleasantly free of dead bodies, don't you think?'

For a moment, Fitzgerald could have sworn the German's face took on a hunted look. As though the devil himself had reached out and laid a hand on his heart. The vision quickly passed being replaced by one of cool impersonality as the German said, 'So we will leave it that you are fully in charge of the operation. From the purchase of the machinery to the setting up of the company Relief Air. Once we have a definite acceptance of the price I will pass the financial details to Lisa, which you will also handle. Everything of course is to be handled outside Geneva . . . in fact outside Switzerland.'

Fitzgerald stood up and put the money into his inside pocket. He held out a hand. 'A pleasure meeting you, Otto . . . until the next time.'

The last thing he heard as he left the office was the wracking cough of the German as he lit his cigarette.

14 October
Zurich, Switzerland
TUESDAY 1030 HOURS

MARIELLA SCHLEGEL PACED her room making alternate patterns of diamonds and squares on the carpet and occasionally glancing at the new Longines watch on her left wrist. Konrad Zwicky was late! Damn the boy. Surely it didn't take this long to fence a few stolen credit cards!

She had arrived at Zurich Flughafen late on the Saturday evening and had met the long-haired Konrad, as arranged, in the airport bar. He had driven her to the Neues Schloss Hotel in the Stockerstrasse, where he had booked her a room. He had promised he would telephone early the following evening.

Once he had gone, she slipped into a warm bubble bath, looking forward to a welcome rest from the more demanding ways her clients expected of her. It was like a breath of Alpine air.

The following day was spent in leisurely fashion, window shopping in the Bahnhofstrasse and strolling by the lake. By early evening she was back in her hotel room waiting for the call from Konrad Zwicky. It came at midnight, when he told her his contact was out of town and would not be back until some time on the Monday afternoon. He promised he would be at the hotel with the money at nine-thirty on the Tuesday morning.

At first she hadn't been unduly worried; she was enjoying the rest. It was only later, when she had undressed and slipped naked into bed that her mind started

47

playing tricks on her. Or were they tricks? The faint background noise when Konrad had telephoned! It had sounded like music. A nightclub! Had he cashed in the credit cards already? Was he spending the money on a bunch of nightclub tarts?

She had slept badly that night and first thing the following morning had tried to reach him via various contact numbers she had. But no one had seen him. Or if they had they were not saying. The Monday had dragged on with a terrible slowness which had twice seen her packing her bags. Both times she had looked at herself in the mirror and issued the same stern reprimand: 'Not this time Mariella. This time we take what is ours. No matter how little. This time we are getting out. No more obscene tricks for fat slobbering businessmen. No more crumbs from their table. This time we take everything . . . every damn thing!' It was after the final admonition that she had swept out of the hotel and taken a taxi to the Bahnhof Strasse. Buying the expensive watch with some of the seven thousand francs she had found in von Klaus's wallet made her feel better.

She was still pacing the room when there was a soft tapping at the door. At first she thought it was the maid who had come to service the room.

'Can you come back . . .' she started to say, opening the door. Her mouth froze on the word 'later'. It was Konrad Zwicky. His eyes were bloodshot and his face grey and unshaven. He gave Mariella a sheepish grin and tumbled into the room.

'Where the hell have you been?' she snapped closing the door. 'Don't you realise I have a business to run!'

Zwicky, who had slumped into a bedside chair, was clutching his briefcase on his lap. He didn't answer. She went over to him and looked him straight in the eyes; then grabbing him by both shoulders, she shook him until his teeth rattled.

'You've spent it, haven't you? You got the money and you've blown the bloody lot . . . How much?' She shook him harder. 'Tell me . . . how much?'

48

Zwicky's head which had already been a little wobbly on his neck, now felt as though it was going to drop off. A weekend of Pernod and water and an infallible system to beat the roulette wheel at the Black Kat Nite Club was going to take some time to purge from the system.

'Six thousand,' he mumbled.

Mariella's mouth dropped open, then she brought her right hand back and slapped him hard across the face. His head rocked some more.

'I'll get it back . . . I promise I'll get it back,' he cried. 'Just give me a few days.'

'Few days,' she shrieked. 'That is it. Finished. Brother or not, you can rot in hell for all I care. This is the last time, Konrad, do you hear me? The last time.'

He looked up a little uncertainly. 'What about last week? You seem to forget it was me who helped you out of a hole.'

'I have forgotten nothing. One favour for the countless favours I have done for you.'

Zwicky laughed nervously. 'Favour! Carrying a dead body through the streets of Geneva, and then taking it miles out into the lake!'

'Yes, favour. Do not think that because of that I am going to keep you in gambling money for the rest of your life. Make sure you understand that, Konrad. Also make sure you understand I do not want to see you again. Ever!' With that she picked up her suitcase from the end of the bed, snatched her handbag from the dressing-table and stormed out of the room.

Konrad Zwicky sat with his head in his hands feeling sorry for himself and trying to remember the mornings he had awoken without a hangover. He knew, however, that if he could suffer a beer or two before the morning was over his remorse would magically disappear. The bedroom minibar was broken into immediately. Fifteen minutes and three bottles of Dunkle Perle later he went into the bathroom, washed his face and combed his hair. The electric razor he carried in his briefcase added the final touch to his ablutions.

He inspected his face closely in the mirror. The brown

eyes seemed a little clearer. Sure there were heavy pouches underneath them, but the eyes still held the same life and intelligence as the youthful photographs which adorned his mother's apartment on the other side of town. Whenever he was broke he would go and visit her and look at the photographs and be an eighteen-year-old again. Indeed his mother hardly treated him any differently. She also failed to see a thirty-three-year-old failure who was always going to make his big start tomorrow.

He smoothed his long brown hair into place, patted his cheeks in an attempt to bring some colour back into the lifeless grey flesh, and went back to the bedroom. He looked at his briefcase with renewed interest. It was empty, but it gave him a feeling of enterprise, as though he was travelling somewhere to conduct business. He opened it now and filled it with the remaining contents of the minibar. Then he left the room and walked quickly down the thickly carpeted corridor to the elevator.

The three beers he had just consumed had put him in an expansive mood and he decided to forgive Mariella for slapping him so hard. He also decided to forgive Xavier da Silva, the owner of the Black Kat, for running an illegal and crooked gambling table because the next time he got his hands on a decent payroll he was going to clean him out. Financial survival in Zurich was becoming a dog eat dog affair anyway. The secret was to think big. Perhaps after the Black Kat he would move south to Monte Carlo! That, however, was tomorrow. The future. Right now he needed breakfast. There was a small café just off the Bahnhofstrasse and the food was cheap. He checked the top pocket of his brown sports jacket and smiled. He always stuffed a hundred francs or so in there before he tied one on. By the time the drink had taken over he had forgotten about it. His hangover survival fund he called it. So far it had never let him down.

The elevator door hissed open and Konrad drifted out and past the reception desk towards the main door. He paused to check the headlines of a hotel newspaper and was about to set off again when he heard an American voice telling the receptionist that he was a tourist, and enquiring what the best sights would be during a one- or two-day visit.

Konrad Zwicky moved quickly across to the desk and the man in black. The receptionist, a thickset girl with a ruddy face had turned to answer a telephone when Konrad said, 'Excuse me, you are an American?'

Chance Fitzgerald looked at the young man. He was about his own height, but underweight so that his clothes seemed to hang from his frame in untidy folds. The face was grey, as though still recovering from some illness which had necessitated the patient being bedridden out of the sun for some considerable time. Only the eyes seemed to be alive. Brown, alert, intelligent.

'Once in a while,' Fitzgerald remarked in the oblique way which was his trademark.

Zwicky shuffled his feet uncomfortably. Usually Americans opened up at that remark. Gave him a brief potted history of Kentucky or Texas or Arizona and how they were just 'doing' Switzerland before moving on to Italy. The young Swiss would listen with rapt attention, pleading for more when they paused to catch breath. Usually, by the end of their monologue, he would have found a patch of common ground to use as a lever in selling his services as Swiss guide extraordinaire. With this American, however, it was different. Possibly the penetrating blue eyes were to blame. They seemed quite hard and friendless, even though the mouth was slightly upturned in what appeared to be a perpetual smile.

Avoiding the man's direct gaze, Zwicky said, 'I overheard you mention that you were a tourist. I usually take tourists around the city and perhaps to Mount Titlis if they have the time . . . then, of course, there is Lake Lucerne.'

Fitzgerald, aware that he needed to play the tourist role for at least a day before he drifted on to the next place, said, 'You could be just the man then, Mr . . .?'

'Zwicky. Konrad Zwicky.'

They shook hands. 'Right, Konrad, when do we start? Name's Chance Fitzgerald by the way.'

Konrad grinned broadly. 'Right away, Mr Fitzgerald.'

Once the American had signed the register and deposited

51

his holdall with the porter, the two men stepped outside into the sunlight on the Stockerstrasse.

'You have had breakfast, Mr Fitzgerald?'

'No, Konrad, been travelling all morning.'

'Good, there is a little café just off the Bahnhof Strasse; not very smart, you understand, like the Neues Schloss, but the food is the best in Zurich.'

'They do eggs and bacon?'

'Everything,' Konrad said confidently, not really knowing if they did or not. And as for the food being the best in Zurich, another slight overstatement, although the tourists all seemed satisfied enough once he had walked their feet off and so built up their appetites. 'So,' he continued, 'what do you know of Zurich?'

'Know? Not a thing. First time here.'

Konrad took a deep breath and launched into the same patter he gave all his customers. 'Zurich is the economic metropolis of Switzerland. By the time of the Knights, the city, whose beginnings go back as far as 400BC was already prosperous . . .'

The two men walked on through the late morning sunshine.

Later that afternoon both men returned to Zurich. Konrad Zwicky's commando course had lasted a shade over six hours and had started with a high speed car dash to the mountain resort of Engelberg. It had been a perfect Alpine day which lit the landscape with a pale translucent blue. In the lower lying pastures before the resort, autumn crocuses were patterned on the vivid green where rivulets of cold clear water tumbled downhill to the river. Once at Engelberg the two men had boarded an aerial cableway and taken the fifteen-minute journey through the many changes of scenery from the green valley up into the high alpine glacier. Following a brief lunch they had descended by cable car and driven to Lucerne. There, a short guided tour on foot and back to the open road. Konrad Zwicky had hardly paused for breath during the entire day.

Now at the same café they had visited earlier in the day, they were weary and footsore.

'One hell of a tour,' Fitzgerald said, stretching in his chair, 'everything at a hundred miles an hour.'

Zwicky laughed. 'You liked it then?'

'Nice when you stop and catch your breath.' Fitzgerald took a sip of the hot chocolate his guide had recommended. 'So, Konrad, what else do you do?'

'Do?' said the Swiss. His mind left the tourist spiel which had been piling up inside his head and attempted to assess which hard luck story to pitch at his latest client. The old white-haired mother with the incurable illness had not been doing too well of late, especially as his last American tourist had turned out to be a retired small-town doctor who had quickly seen through Konrad's cheap lies as a way to increase his gratuity. No, this time he decided to play it straight. Or as straight as Konrad Zwicky could play anything.

'I live on my wits, Mr Fitzgerald. I think I have a good brain but little opportunity in this place to use it.'

'So why not move out?'

'Money, contacts. The usual problems. One day I will though.'

Fitzgerald, who had always had a soft spot for any loser fighting the odds, looked closely at the grey-faced young man. 'Would you consider yourself trustworthy?'

Zwicky wrinkled his brow. When I am sober, he thought. 'A strange question, but yes.' Well, he felt trustworthy at this particular moment. And with a little more effort felt certain he could be most of the time.

'You said you live on your wits. I assume that means turning your hand to anything.'

'Yes. Even if I say so myself I am very adaptable.'

'How would you like to do a job for me?'

'For you!' Konrad said in a high voice, which in the young man was a sign of excitability. He tried to control his eagerness. Too much generally resulted in a lower price. 'What sort of job?'

'Kind of detective work. General investigations. Asking discreet questions and coming up with the right answers.'

Zwicky smiled. His hangover was long since gone and he

had a strong feeling that this discussion was leading to another big pay day. 'Yes, I know what you mean.'

'Good. Next question: how well do you know Geneva?'

'Well enough,' Konrad said quickly, thinking of the previous week when he had been there with his friend Willy Storck. One of those frequent trips he made to sell off stolen goods. One that had unwittingly made him an accomplice to murder.

Fitzgerald leaned forward and said in a low whisper. 'Good. In that happy event, I would like you to check someone out for me. A businessman. He has an office in the Place Bel-Air.'

Zwicky said, 'What exactly do you wish to know?'

'Anything and everything. Personal life; business dealings. A brief appraisal of his integrity, should we say. I'm planning to do some business with him and need to be sure I'm getting a straight deal . . . you understand?'

'Yes, I understand. It is no problem, Mr Fitzgerald . . . my line of world, as you Americans would say.'

Fitzgerald threw back his head and laughed. 'Near enough, Konrad old son, near enough.' The laughter had disappeared when he added quietly. 'Remember, this is to be discreet. No talking to the wrong people.'

'You can trust me, Mr Fitzgerald, and I assure you I will not be talking to the wrong people.' He picked up his coffee cup and swilled the dregs around in circles. 'There is, of course, the matter of money.'

'How does three thousand down and three thousand on completion sound . . . plus expenses of course.'

Zwicky checked his eagerness. It sounded good. 'Could we say four thousand down and another four thousand on completion?' he ventured. 'I think it will be a great deal of work and I may have to pay off the odd person here and there.'

Fitzgerald, with fifty thousand dollars in his pocket – five for his advice on the airplane purchase and the remainder to start the deal rolling – nodded agreement.

Zwicky bit his lip in annoyance and wondered how much higher he could have pushed the American. Perhaps five and five, or even six and six. Forcing a smile he said, 'Who is the man, by the way? You did not yet give me his name.'

'His name is von Klaus. Otto von Klaus. Now, when you have assembled all the information . . .'

But Konrad Zwicky had stopped listening. There was just a loud buzzing sound in his ears. That and a sudden feeling of giddiness. Otto von Klaus! The credit cards he had fenced. And Mariella had been involved! He sensed that this was something big. Far bigger than he had ever undertaken before. He would go to Geneva straightaway – tonight – and talk to Mariella. He could even pay her a thousand francs on account. Then again if he went to the Black Kat Nite Club instead he could double if not treble his money. That would impress his big sister. That would show her that Konrad Zwicky's luck had finally changed. Yes, he would leave first thing tomorrow.

Outside the café the early evening sky was overcast, while further to the west in Geneva it was raining. Otto von Klaus, sitting in the glow of his desk lamp, finished looking through the previous year's accounts. In the short term, as Lisa had remarked, it was the wrong time for selling. Definitely the wrong time. But then when was the right time? What if business dropped off even more? His various enterprises were, in the main, energy related. And with the continuing fall in oil prices! He closed the folder in front of him, then looked at his watch. Seven-thirty. He rubbed his face tiredly. Where had the day gone? He always stopped at six. What was happening? You are tired, Otto, that is all, he told himself. Tomorrow we start again. Fresh. He picked up the phone and dialled Marie's number.

It rang twice, then a sultry voice said, 'Hello.'

'Marie?'

'Yes.'

'It is Otto.'

There was a short silence as Mariella suppressed a gasp. Had he found out about the credit cards? His money! 'Otto, how lovely to hear from you,' she was using her professional voice.

'Lovely be damned. Where have you been?'

'Been, Otto, been? I do not follow.'

'I have tried to call you a dozen times or more since Saturday night.'

'Ah, I see. My mother, in Zurich, she became very ill. I had to fly there at short notice.'

Von Klaus snorted and said, 'I must see you.'

'When?'

'Now.'

'But I am afraid I have a client this evening.'

'Cancel it,' he barked.

There was a pause. 'I think it might be very difficult.

'Marie, I do not give a damn about your difficulties, just cancel the appointment. I will be there in twenty minutes.' He listened for a moment expecting her to argue, but instead there was silence followed by a click. 'Marie!'

'Yes.'

'Nothing. I will see you shortly.' He put the phone down and went through to the outer office. Lisa was audio-typing. The remainder of the staff had long since left. He turned and moved back towards his office.

Lisa stopped typing and looked up. 'Something you want, Otto?'

'No, nothing,' he said tightly.

Perhaps I am hearing things he thought, returning to his desk. So what if there is a click on the telephone line. That does not mean someone is listening to my conversations. What was the name for it? Phone tap! Yes, that was it. He wondered how you could check out that sort of thing.

Half an hour later he arrived at Marie's house. The heavy rain had eased to a fine drizzle now, so that the street-lamps seemed to be suspended like electric haloes above the winding streets. It was only when he reached the entrance to the alleyway leading off the Grande Rue that he paused and held his breath. The nightmare of that night would haunt him forever and that was one more reason for selling up and getting out. Perhaps distance would eventually erase the memory. One thing he felt certain about was that remaining in Geneva and being amidst the old familiar streets would keep the wound open forever. He moved towards the front door of the house, turning up his raincoat collar and pulling his chin down in a vain attempt to conceal his presence from anyone who might be watching.

He rang the bell and waited, looking nervously from side to side. The light in the hallway was dim as Mariella opened the door. He hurried in without a word, making for the sitting-room. She followed, but before she had the opportunity to speak a letter was thrust into her hand.

'Read that,' von Klaus said aggressively, 'and then tell me what the hell you think you are doing . . . and for your sake you had better have a good excuse.'

Mariella, dressed in one of her favourite black gowns, moved across to a table-light and started reading.

'What is this?' she cried spinning around. 'What is this you are giving to me? Blackmail! Blackmail! Damn your eyes, Otto, you should know me better.' Her voice had dropped and tears were filling her heavily made-up eyes, when she added, 'After all these years . . . after all . . .' She sank defeatedly to the sofa, hands clutched tightly together, head bowed.

The sting was removed from the German's voice when he said, 'All right, what about the doctor, the one who stitched my wound?'

She dabbed her cheeks with a tiny lace handkerchief and looked up with glittering eyes. 'Oh no, Otto, not him. He's too much of a gentleman. Besides which, he is very wealthy.'

'What about the two young men, the ones who . . .' His voice faded away. He could not bring himself to discuss dead bodies; it made him feel physically sick.

'No, they are too simple. And uneducated young men do not ask for those sort of figures. To them, fifty thousand francs would be a fortune.'

Von Klaus, still in his wet raincoat, sank wearily into a chair. 'Could I have a drink?'

Mariella leapt to her feet and went to the drinks cabinet. When Otto asked quietly for something he was not at all well. Come to think of it, he did look jaded. She poured a large whisky and handed it to him. 'How is the arm?'

'It itches a lot.'

'It has been bathed and cleaned?'

'Yes.'

'You'd better let me take a look . . . come through to the bedroom.'

He let himself be led to her bedroom and sat heavily on the end of the bed, 'It is very worrying,' he said as if to himself. 'Very worrying.'

Mariella moved close to him, smoothing his brow with her short plump fingers. 'Do not worry,' she said soothingly, 'I will help you.'

He looked up, uncertainty in his eyes. 'You will do that after . . .'

Her fingers silenced his lips as she produced a quick-silver smile. It was a smile full of sincerity and kindness. Or the smile of an actress who had forgotten what sincerity and kindness really were after ten thousand performances.

'Of course I will. And the first thing I will do is to speak to a police inspector client of mine. I will find out how the police would resolve such a problem . . . then we will apply the same method.'

'Do you think that is safe?'

'Oh yes. Anyway, he is always very drunk. He never remembers what has happened.'

'Perhaps it will work.'

'There are no other people you suspect? At your office for instance!'

Von Klaus thought back to the day which had followed the killing. He had gone home. His housekeeper had been there. Then Lisa brought papers from the office for signature. He had told her he had fallen down some steps and badly bruised the muscle in his left shoulder. She stayed for a short while and they drank coffee. And then he had taken a sedative and gone to bed. That was all.

He downed the whisky in one go. 'No one,' he said. 'No one at all.'

Mariella refilled his glass. 'I've just had a thought,' she said, 'something I once saw on the movies. We find out the make of typewriter used to write the letter. That way we could perhaps . . .' her voice droned on, but von Klaus wasn't listening. He was feeling the fire of whisky spread through his belly and picturing the Rubens-like figure beneath the black dress.

17 October

ACCORDING TO THE BBC news it was England's first Indian summer for seven years. In Regent's Park the trees were autumn coloured and the dust lifted by the warm breeze hung like a golden haze in the sunlight. Young couples drifted aimlessly hand in hand, mingling with pram-pushing nannies, truant schoolboys and smartly blazered ex-majors.

Chance Fitzgerald had met Lisa Wendell-Holmes five minutes earlier. They were now walking along the footpath by the lake.

'I thought it would at least be raining,' she said conversationally.

Fitzgerald looked up at the sky. It was cloudless. 'Another few days perhaps . . . If the weather men are to be believed.'

'Almost makes you want to come back here and live.'

'You're from London then?'

'Richmond.'

He smiled. 'Ah, I should have known.'

'Known what?'

'Known they would have written a song about you. "Sweet Lass of Richmond Hill".'

Lisa felt herself blushing. 'Do you have any news from Otto?' she enquired, changing the subject.

Fitzgerald patted his pocket. 'I do indeed. Good and bad.'

'Oh.'

'The good is that I have found the machinery as requested. The bad is that the price is a little heady. Like trying to buy a bottle of the best during prohibition.'

Lisa said: 'Supply and demand. Although I would have thought that surplus military aircraft would have been cheaper than, say, a civil airliner.'

'Machinery, not aircraft. You read the instructions I left with Otto!'

'Yes. Seemed a bit cloak and dagger.'

'Oh, it's that all right. And believe me it needs to be. Talking in riddles confuses the enemy long enough for yours truly to be a long way away when the balloon goes up. Anyway, enough of my problems. How did you know that military machinery was cheaper than the civil?'

'Educated guess. Otto's companies have dealt with third world governments from time to time and I've seen reports condemning a thousand typewriters for no other reason than computers were the "in" thing. I therefore imagined an army surplus typewriter with a condemned label would be sold off for pennies.'

'True.'

'But not your sort of typewriters, is that it?'

'Maybe, but I'm dealing with brokers. They're the guys who are probably third down the line from the dealer who paid peanuts for it to the military.'

'Couldn't we have done that? Bought direct, I mean.'

'If you want to be seen by everyone and listed for what you're doing, sure you could. As it is, we're trying to keep a low profile.'

Lisa stopped and looked across the lake. 'I used to come here when I was a little girl,' she said reminiscently, 'and feed the ducks.'

'And did you ever play the game of wondering where you would be when you were grown up?'

'Yes, I suppose I did.'

'And where did you think that would be?'

Her eyes searched across the water for somewhere which didn't exist any more. 'Still here. Except I would be a mother with my own little girls . . . still feeding the same ducks.'

'You never married then?'

'Yes,' she replied, her voice growing softer. 'My husband died three years ago.'

'I'm sorry . . .'

'It's all right . . . it was a long time ago.' Her voice brightened suddenly. 'Anyway, what about you? Are you married?'

'Once. Then airplanes somehow got in the way . . . we were divorced five years back.'

'And children?'

'A daughter I rarely see . . . she lives with my ex-wife's people in Jersey.'

They were silent for a while, then Lisa said, 'And what else do you do, other than sell machinery as you put it?'

'Apart from a lifetime's study of the card player's catechism and a few years at the sly craft of soldiering, not a lot. Just one of those rebels with all the wrong causes. Tolerated at twenty, frowned on at thirty, and something far worse at forty I shouldn't wonder.'

'That sounds irresponsible!'

'Oh, but it is, dear lady. The Catholic conscience quietened a long while ago. Besides, I couldn't change it now even if I wanted to.'

'Have you tried?'

His blue eyes looked momentarily troubled. 'To try,' he said softly, 'you need three things. Number one is the reason. Number two is the will power, and number three, the money. And the most I've ever held at any one time is a small pair, and without a full house . . .' He left the unfinished sentence hanging in the air.

'I suppose I'd better get the information through to Otto,' she said at length.

'You'll telex it?'

'Yes, we have an office in Piccadilly.'

'One other item not on the list. The price. Twelve million US dollars. Also tell Otto we'll need up-front money for the people in Alaska.'

'How about a letter of credit?'

'Afraid not. Cash or a bank draft's the only way they'll deal.'.

61

'That could be difficult. Otto was hoping to do a back-to-back letter of credit. Not that he said that much, but that's the way all his deals go.'

'Not this one, I'm afraid. Couldn't he bridge a loan with one of the Swiss banks?'

Lisa was thoughtful for a moment. 'If he did,' she said, 'he'd be in hock up to his eyebrows. If anything went wrong he'd be left without a penny.'

'Alchemy!' Fitzgerald said softly.

'What was that?'

'Nothing. Base metal to gold; not important. What is, however, is lunch. Can I interest you?'

She looked at him and felt the resolve slipping. She had told herself she would not become involved, that the pain would be too great. But then how many times in her life had she met a Chance Fitzgerald. 'How long is the telex?'

'Pretty long. About four pages.'

'Oh. In that case I'd better skip lunch. Otto needs the details as soon as possible.'

'Dinner then?'

Their eyes met. He smiled and at that moment she felt as though she could handle all the pain in the world.

Otto von Klaus received the coded telex message from Lisa two hours later. It was three-thirty in Geneva. He deciphered the text using the instruction card left by Fitzgerald, frowning as the last line became clear. Twelve million dollars to be paid to current owner before aircraft released.

He sat back in his chair and lit a cigarette. The next stage was to add fifty per cent – the rule when dealing with Iran. Naturally there would be a protracted period of bargaining, except he, Otto von Klaus, had the whip hand. Fitzgerald had not only sent a fully detailed specification of the aircraft, but he had pointed out that the Iranian Air Force was heavily dependent upon this type of transport aircraft. A leftover from the days of the Shah, when American trade flourished. Naturally the air force of those days had invested heavily in American hardware. Then, with the emergence of the Ayatollah in 1979, the American market place had become a no-go area. Which was fine in principle. Except principles rarely won wars. The ongoing conflict with Iraq proved that. According to Fitzgerald and information he had received, seventy per cent of their Hercules fleet of thirty aircraft was unserviceable either through battle damage or shortage of spare parts. It was obvious, therefore, that transport planes were on the list of priorities. Fitzgerald had concluded his report by saying the C–130 being sold to them would in all probability be used as a 'Christmas Tree' – i.e. parts would be taken from it to make other aircraft airworthy. One aircraft being the 'Santa Claus' which would put ten more in the air. And if that was true the German was not going to back off his price by one cent. No, twelve million became eighteen. The six-million-dollar profit margin made him feel almost happy.

Of course, the method of payment still needed to be agreed. There had to be a way to make the Iranians pay in advance. For a profit of six million dollars Otto von Klaus felt sure he could find it.

The resort of Monte Carlo is one of the three 'Quartiers' of the Principality of Monaco. It is situated on an escarpment at the base of the Maritime Alps along the French Riviera just nine miles north-east of Nice. It is one of those fairy-tale lands, a beautiful and luxurious playground for the world's rich. But apart from the Casino introduced by Charles III of Monaco in 1856 to revitalise a flagging economy and the more recent Monaco Grand Prix, when the narrow winding streets are given over to the best that the Formula One circuit can offer, it is a country of zero income tax. A place from which to run international businesses and retain every last penny of profit.

It was along those lines that Rashid Suliman – a one time seller of death and destruction – had been thinking when the telephone rang in his penthouse suite at the Hotel de Paris. He picked up the gold and ivory instrument and walked out the lead until he reached the balcony. Then, looking down at the tall white yachts lying at anchor in the harbour, he took the receiver from the cradle and pinioned it between his ear and shoulder.

'Hello. Rashid Suliman.' His voice was authoritative and with little accent. He listened for a while then said, 'Yes, Mr von Klaus, that is indeed excellent news.' Another pause, then his voice became almost jovial. 'Eighteen million US dollars . . . no, that sounds very reasonable. I shall expect details by courier this evening then.' He brushed a fly away from his dark face, his left eye still coveting the magnificent white yachts. 'Of course, Mr von Klaus, of course. I will contact you early next week to make the financial arrangements. I alone am not the author of such matters you understand . . . no, no, it is my pleasure, Mr von Klaus.'

He replaced the receiver and put the instrument on a small patio table. So, Rashid Suliman, he thought, we have at last found a Lockheed Hercules, a war steed for our masters. Praise be to Allah, for without him you might have returned to your homeland a failure.

He poked a finger under the eye patch which covered his right eye and scratched the socket. It was a curse. Ever since he had lost the eye eighteen months earlier at a battle in the Faw peninsula, it had been a constant source of irritation. Perhaps there were slivers of metal still inside the stitched-up wound! The army surgeon at the field hospital had assured him it was completely free of debris, or words to that effect. The only problem being the man had been a horse doctor, and not a very good one at that. No, he, Rashid Suliman, would travel to London before long. He would find a Harley Street specialist – the finest in the world. It would take money, of course, lots of money. But that would be the only way.

He took a last envious glance down at the bay of white yachts before returning to the regal splendour of his suite. After years of being bivouacked in the desert with hundreds of his fellow countrymen, smelling their rank body odour day after day and night after night, of ladling soup out of huge black cauldrons in which the grinning heads of sheep were boiling and then washing down the vile concoction with brackish water, this was suddenly paradise. A book with an ending. It was as though he had died. As though he had reached that state when the sun ceased to shine and the stars fell down and the mountains were blown away, and had then been delivered free from all evil by Allah to this place. This paradise. Reclining in robes of silk on soft couches, feeling not the scorching heat or the biting cold. Being served with silver dishes and beakers as large as goblets, silver goblets brimful with ginger-flavoured water from the Fount of Selsabil.

Suliman smiled a smile of deep contentment. He had given the German a large sale. A promise of great profit. But were not promises made to be broken? And would not he, Rashid Suliman, a one-eyed soldier of Islam, benefit beyond his wildest dreams!

Suddenly, as if to be careful of counting his blessings too soon, he sank to his knees and started to pray. 'In the name of Allah, the Compassionate, the Merciful. Praise be to Allah, the creator of heaven and earth. He sends forth the angels as his messengers, with two, three or four pairs of wings. He multiplies his creatures according to His will. Allah has power over all things . . .'

It was midnight in London when Fitzgerald heard the first of the rain brushing against the window pane. He turned to Lisa.

'So much for the BBC and their Indian summer . . .' he started, then stopped. Her eyes were closed. She was asleep. He lay back on the pillow, one arm still wrapped around her soft warm body. It had been a strange sort of day, he decided. A strange sort of week even. Lisa Wendell-Holmes, an English lady who had worked for Otto von Klaus for three years, who spoke a number of languages, who had hazel eyes flecked with green, who was very attractive, who was a widow, who had come to his bed – and that was all he knew. But then, wasn't that always the way?

Gently withdrawing his arm he reached across and switched off the bedside light and whispered 'Goodnight.' As sleep came, a small voice deep inside tried to tell him there was no future in it. But there was no one to hear.

20 October
Norfolk, England
MONDAY 1100 HOURS

IT WAS RAINING hard as Fitzgerald drove down the rutted perimeter track towards the black hangar. The former military aerodrome was one of many scattered throughout East Anglia, the majority of which had long since returned to the plough, leaving only the odd wartime building to mark it out for what it had once been.

Not so with this place. True, the runways were in a bad state of repair and the squat control tower needed a coat of paint, but it was still a place of flying men. It was on the other side of the airfield that they had erected their portacabin flying school and parked their single-engined Cessnas neatly alongside. However, the hangar to which he was now driving belonged to a crop-spraying company, and Guy Stanton was the boss. He was also the man at the top of Fitzgerald's list. The first man he had phoned. A smooth-talking ex-public school scoundrel, elegant dresser, black sheep of a very wealthy family; and an expert on aircraft, armament, and the Middle East.

Fitzgerald braked to a stop outside the hangar and ran for its shelter. Once inside he paused as if in reverence. Old hangars took him that way. It was something about the cathedral-like spaciousness, the air of cold spirituality. The mingling exotic smells of metal and oil and grease and dope – as powerful as any incense from a Catholic altar. It was the sort of place you either loved or hated. To Chance Fitzgerald it was the home he never had.

He moved slowly forward into the dim light thrown down by the inadequate skylight windows. A number of birds, frightened by the echoing footsteps, cried out from the steel rafters above, before the invisible beat of wings carried them through some secret exit to the outside world. It was then that a cultured voice called out.

'Is that you, Chance?'

Hands thrust deep in his raincoat pockets, Fitzgerald moved towards the voice. 'And who else would it be on such a bloody awful day!'

Stanton, dressed in an immaculate light tan suit and smoking a half corona, came forward out of the shadows. 'So, you old rogue, what brings you to this uninspiring backwater?' He laughed. 'No, don't tell me, you took a wrong turn at Jelalabad!'

'Something like that,' Fitzgerald said wearing his customary smile. 'Anyway, that's hardly the gear for a crop-spraying pilot to be wearing now, is it?'

'Day off, or should I say the joys of running one's own company . . . I'm the best boss I ever had.'

'Makes money then?'

'Enough, plus the bonus of not having people shooting at you.'

Fitzgerald looked around the hangar. It was altogether shabby. Two crop-spraying aircraft with big radial engines dripping oil occupied one corner, whilst the remainder was scattered with crates and boxes of chemicals. The concrete floor was pitted and black with oil stains.

'So you don't miss the excitement then! Pitting your wits against the odd missile or two. Running the gauntlet against the reactionary elements of a nice little banana republic!'

Stanton dropped his cigar on the floor and ground it out with the toe of his shoe. 'That was a long time ago, Chance.'

'It doesn't have to be.'

Stanton's aristocratic face showed understanding. 'Ah, so that's what this is all about. For social visit read recruiting drive. Where is it this time? The Jekdalek Valley, Afghanistan, teaching the Mujaheddin how to knock down Soviet gun-ships! Or perhaps Nicaragua to give the

"Contras" more advice on flying vintage kites. Come to that, I hear they're still killing people in the Falls Road. No jet-lag getting there, old boy, and one can even get home for the weekend.'

Fitzgerald said quietly, 'If I didn't know you better I would have said you were growing soft.'

'People change.'

'Not our kind.'

'Not your kind perhaps. My kind, I'm afraid, is through with action-man excursions to hell and back. There's something to be said for going to bed at night and waking in the morning without the stench of death in your nostrils.'

Fitzgerald looked at Stanton. Years earlier they had often been mistaken for brothers, not only in looks but also in attitudes. Now he saw something he had fought against all his life. Age! Not the lines set into the face or the greying hair, but more the defeat in the eyes. Defeat or realisation? Or acceptance of *Ora*, *Labora* and *Vita Communis* – the prayer, labour and communal life of the working man when the dreams have finally been snuffed out.

'Married is it?' Fitzgerald said perceptively.

Stanton shrugged. 'I don't see that that has anything to do with it. Why not face reality, Chance? We're old men now. Wars are for youngsters; fit and healthy types with lightning fast reactions, who have no objections to unloading napalm on a village of innocent civilians.'

Fitzgerald smiled. 'We all die sooner or later, Guy, part of the big game plan . . . or didn't they teach you that at Eton!'

Stanton laughed mockingly. 'Always the man with the words, aren't you, Chance? The only chap I know who makes murder sound like a respectable word.'

Fitzgerald clicked his tongue reprovingly. 'And aren't all soldiers murderers in one way or another, or does being a soldier of the Queen absolve you from sin? Besides, didn't those very Queens and Kings back in the pages of history kill unmercifully to grab the land and the power!'

'That's not the point – '

'It never is, Guy, it never is. And if you're going to tell me that the old mother church has got to you, forget it. I could name a few wars blessed in her name.'

'It's nothing to do with that,' Stanton said lamely. 'It's just that I've had enough.'

'You're talking yourself out of a lot of money.'

'I don't need it.'

'And I haven't even mentioned the word war.'

'I still don't need it.'

'A hundred thousand dollars!'

Stanton turned and started walking across the hangar. He made the half-way point before he stopped.

'For doing what?' he shouted without turning round.

'Delivering a Hercules from Alaska.'

'To where?'

'Iran.'

Stanton laughed loudly and started walking again. 'Iran! Has anyone ever told you, Fitzgerald, that you're bloody crazy?'

'Where are you going?'

'Pub in the village.'

'I'll join you then,' Fitzgerald called.

Stanton stopped and turned. 'On one condition, you lunatic Irishman, and that is I do not want to hear about Alaska and Hercules and ferry flights to Iran. Is that understood?'

Fitzgerald smiled, pushed his hands deep into his raincoat pockets and started walking towards the Englishman. 'As the world advances towards you – retreat! Sure thing, old son, and if that's the way you want it who am I to say otherwise?'

It was also raining as far south as Geneva when a bedraggled Konrad Zwicky rang Mariella Schlegel's doorbell. All in all, it had been a disastrous week. Ever since he had received the first payment of four thousand francs from the American Fitzgerald. Of course he should have left immediately for Geneva. That way he could now be passing information back to London and awaiting the second four thousand. Instead he had gone back to the Black Kat Nite Club.

Initially it had been truly amazing. His luck, it seemed, really had changed. The more he played, the more he won.

And so it was that Tuesday night became Wednesday night and Wednesday became Thursday. He even bought some new clothes on the Friday; a pale blue suit, canary yellow shirt, and white casual shoes. Then he went back to the club and began winning all over again. Of course, the girls had been excited, each one vying for his favour. At the end of the night he had bought them all champagne. He awoke the following morning with a hangover and two of the club's prettier hostesses in his bed.

The amazing sequence of good fortune ended on the Sunday night. By which time he had accumulated a staggering eighty thousand francs. That was when the cheroot-smoking, bald-headed Xavier da Silva had invited him into the backroom. The game for the high rollers as da Silva had put it.

Zwicky was escorted into the smoke-filled room by Lolita, the blonde that all the club's customers drooled over. Her plunging neckline and splendid cleavage were almost legendary in night life circles. What was more, she stood behind him throughout the evening massaging his shoulders and generally putting him off his game with whispered suggestions that brought a blush even to Konrad's face. It was when he was down to his last few hundred francs that she moved away and started the same game with another player in the poker school.

Konrad was feeling sick to the pit of his stomach as he placed his final bet. How could this have happened? Eighty thousand francs in one night! By chance he happened to glance up from the pool of light over the green baize table. In the shadows beyond the circle of players he noticed Lolita moving her fingers above the player's head. Her eyes were looking at the dealer, Xavier da Silva. So that was it! A code. Damn her. Damn him. Damn them all. He had been set up. Anger burned quickly into his head, but he knew it would be folly to accuse da Silva of cheating. No, the only way to combat it was with some cheating of his own. And for that he would need a partner.

The door in the Grande Rue was eventually opened by a heavily made-up Mariella. She was fixing an ear-ring, certain that it was her afternoon client who was early. Her fingers, as her face, froze when she saw who it was.

'What the hell do you want?' she said sharply.

Konrad shuffled his feet in a boyish manner. 'I've . . . I've come to pay you the money I owe you,' he said in a subdued voice.

'You have it?' she replied in disbelief.

'Would I have come if I had not?'

They were in the kitchen when she said, 'Well, where is it?'

Konrad smiled nervously, extracting a crushed packet of cigarettes from his pocket at the same time. He lit one, brushing away the smoke which burned his eyes.

'You don't have it, do you?' Her voice was full of cold anger now.

'Better than that,' he answered.

She looked at him closely and saw the marks of too much drinking about his face. The eyes, however, emanated something which made her reluctant to throw him out. 'I'm listening,' she said.

Konrad dropped into a chair by the kitchen table and quickly outlined his meeting with Fitzgerald in Zurich, making sure he made no mention of the initial payment of four thousand francs.

'And that is it,' she said, when he had finished.

Konrad crunched out his cigarette. His eyes were a long time searching the room before they returned to hers. 'You know this Otto von Klaus, don't you?'

She took a moment to answer, not wanting to say too much. But on the other hand he was her brother. And if she could not confide in him, then who could she? 'Yes, I know Otto.'

'Well, don't you see,' he replied impatiently, 'Fitzgerald wants information. The right sort of information could be worth a lot more than the four thousand francs he's promised me.'

Mariella, who was sitting on the other side of the table, squirmed uncomfortably. How much to tell? That was the question. Finally, she said: 'He is planning to sell his companies. The amount he is hoping to get is twenty million francs.'

71

Konrad let out a low whistle. 'Twenty million . . . how do you know this? How did you find out?'

'He is one of my clients. He keeps a pocket diary in which he writes down important business matters.'

'So how did you . . .'

'While he sleeps, I look in the diary.'

Konrad laughed. 'Good, good. And that is how you got the credit cards?'

She was motionless for a while. 'No, that is not the way. I picked them up in the street. You remember the body you and your friend Willy disposed of.' Konrad nodded, not really wanting to remember. 'Well, Otto was the man who killed him.'

A silence abruptly fell between them and was all the more startling because it descended on the rush of words like a slammed gate. Konrad, who had caught his breath at the revelation, now pressed his lips tightly together to hold back any sound until he could be sure of controlling it. His voice when it came was thin and high-pitched.

'Killed him . . . you are sure of this?'

She nodded. 'It happened outside in the alley.'

Konrad lit another cigarette. 'Could I have a drink?' he asked. 'This needs to be thought out.'

Mariella went through to the sitting-room and returned with two wine glasses filled with neat whisky. 'I will join you. It has been that sort of day.'

Konrad drained the glass in quick little sips, twirling it expertly in his hand each time he took it from his lips.

'Yes,' he said at length, 'Mr Fitzgerald will have to pay a lot of money for this kind of information. There is nothing else you can tell me, for instance about the deal that Mr von Klaus and Mr Fitzgerald are planning?'

'Perhaps your Mr Fitzgerald has something to do with the purchase of Otto's companies!'

Konrad was about to reply when the doorbell sounded.

Mariella threw back the remains of her Scotch, shuddered slightly and stood up. Smoothing down the slinky black dress she said, 'Stay in here, and don't make a sound. This one is old, no stamina, so I won't be long.' She laughed and moved towards the door. 'And while you are here in Geneva you had better stay with me.'

'Until I get the money from Mr Fitzgerald, you mean?'

'Until *we* get the money, brother dear . . . until *we* get the money.'

Back in Norfolk, Fitzgerald was having a harder time convincing Guy Stanton than he had imagined. The Crooked Fiddler was a whitewashed pub, complete with neat thatched roof and typical Norfolk flint walls which ran along the sides and rear of the property. Inside there was a long bar, low black-beamed ceiling and a log fire crackling cheerfully in a large open hearth. The furniture was cottage style: round oak tables and matching chairs with chintzy cushions. A black Alsatian peered up inquisitively as the two men, water dripping from their raincoats, entered the room. Satisfied they were here on legitimate business, the dog muzzled its nose back between its paws and went to sleep. Apart from the dog, three old men sat at a table near the window playing dominoes. Their conversation faltered just long enough for them to inspect the newcomers before returning to their game.

Stanton moved to the bar. 'Good day, Arthur, how's business?'

Arthur Young, the owner of the Crooked Fiddler, shrugged. He was a big countryman with black hair parted in the middle and the type of moustache favoured by long ago sergeant-majors. 'Damned weather's keeping them all at home. And only a few days ago the weather man was promising the sunshine would last for at least another week . . . still, I suppose it's good for the gardens.' He picked up a glass. 'Must have hit your business as well, sir . . . the weather!'

Stanton lit a cigar. 'Luckily there's not much on at the moment.'

'Ah well, one man's meat . . . your usual is it, sir?'

'Thank you, Arthur.' He turned to Fitzgerald. 'Still on the Irish?'

'Bushmills! No thanks, just a mineral water.'

'Mineral water! What happened to the hard stuff?'

'High days and holidays. Besides, I'm in training.' Fitzgerald turned to the barman. 'Nice place you've got here.'

'That it is, sir. Fifteen years I've had it now and the village is still the same as when I first arrived. Not that I'm against change you understand, but it has to be for the better, don't you think?'

The two men smiled agreement and took their drinks to a table by the fire, hanging their raincoats on pegs at the side of the chimney breast to dry.

'So when did you get married?' Fitzgerald asked.

'That noticeable is it?' Stanton replied, taking a sip of his gin and tonic. 'A year last June actually. Tried to contact you but the word on the grapevine was that you'd gone back to Nicaragua.'

'Something like that. Your wife from Norfolk?'

'Norwich. We were married in the registry office there. Never thought I'd see the day though.'

'We usually do in the end. Airplanes and women. Now there's a deadly combination for you.'

'You're not back with Maxine then?'

Fitzgerald let out a long laugh. 'Jesus, Mary and Holy Joseph, I wouldn't wish her on my worst enemy, and that's a fact.'

'You still see your daughter though!'

Fitzgerald's face became serious for a moment. 'Alice, yes, from time to time. She lives with Maxine's folks in Jersey. Seems happy enough.'

Stanton puffed on his cigar. 'So tell me about this Hercules flight.'

'I thought you weren't interested.'

'I'm not, but I'd still like to know what I'm missing.'

Fitzgerald smiled and leaned forward, outlining the plan simply and quickly.

'Looks like plain sailing up to Khartoum,' Stanton remarked when Fitzgerald had finished. 'After that you've got a logistics problem.'

'Routing you mean?'

'Yes. Have you considered that a great deal of the flight from Khartoum will have to be carried out at zero feet?'

'I've considered it, sure, but as you're the expert on east of Suez terrain, not to mention the old Hercules, I figured that any observations I made would be shot down in flames. So tell me.'

'OK. Primarily we have a C–130H which has a service ceiling of around 33,000 feet. Up there and with a light payload you would have a range in the order of 4,300 nautical miles. Down on the deck you can halve that; say 2,150. And that, bear in mind, is in still-air conditions.

'Therefore, if we went direct, overflying Saudi Arabia, we would be fine. Only problem is that without diplomatic clearance we would be intercepted by their fighters and forced down. With me so far?' Fitzgerald nodded. 'Which brings us to the alternative procedure. Low level over Ethiopia into the Gulf of Aden. Once there we pick up a track for Bombay except that half-way across the Arabian Sea we turn left and run into Iran from the south. There's a small town on the southern coast called Chah Bahar. It has an airstrip.'

'And you think we'd pull it off without being intercepted?'

'Better odds than Saudi. Also, once over the Gulf of Aden you could climb and make a high-level cruise towards Bombay. Hopefully you would be taken for commercial airways' traffic.'

'So what's the problem?'

'I didn't say there was one.'

'Except you don't sound very convincing.'

Stanton finished his drink. 'The distance could be the stumbling block. The second routing would be in the order of 2,500 miles. And as I said earlier, range at sea level would be 2,150. Maybe less.'

'But you said we could climb over the Gulf of Aden. That would save fuel.'

'Some, agreed. But the high level cruise would only be to a mid-point in the Arabian Sea. Once you've turned left for Iran you would need to drop down to be sure of staying off someone's radar screen.'

Fitzgerald rubbed his chin thoughtfully. 'According to my reckoning, though, we could still just about make it;

providing we did the high level bit you mentioned.'

'Except you've forgotten about the prevailing winds,' Stanton said. 'December time, the surface winds over the majority of that route will be on the nose.'

'How much?'

'Enough to make it extremely hazardous.'

'So we fit internal ferry tanks.'

Stanton shook his head. 'Someone would smell a rat. A legitimate operation on famine relief in the Sudan would need every cubic inch of space for cargo.'

Fitzgerald said, 'Any ideas?'

'I'd need to go over the figures. Distances, exact fuel burns at specific attitudes. Also an accurate average of upper and lower winds for that route during December.'

'When can you do that?'

Stanton suddenly jerked back in his chair and laughed. 'You're not getting me to talk myself into a corner . . . I see the game now.'

'Game?'

'Yes, game. A damned difficult game come to that.'

'Well it's not going to be easy, that's for sure. But then when was anything in our line of work plain sailing?'

'I still don't need the money,' Stanton said, with less conviction than he had earlier.

'Sure you don't. You'll just hide yourself away in this God-forsaken backwater and fly your toy airplanes until you become too old or lose your medical, and then they'll plant you in some pleasant little marble orchard with only the beech trees and the rooks for company.' Fitzgerald stared into the dancing flames of the fire. A log dropped, sending a flurry of sparks up the chimney. 'No, Guy, you're not the type. If you had been you would have signed up with British Airways years ago. All that respectability and an immaculate uniform, and beautiful young girls to serve you coffee on the flight deck, and God knows what else in your hotel room in the evening. No, old son, you're one of us, like it or not. A tired old bastard as leathery and tough as the Mujaheddin, who will still be lugging his battered flight case across the ramp a hundred years from now, long after the British Airways types have retired to a country

76

cottage in Devon or Cornwall on a fat index-linked pension.

'Climbing up into cockpits of antiquated airplanes with enough snags to have them condemned. Dodging typhoons over the South China Sea to unload stores on a few khaki-coloured rebels who are probably fighting for a more worthy cause than we are. And the joke is, old son, when we get back we'll probably find that the paymaster has absconded with our wages.' Fitzgerald finished his drink. 'But then it won't really matter, because we'll be alive. Adrenalin, Guy, we live on it. Without it we might as well go to our graves right now.'

Stanton was pensive for a long while. He finished his cigar and tossed it into the fire, then sat back in his chair.

'Not so long back,' he said pointedly, 'I read an article in *Time* or *Newsweek*. It was about an American army colonel who was attempting to supply missiles to the Iranians. The colonel, along with a few shady arms dealers, had cooked up a fairly impressive plot to ship the arms out of Miami on a 747. Unfortunately, for them at least, the FBI got wind of the operation and busted the entire gang. In the light of the that wouldn't you think that the FBI, and the CIA come to that, have really tightened up on the military surplus side of the market?'

'But it's not an arms deal, Guy. As I've told you, it's a legitimate cargo operation. Turks and Caicos set up to supply famine relief through the Red Cross to the Sudan. You can't get much more straight arrow than that. That we lose the airplane on the first mission is naturally tragic. That you and your crew walk out of the swamps a week later endorses the "crash" story . . . as well as making you heroes.'

'And you're setting up the company?'

'Yes, but my name will be absent from any official documents. Nominee shareholders usually form the list which appear on the records.'

'And who would they be? The nominee shareholders!'

'Oh, stooges from the accountant's office who set up the company. So if you're worrying about the CIA breathing down your neck, don't.'

'Just the fanatical Iranians!'

'Look, Guy, we need to make a run from Khartoum to Iran. For that I need a minimum of three crew. Two pilots and a flight engineer. Once that's sorted we can check out all the niggling little problems we might have to face when the time comes for the flight to take place, not least of which is getting the crew back from Iran to the Sudan without being spotted.' Fitzgerald was smiling when he added, 'I mean, did I ever let you down before?'

Stanton expelled a tired breath. 'No, and you're not going to get the opportunity to try again.'

Fitzgerald fell silent, his eyes appearing sightless as he stared into some private eternity. 'I checked out your company before I came,' he said eventually, 'which means I know your financial position.'

The veneer cracked ever so slightly. 'Yes, well, it's nothing for you to be concerned about. Slight hiccup in the cash flow; nothing a good season next year won't put right.'

'If you get to next year before the bailiffs move in, you mean!'

'I'll get there.'

'I doubt that. I mean, how do you pay debts without money?'

'I don't have any immediate debts; well a couple maybe, but I can hold them off for a while yet.'

'What about the planes?'

'Both paid – ' Stanton stopped abruptly, his eyes questioning. 'You're not going to call in the loan?' he added with disbelief.

Fitzgerald scratched his head, a mock-serious expression on his face. 'Now let me see, when was it? Two years ago! And you needed forty thousand dollars and I loaned you half of it. Of course with interest that would add up to a pretty penny now.' He laughed. 'No, I'm not calling in the loan, but I am looking for one of my own.'

'Blackmail – transitive verb and noun. Compel, compulsion. To make payment or action in return for concealment of discreditable secret. Figuratively, to make use of threats or moral pressure.' Stanton's voice had an edge of bitterness.

'Now there you go with that superior education of yours. I mean, what would I, a simple Irish-American, know of transitive verbs or blackmail. In fact I'd already decided to write off the loan . . . let's call it a wedding present, shall we?'

'Let's call it blackmail you homeless nomad.'

Fitzgerald laughed at that. 'Occasionally their black tents appear on the outskirts of a city. Men with lean weathered faces and squinted eyes, buying up provisions. Soon the black tents are gone and the Bedouin are back roaming their beloved barrens. Now tell me of a finer life?'

'I would still need to convince my wife,' Stanton said tonelessly.

'I've already thought of that. Tell her you've been hired as a consultant to set up an air-drop programme for the Sudan. You might even mention Bob Geldof's name to add authenticity.'

'One of your better lies, Chance, but I think she deserves the truth.'

The Irishman's face darkened. 'Sorry, Guy, you know the rules. Play about with the truth as much as you like, but never tell it.'

Stanton was silent as he ventured into that abysmal dark place in the mind. It was the place all soldiers went before the battle. The panic area. Viewing all the terrible ways of dying. Staring into the mirror and seeing yourself dead. Looking down on your own corpse as life continues without you. He smiled tensely. It was honour which would commit him in the end. Chivalric figures simply did not turn and run. Even when they belonged to that grimmest of all companies, The Order of St Lazarus – reserved for knights who had contracted leprosy. Or in the twentieth-century way of things – shell shock. And how did you tell a friend that you were afraid? Frightened of guns, bombs and the pagan desert lands which had spawned that fear. Especially when you could not really admit it to yourself.

There was a great sadness in his eyes when he turned to Fitzgerald and said, 'When do we start?'

* * *

In Tehran it was mid-afternoon. A cooling wind which had had its birth over the Caspian Sea before starting its journey south over the Elburz mountains, failed to penetrate the high-walled courtyard where Rashid Suliman sat watching the sunlight glint on the mosaic of window panes. Across the small garden table, his face lost in the shadow of a fig tree, Suliman's guest, Fazlollah Mahallati, sat clicking worry beads between his fingers. Mahallati, head of the Islamic Revolutionary Guards Corps and a representative of the nation's leader, was a rising star in Iran's new political regime. He was also a lifelong friend of Rashid Suliman. Both men, dressed in simple white jellabahs and open sandals, had been sitting in the garden for more than two hours. Their conversation, in the great Arabic tradition, had flowed in wide majestic circles, circumnavigating the heart of the matter up for discussion. Now, during the past five minutes, Mahallati had become silent. His dark eyes were deep in troubled thought.

'You are very quiet, Fazlollah,' Rashid said.

'Forgive me, my friend, I was thinking of this latest battle of Faw. Of the helicopter gun-ships and tanks and rocket launchers. Our brave soldiers told me it was a walking wall of fire.' He sighed deeply. 'Two days ago I was there . . . just hours after the fighting had stopped. And you know, Rashid, walking through the detritus struck me as a foretaste of the day after the end of the world, with not a single birdsong to disturb the grey final silence.'

He put a hand to his forehead. 'It is all here, my faith, but sometimes it weakens. Sometimes I feel like Zacharias who was with a barren wife without an heir. Except he prayed to Allah and was given a son . . . my prayers it seems are less tangible.' He sighed again. 'Sometimes, Rashid . . . sometimes I think I am an unworthy servant of Islam.'

Rashid shook his head. 'No, Fazlollah, not you. Did you not notice, as I have done, that even amongst the ruins hope grows? Flowers reach from the spent cases of shells. Blossoms spring from the implements of war. Just so, we of the Arab nation must be optimistic. Mustn't we?'

Fazlollah leaned forward out of the shadows, the sunlight reflecting the silver in his beard. His eyes had lost some of their sadness when he said, 'And you say I am not unworthy! Against you, Rashid, I am nothing more than a poor sherbet seller.'

Rashid laughed loudly. It was a valve to release his impatience. The new-found irritability which had been building within him ever since his frequent buying trips to Europe had opened the doors to exotic nightclubs, elegant hotels and the beautiful white-skinned girls who had willingly shared his bed. And now, after that breathless, skin-tingling excitement, he had been thrust back into a land as old as time itself. A time which had now become valueless. Where a day passed in idle conversation was considered a day well spent.

'So, my beloved sherbet seller, what of the papers I have brought you? You have read them?'

Fazlollah clicked his worry beads a few more times before answering. 'You remember the old days, Rashid? The old days of happy bargaining, when we would go into the suq and the merchant with the white hair would cry: "Regard it! for only twenty-five rials, a pitcher of pitchers! The sun and the moon of pitchers!" And you would answer: "That! It is dented, worthless. But from charity and because I suffer from a softening of the heart, I will offer you three rials." '

Rashid smiled warmly. 'Yes, my friend, I remember those days with great affection. But now you are rightly thinking that eighteen million dollars for this Hercules aircraft is too much.'

'Perhaps.'

'They are not easy to come by.'

'This is true.'

'One aircraft used for spares will probably put six of our unserviceable Hercules back in the sky.'

'This is also true.'

'But you think I have a trick yet to play!'

Fazlollah gave a sly smile. 'With you, dear friend, I never think. Except perhaps to gauge the distance your audacity might go. So tell me the way of this!'

'The same way you will win your war, Fazlollah.'

'Ah, a riddle . . . the same way I will win my war . . . but surely I am given a clue!'

Rashid absentmindedly poked a finger under his eyepatch and scratched the socket. 'The Persian Archers!' he offered.

'The Persian Archers . . . the Persian Archers! But what is this? Not enough.' Fazlollah paused and clicked his worry beads slowly between his fingers. 'But wait, you were always the scholar of history. When Iran was known as Persia, the Persian Archers were the gold coins that depicted an archer on the obverse of the coin. They were the gold coins of Achaemenids used by the Persians in bribing first one Greek state then another . . . The Peloponnesian war! I am right?'

'Thus far, sherbet seller.'

Fazlollah tugged at his beard, his eyes searching the cloudless sky as if for divine inspiration. 'Thus far you say, thus far. How goes it now?' he muttered to himself. 'At first the Persians encouraged Athens against . . . Sparta. From that they gained the treaty of Callias.' Fazlollah was smiling now as over two thousand years of history slipped into place. 'It was after that that the Persians intervened on Sparta's side, taking away their support for Athens. And so it was that Persian gold and Spartan soldiers brought about Athens' fall.' Fazlollah clapped his hands with obvious glee. 'There you see, I also remember my history.'

Rashid grinned. 'Except you omitted the Treaty of Miletus which was the pivotal point of the war. But no matter, your mind still works and that is good. But what of the riddle? You have still not answered it.'

'The riddle,' Fazlollah said proudly. 'It is simple. The papers you brought me made interesting reading between the lines. I think that your Mr von Klaus in Switzerland, being a broker, will have to buy the aircraft, or at least arrange a bank loan, if your past arms dealings are, shall we say, the normal way of things. And that financial bridging will exist until we take delivery of the aircraft at Khartoum. I am right so far, yes?'

Rashid nodded.

'So, a step further. We arrange a letter of credit on our Italian bank in Milan. And now your Mr von Klaus is happy because the Italian bank has the money and is very trustworthy. Now that we have lulled Athens, nobly played by Mr von Klaus, into a false sense of security we secretly remove our support and pledge it to Sparta . . . this, of course, is your part in the play. So, how do you, Sparta, defeat Athens?'

Fazlollah stroked his beard and pondered the question before continuing. 'Let us say that the flight is late in leaving Khartoum. Shall we make it one minute past the deadline for the letter of credit! A great sadness of course, for now the aircraft is in the sky and on its way to our country. Naturally, the bank in Milan refuses to pay the letter of credit because your telex message from Khartoum has not been received within the appointed time; that is, the terms have not been strictly complied with. Your Mr von Klaus is by this time a very worried man as he will now have to contact our government to re-negotiate new terms.'

Fazlollah looked at Rashid for a supportive gesture. All he saw was a hint of confusion in his friend's eyes.

'Finally and most tragically we find out that the aircraft has "crashed" – in exactly the way it was planned by Mr von Klaus as a brilliant subterfuge in smuggling it out of Africa. We, of course, are far from pleased. How can we possibly discuss handing over all that money for a dented and worthless pitcher, especially as Mr von Klaus, the seller, failed to comply with the letter of credit, which he, by his very own hand, has drawn up. Of course, just to make sure there are no repercussions we will have transferred the Milan funds to another Italian bank at exactly one minute past the deadline.'

Fazlollah sank back into the shadows of the fig tree, his face wreathed in a smile. 'So tell me, my friend, how close was the humble sherbet seller to the trick you had conceived?'

Rashid, who had grown visibly pale, forced a smile across his ravaged features. This was not quite the way he had intended the discussion to go. Even so, he had to admit to himself it was quite brilliant. Brilliant for Fazlollah and brilliant for Iran. But it still left him without the fortune he had planned to extract from the deal.

'What of the crew of the Hercules?' he questioned.

'The crew of the Hercules!' Fazlollah laughed. 'But they were killed, Rashid. An unmarked grave in the Sudan will give an added poignancy to the final chapter in their wretched lives. I believe in Western eyes they will be viewed as heroes. Gallant airmen giving their lives in a brave attempt to help the starving millions of that once great continent . . . that they were executed at Chah Bahar is a secret shared by you and I and Allah . . . but come, you still have not told me how close I came to the trick which you had conceived!'

'Close enough,' Rashid said unconvincingly.

'Good, that is good. I am learning. But tell me; you said "in the way I would win my war!" '

'A longer battle, but yes. Firstly, we look at the geographical situation of our enemy, Iraq. He is sandwiched between, on the east, our great nation, and on the west Syria. So we pay Syria to go to war with Iraq. Not a big war, you understand, but enough to draw the Iraqis to the west of their country. We naturally move into the south.'

Fazlollah frowned. 'And what do we pay Syria with?'

'American arms.'

'American arms!' Fazlollah laughed. 'But we have no American arms. Where would we find such a rich prize?'

Rashid said simply, 'From the Americans.'

Fazlollah laughed again. 'The story is a good one, Rashid, but how do we achieve the impossible?'

'The Syrians. As we know, they have ties with terrorism and support the Shi'ite Moslems in the Lebanon. Therefore the Syrians arrange that the Shi'ites abduct a number of American civilians.'

Fazlollah stared at Rashid for a moment. 'And we hold the Americans as hostages, you mean?'

'Exactly. Except the Western world lays the blame at the house of the Shi'ites. Our next step is to enter secret negotiations with America. A simple exchange. Arms for the lives of their citizens.'

'But what of the Syrians? The arms they have so far received will have been used against the Iraqi. They will want more for their fight with the Israeli.'

Rashid tapped the side of his nose. 'We give them a large amount of the captured Iraqi arms.'

'But in that way we have not outwitted them.'

'Oh, but we have, my brother. Are not the Israelis funded for their war by the Americans?'

'In part . . . yes.'

'And would not the Americans supply us with further arms if we pledged to crush the Syrians from the rear?'

Fazlollah was silent for a while. 'A clever plan, Rashid, but I think it will take a very long time.'

'The Peloponnesian war lasted for fifty-six years, Fazlollah. Fifty-six years. We have all the time in the world.'

Fazlollah clicked his worry beads and made no answers. He was once again at Al-Faw, stumbling through the detritus of war and smelling death in his nostrils. Except now he saw a faint light on the horizon. A faint glimmer of hope.

For Rashid, his friend's silence was a welcome relief. A moment's pause to reconsider his situation. His original plan would still work if he could find a way to ensure that at least a part of the eighteen million dollars would fall safely into his hands.

From somewhere beyond the wall, as if in warning to all unbelievers, a high sweet voice began intoning a sura from the Holy Koran.

Lisa Wendell-Holmes lay in bed, an unread book on the counterpane. The room was lit by a single bedside lamp and from another room the hi-fi system was playing a tape of Wagner's *Lohengrin*. She looked at her watch. It was nearly ten. Chance would be back from Norfolk soon. Chance Fitzgerald. How many times in her life did a woman meet a Chance Fitzgerald? She had asked herself the question over and over again since that first meeting. And now she was panicking. Afraid that it was all a mistake. Had she been too willing? Too eager. Should she have played the waiting game? Besides, what did she know of him? Nothing. Divorced. A daughter he spoke little about. And financially he seemed no better off than herself. Of course, that seemed set to change once the deal with Otto had been concluded.

She rubbed her eyes tiredly. My God, Lisa, you really are crazy. This character comes along when you least expect it – when you have made your own plans for the rest of your life – and surprises you in more ways than one. And you, noble, dedicated female that you are, begin to act like a moonstruck kid hung up over some moody rock star.

But then it shouldn't have been like this. It should have been a long and happy life with Philip. Guilt washed over her as she thought of her husband. This was the first time she had been with a man in three years. Three long, lonely years, and now! She switched out the light and burrowed her face in the pillow and cried herself to sleep.

21 October
Geneva, Switzerland
TUESDAY 0940 HOURS

OTTO VON KLAUS sat at his desk in a state of shock. Up until now the man sitting before him had been nothing more than a name on a file. The voice at the end of a telephone. Now, by his very presence he had become a threat to the German's anonymity in the whole affair.

'You will, of course, forgive me for calling unannounced,' Rashid Suliman was saying, 'but I felt the matter was of such great urgency that I had to speak to you personally.'

Von Klaus nodded. He felt unsure how to handle this man. How to voice his annoyance at the prospect of being found out as being involved in an illegal arms deal. Fitzgerald had been quite clear over that issue. Even so, the dark-skinned Arab with the hawk-like leanness of face and the one cruel unblinking eye, commanded respect.

'It is not a problem,' he said evenly. 'You would like coffee perhaps?'

'Tea in preference. Strong and sweet if that is possible.'

The German pressed a button on the intercom system and passed the order to one of the typists who had taken over Lisa's position.

'So, you were saying . . . a matter of great urgency.'

Rashid fingered the nagging itch under his right eye-patch. 'Quite so, but firstly may I congratulate you on your plan to smuggle the Hercules to Iran. The Red Cross subterfuge is brilliant, quite brilliant . . . you thought of this yourself?'

Von Klaus waved his hands. 'It was nothing. I thought of how a stage magician uses sleight of hand; this is something similar yes . . . a clever trick which deceives the eye.'

'Clever indeed,' Rashid replied admiringly. 'But now to business. The Hercules, of course, lies at the heart of the matter. Or should I say the amount of money you are asking.'

'It is too much?' von Klaus said without thinking.

'In the Arab way all things are too much. We barter for our food, our clothes — even our wives.' Then, with a slightly sardonic smile added, 'I think we would also barter for our souls given the chance.'

'So how much are you offering?'

Rashid Suliman smiled openly. 'To be precise, all and nothing!'

'I do not follow.'

'Understandably so, Mr von Klaus, but perhaps when I have finished you will.' He outlined his meeting with Fazlollah Mahallati in Tehran, modifying the story strongly in his own favour.

Von Klaus was dumbfounded. It was some time before he found his voice. 'I am most grateful to you; most grateful indeed . . . except one matter puzzles me. The reason! The reason you have told me this. Surely it is against your country's interests?'

'My country's interests exactly. And in that you have the reason. Quite simply I prefer your style of country, and shall we say I wish to purchase a small part of it . . . except for that I need money.'

The German's face showed immediate understanding. 'Ah, I see. You can arrange for the money to be paid within the terms of the letter of credit providing I pay you a commission. This is so?'

'Yes.'

'Yes,' echoed von Klaus distantly. 'There is, however, a problem, and that is I cannot work within the usual confines of a letter of credit. What I mean is that I am not a part of this matter, on the surface at least. Therefore an agent working on my behalf would have to collect the money in person in Milan.'

'This can be arranged I think.'

'Secondly, I am not a banker but I am aware of the problems with exchange control in Italy. So how does your bank justify the payment in its records, and more importantly how can it pay out so many American dollars? The authorities, you understand . . .'

Suliman said, 'This is not a problem. We – my country you understand – have many interests throughout the Western world, a leftover from the days of the Shah. Not least is a remarkable amount of American dollars unofficially lying in vaults all over Italy. The transaction will be confidential; the authorities will never know.'

Von Klaus lit a cigarette and coughed out of habit, before tackling the earlier question. 'You mentioned a commission. How much would that be?'

'I am not a greedy man, you understand, as I am sure you equally are not. Shall we say two million dollars.'

'Two . . . two million dollars!' von Klaus stammered. The tea arrived at that moment giving the German time to marshal his shattered thoughts. Two million was a great deal of money. A third of the gross profit, in fact. But at least this way he would be assured of receiving the remaining four million. And if it had not been for Suliman's devious mind he would have ended up losing everything. Even so, he was enough of a businessman to know that the first offer on the table was generally a 'feeler'.

Rashid Suliman was watching and admiring the young blonde-haired girl leaving the room when von Klaus said: 'Perhaps one million would be fairer. I am not, you understand, making much on this deal. A great many people to pay – '

'A very pretty girl,' Rashid interrupted, motioning towards the door. 'What the Koran would refer to as a virgin as fair as corals and rubies.'

Von Klaus, whose mind was caught up in more important matters and who had not even looked at the girl, said, 'Yes, very pretty. A good figure too. Perhaps you would like her to escort you to dinner this evening?'

Suliman's face lit up. 'Splendid, I look forward to it. Could we not call it a small reward for the automobile spares my country has purchased through your Monaco company?'

'A very satisfactory arrangement, yes?'

'Yes, without doubt. And of course I completely understand that the fifty per cent surcharge you levy on the normal retail price is a necessary evil in these difficult days of spiralling inflation. Not to mention the overheads you obviously have to meet.'

Von Klaus puffed nervously on his cigarette. 'As you say, overheads. These are extremely high . . . another factor in these hard times I think you will agree.'

'Indeed I do. Although I would have thought a fifty per cent increase might be construed as . . . shall we say excessive!'

Von Klaus stubbed out his cigarette and inwardly cursed the man. He was even more devious than he had first thought. 'The figure you mentioned earlier was two millions. This is correct?'

The Arab smiled. 'My tastes alas; they are not as simple as they once were.'

'But what happens once the letter of credit is paid by your Italian bankers? Surely they . . . your country that is, will arrest you . . . and what about me? What if they think I have been involved in a conspiracy?'

'Trust me.'

'It is not that, it is just . . .'

'Just that you want peace of mind.' Suliman laced his fingers together across his stomach. 'Have I not lifted up your heart and relieved you of the burden which weighed down your back?'

'Yes but – '

'And in this matter I will also offer such comfort.' The Arab's voice had lost its warmth as he outlined his plan to guarantee them both a safe future as well as the eighteen million dollars from his government.

It was early afternoon in London when Lisa received the telephone call from Otto von Klaus. She was in the elegant boardroom of the Piccadilly office, sitting at the head of the long mahogany conference table.

'Hello, Otto.'

'Lisa, how is everything?'

'Fine. Chance has recruited the crew members he requires. He's just waiting to hear from you now before he goes ahead and sets up the offshore company.'

'That is good, however matters here are more difficult.'

'Difficult?'

'This morning I had a visit from Mr Suliman.'

'Suliman?'

'The buyer.'

'Was that wise?'

'I could do nothing about that. He just arrived.'

'And?'

'A problem with the payment, one which he has resolved . . . except it will cost me a great deal of money. A commission, you understand.'

'How much?'

'That is not important; it has now been agreed. What, however, is important – in fact critical – is that I have to bridge the twelve million dollars from date of purchase to delivery out of Khartoum.'

Lisa's eyes widened. 'Bridge the twelve million! Is that safe, Otto? What if something goes wrong?'

There was an empty silence.

'That is why I am calling you, Lisa. You must do everything possible to ensure that everything goes smoothly. I do not want to borrow that kind of money for more than a few days . . . even then it will be very expensive. Perhaps you can stress the urgency of this to Chance.'

Lisa stood up and carried the telephone across to the tall window. The scene beyond the glass could be any city in the Western world. Fender-to-fender traffic and bustling pedestrians with downcast eyes and serious unsmiling faces.

'Yes of course,' she said. 'When do you think the funds will be available?'

'A few days perhaps; then another few days to transmit them via New York to the Alaska company.'

'Perhaps they have an account in New York. That could save a day or so's interest.' There was a chilly silence. She

91

was leading again. Seeking to redress the situation she added, 'Did Chance say if the purchase price was negotiable?'

'He said unlikely. Although if his inspection of the machinery found it to be not in accordance with the telexed details then there might be room for manoeuvre. Why do you ask?'

'No reason. Other than your interest of course.'

'Perhaps,' he said after a thoughtful silence, 'perhaps you should go with him.'

'To Alaska, you mean?'

'Exactly.'

'A good idea, Otto. To ensure we are getting the best deal possible you mean?'

'Of course. And finally you can find out the exact costs of hiring the crew and setting up the company . . . also the lowest figure that Chance will himself require. He and the crew will, of course, be paid following completion of the deal. That is, after the machinery has arrived safely at its destination. You understand?'

'Yes, Otto, I understand.'

'That is all then,' von Klaus said abruptly. 'I will be in touch.'

Lisa arrived at the apartment at four-thirty. Chance was sitting at his desk by the window tapping inexpertly at a portable typewriter. He stood up and kissed her lightly on the cheek.

'You look like you need a cup of coffee.'

She smiled and tugged off her wet raincoat. 'I'll make it . . . real coffee.'

'That sounds like a judgement on my instant brew.'

She laughed and went through to the kitchen. He followed.

'I've decided,' she said lightly, that all pilots must secretly bless the advent of fast food . . . matches their pace of life.'

Fitzgerald pulled her towards him. 'Next you'll be saying we go for fast women.'

Lisa said uncertainly, 'Well!'

'I wouldn't say you were fast.'

'Even after the speed with which I came to your bed?'

He kissed her again. 'And there you have your answer. Fast women don't ask those sort of questions.'

She returned his kiss before moving away and plugging in the percolator. 'So what sort of day have you had?'

'Quiet,' he replied. 'Any news from Otto?'

'Yes, he called after lunch.'

'And?'

'A few problems,' she said grimly. 'He has to bridge the twelve million dollars.'

'But he can do it?'

'Yes, except he'll be at full stretch should anything go wrong. Do you have any doubts about the aircraft and the delivery?'

'Not a one, dear girl. I'll run through the entire plan of action with you if that will put your mind at rest.'

'Yes, perhaps . . . also Otto needs an actual breakdown of costs involved.'

'No more than half a million dollars total.'

'Is that everything?'

'Except my fee.'

'And you have a figure in mind?'

'I seem to recall Otto mentioning we would split the profit fifty-fifty.'

'He said that?' Lisa said with some surprise.

'When he picked me up at the airport in Geneva last week. I seem to recall we agreed on that, especially as I'm taking all the risks.'

'I think Otto might disagree with you on that point . . . in the light of this financing problem, that is.'

He smiled again. 'I'm sure he will; but business is business as they say. Anyway, enough of this. How would you like to come to Jersey with me?'

'Jersey? When?'

'In the morning.'

Her face showed disappointment. 'I'd love to, but I have a great deal of work to do; not least helping Otto sort out the bridging loan. Then I promised an aunt I would go and see her tomorrow evening.'

'Will you need the car?'

'If that's OK.'

'No problem. Why don't you drop me off at the airport in the morning. Then you've got it until I come back.'

'When will that be?'

'Thursday afternoon . . . evening.'

Lisa took the cream from the fridge. 'You're going to see your daughter when you get to Jersey?'

'Amongst other things, but the main reason is to set up Relief Air. A word with the right offshore specialist might save me a lot of time, and Otto a lot of money.'

'And your ex-wife will be there?' She regretted the words as soon as they were uttered, was angry with herself for showing weakness.

Fitzgerald laughed. 'Maxine! Good God, no. She's never there. More than likely roughing it on some sun-kissed beach in the South Pacific; although I'm glad you asked.'

'Glad! Why?'

'A little bit of jealousy never did no harm. Besides, it shows you care.'

'I might not,' she replied in a small voice.

'And there's the pity,' he said rolling out the bog Irish. 'So I'll need to be sending the tickets back after all.'

'Tickets?'

'For the theatre.'

'Which theatre?'

'Ah, but that would be telling. Wouldn't you rather the surprise?'

She digged him playfully in the ribs. 'I hate surprises. You should know that by now.'

'Is it worth a kiss?'

'After you tell me.'

'In the bedroom, on your pillow.'

She pulled away from him and ran out of the kitchen, screaming with laughter as he chased her.

'A lie, Chance Fitzgerald,' she said breathlessly, throwing the pillow aside.

He caught her by the waist and pulled her down on the bed.

'But it got you here didn't it?'

'Oh no,' she cried, struggling to break free. 'I'm in the middle of making coffee.'

'What about my kiss?'

'No tickets, no kiss.'

'Ah, 'tis a cruel tongue you have my colleen of Raglan Road.'

'Where's that?'

'In Dublin . . . something out of a poem written by Patrick Kavanagh.'

'Do you remember it?'

'A little,' He thought for a moment, then recited softly:

On Raglan Road on an autumn day
I met her first and knew,
That her fair hair would weave a snare
That I might one day rue;
I saw the danger, yet I walked
Along the enchanted way,
And I said, let grief be a fallen leaf
At the dawning of the day.

'That's beautiful,' she said.

'It's the Irish,' he answered. 'They know a thing or two about words . . . now about that kiss.'

'Now about those tickets,' she mimicked.

He grinned, reached into his jacket pocket and pulled them out. Holding them high above her head, he said, 'Now the kiss.'

'I can't see them.' She struggled to pull his arm down as his lips found hers. The gyrations continued a moment longer before the hunger of new love consumed them both.

The tickets fell unnoticed to the floor.

22 October

Jersey, Channel Islands

WEDNESDAY 1000 HOURS

JERSEY IS THE most southerly of the Channel Islands and lies in the bay of St Michel between the Contentin and Brittany coasts. It is the largest of the island group, measuring nine miles long by five miles wide and is a natural sun trap sloping gently from north to south. When Chance Fitzgerald arrived, however, it was raining, a strong wind driving out of the south-west.

Having collected his hire-car from the parking bay near the airport terminal he drove in the direction of St Helier. After London it was a small step back in time. The pace of life was less frenetic and the people still found time to smile and be friendly. He had been to the island a number of times over the years to visit Alice, and she had taken great pride in showing him the sights. Each meeting had been carefully stored and treasured in Fitzgerald's mind, from the zoo and her favourite animal – the spectacled bear – to Mont Orgueil Castle which she had assured him had been saved from demolition by Sir Walter Raleigh in 1600, and their walks along the sands at St Ouen's bay. That had been the last time. Nearly two years ago. He had been acting the clown; she, a ten year old full of giggles. At some stage she had said: 'Oh, Daddy, even the seagulls are laughing at you.' He smiled at the memory. She was a fine girl. And he had been away too long.

By the time he reached St Helier he had changed his mind about checking in at the hotel first and kept on driving towards St Clement. Jack Audley's house was set in a few dozen acres of well-manicured gardens. The high wind was stripping the red and gold leaves from the trees as he drove the Ford Fiesta up the long gravel driveway. He braked to a stop at the front of the house. There were two other cars there. One was a silver-blue Rolls-Royce, the other an Italian racing red Ferrari. Fitzgerald smiled to himself. With an island speed limit of forty miles an hour they represented nothing more than the owners' status. Excessively wealthy.

He climbed out of his car and walked around the side of the house. The main structure was over three hundred years old and was constructed in pink granite. The windows were white-framed. Towards the rear of the property was a massive courtyard, laid in a concentric pattern of gunmetal grey cobblestones. What may once have been stables had been tastefully converted to garages beyond which the land fell away in floral tiers to a pink flagstone patio and an Olympic-sized swimming-pool. Beyond that, a newly built pool-house had a distinct Spanish flavour.

A white Range Rover coasted into the courtyard and braked gently to a stop. The door opened and out climbed Jack Audley. The hair was whiter than Fitzgerald remembered from his last visit and the pink face a touch fleshier. Other than that, he was playing the country squire to the hilt. Bespoke Donegal tweed by Gieves and Hawkes, shirt by Harvie and Hudson of Jermyn Street, shoes handmade by Trickers and gold watch from Patek Philippe of Geneva. All he needed now, thought Fitzgerald, was an over-and-under by Purdy and Sons and a brace of pheasant at his feet and the picture would be complete.

'What the bloody hell,' Jack Audley exclaimed in his no-nonsense Yorkshire accent. 'Is that you, Chance?'

'The prodigal ex-son-in-law returned. How are you, Jack?'

Audley came forward and thrust out a big flabby hand. 'Well, I'll be damned. Been here long?'

'No, just arrived . . . I was admiring the estate.'

Audley smiled. 'Pool's new. Come down, I'll show you around.'

Fitzgerald followed the Yorkshireman down the sweep of stone steps.

'Pool-house is not quite finished,' Audley mentioned, as they went through the door. 'Up this end are the changing-rooms, that sort of thing. Down there a sauna and jacuzzi.'

'I'm impressed,' murmured Fitzgerald.

'Should bloody well hope so. Cost me sixty thousand so far.'

Fitzgerald smiled at that; Jack liked to tell you the cost of things.

'Upstairs here,' Audley continued, leading the Irishman up a circular wrought-iron staircase, 'are spare rooms for guests . . . and a small gym.'

The tour continued for a while before the two men ended up at the main house. They went into a large sitting-room, elegantly furnished, the furniture a blend of George I and Louis XV, the walls hung with Turners and Constables. By the doors, as elsewhere in the house, small white cameras pointed in every direction.

'New burglar alarm system,' Audley announced, answering Fitzgerald's unspoken question. 'Cost a small fortune.'

'You've been burgled then!'

'Not over here, but you remember the business back in England years ago, when I had that rare collection of Greek coins pinched, not to mention a number of priceless Ming vases . . . this is insurance. Making sure it doesn't happen again. Drink?'

'Bit early for me, Jack, any coffee going?'

'Kitchen. The missus is out; fashion show in town somewhere, and Mrs Le Brun, the daily, went early, so you'll have to fix it yourself. You know me and bloody kitchens.'

Fitzgerald followed Audley out of the room.

'So, lad, how long are you over for?'

'Depends, day or so.'

'You'll stay here, of course.'

'Thanks, but I've already made a reservation at the Pomme d'Or in St Helier.'

'That's easy, I'll phone and cancel it.'

'No need, I don't want to put you out.'

Jack Audley spun around, his eyes dark and angry. 'There you bloody well go again. Every time I offer you something you throw it back in my face.'

'It's not that,' Fitzgerald replied quietly, 'just that I don't much go in for charity.'

'Charity. Charity! Who said anything about bloody charity? You're family for Christ's sake.'

'Not any more.'

'And who the hell do you think is raising your daughter?'

'Not my daughter, Jack; your daughter's daughter. Even so I'm grateful and if you want to hear it again I am forever in your debt. The problem is I don't like owing any man.'

Audley moved towards a kitchen cupboard and pulled out a bottle of malt whisky. 'And the missus calls me stubborn . . . sure you don't want one of these?'

Fitzgerald shook his head and busied himself with making a cup of instant coffee.

'There is one small favour, however.'

'Fire away.'

'Do you know any good accountants?'

Audley, who had seated himself at the long oak kitchen table and was now pouring his second drink, said, 'Accountants. What did you have in mind, tax avoidance?'

'Need to set up an offshore company. No names, just nominee shareholders.'

Audley, who had run his fair share of crooked deals, smiled. 'How illegal?'

'Illegal! Wrong man, Jack. You know me, a good Catholic boy from way back.'

'Exactly. So how illegal?'

Fitzgerald poured the hot water into the cup. 'In theory it's not. In practice, should anything go wrong, that is, I don't want my name on it.'

Audley laughed. 'Bloody amazing. All those years I gave you the opportunity to come into business with me and you turned me down flat to go and fly those silly bloody airplanes of yours, and here you are doing it anyway.'

Fitzgerald sat down at the other end of the table. 'With a difference, Jack, with a difference. This time it's my game. My own skills . . . no hand-outs.'

'Hand-outs!' Audley flared. 'You and your holier than bloody thou attitude seems more to the point. Didn't it ever occur to you I just wanted to help?'

A door opened and a shrill voice said. 'Jack Audley, I can hear your voice on the other side of the house. Whatever – ' Jennifer Audley stopped dead in her tracks. 'Oh, hello, it's you,' she said icily to Fitzgerald. 'I should have realised. Whenever you two are together you behave like schoolboys.' She pulled her mink coat a little tighter around her plump body, cast a disapproving eye at the men littering her immaculate kitchen and turned to leave.

Audley said, 'By the way, Jen, Chance will be staying with us tonight. And possibly tomorrow.'

She turned back to her husband. 'Rather difficult tonight, Jack, the party and everything.'

'He'll be coming to the party as well,' Audley said firmly.

Jennifer shrugged. 'Oh well, if you insist. He'll have to stay in the blue room. I'll telephone Mrs Le Brun's daughter; she can come in and make it up.' With that she turned on her heel and stalked out of the kitchen.

Fitzgerald, feeling the uncomfortable air of tension which had suddenly descended, said, 'I think the hotel would be better, Jack. Besides, with a party going on as well, I'm sure Jennifer has enough to worry about.'

Audley poured another whisky. 'Enough to worry about be damned, unless you consider what new dress to wear and what shoes go with which outfit. No, I've told her you're staying and if you go to the hotel now she'll think she's won some kind of moral victory . . . then life will be even more bloody unbearable.' He looked up and saw the resolution in Fitzgerald's eyes, so quickly added. 'You can pay me the going rate for a hotel if you like. That way I won't be doing you any favours. Right!'

Fitzgerald finished his coffee. 'Is Alice at school?'

'No, it's half-term. She's staying with a schoolfriend, though . . . the party and that. She's got a horse now.'

'A horse!'

'Out riding most days after school. Gets on well with animals; in fact she's won quite a few rosettes at the local gymkhanas.'

'Really; that's great. Does she keep it here . . . the horse?'

'No, we'd already converted the stables to garages. Keeps it over at her friend's place. Charlie Blaine's her father, the chap that owns the local air-taxi company. I think you met him the last time you were here; at one of Jen's garden parties, if memory serves me.'

'Perhaps, I don't remember.'

'No, well, not to worry. If you've finished your coffee I'll take you up to the blue room. Last bloody year it was green, then she decides blue would be prettier.' He threw back the remains of his whisky. 'Cost me over five grand to do it the way she wanted. I ask you, five bloody grand . . . she'll have me in the poor house yet, mark my words.'

'About that accountant, you never did say.'

'That's easy,' Audley remarked. 'Philippe Dupres. Looks after some of my business interests.'

'What is he, French?'

'Jerseyman, young, bright as a button. He'll be at the party tonight. I'll call him if you like, ask him to come round early.'

'Perhaps it would be better if I dropped by his office.'

Audrey pulled himself up from the table. 'Aye, maybe you're right. Come through to the study and I'll give you his address.'

It was two o'clock in Geneva when Otto von Klaus walked up the Rue de Hollande. The sky was overcast and a chill wind coursed down the long curve of street. The barred ground-floor windows of the building gave it the depressing air of a penal institution rather than a place of private banks.

He pressed the doorbell and waited for the buzz of the electronic lock. Inside the door he entered a bullet-proof glass cage, where he pressed another button attached to a small microphone. A female voice said, '*Bonjour, comment vous-appelez vous?*'

'*Monsieur von Klaus, j'ai un rendezvous avec Monsieur Lesquereux.*'

Seconds later, a young girl appeared and escorted him in the elevator to the fourth floor.

André Lesquereux was seated at his desk when von Klaus entered. He was small and wizened, with black glittering eyes and no hair. His skull shone parchment yellow in the light of the desk lamp. The small window to the right of his desk afforded little light even on the brightest of days. Lesquereux stood up, made a stiff little bow, and held out a frail bony hand.

'Otto, how nice to see you again. It has been a long time. Please' – he waved to a carefully placed chair – 'be seated.'

The German lowered himself into the chair, his eyes taking in the furnishings. They were old like the man. They even carried a faint smell of decay, as though after two hundred years of trading as a private family bank it was all nearing the end of its life. In a way perhaps it was. André Lesquereux had been an only child and he had no heir to carry on the tradition.

'You look well,' von Klaus said. 'Business must be good.'

The banker waved his hands in the air. 'Not as good as the old days, I think. Too much legislation; they have tied our hands and loosened our tongues.'

Von Klaus nodded. He knew to what Lesquereux was referring. The tightening up of laws in recent years which gave access in certain cases to private accounts. The numbered Swiss account was therefore becoming less secure as a hiding place for investors to store their money. Especially those attempting to dry-clean criminally obtained fortunes.

'Nothing, I think, is as good as the old days, André.'

'No, Otto, nothing. May I offer you coffee?'

The German smiled. 'Thank you.'

Lesquereux passed a message via a desk intercom before turning back to his client. 'So, business. You mentioned a short term loan over the telephone. Do you have a figure in mind?'

Von Klaus said firmly, 'Twelve million dollars over ten days.'

The banker turned the page of a document on his desk. 'That should not be a problem. But what of security? From your portfolio, I see' – he glanced quickly down at the page before him – 'that you have only a little over one million francs with the bank.'

Von Klaus produced a sheaf of documents from his pocket. He handed them to Lesquereux.

'I am selling my companies. In there you will find an outline of the current discussions with N.L.T. in Paris. The proceeds from the sale will, of course, be deposited with you before I activate the loan.'

Lesquereux read quickly and expertly through the documents, transferring the figures mentally as he went from francs into dollars and finally back into francs.

'This will still leave you one point eight million francs short,' he stated, placing the papers on his desk.

Von Klaus swallowed. It was against his better judgement, of that he was sure; but it was the only way. 'The deeds to my house . . . and my collection of paintings. That will be more than adequate.'

For the first time during the meeting, André Lesquereux looked troubled. This was because private bankers, unlike the larger commercial organisations, nurtured a relationship with their clients. It was something that extended beyond the traditional role of banker, and included advising on such matters as estate planning, corporate takeovers, tax returns, setting up new corporations, reorganising ailing ones and even such mundane matters as travel arrangements, secretarial help and occasionally, where to go for an enjoyable vacation without overdrawing your bank account.

'I have known you a long time, Otto, and in that time I have formed the opinion that you are an excellent businessman. Much like myself, I think you have a basically conservative investment philosophy, aimed at preservation of capital, rather than running down the first performance alley for capital gains at any cost. This is not so?' Von Klaus allowed himself a perfunctory nod, but said nothing. 'If there is anything you wish my advice upon, Otto, you only need to ask, you know that. You also know that any discussion held within these four walls is strictly confidential . . . You remember, I did not let the Frenchman down!'

Von Klaus looked puzzled. 'The Frenchman?'

'The fifty million francs in the sack!'

'Ah, yes, I remember. No, André, it is nothing like that.'

'You are sure? It is not that I wish to press you, Otto, it is just that your request concerns me. After all, we both know that personal guarantees in business can be very dangerous.'

'I appreciate your concern my friend but this personal guarantee is quite different from the usual. Quite, quite safe.' With that, von Klaus stood up and held out his hand. 'Now, if you will forgive me I have another important meeting.'

'But the coffee . . . I must apologise for it taking so long.'

'Von Klaus raised a hand. 'Never mind. Perhaps we should have lunch together. You can tell me some more of your fascinating stories of the old banking days.'

'You would like that?' Lesquereux said enthusiastically, walking round his desk to the door.

'Of course, of course. And perhaps we will have a bottle of the Château Haut-Brion!'

'The sixty-six?'

'Naturally, André. Only the best.'

Lesquereux opened the door and led von Klaus to the elevator. 'I will come down with you.'

'No, it is not a problem. I will show myself out.'

'You are sure?'

The elevator doors swished open. 'Yes. Goodbye then, André.'

'Goodbye, Otto.'

Out on the street, von Klaus gulped in the cold damp air, then set off along the Rue de Hollande at a brisk pace. Damned bankers, he thought to himself. He was remembering his early days, the days he would have progressed no further than an assistant manager, and even then his application for a loan would have been rejected. Age, wisdom and business acumen had, however, changed him. He now knew the game. Knew that a bank would never refuse to lend you money. And the larger the amount, the easier it was. Of course they needed security, of which there were many forms. One of the unacceptable ones however was aircraft, being classed as a high capital cost movable asset. Something that could be operated without insurance. Something which could crash and be worthless. Or be stolen and be equally worthless. Still, that was not important now. He had satisfactorily set up a deal with N.L.T. in Paris for more money than the London people had offered, had concluded an arrangement with Rashid Suliman which made his investment 'blue chip', and was now going to Marie's house. The stitches from his wounded arm were to be removed by the doctor who had put them there in the first place. He wanted to meet the man again. Form his own opinion, although, since that first blackmail letter, there had been no further contact by whoever was responsible. To Otto von Klaus this was a lucky omen. He felt certain that the blackmailer had had second thoughts over their course of action, which brought him to the unanswered question. Who stood to lose the most? And so far the only answer was the tall elegant doctor wearing the expensive cashmere topcoat.

It was cold now and he regretted leaving his car at the office. It was much too far to walk. He looked around for a taxi but without success. In the end he let the story of André's Frenchman run through his mind; that way he would cover a part of the distance without even realising it.

It had been some years earlier, following a purge by the Federal Banking Commission, and when the law had required banks to notify the police if they suspected deposits to be 'black' money. This was really to stop sackfuls of Italian lire flooding into Switzerland, but it so happened at that time that the French police were looking for a thief who was on the loose with fifty million French francs. The banks were on the alert.

Two days after the police bulletin, a scruffy old man appeared at André's bank wishing to open an account. André, feeling he was not quite what they were looking for in a client, explained that his bank only dealt with the wealthier citizens – that is, people who ran six-figure accounts.

The scruffy, unshaven man said that was quite all right because he had fifty million francs. André was seized with panic. Hadn't this man killed to get the money! The story stretched out at this point, but ended with André diplomatically suggesting the man try another bank. One that he felt sure would handle the account better than his own. In reality, the banker did not want to call the police. His bank simply did not do that sort of thing.

So it was that the unkempt old man went to another bank. They, however, turned him in, and minutes after his arrival he was dragged away and thrown into the cells. It took four days for the truth to emerge. Then it was found that the old man with the countenance of a tramp had in fact been a farmer in some remote area of southern France. He had lost both his sons through illnesses years earlier, after which he and his wife had devoted themselves to work. She had died a month earlier and he had taken her body and buried it on a hillside near the farm. He then sold the property and the many thousands of acres which went with it. He had insisted on cash, and distrusting French banks and knowing that Switzerland could be used as a tax shelter, eventually arrived in Geneva. The story had no known ending, for after his release from jail, the man took his money and disappeared.

An amazing tale, thought Otto. Even though he felt slightly annoyed that André should have considered that he was dealing in something dishonest. Even if he was.

In Norfolk it was a sunny day. Even so, the air was brittle and cold. Guy Stanton had the doors of the large black hangar open and had just pulled one of his crop-spraying aircraft out to carry out an engine run, when the green MG sports car roared up and braked to a skidding stop. The two men who emerged were expected. The first, the driver, was a short thickset man with oily black hair. His name was Michael Chan and he was of Chinese extraction as was obvious from his yellowed complexion and slanting eyes. Even so, he had been born in the West Midlands and spoke with a gravelly accent of flattened vowels, interspersed with the odd dash of Hollywood. He had been a great fan of the cinema, especially the old gangster movies of the Cagney, Bogart era. It was from his love of the cinema that the nickname Pedro had arisen, except it had been so long ago that neither he, nor anyone else could recall the precise reason for so obscure an appellation to someone of oriental lineage. Besides that, Pedro was fifty-five years old, suffered badly with asthma and was the finest flight engineer Stanton had ever known. He was also the quietest; not being much given to words. Indeed, on some days he never spoke at all.

The second man was something of an enigma. Tall, slightly stooped. Silver-grey hair and washed out pale blue eyes. He carried a silver-coloured alloy briefcase which contained a bottle of vermouth, a bottle of gin and a cocktail shaker. His hands were unsteady first thing in the morning, but two very dry martinis always did the trick. Other than that he had flown in three major wars, been shot down six times and in most flying men's opinions could still teach the birds a trick or two. His name was Hiram P. Gaylord III. He was a southern gentleman with an accent honed in Vacherie, Louisiana. He was a worn sixty-two years of age and talked constantly of going home. He had been using the same words for close on forty years. So far he had not made it.

The three men greeted each other with silent handshakes. Following that, Gaylord carefully placed his briefcase on the wing of the Pawnee aircraft, opened it and mixed a martini. He handed out the small silver cups. Raising his so that it glinted in the sunlight, he said. 'To absent friends.' They drank.

It had been the same ever since Stanton could remember. No hellos to bind their coming together, and no goodbyes to sever their kinsmanship. And always the brief ceremony with the silver cups. Always the few silent moments to cherish those friends left in shallow unmarked graves somewhere at the end of the world.

'So, where's the war?' Gaylord enquired briskly.

'No war,' replied Stanton. 'Merely a delivery flight. We're taking a Hercules out of Alaska.'

Gaylord looked confused. 'A delivery flight! But you said

on the phone that the contract was worth a hundred thousand dollars. No one pays that kind of money just to ship airplanes.'

'No, perhaps not, but this isn't exactly your run-of-the-mill operation.'

'How much not run-of-the-mill?'

'Iran.'

The American's eyes narrowed in concern. 'Sounds kind of risky.'

'More or less what I said to Chance.'

'And what did he say?'

'When I laughed in his face he said, as the world advances towards you — retreat.'

'But you took the deal anyway.'

'Yes . . . however, there is a little more to it.'

'I somehow guessed there might be.'

Five minutes later, Stanton had outlined the operation. He now waited for a reaction.

'How do we get back to the Sudan?' Gaylord enquired, 'after we've dropped the airplane off in Iran.'

Stanton said, 'We haven't cleared that one up yet.'

'But once we get back we need to lie low in the swamps for a few days, is that what you figure?'

'More or less.'

Gaylord rubbed his chin thoughtfully. 'And what's your appraisal of the situation?'

'I think it's eminently feasible, although I must admit to reservations about the Iranians. We've all operated in that part of the world at some time or other and we all know how cheaply they regard life.'

'Throw us in the caboose after we've delivered the ship you mean?'

'Why jail? Bullets are quicker and cheaper.'

'You figure they're going to gain something by that kind of action?'

'I don't know. Except I've never considered an Arab needs a reason for doing anything.' He moved away from the Pawnee and looked skyward at a light training plane crossing the airfield. 'Anyway, that's it. Nothing more I can tell you at this moment in time. Chance will fill in the gaps.

If you decide to change your mind I'll understand . . . after all it's hardly our usual kind of work is it?'

Gaylord paced up and down for a while, weighing up the pros and cons of the situation. 'Well, I figure it this way,' he drawled at last. 'I've been with airplanes all my life, and as age is kind of against me getting a legitimate flying job; I might just as well string along for the laughs. And hell, we've had a few of those over the years haven't we?'

Stanton managed a weak smile. 'And Pedro?'

They both turned, but the Chinaman had drifted quietly away. He was inspecting the decowled engine of the other aircraft inside the hangar.

'He'll be OK,' Gaylord replied.

'He's fit enough then . . . his chest!'

'The asthma you mean . . . well he still wheezes and rattles like an old Canadian Pacific loco, but I guess he'll last the course.'

Stanton sighed. 'I was hoping to remove the element of guesswork from this operation. No matter, I'll leave it to you. He's your responsibility. OK?'

'That's fine. By the way I never properly welcomed you back to the merc game.'

'A cameo appearance only, old boy. After this I intend to live to a ripe old age and die peacefully in my sleep in an elegant four-poster bed.'

Gaylord smiled. 'That sounds like the oats that just went through the horse.'

Stanton's face was bleak when he said, 'No shit, Hiram . . . this is the last time for me. The very last time.'

Back in Geneva Otto von Klaus was sitting in tight-lipped silence as the nurse removed the stitches from his left arm. His anger was slowly boiling over. He looked again at the woman. She was short and heavily built. Her age, he guessed, was about sixty and she had thorny grey hair and a faint moustache which was discreetly powdered. Besides that, she was quite the ugliest person he had ever seen.

'Why did the doctor not come?' he said in German.

'Ach, the doctor is a busy man. Today he is at the Zurich Kantonspital. Anyway, this is not work for so important a man . . . there!' She stepped back and admired her work. 'Now you are as good as new.' She moved across to the kitchen sink, washed her hands and dried them carefully, then picking up her coat and bag she gave a brief stern-faced nod to von Klaus and went out the door. Her voice lingered a moment in the hallway, as she said something to Mariella, then the street door banged shut.

Mariella came into the kitchen moments later. She was wearing a full-length silver fox coat, held together at the front by her left hand. Her hair was pulled back from her face and pinned up in a high pyramid. Her make-up had been carefully applied in the fashion of a common tart.

Von Klaus chose not to notice. 'So where is the doctor?' he questioned sharply.

'The nurse told me Zurich.'

'Have you spoken to him on this matter . . . the letter!'

Mariella, using her sultry business voice, said, 'No, Otto, I have already told you I have not seen him since that night.'

Von Klaus stood up and rubbed his arm gently. It still itched. He took his shirt from the back of the chair and began to dress. 'I still think it was him,' he persisted.

'You have had another letter?'

'No.'

'Isn't that good?'

'It is strange. It is as though someone has become afraid of continuing, knowing that they could also harm themselves. That is why I think it is the doctor. As you yourself said, his coming here to visit you could damage his reputation permanently. I think he realised this after he sent that letter . . . or spoke to you!'

Mariella took on a hurt expression. 'But I have told you, I have not seen this man since. I swear on my mother's life. And you should know I would not say such a thing lightly.'

'I still need to know,' von Klaus snapped, tucking his shirt into his trousers. 'What about that police inspector friend of yours! Did you find anything out?'

'About the letter, you mean? No, not really. It seems all the police would do is wait for more leads . . . clues. Even checking what sort of typewriter was used to write the letter doesn't mean a thing. He said there were perhaps many thousands of every model of typewriter – even here in Geneva.'

She moved to one of the kitchen cupboards. 'Drink?'

'Not just now, Marie. I must go into the office. I have some important matters to clear up.'

She took a tumbler from the cupboard and poured a large measure of neat whisky. 'But you will be back later?'

'I don't think so. I will telephone you.'

Just as she had expected, and as Konrad had called Mr Fitzgerald in London and been told by a female voice that he would be back on Thursday – tomorrow – it seemed prudent to make a final check on Otto's diary for any last minute information. Konrad had convinced her that the more details they had to string on to the killing, the more money they could expect.

She turned from the kitchen worktop, still holding her fur coat closely to her body. Her free hand carried the glass of whisky. 'Have this, anyway, before you go. The nurse mentioned that a drink would probably be good for you; something about trauma.' She pushed the glass into his hand.

He took a sip, then threw it back in one go.

'You haven't said anything about my hair,' she said huskily.

'Hair!' He turned and looked. 'Yes, very nice.'

'Or the fur coat.'

'I have seen it before,' he replied shortly, moving towards the kitchen door.

'Otto,' she called. It was as he turned that she flung open the coat. She was quite naked except for a lacy red suspender belt and black stockings of the sheerest denier. For Otto, with the taste of whisky in his mouth and the burning sensation surging through his body, the sight of her heavy breasts and magnificent thighs was too much. He rushed forward and grabbed her savagely.

'Oh, Otto,' she cooed, 'you're so strong . . . no, no, not here. Take me to the bedroom.'

He did as he was told, while she quickly and expertly ran her fingers over the outside of his jacket pocket. The diary was there.

*   *   *

It was nine o'clock in Jersey when Chance Fitzgerald found out the reason for Jack Audley's pressing invitation. Up until then, it had the beginnings of a rich man's party. The chandelier-hung dining-room had been cleared to make a dance floor for the rock band brought in to entertain the younger generation. The courtyard was filling up with a sparkling selection of Porsches, Ferraris and Mercedes. And the plummy conversations that filled the air were of polo and driving a ball three and a half inches in diameter with a strangely balanced mallet from the top of a galloping horse to Cowes week and thirty-six-footers with billowing spinnakers and the forthcoming skiing season at Gstaad.

Jack Audley had appeared at some stage, red-faced and smiling, and mentioned Maxine would be along shortly. Slipped his mind earlier, he had added. And then with a sly wink, the parting shot: 'She'll be glad to see you, lad.'

Fitzgerald had drifted away moments later to the sanctuary of his room. He should have realised that Jack had been up to something.

His first thought, as he closed the bedroom door and turned the key softly in the lock, was that he could not remember leaving a light on in the room. The second thought, as he moved slowly down the short corridor past the dressing-room, was that he vaguely recognised the perfume from somewhere. But where? It was as the room opened out that the question was answered.

She was lying on the bed, her head propped up by a number of pillows. He looked in stunned silence at the short black hair, the full red lips and the trim figure in the simple black evening dress. The high-heeled shoes had been carelessly discarded and were lying on the floor.

'You look as though you've seen a ghost,' Maxine Audley laughed, twisting the champagne glass in her fingers.

Fitzgerald walked across to the big bay window. 'I wasn't expecting you,' he said at length.

'Especially languishing on your bed you mean?' When he didn't answer she added, 'Mummy mentioned you were staying. Said something about a business venture . . . you're not flying any more then?'

'Not so much.'

'So what type of business are you in?'

'Buying and selling.'

'Ah,' she raised her plucked eyebrows. 'Buying and selling! The sort of remark which covers endless ground, and I don't suppose for one moment you're going to tell me exactly what it is you're buying and selling?'

Fitzgerald managed a wry smile. 'Would you believe me if I said ladies' knickers?'

Maxine pulled a face. 'Well, at least you've still got your salesman's sense of humour . . . coarse but amusing. Anyway, how long are we to be honoured with your company?'

'Until tomorrow.'

'Nice party downstairs; lots of champagne. Wouldn't you like to escort your ex-wife?'

He was staring down from the window at the brightly lit swimming-pool. The covers had been removed in preparation for the midnight dip. 'And what about your boyfriend? You're hardly the type to arrive without the attendance of some handsome young Lothario.'

She shrugged her shoulders. 'Oh he's just a naval type. Becomes a bore after a couple of days . . . he won't mind.'

Fitzgerald left the window and went to sit on the end of the bed. He looked at her, a beautiful woman with the mind of a spoiled child, and sighed. 'What is it you want, Maxine?'

'Want!' she pouted, looking into his unbelievably blue eyes and feeling her stomach turn to jelly. 'I want you to take me to the party.'

'I have an early start in the morning. Lots of work to do.'

She tossed the champagne glass aside and ran her long fingers through her hair. 'Don't you find me attractive?'

'Yes, very attractive. The trouble is we've already been down that road and found it leads nowhere.'

She eased the strap of her dress from her shoulder, partially exposing her right breast. 'Wouldn't you like to find out if we still go well together between the sheets?'

'Oh, dear girl, when will you ever learn? Everything has changed. It's all over, past. Besides I have someone else.'

She gave no reply. She was sulking. Only then did he

realise he had gone too far. Touched some source of secret inner hurt. She jumped off the bed and picked up her shoes. When she turned to look at him again her eyes were full of cold hatred and contempt. 'You mean you're about to screw up someone else's life, is that it?' Her voice broke with rage and hatred. 'I wasn't enough. You left me with a daughter to raise and worry over while you went off to play the big hero fighting other people's wars . . . and now, you selfish bastard, you're going to do the same thing all over again . . . except you're not going to contaminate my daughter, do you understand?'

Fitzgerald was silent. Shaking with anger, she watched him pick up the glass from the bed and walk slowly past her and place it carefully on the bedside table. When he turned his face was quite empty of any emotion, his eyes almost sad.

'Not now,' he said quietly. 'I'll talk to you in the morning if you like, but not now.'

'In the morning when I'm sober,' she spat. 'Is that what you mean?'

'I didn't say that.'

'You didn't have to you hard-headed bastard.' Her hand lashed out and struck him a stinging blow across the cheek. He didn't move. 'I meant what I said about Alice. I want you to stay away from her. I don't want you to see her . . . ever again.'

He sat for a long time after she had gone. It still hurt him, even now. Even after all these years. He could be alone in a strange city and hear a small girl calling out to her father. See them walking happily hand in hand through some big department store. Feel the wrench at his heart when he realised he would always be an alien to that happy world of ordinary people. It was an incurable illness. A craving for excitement that would not and could not be stilled. A morbid fear of the mundane, clock-in, clock-out, nine-to-five existence. Something he felt sure would follow him to his grave. In the old days, of course, he had simply hit the bottle. There had been solace in the alcoholic haze. But now that he was sworn off the stuff the heartache was sometimes too much to bear. Perhaps she was right.

Perhaps he should stay away from Alice. Perhaps that had been the answer all along.

He looked down at the carpet and saw the sparkling diamond ear-ring. He picked it up and turned it slowly in his fingers. Expensive trinkets and Maxine went together. He idly wondered which rich boyfriend had bought it for her before dropping it into the bedside drawer.

23 October

Geneva, Switzerland
THURSDAY 0955 HOURS

THE LETTER HAD arrived with the morning mail. It had a local postmark. It was from the blackmailer. A day earlier and Otto von Klaus would have been at least fraught with anger knowing he was hopelessly cornered. Trapped in a million-dollar labyrinth of nailbiting complexity. Now it was as though he was on mescalin, seeing no reason for doing anything in particular and finding the cause for which he was prepared to act and possibly suffer, profoundly uninteresting. Except it wasn't mescalin. He had found out who the blackmailer was. He, Otto von Klaus, self-made multi-millionaire, had succeeded where the police, he felt certain, would have failed. But then the police would have been working from the outside. He had been very much on the inside.

The two letters were on the desk before him. The stationery was the same. The typeface different. And whereas the first letter had been sent to his home address, the second had come to the office.

Now he was confronted with a different type of problem. What to do about it? Letting the blackmailer know he knew could be dangerous. Which left a counter-move. A black-mail of his own. A threat issued by a strong-arm man! Or an accident! His stomach churned at the thought as he unconsciously reached out and screwed up the letters in his hands. No, Otto, it is the only way. You must be strong. One killing or two, it makes no difference. No difference at all. No one must be allowed to get their hands on your money . . . not now.

It was four o'clock when Chance Fitzgerald arrived back at his apartment in Clapham. For a round thousand pounds he had set up a corporation tax company in Jersey, which simply meant that the company's activities would be conducted outside the island and would attract no local tax. Upon the advice of the Jersey accountant – Philippe Dupres – the company Relief Air would be a Panamanian registered company, which was exactly the same as his Turks and Caicos idea, but easier to handle from the accountant's point of view. This now left him with a meeting with the Red Cross and the story of the anonymous benefactor who wished to supply the Hercules aircraft with crew for a period of six months free of all charges, providing the aircraft was used in Africa to help in the Food Aid programme. Before that, however, he needed to go to Alaska and survey the Hercules before payment was made.

Before leaving Jersey he had driven out to the stables. Jack Audley had said she would be there. And she was. He parked the car by the side of the road and looked through the thin winter hedge. There were three horses and only one was a yellow dun. That had to be Long Shot. And the tightly jodhpured rider wearing the black windcheater, Alice. They were working in the sandschool. He climbed out of the car, pulling his collar up against the premature snow wind which swept down from the north. Voices drifted across to him. Young girls of twelve or thirteen issuing stern reprimands to highly strung animals of indeterminate weight and power, in much the same way as one might dress down a puppy for chewing your favourite slippers. He looked on with all the admiration of a father, quite certain that his daughter was by far the best rider there. He had ridden in his youth and out of some vague memory knew that she sat her horse well. After a while, they stopped and dismounted. Alice removed her helmet and shook out her long blonde hair. Good God, she was almost a woman. It was then that fear overtook him. Fear of suddenly appearing and saying the wrong thing. Fear that she may not want to see him after all this time. Fear that Maxine had already spoken to her. The girls were leaving the sandschool now, leading their horses towards the distant stables. Fitzgerald, reaching out with his heart, smiled a smile of infinite sadness and whispered, 'Sorry, my darling girl . . . sorry.' Then he climbed back in the car and drove away.

Now, back at the apartment he was wandering around in a quiet rage. It would pass eventually, he knew that. It was a controlled rage, something of his peculiar brand of Irishness. As his Dublin grandfather had once told him: 'Be loud neither in dress nor voice. For as well as speaking vacant minds, loud voices for the Irish carry deadly Imperial echoes.'

Lisa arrived back shortly after six. By then he had unwound and was sitting with his feet up listening to a tape of Johann Strauss. He hadn't heard the door above the sound of the music and she was practically in his lap before he realised it.

'Welcome home. Why didn't you phone? How was the trip?' she said in one breath.

He laughed and kissed her and felt happier than he had been all day. 'Thank you. I did, but there was no reply. And the trip went well enough . . . does that answer your questions?'

She kissed him back. 'It does.'

'Is that all you're going to say?'

'I'm looking at you.'

'And what do you see?

She smiled coyly. 'I couldn't possibly tell you, handsome young Mars . . it might go to your head.'

'Young! I thought those sorts of compliments were supposed to be paid to the lady, or is this a taste of women's lib?'

'If you like . . . have you eaten by the way?'

'Sandwich at the airport.'

'Do you want to eat?'

'Do you?' he asked nuzzling at her neck.

'I asked first.'

'I'll take you out for a meal if you like.'

'I could always make you something.'

He kissed her on the cheek. 'Or we could forget the whole idea and go to bed?'

Her face lit up as she laughed. 'I thought you'd never ask.'

She had gone through to the bedroom when the telephone rang. He lowered the volume on the hi-fi and answered it.

'Mr Fitzgerald?' It was an accented voice he failed to recognise at first.

'Speaking.'

'Konrad Zwicky, Mr Fitzgerald, I have been trying to reach you for two days.'

Fitzgerald reached out with a foot and pushed the hallway door closed. 'Yes, I'm sorry, Konrad. I've been out of town for two days; anyway, how are you?'

'Well, Mr Fitzgerald, quite well.'

'You have some news for me?'

There was a businesslike quality to Zwicky's voice when he said, 'Rather more than you might have bargained for, Mr Fitzgerald. Could we perhaps meet to discuss it?'

'Can't you outline it over the phone?'

'I'm afraid not. I am working with a contact here in Geneva. The news is of the most confidential nature.'

'I see, so where would you like to meet?'

There was something curiously like a sigh of relief from Zwicky.

'Zurich. If that is possible of course.'

'I can't make it this week . . . call me back Monday morning, we'll fix a date.'

'I will do that, Mr Fitzgerald. Also because the information is very confidential my contact is asking a high price for it. I know we agreed a figure but I am certain you will understand once you have heard the full report.'

'Perhaps, Konrad, perhaps. Anyway, call me back early on Monday, we'll take it from there.'

Replacing the receiver, he wondered what could be so confidential that it couldn't be discussed on the phone. Or was it merely Konrad Zwicky's way of trying to obtain more money? His mind was still turning over the strange

119

conversation as he went through to the bedroom. Lisa was sitting at the dressing-table combing her hair. She turned around, a questioning look in her eyes.

'Phone,' he said absently.

'About the deal?'

'One of the crew fallen ill,' he lied. 'But I don't think we'll be moving out just yet, will we?'

'Two weeks before the funds are ready for transaction. Otto says less, but I doubt it.' She stood up and moved towards the bed. 'Oh and before I forget, you had a call yesterday evening. He wouldn't leave a name, but he sounded German.'

'German?'

'Maybe Swiss.'

That sounded like Zwicky. And if it was he had forgotten the code – if a female answers replace the receiver and try on the next hour. Damn, he would have to speak with him. Security was critical in this type of operation.

'Perhaps the Red Cross!' he said hopefully.

'But surely they would have left a message with me.'

'Security,' he answered and took her in his arms. But the moment had passed. His mind was a million miles away. It was nothing more than a gut feeling, but something was not right.

1 November

Nikolaevsk, Alaska

SATURDAY 0720 HOURS

THE WIND WAS like the echo of some ancient song, as though it belonged as much as the snow and the tall firs which framed the sleeping village of Nikolaevsk on the sparsely settled Kenai Peninsula. Lisa Wendell-Holmes was awake, had been for an hour or more. The wind had been responsible and at first she had been annoyed because she couldn't get back to sleep. But the more she listened, the more she became entranced by what Kiril had called the Devil Music.

She and Chance had been in Alaska for three days now, during which time he had surveyed the aircraft at Anchorage airport. She had been impressed by its size and by Chance's knowledge of so complex looking a machine. The test flight in the cold blue of an arctic sky had been quite magical. She had never sat on the flight deck of a large aircraft before, let alone remain there for a flight. And in her mind it became another reason for loving him. A reason which would see her walking through the fires of hell if he asked her. Watching him fly the plane, she sensed a different person, a man who somehow became a part of the alien electronic systems. She noticed his hands, how gently they touched levers and the control wheel evoking a graceful ballet against the music of engines. The landing, when it eventually came, was unbelievably smooth, the point of contact between wheels and runway being impossible to perceive. Her admiration had not been one-sided either. The flight engineer, a gnarled old veteran with a slow Canadian accent, had confided in her as they deplaned: 'I thought I'd seen them all in thirty years. Figured that pilots were either lousy, average or good. Not so this guy. This guy's a bird.' Then he had gone over to Chance and said: 'Sir, it was a pleasure to fly with you.'

Chance had given him a wry little smile and replied, 'Didn't scare you too much then?'

'Not more than twice in every ten minutes.'

'Hell, I must be losing my touch.'

Both men had laughed and Lisa had understood the casual deprecatory banter as being part of the airmen's lore. It was as though praise was frowned upon, whereas thinly disguised admonitions were an acceptable form of respect.

So the deal was struck. The price firm at twelve million US dollars. She had readily accepted Chance's word that it was worth every last cent. The thought that she was working for Otto and therefore protecting his interests was fading fast. Her life, it seemed, was becoming more entwined with Chance's with each passing day.

On the Friday they had accepted the offer of Kiril Fefelov, an executive of the airline that owned the Hercules, and driven south to the village of Nikolaevsk. It had been a bitterly cold minus fifteen, belying the clear blue sky and dazzling sunshine.

Throughout the journey Kiril had told them about the origins of the little hamlet to which they were now journeying. How it was made up of Russians who began their quest for religious freedom in the 1920s after communism came to Russia. The talk went on to braga, an amber alcoholic drink made from raisins, yeast, sugar and berrie and how the site of the village was only twelve miles north of Kachemak Bay, where the glacier-hung Kenai mountains and deep lovely fjords ringed the southern shore.

They arrived as darkness was descending and from the top of a ridge it was just as beautiful as Lisa had imagined. There was a single snowbound main street lined by neat wooden houses. The windows were already yellow lit and the blue smoke from the chimneys hung like a wreath above the clearing in the tall pine forest.

Kiril, whose wife had died three years earlier, still kept a home in the village so as not to lose contact with his people. Because it was Friday Kiril's religious beliefs forbade him to eat meat and eggs, or to drink milk. However, he made his guests a Ukrainian stew with dumplings, while he ate nothing more than a small plate of boiled vegetables. After that they drank braga around the crackling log fire and listened to stories of the Old Believers – those who had refused to accept the reform of the rites of the Russian Orthodox Church as long ago as the seventeenth century. Finally and with more than enough of the amber liquid imbibed, she and Chance had gone to bed. They hadn't made love straightaway, but lay listening to the wind moaning through the top of the surrounding forest.

At first she had been concerned by his silence. Perhaps he didn't want her in the same way she wanted him. Or perhaps it was the result of the telephone conversation she had had a few days earlier with Otto when she had relayed Chance's message that his payment was to be fifty per cent of the profit. Otto had actually laughed and said, 'Of course, how stupid of me to forget. You can tell Chance that our net profit will be at least two million dollars; so he, of course, will receive one.' She had been dumbfounded at this sudden change in character of her employer. But then, hadn't she always wanted him to be a little more human? And didn't this change of attitude over money augur well for her in the long run? Even so Chance had not seemed overly impressed at the prospect of becoming a millionaire. The promise of great wealth, she had thought then, didn't seem to have the effect on him as it might with other people. Now, however, she wasn't sure. Perhaps the idea had finally sunk in and he was realising with all that money he could find a younger, more beautiful woman to be by his side. It was as these thoughts were plaguing her mind that he suddenly turned and wriggled an arm beneath her body.

'Lisa.'

'Yes.' She looked at him. His blue eyes seemed troubled.

Was this it? Was this the moment he was going to tell her that they couldn't go on together! That it had all been a mistake. That he liked her a lot but . . .

'What do you intend to do when all of this is over?'

'Do?'

'Will you be going back to Switzerland?'

'I suppose so. And you? What will you do?'

'And there's the rub, to coin a quaint old English expression. I don't know. Look for another third world that needs pilots.'

'You don't sound very convincing.'

'No. I did once though. It was all cut and dried then; one road without any turnings.'

'But after this you'll have money. You won't need to go back to flying. You can start a new life.'

'Like Aladdin and his lamp you mean! New lives for old.'

'Why not?'

He smiled and pulled her close to him. 'Because they pulled the dream factory down a long time ago. When I stopped being a child to be exact.'

'I wouldn't have taken you for a defeatist,' she said.

'I'm not, my lovely girl; I'm of the other variety . . . a realist.'

Now it was nearing the dawn and she lay listening to the wind playing its mournful song. She snuggled closer to him, feeling his warmth against her limbs. If only we could stay, she thought. Stay forever in this log cabin with the mountains and the snow and the winds then it would be perfect. Even the million dollars seemed an intrusion into their happiness.

Somewhere beyond the window the devil music played on. And Kiril had said that one had to make many prayers in church for it. For without the prayers it would be an ill omen. She pulled herself closer to the man she loved and screwed up her eyes. 'Dear God,' she prayed, 'don't let anything happen to our love. Please, please . . .'

3 November

Zurich, Switzerland

MONDAY 1300 HOURS

CHANCE FITZGERALD WAS met at the airport by Konrad Zwicky. They went to the bar and took a seat by the window. It was snowing now, thick dense flakes driving relentlessly across the airfield.

'Not a nice day for flying, I think,' Konrad said conversationally.

Fitzgerald, who had returned from Alaska the previous day and was still feeling the effects of jet lag, took a sip of his mineral water. 'You're not wrong, Konrad. Mind you, where I've just come from it's a damn sight worse. Anyway, what's the news? My return flight leaves in an hour.'

Konrad finished his glass of Dunkle Perle and wiped his mouth nervously with the back of his hand. 'That is better,' he exclaimed. 'Yes, the news.' He produced a small notebook from his pocket and flipped it open. Mariella had suggested that. He looked at the small notations she had made.

'Firstly, my contact will need fifty thousand francs for the information.' Konrad's hands were shaking even as he said it. He felt certain the man before him would laugh and turn him down flat. He had said as much to Mariella. Another ten thousand he had suggested, at the most fifteen . . . but fifty, that was crazy. She had instructed him to say exactly what she had written. No more, no less.

Fitzgerald's eyes widened in mild surprise. 'Lot of money,

Konrad. But then you must feel that the information is worth it.'

Konrad nodded eagerly. Was that a yes or a no? What was it about this man that made him feel so uncomfortable? It was as though he were made of steel. Nerveless. Jesus, he hadn't underpriced himself again had he? 'Otto von Klaus is selling his companies,' he said.

'Go on,' Fitzgerald replied quietly.

Konrad outlined the information before him. The amount. The buyer in Paris. And the date of the transaction.

'Interesting,' Fitzgerald smiled, 'but hardly worth fifty thousand.'

Konrad moved quickly on to the next item. 'Then there is the Arab. A man by the name of Rashid Suliman. He is buying an aircraft from Mr von Klaus. They met in Geneva last week.'

Fitzgerald's smile disappeared. 'You're sure of this?'

'Yes, I am positive.'

'What was the meeting about?'

'I do not really know. The information was in a code.'

'What about the price of the aircraft . . . were figures discussed?'

Konrad cleared his throat. 'My contact did say there was a number 18 written in brackets . . . She, my contact that is, was unsure if this was of importance.'

Fitzgerald turned back towards the window and watched the sticking snowflakes slowly melt and slide down the glass. Eighteen! Perhaps eighteen million dollars, asking price to the Iranians. But Otto had told Lisa the profit would be about two millions. But then there was the cost of setting up the operation and paying the crew, not forgetting the cost to bridge the twelve million dollars for a number of days. All of that would greatly reduce the net profit. And even if Otto was asking eighteen millions there was still the Arab factor – they would always knock you down. No, there seemed nothing unusual about that. Nothing, except his clandestine meeting with Rashid Suliman. He would need to check that out in more detail, especially as Otto had insisted he wished to remain anonymous in every sense of the word.

He turned back to Konrad. 'Still not worth fifty thousand my friend.'

'Then there is the killing,' Konrad said in a strained voice. He suddenly realised that everything had gone silent, as though he had spoken too loud. He was sure the old people at the next table were listening. As for Fitzgerald, he had been lifting his glass to his lips; now he was lowering it back to the table.

'Killing!' he whispered. 'What killing?'

Konrad pulled his chair a little closer to the table, then leaned forward and in a low voice told him about the stabbing and the blackmail letters which had followed.

'And who was the man who was killed? Did he have anything to do with this aircraft business?'

Konrad looked at the notes in the small booklet. 'I cannot say. I do not have this information.'

Fitzgerald took his wallet from his pocket. 'Tell me, Konrad. How trustworthy is your contact. How good is all this information?'

Zwicky, sensing that payment hinged on proof positive, threw away the script. 'She is my sister.'

Fitzgerald, who had passed the stage of being surprised by anything the young Swiss told him, merely nodded. 'And she knows Otto . . . Mr von Klaus?'

'She is his mistress.'

'Ah, I see. And the blackmailer? Von Klaus or your contact . . . your sister . . . has no idea who this could be?'

'Apparently not. Although Mariella, my sister, said that Mr von Klaus had accused her, as she was one of the few people who knew of it.'

'Few people, you say. Who else knows?'

Konrad went hot under the collar. What was he saying? 'I am not sure,' he said hesitantly. 'I can ask my sister though.'

Fitzgerald nodded and counted out some money from his wallet. 'Five thousand on account, Konrad. I will also give you a letter stating that I owe you a balance of forty-five thousand.'

Konrad smiled nervously. He didn't like asking people for money. 'My sister said I was to get the full amount now.'

'Sounds a good business lady, but I'm afraid I haven't got it yet. Tell her she has my word, and where I come from that still stands for something.' He took a pen from his inside pocket, found a piece of paper in his wallet, and began writing. 'One other thing, Konrad. I want you to go back to Geneva straightaway and check out the following.' He pushed the piece of paper across the table.

'And the letter . . . the forty-five thousand francs?'

'Give me your address, I'll send it tomorrow.'

An hour later the bar had emptied. Konrad had watched the London flight take off and be instantly swallowed by the dark snow clouds. Now he was alone. He looked down at his empty beer glass and considered ordering another. Instead he shook his head and lit a cigarette. No, for once he would do things the right way. For once he would do exactly as Mariella had told him. He left the bar and went in search of a telephone.

'Mariella!' The line was bad. The background hissed and rushed like the sea, so that his sister's voice seemed to come from a long way away.

'Yes, Konrad, how did everything go?'

'As you said it would. Perhaps we should have asked for more.'

Mariella's voice sounded excited. 'You have the money then; the fifty thousand?'

Konrad coughed, feeling the familiar twinge of guilt when he hadn't done something quite right. 'Not exactly.'

'What is that? What do you say . . . speak up it is a very bad line.'

'We have five thousand,' Konrad said in a louder voice. 'And Mr Fitzgerald is sending a letter tomorrow to confirm he will pay the remainder.'

There was a long hissing silence and for a moment he thought he had lost contact.

'How can you be so stupid, Konrad,' she suddenly yelled. 'Why can't you do as I tell you for once . . . how do you know the man is trustworthy? Tell me,' she screamed, 'how do you know?'

Konrad's eyes were pricking with tears and his hands

were shaking. 'It is all right, Mariella, he is a fair man. I am sure of that.'

'You are sure! You are sure! You, the world's biggest failure. You, the idiot with less sense than the day you were born . . . you, Konrad, can be sure of nothing. Nothing! Do you hear me?'

'Yes, Mariella.'

'What flight are you on?'

He fumbled through his pockets and produced a crumpled ticket. 'I will be home by four o'clock,' he said quietly.

'When? Speak up.'

'At four. Four o'clock . . . and I am sorry. But I can assure you there will not be a problem. Mariella . . .' The sea rushed back at him and he knew she had put the phone down.

He wiped the tears from his eyes quickly, pushed the crumpled airline ticket into his pocket and made his way dejectedly back to the bar. Why did she always shout at him? Ever since he was a small boy. And always she would hit him across the face. Why? Why? He had tried harder this time, hadn't he? He had stayed sober. He had made her meals. Even done the housework while he had been staying with her. He had even begged her to come to Zurich with him. To come and sort out the business with Mr Fitzgerald. Instead she had bought him a return airline ticket to Zurich and given him a carefully worded few pages of notes and instructions, adding that she must remain anonymous at all costs. And now she was screaming at him because the man hadn't paid in full. He ordered a beer and a whisky, drank them quickly and took a fresh set of drinks to the table by the window. It had stopped snowing now but the sky was growing darker. The cleared runways stood out against the snow like dykes, while vehicles with amber flashing lights threaded their way between a row of parked airliners. With an hour to kill and a few degrees of frost on the other side of the window, the drinking should at least have been fun. Except he didn't have any company.

His hand went instinctively to his inside pocket and the five thousand francs which Fitzgerald had given him. Why not, he thought. He hadn't been to the Black Kat for what seemed like months. As long as he stayed out of the backroom and Xavier da Silva's crooked poker table, he knew he could at least double his money. That would certainly make Mariella happy. He finished his drinks and went off to the airline desk to change his return ticket. The morning flight would be early enough. There was a spring in his step now and he was smiling. Soon he would be walking down his beloved Bahnhofstrasse, lined with lime trees and bustling with the familiar blue and white trams. And the luxury shops with their elegant window displays. And tomorrow he could be a rich man!

In Geneva, Otto von Klaus sat at his desk and rolled a half-filled tumbler of whisky between his hands. His face had a grey pallor and his eyes were bloodshot through lack of sleep. He drank the whisky in one gulp and swivelled his chair towards the window. The thick snowflakes falling from a darkening sky seemed to reach into the room and suck the very warmth from his body. He shivered, then yawned, and became conscious of an ache behind the eyes. Cautiously he pressed his fingers against the closed eyelids, morbidly enjoying the pain it gave.

Perhaps tomorrow, he thought. Perhaps by then he would have found a better idea. The false hope withered swiftly for he knew he had been over the same ground time and time again. No, the second blackmail letter had given a deadline of 5 November. The drop was to be made at the airport in a left-luggage locker, the key for which had been neatly taped to the letter.

He once again considered silencing the blackmailer by employing outside help, but his mind returned to the same quandary. The fear that once someone else knew they too could turn to blackmail. He turned back to his desk and unlocked the top right-hand drawer. His hand was shaking and his eyes were filled with a fascinated horror as he picked up the revolver. It was a Smith and Wesson .38 and carried no bullets in the chamber. It was something he had been given years ago in Germany when he had been involved with a minor racketeer in the fur business. The man with a pock-marked Levantine face had insisted that Otto keep it under his pillow, saying that the underworld would send its assassins in the night to cut a man's throat if they suspected he was working against them. Otto did better than keep it under his pillow. He sold up and left the city as fast as his frightened legs would carry him. Now, after all this time, he was steeled to using it in anger.

He put the gun back and picked up the clear plastic container of dark green sleeping tablets which the elegant doctor had left him following the stabbing incident in the Grand Rue. He weighed the container in his hand. It was the perfect murder after all. No, he shuddered at the word. Accident sounded better. And self-inflicted accident better still. He got up from the desk and went to the drinks cabinet. Another large Johnny Walker and he felt himself grinning. A little nerve twitched and jumped in his cheek and he touched it with a fingertip to try and still it.

Suddenly he was ready. Without realising it, the fear had been responsible. The fear of losing his hard-earned money. The fear of being found out as someone who had accidently stabbed a man to death. The fear which had driven him a little mad and forced him to drink too much. And it was the drink which had completed the cycle. Given him the courage he had thus far lacked. He straightened his tie and went back to the desk and picked up the pile of letters and packages.

Anna, the young secretary who had taken over Lisa's job was painting her nails a blood-red colour when Otto went through to the outer office. Ever since she had acted as a 'hostess' to the Arab client she was taking her work far less seriously. Otto did not mind, he might be in need of her services again, and also on this day her idleness would be beneficial. He gave her the various packages, all for hand delivery – something he himself had timed as taking a minimum of one hour and ten minutes – and told her not to worry about the switchboard as he would take care of it. He then went through to the adjoining office and told his chief accountant he was not to be disturbed for the next hour and a quarter as he was conducting an urgent meeting with a very important client. Finally, he placed a call to Lisa in London, interrupting his own conversation after a matter of seconds by announcing that a client had just arrived and asking her to call him back in one hour. Then, taking the new camel-coloured cashmere topcoat and the black astrakhan hat from the plastic bag by the side of his desk, he put them on. With the revolver and the phial of sleeping tablets tucked safely in his pocket, he went back to Anna's desk and placed the switchboard to night service. Then he hurried out into the cold afternoon.

Five minutes and forty-two seconds later he had parked his Mercedes in the old town and was half-running, half-walking down the Grande Rue. The snow was thickening now and what few people were in the street had their heads cast down. It was even better than he could have hoped for. No one would remember seeing him in this weather. He rushed into the alley at the side of Marie's house and banged on the door.

She was wearing a white Turkish towelling robe and her head was turbanned in blue silk. Her face was pink and well scrubbed as though she had just come from the bath.

'Otto,' she said warmly, 'you are very early. You said six o'clock.'

He mumbled something and went through to the kitchen. She followed.

'A drink, Marie, we have a small celebration.' He tugged off his coat and placed it with the hat on a chair.

'Whisky,' she said brightly.

'Of course whisky,' he snapped. 'What else?'

'So,' she said, raising her glass, 'what is the celebration about?'

Otto, with a sudden hiss of indrawn breath, said, 'About, my dear Marie? It is about money of course. Money, money, money.' He laughed. He loved the sound of that word. It had a musical tinkling sound. 'I have sold my companies. You are now looking at a very rich man.'

She joined in his laughter. 'But you were always rich, Otto.'

He took a sip of his drink. 'In assets only. But now I have sold them. Now I have just money. Drink up,' he beckoned.

She tipped back her glass and shuddered as the raw whisky burned down her throat. Otto picked up the bottle and refilled her glass.

'That is too much, Otto, you will make me drunk.'

'And why not? Come, we get drunk together.'

Mariella laughed and entered into the spirit of things. This was, after all, a part of her business, she thought. And if the customer says get drunk, you get drunk. He, after all, is footing the bill. She dropped down into a chair by the kitchen table, her robe falling open to expose her large breasts. She made no move to cover herself. The customer was paying for that as well.

By the third whisky she could feel a soft warm glow pulsating through her body. She was feeling good, very good, but even so there was something about Otto's manner which was not quite right. His eyes looked glazed, as though he was ill. And his voice although appearing to be friendly was somehow cold and distant.

'You could have at least asked me,' he was saying in a strange voice.

'Asked you!'

'For money! If you needed it that badly you could have asked me.'

'I do not understand, Otto . . . what are you saying?'

He looked up, his grey eyes lit with an almost savage quality. 'You know what I am saying, Marie. The black-mail!'

'The blackmail!' she repeated falteringly.

His eyes dropped back to the glass in his hands. 'You were the one all along. And all the time I believed you. And all the time it was a lie.'

'But Otto, I have told you. I know nothing of this. Nothing. You must believe . . .' Her voice stopped with a small strangled gasp as his hands appeared above the table. The dull black gun wavered slightly. Her face turned ghastly white as fear and shock combined within her and her entire body trembled.

'My pocket diary,' he continued, in the same faraway voice. 'I have watched you when you thought I was asleep. My mistake, of course, for writing down important business matters which were highly confidential. But still you had no right to do that.'

'But, Otto,' she pleaded, 'I can explain . . .'

'Not that that entirely convinced me of course. But the last time I was here you made me coffee. You were out of the kitchen and I was looking for some sweetener. I took a container,' he pointed with the gun, 'from over there, on the shelf. The one marked *Sucre*. And what did I find inside? My wallet. Empty, of course.' His voice lifted fractionally. 'So what did you do with the money, you bitch? And the credit cards!'

She broke down at that, lowering her face into her hands and sobbing violently.

'Stop that,' he yelled. 'No more of this play acting.' He staggered from his chair and moved around the table.

She looked up, her eyes full of fear. 'What . . . what are you going to do?'

He took a pen and paper from his pocket. 'Write down what I tell you,' he snarled.

She took up the pen and in a shaking hand did as she was told.

'Now,' he said, 'you have a choice.'

'A choice?' She didn't understand.

He waved the gun menacingly in front of her face. 'Either you die with this, or you can choose a more peaceful way.' He dropped the plastic container on the table.

'What are these?' she sobbed, picking them up.

'Sleeping tablets. There are thirty of them. You will take them all.'

Her eyes were wide with fright when she cried, 'Otto, please. I swear on my mother's life that I know nothing of the blackmail . . . and the wallet I can explain. I will pay you back. Every last sou.'

He reached out and struck her violently across the face. 'You will pay me back! You? You whore who does not know truth from lies. Why should I believe you?' He pushed his glass of whisky before her. 'The tablets,' he ordered. 'Now.'

Her mind was in a turmoil as she glanced at the note and realised what she had written. Desperately, she tried to clear the fog which seemed to shroud her mind. He was mad. Not drunk mad, but crazy mad. And weren't mad men dangerous? Other than that, he had given her a choice. One way she was dead instantly. The other! She glanced nervously at her watch. Twenty minutes to four. A glimmer of hope shone in her eyes. Konrad would be back at four. Then there was Mitzi, a girl who had been on the game in Zurich. One who had taken an overdose. The pills had taken some time to work, to put her to sleep, and it had been during those fateful last minutes that she had changed her mind and telephoned the hospital. Within an hour they had pumped her stomach out and saved her life.

Von Klaus forced the drink into her hands. Even though she knew it was the only way she was terrified. The barrel of the gun was pressing hard against the temple now. She emptied the pills into her sweating palm and took three, washing them down with the whisky. She almost gagged as they caught in the back of her throat.

Von Klaus pushed the gun harder against her head. 'More, you bitch,' he yelled. 'Faster, faster.'

When it was done she felt no different, except her brain was working rapidly. She had to feign sleep. Once he had left she could phone the hospital. And failing that there was Konrad. She staggered to her feet and took a few steps forward reaching out for support. Finding none she weaved drunkenly back to the chair and fell into it. She made her body tremble all over for effect before saying in a small voice, 'Why . . . why?' When no answer came she lowered her head to the table and closed her eyes.

Von Klaus, being uncertain how quickly the tablets would take to act, took his whisky glass and emptied it in the sink. Then he washed and dried the glass and returned it to the cupboard. Next he put on the cashmere coat and the astrakhan hat and moved slowly towards her. His fingers were shaking as he reached out and touched her forehead. She didn't move. He expelled a frightened gasp of air and, certain she was unconscious, went quickly to the rear door and let himself out.

The snow was falling in a white fluid wall as he stumbled and slithered along the Grand Rue. He laughed to himself,

And again. And again. A man in a camel-coloured cashmere coat with a close-fitting black astrakhan hat, which at first glance could be mistaken for black hair. A good disguise, he decided. One that did not look unlike the elegant Swiss doctor. He checked his watch as he climbed into the Mercedes. Six minutes and a few seconds to four. He could just make it back to the office before he was missed.

Back at the house, Mariella had listened for the slamming of the back door. Thank God he had gone. Even so she waited a short while to make sure he wasn't playing a trick. Eventually she opened her eyes and looked slowly around the kitchen. She was alone. She had fooled him. She pulled herself up from the chair. It was the strangest feeling. As though her entire body was stuffed full of cotton wool. It felt detached, numb. She moved uncertainly towards the living-room.

Her mind was still clear enough to phrase the words. She knew exactly what had to be done. Besides, she consoled herself, the girl in Zurich had told her the pills had taken the best part of half an hour to knock her out. She dialled the hospital with thick sausage-like fingers and waited for a voice. Then the nightmare began. Someone was speaking to her and she was trying to reply, except the words were hopelessly slurred, running over themselves in a stream of unintelligible gibberish. Tears of frustration and anger were flowing down her cheeks as she tried to form the words; 'Send an ambulance quickly.' The voice on the other end of the telephone was becoming impatient, almost cross. Mariella tried again. But the line was dead. Now her mind was flooded with panic as she frantically redialled. Without noticing it, the number was incorrect. She listened to the distant bleeping sound, but no one answered. She looked down at her watch. The wavering figures said five minutes to four. Konrad! Konrad would walk through the door any moment now. Any moment. She gathered the towelling robe around her and stumbled into the hallway, and fell. It took some time before the realisation struck her. What if he was late? What if the plane was held up! Or the traffic from the airport had delayed him! Now there were voices screaming inside her head. She had to reach somebody. Outside. The street. She knew the man who owned the antique shop opposite her house. Yes, that was it. That was the answer.

Clawing her way gradually up the wall, she made it to her feet and shuffled towards the front door. Her entire body seemed devoid of feeling now, so that at each lurching step she almost fell. Then she was against the door, her breath coming in short laboured gasps. She lifted her hands to the catch and tried to turn it, but her fingers would not work. She was looking at them, commanding them to turn the catch and they would not obey. It was as if they belonged to someone else. To some great fat balloon of a person blown hard with air. How long she stood there crying and fumbling with the door catch she didn't know, but in the end her legs gave way and she collapsed on the floor. There was a roaring sound in her ears now. It was not unlike the sea and felt strangely soothing. No Mariella, she chastised herself. It is not soothing. It is wicked and cruel. It is trying to take you away. You must stay awake.

She remembered the letter and the words he had made her write. 'I have decided I cannot go on this way. Now I must repent for my sins. May God forgive me. Marie.' At first she had not understood; now, however, she realised it was a suicide note. But it was the thought that Otto would get away with it which made the anger rise within her one last time. The scream was an agonised sound from the very depths of her being and took with it the last of her strength.

When no one came, she huddled into the foetal position and closed her eyes. She felt tired now. Very, very tired. Perhaps after a short rest she would feel refreshed. Then she would call out again. Even so, and this pleased her, Konrad would walk through the door very soon now.

Her mind drifted back to the girl in Zurich and wondered how the sleeping tablets had taken so long to act in her case. Still it wasn't important. She wiped the tears from her eyes and forced herself to smile. Beyond the door she imagined she heard muffled footsteps in the snow. 'I'm never going to shout at you again, Konrad,' she whispered. 'Never again . . . I swear on Mama's life.'

Otto von Klaus pulled up outside his office a few seconds before four o'clock. He took off the cashmere coat and astrakhan hat and stuffed them under the passenger seat, then ran into the building.

Anna, as expected, was still absent. He placed the switchboard back to normal service and went through to his office. His hands were shaking violently as he poured a large whisky. But he had done it, had saved himself a million dollars. Never again, he decided there and then, would he have anything to do with women. In fact, after this aircraft transaction was concluded he would avoid people altogether. That way his money would be safe and he would be happy.

He moved over to his desk and sat down, feeling his heard pounding noisily against his chest and smelling his own body sweat. He laughed suddenly. It was amazing. The perfect crime. Mixing whisky with the sleeping tables had been a clever touch. Knocked her out almost instantaneously. And the letter, of course that had been quite masterly.

The telephone rang and he jumped in fright. He picked it up and forced calmness into his voice. It was Lisa. He smiled to himself and picked up the paper which outlined the details of the financial arrangements he wished her to conduct with the Alaska company.

In Tehran it was early evening. The mosaic tiled floor of the mosque was cool to Rashid Suliman's bare feet. He moved slowly along the colonnade which supported the high arch of the ceiling. The hall was massive and could have held more than a thousand worshippers. As it was, there were no more than fifty present. From the high narrow slits in the walls he caught glimpses of a starry sky and his nostrils were filled with the dry flinty smell of the desert.

The muezzin's voice rang out then with the oft repeated 'Allahu akbar' and Suliman turned to face Mecca. It was at moments like these that he was torn between his religion and his country and the great exciting freedom which the Western world offered. Truly, at this moment he would lay down his life for Islam. There was something here, some great spiritual magic which belonged only to the desert, where a wind gusting down from the north seemed to roll the whole world away to the horizon. It was simply old and timeless and hauntingly beautiful. He touched his ears with his hands, then clasped his hands in front of him, the left within the right. He bowed then knelt down, touching his forehead on the floor at the appropriate moments and recited: 'In the name of Allah, the compassionate, the merciful, I seek refuge in the Lord of men, the King of men, the God of men, from the mischief of the slinking prompter who whispers in the heart of men; from jinn and men.' He looked over his right shoulder then his left, to greet the two recording angels who wrote down his good and bad acts.

It was as he was standing to leave that Fazlollah Mahallati drifted silently to his side. Both men left the mosque together.

Fazlollah said, 'Your faith is still strong, Rashid.'

Suliman nodded. He was unsure what the 'still' was supposed to mean. Another of Fazlollah's little games perhaps! He would need to watch his old friend very carefully; age it seemed had made him a worthy adversary.

'Always strong, Fazlollah,' he replied. 'As Arabic is the most dazzling of languages, so is Islam the brightest star in the firmament.'

Fazlollah smiled in the darkness. 'You will come to my house to take tea and share a nargileh with me?'

Suliman, wishing to avoid his friend's company and having no desire to take hashish, said sadly, 'A thousand pardons, my friend, but tonight I sit with my father.'

'Ah yes, you must give him my respects. And the illness, how goes it?'

'He is thankful to Allah for little pain; no more.' The two men walked on in silence for a while, then Rashid said, 'And your war! It goes well?'

'Indeed. We have drawn the Iraqi troops into counter-attacking at Faw. Of course our losses are heavy and the Iraqis smelling victory are committing their best soldiers to this battle.'

'But this battle is only a feint,' Rashid observed perceptively.

139

'Indeed. At this very moment thousands of our regular troops are massing near Susangerd. An arrowhead advance across the border before we sweep south, driving the Iraqis into the sea.'

'And then?'

'And then, my friend, Kuwait. Of course our air support is still too weak to think that far ahead; which brings me to the matter of the Hercules. This still goes well?'

'As planned.'

Fazlollah smiled tensely and made no comment. Eventually they came to the edge of the old city and the place they would part. Fazlollah said, 'Goodbye, my friend.'

'Until the next time,' Rashid replied and was soon swallowed up by the dark night.

Fazlollah remained a few moments pondering the imponderable. Why had Rashid, a true merchant when it came to bartering, allowed the deal with the Hercules to be concluded at the full asking price? He had seen the written reports at the ministry that very day and knew this to be true. Of course, it was already decided that they would obtain the aircraft for nothing. But that was not the point. No, the point was that Rashid, for the first time in his life, had not played the game. Had not haggled for a fairer price.

Fazlollah stroked his beard thoughtfully, and wondered why so unimportant a matter should trouble him.

In Norfolk, the rain had been dying away. As Fitzgerald pulled up to the side of the old hangar, only a few drops spat tiredly against the car's windshield. He switched off the headlights and left the car, stumbling through the pitch blackness towards the hangar door. The latest problem had arisen following his return from Zurich. It was something he had never even considered. In his mind the Red Cross was a charitable organisation which would be only too willing to avail themselves of a Hercules cargo aircraft. Not so. He had read the report Lisa had prepared. It had commenced by outlining a few pertinent facts.

'The International Red Cross has national affiliates in almost every country in the world. It was first established to care for victims of battle in time of war, but later turned its help to include the prevention and relief of human suffering in general.

'Peacetime activities include: first aid, accident prevention, water safety, training of nurses' aides and mothers' assistants, maintenance of maternal and child welfare centres and medical clinics, and numerous other services. Its emblem is a red cross. In Muslim countries it is a red crescent, while in Iran it is a red lion and sun.

'From an historical point of view, and as an *aide-mémoire*, should you be interviewed by one of the Red Cross committees, the Red Cross arose out of the work of Jean-Henri Dunant, a Swiss humanitarian, who, at the battle of Solferino in June 1859 organised emergency aid services for Austrian and French wounded. Further to this, the Geneva Convention of 1864 was the first multilateral agreement by the Red Cross and committed signatory governments to care for the wounded of war, whether enemy or friend.

'The present problem is that the international committee – made up of twenty-five Swiss citizens – in Geneva, have to approve all large donations of the type offered. It seems they do not accept the offer of aircraft out of hand. Proof of ownership and moral standing of company or individual would appear to be a factor. The next meeting of the committee, when it will either accept or reject the offer put forward by Relief Air, is not until Monday 1 December.'

He had sworn softly after reading it, and then put a call through to Guy Stanton in Norfolk to arrange a meeting of the crew that night. Amongst other things, they had to consider an alternative way of delivering the aircraft to Iran. With that done he had told Lisa to contact Otto and see if he could pull any strings in Geneva to bypass the Red Cross system, and departed for Norfolk.

Now, inside the darkened hangar, he was feeling his way past Guy's crop-spraying aircraft. The dull yellow light in the far corner came from a partly opened door. Chance eased it a few more inches and through the thick fug of cigar smoke and fumes from a paraffin heater saw the three men sitting around a small table playing cards.

'The life of Riley for some, it is, it is,' he said in a thick Irish brogue.

Three heads simultaneously spun round and Stanton said, 'I wish you bloody well wouldn't do that.'

'Do what?'

'The creeping Jesus act.'

Fitzgerald smiled. 'Stealth and soldiers, old son.' He pulled up a chair and sat down, dropping an arm around Pedro's shoulder. 'Winning?' Pedro grinned, his eyes motioning towards the pile of money in front of him.

Gaylord laughed. 'When did he ever do anything else? Especially when there's money on the table . . . anyway, how's it going?'

Fitzgerald looked across at the silver-haired southern gentleman. His face was more gaunt than he remembered. Other than that, he was still the Mississippi river-boat gambler of old. 'Fine, Hiram, just fine. And you?'

'Never been better. Especially with this quaint little business transaction you've cooked up. Yessir, we'll soon be walking in tall cotton . . . my ticket back to Vacherie, first class all the way.'

Stanton who had left the table to pour coffee for his latest guest returned to his chair and slid the tin mug across to Chance. 'Are you playing, or are we talking?'

'I think we'd better talk first.' He ran over the hold-up on delivery due to the delay in obtaining the necessary permission from the Red Cross.

Stanton, cigar clenched between his teeth, was first to meet. 'Bloody amazing, and I thought that that long-haired pop star, Bob Geldof, was out of order when he blasted the UN recently. But if this is the type of bureaucracy he ran into in Ethiopia and the Sudan I can quite understand his anger.'

'Not forgetting the corruption,' Gaylord added. 'Like, for every ten dollars' worth of food that gets through, maybe fifty cents' worth ends up with the people who need it, while the remainder lines the pockets of the wealthy.'

'Life!' stated Fitzgerald. 'Still, that's not our problem. What we're faced with is trying to come up with a back-up plan to ship this machine to Iran.'

Stanton puffed thoughtfully on his cigar. 'Still using the same cover though!'

'Unless you know better.'

Stanton shook his head. 'No. Any other way and the CIA would be falling all over us.'

Gaylord picked up the deck of playing cards and fanned them out expertly. 'I figure it this way. The Red Cross approval will come after December one, right?'

Fitzgerald shook his head. 'Approval or disapproval.'

'Yeah, OK. Approval or disapproval. So what's to stop us positioning the plane into Khartoum by say the end of November and sitting and waiting for the word. Then either way, good or bad, we light outa there when the news breaks.'

Fitzgerald lowered the mug of coffee from his lips. 'One problem with that is if the Red Cross have rejected our offer, we – that is, each and every one of us – will have the gentlemen of the Central Intelligence Agency tracking us. It's not like being on some African dictator's black list for flying fighters for the losing side; these guys mean it. They'll follow you to the gates of hell and beyond . . . and what is more they won't be too particular about bringing you back for trial.'

'Impasse, I think, gentlemen,' Stanton pronounced standing up. 'There's still an hour of drinking time left at the Crooked Fiddler. What say we adjourn there. Damn sight more comfortable than this draughty old tomb.'

As they were making their way through the darkened hangar, Stanton pulled the Irishman aside. 'I'm not too happy about Pedro,' he said in a low voice. 'His asthma is very bad. It could jeopardise the entire mission.'

'Did you speak to Hiram?'

'Yes. He reckons he'll live forever.'

'So what's the problem?'

'The problem is that I've been appointed commander of a bloody aircraft to run a hazardous mission, and for that I at least expect a fit and able crew. What if he becomes seriously ill during the operation?'

'The same thing that always happens. He's left behind. We carry no passengers, get that one solitary fact through

143

that public school brain of yours . . . and don't get on your high horse of noblesse oblige, or whatever you call it because I'm not particularly interested. Pedro is just another merc looking for a big payday. If he survives he'll get to spend his ill gotten gains. If not it will be forwarded to his next of kin. Any questions?'

'Just one. How do I get out?'

Fitzgerald laughed. 'That's easy old son . . . you don't.'

In Jersey, Maxine Audley was pacing up and down her bedroom. She was dressed in a bright red jersey and tightly fitting grey skirt. Her face was pale, accentuating the crimson of her lips, the dark glittering eyes and the vivid blackness of her hair.

'Damn it,' she said out loud. She had searched everywhere for the diamond ear-ring. And tomorrow she was going away with Rupert for two weeks in the Greek islands. As Rupert had bought her the ear-rings as a birthday present she considered it politic at least to be wearing them. He fussed so much and she knew he would be the first to spot if they were missing. Not that she was desperately keen on the man, but he could be entertaining in short bursts. Besides she needed the break. She had been on the island now for eight weeks. Eight boringly long weeks. To Maxine, who was not an islander by birth or nature, each day had seemed like the passing of a jail sentence.

She returned to the dressing-table, sat down, and began working her way methodically through her various jewellery boxes. The collection was impressive for anyone other than Maxine. She found most of the pieces dull. There was an Edwardian two-stone fancy step-cut diamond ring which she hated. Then a Demantoid garnet-and-diamond cluster ring and a diamond eleven-stone Collet line bracelet which she liked even less. The sapphire-and-diamond target cluster ring was something she wore occasionally, as she did the Edwardian Peridot and pearl necklet. Perhaps her favourite ring of the moment was the Ceylon sapphire and baguette diamond. She carried on emptying the boxes, pausing every now and then to admire a piece she had forgotten about. At the end of the search, however, there was only the one ear-ring.

She cupped her chin in her hands and tried to think when she had lost worn them. Last Saturday, at Clive and Val's party? Or the midweek bash at Julie and Alfie's place! No, that had been the gold seahorses which John had given her. God, why was life so complicated, she thought, always having to be so careful what jewellery she wore and always having to remember who had given her what. She swore angrily to herself and stormed off to the bathroom.

Lowering herself into the soft perfumed bubbles acted as a kind of herbalist's balm and she let out a small laugh.

'Really, Maxine, you are silly,' she told herself. 'Just wait for the right moment and use your feminine wiles; he'll probably buy you two new pairs to replace them.'

As she was washing herself the thought struck her. She had last seen Rupert at the party at this house. So she must have been wearing them that evening. The only problem was she had drunk far too much and couldn't remember a great deal about that night. As she was attempting to reconstruct the events, her thoughts alighted on the man she hated. Chance Fitzgerald. She had been lying on the bed in the blue room. Perhaps the ear-ring had come off there! She squeezed the water out of the sponge and watched the soapy trickle run down her breasts. Chance Fitzgerald, she thought again, and then smiled spitefully. She had really fixed him this time. Really and truly. That would teach the arrogant bastard. No one refused her. No one.

It had been the afternoon following the party when Alice had returned from her friend's house. She had been bubbling over with enthusiasm, chattering about her horse Long Shot as though he was a human being, and talking of things like New Zealand rugs, over-reach boots and her progress in cavaletti work. Finally, through boredom at listening to the childish gibberish, Maxine had said, 'Did you have a visitor at the stables today, darling?'

'Visitor, Mummy!'

'Yes, darling, did anyone come and see you today?'

Alice's blue eyes had been puzzled. 'No, why? Who was supposed to come?'

Maxine had feigned embarrassment and turned away. 'It doesn't matter.'

'Tell me, tell me,' Alice had pleaded.

'I know I shouldn't, darling, but perhaps it's for the best.' She turned to her daughter with a wistful smile on her face. 'It was your father; he was here on business. He stayed here last night. I did ask him to come and see you of course.'

Alice had been crestfallen. 'Perhaps,' she started, 'perhaps he will come here, to the house.'

'No, I'm afraid not. He will have flown back to London by now.' She had gathered her daughter in her arms then and held her tightly. That was when Jack Audley came into the room.

'What's happening then,' he boomed. 'Hasn't fallen off her horse again!'

Maxine had motioned him to silence and sent a tearful Alice to her room to get changed. When the child had gone she had turned to her father and told him how Chance had promised he would call in at the stables and see Alice.

'And he didn't, you mean?'

'No.'

Audley had gone over to the sideboard and poured himself a whisky. 'Perhaps his business meeting with Philippe went on longer than usual,' he said at length. 'He'll be back.'

'No, father,' she had replied almost vehemently. 'He will not be back. It has been two years since he visited his daughter. Two years. Now he breezes in, stays at your house, and doesn't have the decency to even stop and spend one minute with his child . . . of course he's got time to rush back to London and that other woman.'

Audley's ears had pricked up at that. 'Other woman! Chance? Who told you that?'

'He did,' Maxine replied, knowing it was her father's abiding wish that they would one day re-marry.

'When?'

'Last night. At the party.'

Audley downed his whisky and left the room, his face a mask of quiet anger.

Maxine climbed out of the tub and rubbed herself down, enjoying the softness of the Turkish towelling against her skin. Then, slipping into a cream silk dressing-gown she went up to the next floor and the blue room. The bed had been stripped and Mrs Le Brun had obviously vacuumed, but she looked anyway. On the bed. Underneath it. Even in the bathroom. There was not a sign of the other half of Rupert's present.

It was as she reached down to switch off the beside light that her hand fell on the drawer of the small bedside table. She opened it without thinking. The diamond ear-ring looked up at her. She picked it up and gave a sigh of relief. Thank goodness, she thought. Must keep Rupert sweet.

She was turning to go when she froze in mid-stride. 'No, no,' she said firmly. 'To hell with Rupert he can buy you a new pair. And as for you, Chance Fitzgerald, I haven't finished with you yet . . . not by any stretch of the imagination.' She was smiling as she left the room, her eyes full of evil as she anticipated some long awaited triumph.

In Norfolk, the four mercenaries were hunched over a table at the Crooked Fiddler. The main bar lights had been turned out and the landlord had called, 'Time, gentlemen, please.' The four didn't move and their faces seemed set as the shadows flitted over them from the flickering flames of the log fire. Stanton had briefed them a few minutes earlier not to make too much noise and wait for the pub to empty. Once the landlord had locked up he would serve them with a fresh round of drinks and they could stay as long as they wished.

Arthur Young came over presently with a tray of drinks, then went about his business, clearing up the empty glasses.

'So where were we?' Fitzgerald asked.

'We, old boy,' Stanton replied, 'we're up shit creek in a barbed wire canoe; metaphorically speaking of course.'

There were a few smiles at the remark before Gaylord

leaned forward. 'OK, Chance, let's run over the second phase for a moment. I appreciate we haven't solved the first one yet, but to my way of figuring the second looks to be a major problem.'

'Getting the three of you back from Iran and into the Sudan, you mean?'

'Something along those lines.'

'Two ways,' Fitzgerald answered. 'By air or sea. The first one poses too many problems for me. The second means a ship from Chah Bahar in southern Iran with a drop-off somewhere near Djibouti.'

Stanton, who had been lighting a cigar, nearly choked. 'Djibouti! Djibouti! And how in God's name do we get from there to Juba?'

Fitzgerald said, 'You tell me, you're the expert.'

'OK, I'll tell you. Number one, the range is a minimum of one thousand miles. Number two, the terrain is hostile. By that, I mean it is possible for a team of young fit commando types equipped with all the right gear to make it. But us? Take a look around, we're old men. Force march any one of us a couple of miles, even on these flat Norfolk roads, and you'd end up with the walking wounded. Try it in desert terrain with the sun beating down on your back and I'll leave you to draw your own conclusions.'

Fitzgerald's face maintained its half smile. 'I wasn't exactly suggesting you walk. How about vehicles?'

'Two problems. One, what bush roads there are will have been washed out by the rains, meaning we could spend as much time out of the vehicles as in them . . . road building, that is. Two, if you're trying to maintain a low profile, a vehicle in that part of Africa is hardly the answer.'

'Puts me in mind of the man asking directions in a Dublin pub and being told, "If I was you I wouldn't start from here at all". But you're quite right, it's too far a journey overland. That's why I'll be picking you up in a light plane.'

Stanton's eyebrows arched. 'And how do you propose to do that?'

'Easy enough. Let's say the sea voyage takes five days. During that period search parties will be out looking for a crashed Hercules. I, being a concerned director of Relief Air, will naturally appear on the scene and rent a light plane to help with the search. Running daily out of Juba I'll arrange to lift you out of some bush strip near the coast and return you to somewhere north of Juba. You then sit tight for a few days before walking into town.'

'You said a light plane. Would it have the range to fly Juba, Djibouti and return?'

'Probably not, so I'll build up a fuel cache somewhere at the mid-point during the first few fruitless days of the air search.'

'And the boat?' Gaylord asked.

'Leave it to me. I'll fix it up with the people concerned. You'll probably be dropped a few miles off the coast with a motor-powered rubber dinghy. Just make sure it's night when you make your run ashore. If anyone spots you make sure you get rid of them; remember, they could blow the whole deal wide open on the very last lap.'

Stanton lit a fresh cigar and blew out a cloud of blue smoke. 'Of course,' he remarked, 'we're assuming that we'll be working for the Red Cross when we go missing. But if your negotiations with them fail, so does stage two. I mean, no point in returning to the Sudan in that case is there?'

Fitzgerald stretched in his chair. 'You're not wrong, Guy. However, you can also leave that to me. I'm banking on a man in Geneva to sort it out for us.'

'And if he doesn't?'

'One for all of us to be thinking about. Clandestine night operations. And we've all done enough of those.' He turned to Pedro who had spoken no more than half a dozen words all evening. 'What do you think, pal?'

'I think whatever we do,' he wheezed, 'still beats working for a living.'

Stanton glowered at the Chinaman and said sharply. 'That's all we bloody well need . . . romantic notions about mercenary aviators from an oriental.'

Fitzgerald noticed a dark look flit across the usually benign features of Hiram Gaylord. 'Well, gentlemen,' he said quickly, 'I think we can call it a night. If you can let me have the usual breakdowns, Guy, on stages one and two.

Other than that I'll keep you informed on movements. Say Friday at the latest.'

The drive back to London was long and tiring. It was raining again and the night was as black as any Fitzgerald could remember. With the radio playing softly, his mind was drifting back over a lot of operations in war zones on similar nights. The unwarranted remark from Stanton at the end of the evening and the look Gaylord had given him were part of the pre-game tension. The nervy build-up to a most dangerous game. And no matter how often you went out and did it, it never became any easier.

For the first time since it had all started he felt unsure of himself. Nagging doubts. Morality. It was the Catholicism again: the flickering candles, the incense-laden air, the bejewelled chalice and the taking of bread. And the low voices, out of Latin now: 'What game is it, Sean Eugene Fitzgerald? What are you now playing? And why would you be holding the souls of three men in your hand?'

It was a twist on the old saw, 'Show me your friends and I'll tell you who you are.'

He reached forward and turned up the volume of the radio and eased his foot hard down on the accelerator, as though sound and speed could escape conscience.

4 November

Geneva, Switzerland

TUESDAY 1005 HOURS

THE SKY WAS clear and blue and sun rays glittered from the windows of tall buildings as Konrad Zwicky made his way jauntily up the hill towards the old town. The back streets, as places out of the sun, were still deep with the previous day's snow and the air was brittle cold, condensing his warm breath into small puffy white clouds. He patted his jacket pocket to reassure himself. The wallet was still there. 'Perhaps if I had quit the game earlier,' he thought for the hundredth time, 'then I would have at least quadrupled my money.' As it was, he had hung on and seen his luck change. Watched his winnings gradually dwindle. It was when the chips before him totalled 5,500 francs that he stopped playing. It was totally out of character, of course, but he was thinking of Mariella. And to return to Geneva without the 5,000 francs Mr Fitzgerald had paid him would be fatal. She would at least kill him. As it was he was still a few hundred francs up on the deal. Also, he had had a good night's sleep.

The forty-minute flight from Zurich had made him feel slightly sick, but then he always felt that way in airliners. They frightened him. Not enough to stop him flying, but enough to bring him out in a cold sweat, especially on take-off when they seemed to climb at an impossibly steep angle. And then there was a change in the engine note. Quite alarming.

On arrival at Geneva-Cointrin airport he had caught a

bus to the city centre. This was another concession. Usually he would have squandered his last few francs on a taxi, carrying on the charade of being a rich man – if not today, then tomorrow.

He turned into the Grande Rue slightly breathless and solicited a smile from a pretty blonde girl, pausing to turn and watch her shapeiy legs until she turned a corner and was lost from sight. He was sure he had seen her before. Perhaps she lived nearby! He made a mental note to look out for her in the future. Then, concentrating on the excuse he had carefully prepared for failing to return on the previous afternoon, he continued up the Grande Rue.

Turning the key in the lock he started to push the door open. It stopped within a matter of inches. He pushed again, harder this time. It gave a little more and he squeezed his thin body through the narrow opening.

'Mariella,' he called. There was no answer. The word was in his throat for the second time when his eyes picked up the huddled shape at the edge of his vision. He looked down and his expression changed to shocked disbelief. He sank slowly to his knees and reached out to touch her face. It was blue and cold and smooth as marble. His voice was a broken whisper when he spoke her name again, while his eyes had a look of incomprehension. He stared at her face, every feature of which he knew. Down to the last little wrinkle. Except now it seemed strange to him, with its set lips, its blue pallor, its stony silence.

'Mariella,' he said gently. 'Mariella. Wake up, wake up.' He tried to shake her, but she was too heavy. Too stiff. He knew then that she was dead. He felt the hot tears filling his eyes as he slumped against the wall.

It was some time before he took the wallet from his pocket and extricated the five thousand francs. There was a boyish smile on his face and his voice was filled with the desperate optimism he had carried within him for more years than he could recall.

'You see, Mariella, the first payment. You see, I did not spend it. I did not let you down.' He reached out and tried to unclench her fingers which had tightened like crooked claws into the palms of her hands. They wouldn't move.

'The first payment, Mariella,' he said again. 'The first payment . . .' He broke down then and pressing his face against hers began to cry.

In London, the sun was breaking through the scattered remnants of clouds. The cold front was being pushed to the east by a force eight wind. Lisa Wendell-Holmes had been up since seven o'clock. Not that she had any reason to be, but after so many years of rising at that hour she now felt it difficult to break the habit. She had showered and washed her hair and then gone to the kitchen. While the coffee had been percolating she had styled and dried her hair and spent a great deal of time applying her make-up. After that she had dressed in a white silk accordion-pleated blouse and knee-length black shirt. The fine denier black stockings and black high-heeled shoes had added the finishing touch. She felt slimmer already.

Now she was looking in the small mirror she had used to apply her make-up, and frowning at the tell-tale age lines around the eyes and corners of her lips. She wondered how she would manage to hang on to Chance. There would always be competition, that went without saying. And if he was handsome now, she couldn't bear to think what he would be like ten years hence when greying hair and deeper etched lines in his face would give him that rugged look that women went for. While she? What would she be like? Completely grey and spreading in all the wrong places! What the hell, she had to hang on to him. It was going to be like shooting the rapids in a fragile canoe with rocks and whirlpools everywhere. It would never be secure, not to her way of thinking, and she would never know what would be waiting around the next corner; but she had at least to give it a try.

'Penny for them!'

She spun round and saw him standing in the doorway. 'I didn't hear you. How long have you been standing there?'

He came over to her and kissed her neck. 'Long enough to wish I hadn't arrived back so late and found you asleep. And long enough to wish I'd been awake before you left my bed.'

'Chance Fitzgerald,' she scolded, 'is that all you ever think about?'

He looked appealingly at her. 'And what would you say if I said yes?'

She laughed and tried to hide her embarrassment. 'Sit down and I'll make you breakfast.'

'Just coffee, my lovely girl, and speaking of lovely girls, the outfit is quite stunning.'

'You like it?' she said and did a quick twirl in the middle of the kitchen.

'Like it would be an understatement.' He gave her a cheeky wink.

'So tell me what happened last night,' she said, pouring the coffee.

'Well, apart from solving the problem of getting the crew back, not a lot. Without Red Cross approval to act under their banner, we still have to find a way to deliver the goods.'

She put the coffee on the table and sat down. 'Why the Red Cross? Couldn't you approach the Sudanese government direct, or some other charity come to that.'

'Sure we could, but I'm looking for the best possible cover. To be seen to be working in conjunction with the Red Cross gives us something like the good housekeeping seal of approval. It also should dissuade certain people investigating our movements.'

'What certain people?'

'The CIA.'

She looked surprised. 'The CIA! But they're American. Why would they be involved?'

'How about I hold an American passport for starters? Then, of course, we have, or are in the process of purchasing, an American airplane, which being built to a military specification can be construed as a weapon of war. And as we're selling it to a non-friendly country!' He lifted his hands in the French way, palms up.

'Why didn't you tell me this before, about the CIA I mean. It sounds dangerous.'

He reached across the table and took her hand in his. 'Because before I thought you were a rather stern English lady who was frighteningly efficient, and who only needed to know the pertinent facts.'

'Stern!' She rolled the word experimentally around her mouth and gave him a mock frown of disapproval. 'I see. So what changed your mind?'

'Let's say getting to know you and finding an ecstatic state of mind which makes a mockery of reason.'

She smiled at him. 'Did anyone ever tell you, you sound more Irish than American?'

'Once in a while. But then my roots are there; or at least my father's roots. I even lived there for a while.'

'When was that?'

'After Vietnam . . . I was looking for something.'

'And did you find it?'

He laughed. 'Heavy conversation for so early in the morning.'

'It's nice. Besides, I'm getting to know you.'

'Ah, a glutton for punishment I see.'

'I wouldn't say that.'

'No,' he gave her a quick smile. 'Anyway, let me know what you find; I've been trying to know me for a long time.' He finished his coffee and took the cup over to the sink and rinsed it out.

'Leave that,' she said, 'I'll do it.'

He placed the cup on the draining-board. 'So, down to business. We still have to solve the problem of delivering this machine of ours. Did you speak to Otto by the way?'

'Yes. He promised to look into it today.'

'Did he think it was a big problem?'

'He wouldn't say if he did. But if there are any strings to be pulled, he'll find them.'

'Quite an influential guy then?'

'Money influential. He equates everything to dollars or francs.'

'It seems to work though.'

'In Otto's case it does but then he's tunnel visioned enough to shut out what other people would see as problems.'

'A ruthless streak, you mean?'

'Depends on what you call ruthless.'

155

'I would call it stopping at nothing to achieve your aims.'

She thought about that for a moment. 'Perhaps. I've never really thought about it.'

'Is he married?'

'Married!' She laughed. 'Only to his money.'

'And no lady friends!'

She paused, her eyes uncertain. 'I doubt it,' she replied. 'Anyway, why this sudden interest in Otto? We were talking about you.'

'No. We were talking about moving a certain piece of machinery half-way across the world.'

'Oh, yes. Must make a note. Makes a point of sidestepping questions on himself.'

'What about trustworthy?'

'Trustworthy?'

'Otto. Would you consider him a man of his word?'

'Yes, I think so. Why do you ask?'

'No reason, other than I like to know the people I'm working with. Nothing too deep you understand, just the basic truth and honour bit.'

'He'll give you a contract if that's what you're worried about.'

Fitzgerald laughed. 'Contract! No, no, no. We have a word in this business. KISS. Keep it simple, stupid. Something of a predilection for words of one syllable and a quiet handshake after the business is agreed.'

She looked at him and for a moment saw a man she didn't know. A cool, calculating individual. The light, carefree attitude to life, she decided, was an elaborate disguise; because in that passing second she had caught a glimpse of the real man. Assured. Unafraid. And perhaps a little frightening. She felt a shiver run through her body as she stood up and went to him.

'What's this?' he said, as she put her arms around his waist and laid her head on his chest.

'Just loving you,' she said quietly. 'Just loving you.'

Konrad Zwicky had never liked the police. It was a dislike which bordered on fear; so much so that just to see a policeman walking towards him in the street made him go hot under the collar. The scalp-tingling sensation would be accompanied by a fidgeting of the hands and nervous sideways glances of the eyes. If there was no side street to dodge into he would normally cross the street. If the traffic was too heavy he would pause and look interestedly in the first shop window. Sometimes, when not a single diversion was available, he would force his unwilling legs on and concentrate his mind on something totally ridiculous. This applied mental concentration would last until the uniformed shape at the periphery of his vision disappeared; then he would let out a shaky breath and return to whatever had occupied his mind previously. As those thoughts invariably bordered on, or embraced, criminality it seemed logical that he should be afraid of those who would seek to maintain law and order.

He felt afraid now, sitting in the corner of Mariella's house. True, the man was not wearing a uniform, but he still retained that look. Almost a smell. An air of antiseptic righteousness. Of course he was pretending to be kind, Konrad thought. But that was always the way. The soft understanding approach, the conciliatory words. Then the casual question from the smiling mouth. Then more questions, and more, and more. And all the time the cold, calculating eyes probing inside your head. It was when the lips stopped smiling that the problems began. Konrad knew that. Not so much from personal experience, but from stories he had heard from some of his friends. The ones who had pushed their luck too far and ended up doing a stretch in the local prison.

The inspector, with Konrad's permission, had made fresh coffee, and now brought two cups to the table. He handed one to Konrad.

'You are sure you do not want a doctor,' he asked. 'A sedative, you understand. Something to ease the shock.'

Konrad looked around the kitchen. At the white-washed walls and the pinewood cabinets and the bright red curtains over the little window above the sink. There was a vase on the top of the washing machine. The flowers, Konrad noticed, were dead. Withered and brown and quite lifeless.

'No, nothing,' he croaked. 'I'll be all right . . . I'll be fine.'

'There are one or two questions, you understand. But perhaps you would like me to come back tomorrow.'

Tomorrow, today, thought Konrad, what difference does it make? Nothing was going to bring Mariella back. He had watched her body being loaded into the ambulance. There had been a white sheet pulled up over her face. Why did it have to be white? Why not black? Black was the colour for death after all.

'No, not tomorrow. Ask me now. Tomorrow I must go to Zurich; to my mother, you understand. She will need me.'

The inspector said in a sympathetic voice, 'Firstly, if I could ask your sister's full name.'

'Mariella Theresa Genevieve Zwicky.'

The inspector started writing, then stopped. 'Zwicky, you say. But we have her family name as Schlegel.'

'Her professional name.'

'An actress was she?'

Konrad lifted his eyes from the kitchen table. 'An actress . . . yes,' he said with some pride. 'A great actress. The West End in London. Broadway, New York . . . she played all the best theatres . . . when she was younger of course.'

'Of course,' replied the inspector respectfully. 'She has not been in anything recently then; I only ask that because I do not recall the name.'

Konrad nodded gravely. 'Recently! No, she has been resting for some years now. They have sent her many scripts to read naturally. But after you have been at the top I think it must be difficult.'

The inspector said, 'Yes, I suppose it must. And your full name sir, for the records once again.'

'Konrad Alain Zwicky.'

'And you said you arrived from Zurich this morning?'

Konrad pulled a crumpled flight ticket from his pocket and looked at it. 'Flight SR204. It arrived in Geneva at nine-thirty.' He pushed the ticket across the table.

'And your reason for being in Zurich?'

'I live there.'

'But you said earlier you were living here.'

'I split my time between my mother in Zurich and my sister . . .' He stopped as a lump came to his throat.

The inspector smiled understandingly. 'Take your time, sir. No hurry.'

'I spend some time in Zurich and some here in Geneva, that is all.'

'And your business?'

Konrad's eyes swept round the kitchen again. 'Business? I am a tour guide while I am in Zurich.'

'May I ask for which company, sir?'

'Myself. I am self-employed.'

'Self-employed,' the inspector repeated to himself, writing as he spoke. 'And you say you arrived back at approximately ten o'clock this morning. This is so?'

'Yes.'

'And you telephoned the hospital at eleven.'

Konrad fumbled through his pockets and produced a packet of Marlboro cigarettes. He lit one and inhaled deeply. 'I'm sorry, you were saying?'

'You telephoned the hospital at eleven, this is correct?'

'I don't know what the time was . . . I just phoned.'

The inspector finished his coffee and went back to the percolator to refill his cup. When that was done he returned to the table and sat down.

'It was two minutes past eleven to be precise,' the inspector said consulting his notes. He closed the little notebook with great precision. 'Was there any reason for the delay? If you arrived back at ten and found your sister, I would have thought you might have telephoned someone immediately.'

Konrad looked at the man. Heavy jowled. Mouth still smiling. What was he saying now, he thought. One hour or two, or three or four. What the hell did it matter? She was dead. Time was not going to change that. 'I am very sorry, Inspector. I was too upset. We were very close, my sister and I.'

The inspector took a sip of his coffee. 'Yes, well, this is understandable. Now, to this note.' He picked up the piece of paper before him. 'Can you say exactly what your sister meant by it?'

'No.'

'But you said you were very close. Surely you must have

some idea what she meant by "I must repent for my sins".'

Konrad crushed out his cigarette. 'No,' he said tiredly. 'She was a theatrical type of person. They say things like that. Things that we do not understand. Perhaps her sins were an admission of failure to herself. Stage people can be melodramatic after all.'

The inspector stood up. 'Well, I think that is all for now, sir. Of course there will be an autopsy to ascertain the exact cause . . . you understand.'

Konrad said, 'Yes, I understand.'

'And you will be at your mother's address for the next few days should I need to contact you again?'

'Yes.' Konrad made a move to stand up.

'Don't bother, sir. You stay there, I'll see myself out. And once again may I offer you my condolences.'

Konrad nodded dumbly and watched him go. The slamming door was next. Then silence. Now what was he supposed to do? What about the funeral? How did you go about such things? He smashed the table with his fist. Why the hell didn't they teach you about life when you went to school? Why did you have to wait until it happened? He lit another cigarette. Actress! She would have liked that. It was something she had wanted to do as a small girl, and now, in one person's eyes at least, she had achieved her ambition.

His head was thudding when he went to the bathroom to find some aspirin. Faced with so many problems he didn't know where to start. One thing, however, was for certain. His sister's death was not all it appeared to be. The suicide note with the signature Marie was all wrong. She had always referred to herself as Mariella.

5 November

Zurich, Switzerland

WEDNESDAY 0525 HOURS

THE VENICE–SIMPLON Orient Express, does not include the Simplon as it used to, but has diverted instead to the Arlberg pass, going through the scenic landscape of Switzerland, the lake of Zurich, the Austrian mountains, Innsbruck, and finally crosses the Italian Alps via the Brenner pass to Venice.

The sense of history and elegance is maintained as it was in the days of classic trains, when Pullman of the USA and Wagons-Lits of René Nagelmackers of Belgium pioneered travel as a luxurious way of life. André Lesquereux now stood in one of the sleeping cars built in 1926 in Belgium and decorated by René Prou, a leading designer of the art deco period. As an ageing banker who rarely rose before eight o'clock, and only then to sit in musty smelling boardrooms listening to the incessant drone of financial jargon, it had all the headiness of an adventure. Not that he would have thought so a matter of years earlier, but now that his life was nearly over he was having regrets. Too cloistered a life had led to too few happy memories for his old age.

The telephone call the previous afternoon, at the bank in Geneva, had been to invite him to a special lunch. A flight to Zurich that evening and a night in a hotel would precede the luncheon, Otto had said. He had also mentioned that they would not return to Geneva until the Thursday morning. When pressed, Otto would say no more, other than it was a small gift to André for all the years of excellent banking advice. The intrigue had been too much and being a gourmet who had been assured of something out of the ordinary, he had handed over the reins to one of his managers and gone home to pack. The arrival at Zurich's Hauptbahnhof on a dark bitterly cold morning, had only heightened the banker's curiosity. Otto had said little, but guided him to a platform, where a few other people were making their way towards a train. André had breathed deeply of the unfamiliar air, a blend of damp stone, metal and wood, mixed with the sharper aroma of diesel fuel.

'So, Otto,' he had said, 'you still have not told me the place for our special lunch.'

Otto had stopped suddenly and raised a hand. 'There it is, André . . . the Orient Express.'

Now, after the smiling steward with the white gloves had shown them to their cabins, he was standing in quiet amazement. There was a knock on the adjoining cabin door and von Klaus came in. 'Well, André, what do you think?'

'Think, Otto! I am too overawed to think.' His eyes narrowed slightly. 'But isn't it a trifle extravagant?'

The German sat down heavily and took his gold cigarette case from his pocket. 'Do you mind?' He held up the case.

'No, go ahead please.'

Otto lit his cigarette. 'Much too early for these,' he coughed. 'Extravagant, you say. Yes it is, but as I am nearly a man of leisure I think a few francs will do no harm. A few hours' enjoyment for once, André; we are entitled I think.'

The banker smiled and sat down as the train rolled out of the station towards Lanquat. 'Yes, Otto, we are entitled. A few hours in exchange for the fifty years' hard labour.' For a moment his eyes filled with past reminiscences and future regrets, then he shrugged it off and said, 'So tell me what happens now?'

Otto drew heavily on his cigarette. 'Well, shortly we will be served breakfast and the morning's newpspaper. After that, you may want to rest. The bedside light is there beside the door,' he pointed. 'A little after ten we will go down to the bar.'

'And then what?'

'Lunch.'

'Lunch!'

'A special lunch. You will see. Now I go back to my cabin to take breakfast and have a nap.' He handed André some brochures. 'They tell me this is interesting reading, something of the history of the Orient Express.'

'You have read it?'

'No,' Otto replied dismissively. 'Something a businessman's life has no time for.'

'So you have never read Agatha Christie?'

'No.'

André, who had always found reading the perfect way to unwind, smiled, 'No matter, Otto, I will see you later.'

The telephone at Chance Fitzgerald's apartment rang at nine o'clock. Just once. Sixty seconds later it rang again. Fitzgerald picked it up, knowing it was Konrad Zwicky, and glad he had remembered to use the code. He didn't want Lisa answering it, although his directive had stated that if any other voice answered on the second call he was to put the phone down and try again on the next hour.

'Hello, Konrad.'

'Mr Fitzgerald?'

'Any news?'

'My sister, Mr Fitzgerald. Mariella. She is dead.' Konrad's voice sounded empty and old.

'Dead!' Fitzgerald exclaimed. 'How? What happened?'

'I don't know . . . she took sleeping tablets. An overdose the police said.'

Fitzgerald was quiet for a moment. 'I'm sorry, Konrad, very sorry. Is there anything I can do for you?'

'Thank you, no. Everything is now arranged.'

'You're sure?'

'Yes, Mr Fitzgerald, I am sure.'

'Regarding the information I asked you to obtain, Konrad, I appreciate that this may now be difficult. If you want to drop the entire matter I will understand.'

'No,' Konrad said quickly. 'I would still like to work for you. I can still help.'

'You've got the list I gave you in Zurich?'

'Yes.'

'OK, follow up as much of that as you can. And stick to the same phone code for the time being.'

'I will,' Konrad said distantly. 'Also there is one other matter.'

'Yes.'

'Mariella did not take her own life.'

'How do you know?'

'I just know. A note she left . . . it was all wrong.'

'Have you mentioned that to the police?'

'No police,' Konrad said determinedly. 'I will find the truth myself.'

'Yes, well, be careful. Let me know if I can help you.'

'Thank you, Mr Fitzgerald.'

'Konrad.'

'Yes.'

'I think we can drop the mister now, just call me Chance. Everyone else does.'

'Yes . . . Mr Fitzgerald . . . I will call you soon.'

Fitzgerald put down the phone and went over to the window. It was not his business, he told himself. You cannot afford to get involved with every cripple and orphan who appears on the scene. So his sister had taken an overdose of sleeping tablets. Or maybe drugs. And according to Konrad she had been Otto's mistress. So what if Otto had dropped her and she in a fit of despair had taken the easy way out! Happens every day. 'But what if she died as a direct result of helping Konrad with his enquiries?' a little voice deep within him asked. 'Doesn't that make you responsible?'

'Why the hell should it?'

'Because you are in part an Irishman, in part a romantic sentimentalist.'

'How about in part a fighting drunk?'

'You're too pious for that, I think. Besides there's goodness in all of us, Chance Fitzgerald.'

'You sound like an old father I once knew . . . as a boy. Always preaching to old men and children. And it's easy enough to convince addled and empty minds.'

'Do you really believe that?'

There was a vision of a lonely childhood with no brothers or sisters, an adolescence with few friends, and a middle life which seemed emptier still. The future looked just as bleak as the past. And for one of the few times in his life he didn't have an answer.

There are two sittings for lunch on the Orient Express, one being at twelve o'clock and the other one-thirty. Otto and André took the noon sitting for no other reason than the maître d'hôtel's advice that everything would be absolutely fresh, whereas the second sitting sometimes carried warmed-up dishes from midday.

The table setting was quite exquisite. Silver, Limoges china and special crystal glasses to balance the mild jerks of the train. The beautiful brass table lamp with the pale tangerine shade and the slender vase of deep red orchids added the final touch.

'Breathtaking,' André effused, sitting down and admiring the snow covered mountains set with deep green firs. 'Quite breathtaking.'

'You noticed the menu?' Otto enquired.

'Ah, the menu,' André chuckled. 'Foie gras de Canard aux truffes du Périgord . . . le caviar Beluga.' He licked his lips in anticipation. 'And then les Délices de Veau aux épinards gratinés.'

'And the dessert . . . what of the dessert!' Otto prompted.

'Le Bavarois Glace ay Kirsch, you mean?'

'Indeed . . . and the wine list. The Graves in particular.'

'The Château Haut-Brion!'

'Premier grand cru classe 1966 . . . your favourite.'

'Otto, Otto, you spoil me.'

The German forced a smile. He was indeed spoiling the banker. The Graves at seven hundred Swiss francs a bottle was proof of that. He took a sip of his mineral water to prepare his palate for the start of the seven course lunch, and hoped it would all be worth it.

In London, Chance Fitzgerald was alone at his apartment. He was seated on the floor of his bedroom in the

Padmasana, also known as the full Lotus position. Of the three meditation poses it is the most difficult to achieve. It is, however, the most beneficial. His purpose was to seek the solution to a problem, and as one who had been practising concentration and meditation for many years now, he knew the answer was within himself. From his early days when the object of his concentration had been a candle flame and his meditation had centred on the petals of a flower, he could now apply the same techniques to solving real problems. He would consider the aspects of the situation in question from all sides, weighing the pros and cons and projecting himself into the future where he could visualise the outcome of the matter which concerned him.

The way was not to daydream, but really to concentrate and wait for the answers to come like pieces of a puzzle, slowly falling into place to form a whole.

Chance's problem was his daughter Alice. He had worried for a number of years over her future, knowing that when Jack Audley and his wife finally died, their entire estate would pass to their only child – Maxine. And Maxine being Maxine would go through the millions as though there were no tomorrow. As for Alice, she would probably end up as her mother's impoverished companion. Unless she had money of her own!

He may have failed as a father, he thought, but he would do his damnedest to ensure she would never want for money.

The Orient Express reached Venice at six-thirty that evening. In the tradition of luxury travel everything had been taken care of, from the passports and the Customs to the transportation of baggage. It was thus, after a brief afternoon nap, that Otto and André arrived at the elegant Danieli refreshed and ready to tackle the German's final gift of dinner.

Some men you bribe with money, thought Otto as they registered, others with beautiful women, while gourmets, like André, required merely food and wine.

'Did you know that this is an old Venetian castle?' he said, mindful of his role as host.

166

André looked around the spacious lobby with its tall marble pillars. The ornately carved wood and stone and the concealed lighting gave it an air of great richness. 'A castle,' he murmured. 'No. But now I see why. It is very beautiful.'

'The bar is just through there,' Otto indicated across the foyer. 'Let me order you a Kir Royale before we go and change for dinner.'

'Yes thank you, that would be very nice.'

'But first, André, if you will excuse me I have to make a quick telephone call to my office . . . the Paris deal, you understand!'

Von Klaus appeared in the bar ten minutes later. His face was troubled. 'Ah, you have ordered,' he said sitting down at the corner table that André had selected.

The banker, who had finished his drink, signalled the waiter. 'Another?' he said, addressing Otto.

'Shortly, André, shortly.' He took a cigarette from his gold cigarette case and lit it.

'You are quiet all of a sudden, Otto. There is nothing wrong, I hope.'

Otto jerked upright and smiled with his eyes. 'Forgive me, André. No, nothing. Well nothing of importance that is.' He took a sip of his Kir Royale. 'Just one of those niggling little matters that tend to get forgotten.'

'Yes, I know the sort of thing. It happens to me a lot these days. I think we must be growing old.'

'Yes, yes. Especially when it comes to favours for old business friends. This particular one asked me to make some enquiries for him in Geneva and I quite forgot. Very embarrassing of course, especially in view of all the business he has pushed my way over the years. Mind you,' Otto drew heavily on his cigarette and exhaled the blue smoke at the high ceiling, 'mind you I doubt I could have done much anyway.' He raised his glass. 'Anyway, enough of my problems. I give you a toast. To a true gentleman of the banking profession, a connoisseur of good food and wine, and a man I am honoured to call a friend.'

André lifted his glass and drank, his old eyes slightly moist with emotion. 'A gracious toast, Otto, a very gracious toast. And I in turn would like to raise my glass to a gentleman of the business world who I feel has the ability to be anything he wishes to be, such is the force of his personality. Not only that but may I reciprocate and say, a man I am honoured to call my friend.' They drank. 'Too many words I fear, Otto. And on a stomach of too much wine.'

Von Klaus laughed. 'I have never known the wine to be too much, André. Not for you.'

'I could still drink the young ones under the table, you mean?'

'I am sure of it.'

'Yes,' André said modestly, 'Perhaps I could. So to your problem. Is there anything I can do?'

'Problem?' Otto looked slightly surprised.

'Your business acquaintance. The favour!'

'Oh that. No, no. I would not dream of asking such a favour. We are here to celebrate our years of working together. It is our special treat. No business.'

André clicked his tongue. 'No business! What is this? I know you, Otto. I know that it will remain on your mind all evening and all morning until we return to Geneva. And that is not good . . . it will spoil your appetite.'

'Yes, perhaps. It is as I said, an old friend of mine. An Englishman. He lives in Jersey, you know it of course?'

'Of course.'

'Well he is something of a philanthropist. He has no children and has lately been helping various charities around the world.'

'A very noble gesture,' André remarked.

'Indeed, very noble.'

'And his problem?'

'A strange one, but he has a fixation about the Sudan and the dying children. To this end he has purchased a cargo plane and wishes to loan it, free of charge of course, to the Red Cross. However it appears the Red Cross screen all benefactors before they will accept gifts. This creates a problem for my friend as he wishes to remain anonymous.' Otto crushed out his cigarette in the crested ashtray at the centre of the table. 'He is, apart from being wealthy, a very private man . . . almost a recluse. Anyway, that is it. He wished me to help in this matter.'

André laughed. The thin high-pitched laugh of a frail old man. 'Is that all?' he said.

Otto frowned. 'All! To me it poses a difficult problem. The Red Cross is a very large organisation after all.'

'Not so large. Still, that is of no matter. What is, however, is that the main committee of the Red Cross is based in Geneva and more than half of them are close personal friends of mine. Let me know exactly what you want and it will be done before the week is out.'

Otto managed a suitable wide-eyed look of surprise. 'Thank you, André. It is a weight off my mind.'

'Now, no more business. Now we drink. Yes?'

Otto raised a hand and waved the waiter to their table.

20 November

London, England
THURSDAY 0655 HOURS

CHANCE FITZGERALD WAS sitting in a chair by the window. The curtains were drawn back a few inches and showed a grey dawn breaking over the rooftops and low scudding clouds which threatened rain. Lisa stirred in the bed and he turned and looked across at her. She didn't wake and presently his eyes returned to the window and the sky. Somewhere up there, ten or twelve thousand feet perhaps, there would be eye-aching sunshine flooding out of the eastern sky. No birds, no people, no noise. Just that ultimate emptiness, full of tall silence and Byzantine halls sculpted from clouds. He had been down too long now. He could feel the withdrawal symptoms. A growing tension within his body; an edginess which too much ground time produced. It was only his meditation which kept him in control. Calmed his spirit. As if being tested yet again he heard Maxine's mocking voice, 'You mean you're about to screw up someone else's life, is that it? I wasn't enough. You left me with a daughter to raise and worry over while you went off to play with your airplanes and fight other people's wars . . .'

He looked briefly back at Lisa's sleeping form. At least he wasn't the arch-bastard he had once been. In those days he would have written a beautiful little note and propped it up on the bedside table before tiptoeing out into a cold dewy dawn. Something that the French referred to as *filer à l'anglaise* – an English farewell. One of those lovely sayings with a *double entendre*. The first was good and meant, to go on your tiptoe discreetly; the second was bad – to run away like a coward. Up until today his goodbyes had been of the latter variety.

Now he was waiting for her to wake up. Not that he had to go, of course. Guy was an excellent pilot who had spent a great part of his life kicking around the watering holes of the Middle East. Hiram, on the other hand, was almost legendary, more bird than man. The type of natural flyer you meet maybe once in a lifetime and only then if you're lucky. No, they didn't need him, but he needed them. Needed the flight deck discipline, the electronically distorted voices running check lists, the background noise of engines, the sighs of hydraulic systems, the familiar smells. And the unforgettable settings that only mother nature could pull from a hat of light and cloud and shadow.

Of course he would have to leave them at Khartoum and fly to Milan to ensure the payment was made in accordance with the letter of credit. Once again, not that he had to. Bankers were efficient, respectable people in the eyes of most men. Not so with Chance Fitzgerald. He viewed them as simply human. Prone to error. In his line of business they wouldn't last sixty seconds. And that had been his yardstick for survival – 'Trust is for God, not mankind.' After Milan he would return to Khartoum and the planned pick-up near Djibouti.

'You're up,' Lisa's voice startled him. 'What time is it?'

'Seven-ish,' he said, going across to the bed.

'And you're dressed! Why so early?'

'Couldn't sleep.'

She looked up at him with sleepy eyes. 'What sort of day is it?'

'Looks like rain.'

She burrowed back under the bedclothes. 'Sounds like England.'

' "Which through Albion winds forever lashing with melodious wave many a sacred poet's grave." '

'Who said that?'

'And you being English, shame on you . . . Shelley . . .

171

Anyway, enough of this. I'll go and make some coffee.' He made a move to leave.

'Not yet. Stay and talk to me.'

'At seven in the morning! No, no. Voices are far too strident then.'

'Come back to bed then.'

He smiled. 'And just a few weeks ago you were a shy lady.'

'Not so my teacher, though.'

He reached down and kissed her gently on the lips, then said firmly, 'Coffee.'

'And loving?'

'Maybe . . . if you're a good girl.'

'I like you in black,' she called as he left the room. 'Very handsome.'

He chose not to hear as he made his way through to the kitchen. It was a psychological thing. Had been ever since the time of Maxine. The first inkling he was going had produced a change in her, what had become a predictable chain of events. The cessation of all but the most essential conversation. The sleeping in the spare room. The absence of any meals. The 'accidental' breaking of one or two of his favourite ornaments. The lifted voice, harsher than that of an enemy. And on the dawn of his departure an empty, unslept-in bed in the spare room, which told him she had been out all night. Yes, it had been psychological. Searching out his weak spots. But if she found them he never let on.

Now, with Lisa, he wasn't sure. He was almost afraid to say anything, especially that he loved her; because he didn't want to find beneath that pretty face there lurked another Maxine.

He took the coffee and the newspaper from the letter-box, and went through to the bedroom.

'And what's the occasion?' Lisa said, as he placed the tray on the bedside table.

'Occasion?'

'The room service. Coffee and the morning paper.'

Fitzgerald went silent. He had picked up the paper and was reading the front page. His face was as bleak as his voice when he said, 'Would you look at that now.'

'What is it?'

'Read it,' he said dropping the paper on her lap.

She picked it up. 'What am I supposed to be reading?'

'Iran crisis . . . out loud.'

' "President Reagan is under pressure to sack two top advisers over a secret Iran deal concerning arms shipments. White House chief of staff Donald Regan and national security adviser Admiral John Poindexter could both fall in the light of this crisis.

' "They apparently were at the heart of secret arms-for-hostages negotiations uncovered yesterday. It has also been disclosed that the President ordered the CIA to keep the talks secret from Congress . . ." '

Lisa looked across at Chance who was standing by the window. 'I don't understand,' she said. 'Will this have implications on our transaction?'

'Maybe, maybe not,' he replied without turning round.

'But the Red Cross cover. You said it was foolproof.'

He turned and looked across the room, his face unsmiling. 'That was then. Sad to say things change rapidly in this business.' He dropped wearily into the chair by the window. 'Let me tell you a story, unrelated in some ways, but significant in others. It was 1967. I was a fighter pilot. I was also unemployed having just left Vietnam and the US Air Force. As luck would have it, however, I strayed across to England and got a job with a company which was contracted to supply armaments and personnel to the Saudi Air Force. The oil wealth had given them a penchant for military things.' He shifted in his chair and found a more comfortable position. 'So that was it. A straightforward job with a large tax-free pay cheque at the end of it. The problems, however, began when I arrived. The Saudis had built a new military base at a place called Khamis Mushayt. It was in the south, near the Yemen border. No big deal of course, except that the Yemenis had Russian-built aircraft and arms and were starting daily bombing runs on the border villages. That turned out to be problem number one. We were suddenly mercenaries. I knew that when they took away our passports and issued us with side-arms, a money belt and a gooley chit . . .'

'Gooley chit . . . what's that?'

'Not nice, you wouldn't want to know.'

'I'm over twenty-one.'

'Yes, I suppose you are. First off, gooley. Slang for testicles.' A half-embarrassed look flickered across her face. 'Secondly, the reason. Get shot down and picked up by the wrong Arab side and they have an impressive line in tortures. Slow death is preferable to a quick bullet through the head. What they do among other things is to cut off your testicles, stuff them in your mouth, then stitch up your lips. When that part is over, they bury you in the sand up to your chin.'

Lisa's cup rattled in the saucer. Her face was quite pale. 'My God, that's horrible. Barbaric.'

Chance gave her a wintry smile. 'Funny too. You can make Arabic out of barbaric . . . hadn't thought of that before. Anyway, the gooley chit was a piece of paper from the country you were flying for and promised to pay the capturing army the sum of fifty thousand dollars in gold on safe return of the individual concerned. The fifty thousand was then, of course. Lot more these days.'

She drank some coffee with an unsteady hand. 'So what happened after you found out you were a mercenary?'

'Not a lot. The planes we operated were pretty old and after a time we had all settled into a happy routine of no women, no booze . . . other than the illegal stuff some of the guys brewed, and making friends with the Saudi Air Force guys on the base. Then, out of the blue the Six Day War. That was when the Israelis hit the Egyptians into the middle of Ramadan. And that was problem number two. Because President Nasser put it out over Cairo Radio that the Royal Air Force had been assisting the Israelis, and that English Vulcan bombers had been seen over Cairo. It was all propaganda of course, except the Saudis believed it. They preferred to accept the word of another Arab country. So, a few hundred ex-pats were put under house arrest. The electricity and the water were cut off and we sat and waited. Our huts were guarded day and night. There was no way out.

'The diplomats won in the end, of course. It was after the

174

event that we learned of the all-night meetings and the schemes which had been proposed to try and pull us out. Personally, if the dice had fallen the wrong way I don't think they would have given a damn. A front-page story without a newspaper.'

'And what happened after the Six Day War?'

'A gradual wind down by our people and a new contract given to the Pakistanis. Some people might call that racist.'

'And you?'

'Good and bad on every side. Some of the nicest guys I've known have been black. Some of the worst, white. It's what's inside that counts.'

'Funny point of view for a soldier of fortune.'

'Why?'

'You might be killing some of the nice people.'

'Governments do it every day and make a big show about morals and equality at the same time. Only difference with me is that I'm not a hypocrite.'

She looked at him with uncertainty in her eyes. 'And the connection with the Iranian business?'

'Interrelated pressure. In the same way the Saudis were forced to review their defence policy and personnel through a common link of the Islamic religion, so will the US — from Congress right on down — be tightening up on anything and everything military . . . or ex-military in our case.'

'But the money's on its way. It left yesterday.'

He stood up and walked across to the bed. 'I'll be going out with the crew,' he said quietly. 'Just in case.'

He sat down on the edge of the bed and took her hands in his.

'You were going before this though, weren't you,' she said.

'Yes.'

She pulled him to her. 'Be careful . . . you know I love you, don't you?'

'I know . . . you tell me every day.'

'You're not complaining, are you?'

'No, my lovely girl, I'll never do that. I promise.' He

kissed her on each eye and then on the tip of the nose. 'The taxi will be along shortly.'

Her face became sad. 'You've already called one?'

'Yes.'

'I could have run you to the airport.'

'No, you couldn't,' he answered. 'I don't like airports and goodbyes. There have been too many in my life already.'

'Milan then?'

'Milan. You've got all the details?'

'Yes.'

'We'll do some Christmas shopping.'

'Take care.'

'I will.'

'And phone . . .'

'Every day,' he called as he went through the bedroom door, 'every day.'

The taxi was waiting at the end of the street. He stopped to mail the letters he had written earlier, then climbed into the cab. The sky was still threatening rain as he settled into the back seat, but he was smiling. Soon he would be back where he belonged.

It was late afternoon in Tehran. Rashid Suliman had left the city an hour earlier accompanied by two Iranian army officers. The olive-coloured Land Rover was now approaching the storm-shrouded foothills of Mount Damavand on the southern fringe of the Elburz range.

Suliman had at first been inclined to turn down the invitation from Fazlollah Mahallati, but that would have been churlish. Besides which, Fazlollah was becoming a very powerful man. It was, therefore, wise to do as bid. Or at least appear to. Anyway, and this was a great consolation to Rashid, he was now prepared for his journey to Khartoum in less than twenty-four hours' time. The plastic explosive (PE) had been difficult to obtain, as he thought it would. But as a former army officer he had his contacts, men with more moderate leanings than the present regime considered healthy. The PE, neatly concealed in a false compartment of a briefcase, along with the timer and detonator, were hidden at his home. Other than that, he had visited Mehrabad airport in western Tehran and inspected a Hercules transport aircraft. For this he had obtained the permission of Fazlollah, the pretext being that he should at least appear to know something of the type of aircraft he was about to return with from Africa. Fazlollah had agreed, voicing the opinion that a servant of Islam should not appear unwise in the eyes of the unbelievers who would be flying the plane. From his inspection of the machine Rashid had found at least a dozen places he could conceal the bomb. A dozen places which would send it crashing to earth like a fireball.

He smiled to himself and pushed a finger under the eyepatch to scratch the empty socket. Yes, within a few short days it would be over. The aircraft would be nothing more than a charred shell, lying in the swamps of the southern Sudan. And he, a true soldier of Islam would be recorded as dead. A truly tragic end for so gallant a man.

As for the repercussions which would echo over the eighteen million US dollars, he would not be alive to answer − in theory at least. In practice he would be the proud possessor of two million dollars and a new lifestyle in the West.

The Land Rover lurched up a twisting dirt track that nearly defeated the vehicle's four-wheel drive capacity. Rashid clung to the side of his seat and shivered. The temperature was dropping, gusts of icy rain lashing the windshield.

It was some way higher up that the vehicle stopped and the two officers climbed out. Rashid followed. A fog was closing in now and the rain had turned to snow, stinging his face in squally flurries. The three men moved towards a concrete bunker which seemed to come and go in the swirling mist. Two sentries in lumpy overcoats pulled themselves to attention and presented arms. Rashid shivered again, more violently this time. His reputation as a disciplined and ferocious soldier had contained one secret and hidden flaw. He could not tolerate the cold. For short periods yes, but only that.

Inside, the bunker was a claustrophobic shell of dim concrete walls dripping condensation. Wooden planks and sheets of plastic had been hastily fixed over the slits to the outside world. In the centre of the low-ceilinged room was a roughly made table. A pressure lamp stood at its centre, flaring with a harsh white light. A few feet from the table a broken down kerosene stove emitted a sparse halo of warmth. Rashid took the glass of hot sweet tea he had been handed and went straight to the stove.

Fazlollah Mahallati appeared in the doorway some minutes later. He was dressed in a heavy army greatcoat which carried no badges of rank. His greying hair and beard were full of melting snow.

'Rashid, my friend,' he cried and rushed over and embraced him in the Arab way. A touch of the lips to either cheek. 'And how was the journey?'

'The journey! The Land Rover is a very versatile vehicle, a good machine-gun platform also.'

Fazlollah nodded. 'Ah yes, you have used them in the battlefield.'

'Except I seem to recall we needed more.'

'This is not a problem. We have just ordered another three thousand from the British. The long wheel base model, of course.'

'This is possible?' Rashid said with some surprise. 'I thought the British followed the American lead and had stopped supply of arms.'

'Military equipment, Rashid, not arms. The British Foreign Office will give permission for deals in military equipment if they are not designed to give either side a military advantage in a war in which Britain is strictly neutral.'

Rashid took a sip of hot tea. 'And the Land Rover is nothing more than surface transport for our soldiers!'

'Exactly. The fact that we modify them into light weapon carriers is something else entirely.'

'And the cost of so many vehicles?'

Fazlollah waved a hand. 'I think in the order of twenty-seven million English pounds.'

'That much?'

'But the war will be won, Rashid . . . it will be worth every last rial.'

'Yes, Fazlollah, I am sure it will. So tell me of this new listening post. I am at a loss to understand its strategic location.'

Fazlollah smiled. 'A listening post in name only, my friend.' He rubbed his hands together in the warmth of the stove. 'We also use it as an interrogation centre.'

'Interrogation?' Rashid replied uncertainly.

'You are aware that there are still those who would wish to see a return to the old ways, yes?'

'I have heard this.'

'And you have no doubt also heard that Gasr prison is full of such people. Those who do not follow in the ways of Islam.'

'Of course.'

There was a long silence. The lamp threw distorted shadows on to the walls. Rashid felt his skin begin to creep. What was this? What was the purpose of the invitation?

Fazlollah smiled and continued. 'Quite simply, we bring the more important political prisoners here to be interrogated. It is a way to ensure there are no martyrs . . . come, I will show you.'

Rashid followed Fazlollah out of the bunker, back into the buffeting wind and stinging snow. They walked quickly up the rough dirt track to another concrete bunker. It was similar to the first, only larger. Inside, an army officer was shouting at an Arab woman. She was dressed in traditional black and her head was held erect and proud.

Fazlollah pulled Rashid aside. They were less than twenty feet away from the scene.

'You recognise her?' Fazlollah asked.

'No, I do not think so,' Rashid replied in a shaky voice.

'No matter. She is the wife of a senior lecturer at the university. She is also the sister of Hassan Shah-Cheraghi, head of the Kayhan group of newspapers.'

There was a spark of recognition in Rashid's eye. 'I have heard of him.'

'We have evidence they have been involved in a plot to overthrow the Ayatollah.'

'Ah.' It was nothing more than an expulsion of air from Rashid's lips. An expulsion which had encapsulated a brief sound. An eloquent 'ah', which said: 'Yes, I understand the seriousness of such a crime. I also understand there can be only one penalty.'

Fazlollah made no further comment and both men stood quite still, listening to the raised voice of the young officer as he tried to browbeat the woman into submission. She remained silent, her head still held high. Her rebellious eyes stared intently towards the two men who had just entered the bunker. For Rashid, it was a traumatic moment. He had seen it all before, except now it frightened him. He tried to concentrate on the woman's face. It was beautiful he decided. Also, she was young, she would have a good body. It was a waste, a shameful waste.

The officer conducting the interrogation had stopped shouting now. He was smiling thinly and fingering a pistol with the same passion he might have used on the woman herself. Rashid conceded that the man had probably taken her anyway, as would most of the other officers.

The interrogator spoke again to the woman. Her manner remained unchanged. The gun was raised to her temple. Rashid watched with horrific fascination, willing the woman to break her silence. She did not. He felt the sweat running down his back, as though he was the one facing death. The explosion slammed into his ears, except it was more than an explosion in such a confined space. It was a deep incisive pain which cut to the very heart. But even through such pain his eyes remained open, watched her face disappear, disintegrate into a mask of bloody pulp, as her body slammed against the wall. It remained defiantly upright for a moment before slithering to the floor, and all that was left was the stench of cordite and the faint blue smoke from the gun. That, and the warm brains and blood splattered across the wall. And that smell would shortly mask everything else.

Fazlollah pulled his greatcoat collar high around his neck and turned to leave. Rashid followed with the sound of the explosion still ringing in his ears.

They were standing by the Land Rover, the fog closing in like a dense smoke.

'This country,' Fazlollah said passionately, 'could be

paradise. But for that we must cleanse it completely. You agree, Rashid?'

'This is indeed so, my friend. The woman's end was just. We must make sure that all unbelievers are accorded the same fate.'

Fazlollah slapped him on the shoulder. 'Good. I knew you would agree with what I am doing. Perhaps after you return with the Hercules we will talk again of this. I would like you to join us.'

'Join you!'

'In the Islamic Revolutionary Guards Corps.'

'Ah.' That sound escaped once more from Rashid's lips.

'You seem uncertain my friend.'

'Uncertain!' Rashid laughed. 'Never that, Fazlollah. Never could I be uncertain. I am a soldier of Islam, therefore it is not possible. I, like you, am devoted to winning this war.'

Fazlollah smiled tensely. 'You are sure of this, Rashid?'

'Yes, I am sure.'

On the drive down the mountain Rashid found himself becoming more concerned. The invitation to the new listening post had been nothing more than a warning. He felt a fleeting sorrow for the woman who had had her face blown away for no other reason than an object lesson. But then she was only a woman. And in the Arab way that meant very little.

No, if there were any sorrow to be felt he should direct it at himself. Fazlollah, he knew, had come to a conclusion. And the conclusion was that his friend Rashid was up to something. How much did he know, that was the question. How much? And how could he have ever begun to suspect? His thinking spilled over to the briefcase and the plastic explosive. It was possible that his house was being searched at this very moment. Another reason for calling him away!

He gripped the side of his seat with sweaty hands as the Land Rover lurched and bumped down the dirt track towards the plains below. Outside the snow had changed back to icy rain.

* * *

181

In Jersey it was also raining. A cold north-westerly wind drove low storm clouds across the island. Maxine had arrived back from Greece that evening with Rupert. They had sat round and chatted with her parents, relating the usual holiday stories. Rupert had, of course, asked her out to dinner, but having spent two and a half weeks with the same man she had had enough. She despatched him with a flurry of promises and went up to her room to unpack and read the mail which had accumulated in her absence.

The first letter she opened was from Mr Woodley, the private investigator she had hired. She read it and smiled to herself, then went through to the bathroom to run a bath. Holidays were all very well, she decided, except you needed another one to get over the first. Unfortunately, her skiing trip to Gstaad was some weeks away. She pouted and checked the temperature of the water, then added a liberal amount of *lait pour le bain*. She was about to step in when she remembered the letter. She could read it again as she soaked. Plan her final attack on that bastard Chance Fitzgerald.

Collecting it from the dressing-table she paused to admire her body in the full-length mirror. The light golden tan she had worked so hard to get right in Greece was perfect. All-over perfect. It added that final touch to her exquisitely shaped body. She stood sideways and patted her tummy. Perfectly flat. Placing a hand under each breast in turn she checked for sagging. They were as firm as ever. As for her hips and legs, they were somewhere beyond perfection, if she was to believe what her gentlemen friends told her. And all of them couldn't be wrong. More beautiful than ever, she concluded, then poked her tongue out cheekily at her reflection, laughed and ran back to the bathroom.

After a day of travelling by car and aircraft the fragrant water was a soothing balm. It was the moment she had visualised throughout the day. She closed her eyes and sighed. It was a truly wonderful life, especially if you were rich. And speaking of rich she would go to London tomorrow, not on the airline, however. She had had quite enough of being cattle-herded through security checks by working-class peasants, and being fed plastic food by spotty-faced young girls who had somehow carried arrogance into the realms of waitressing. No, damn the airlines. She would telephone the local air-taxi company and charter a private jet to fly her to Gatwick.

She held up the letter and read the name again. Lisa Wendell-Holmes. The description seemed to complement the name perfectly. Age: fortyish. Straw-coloured hair. Thickening figure. Dresses in conservative fashion. Facially: nothing remarkable, pretty but plain. Bless you, Mr Woodley. You may not have a way with words, but the ones you use are the right ones. She let the letter drop to the floor and sank lower into the milky white water.

'Tomorrow, Lisa Wendell-Holmes,' she said out loud. 'Tomorrow, your house of cards comes crashing down.'

21 November

Geneva, Switzerland

FRIDAY 0800 HOURS

OTTO VON KLAUS had been awake most of the night, alternately dozing in an armchair, then pacing up and down. Every light in the house had been on, simulating daylight. Now at eight o'clock he was standing in the shower, his flabby skin being bruised by the intense jets of water. It was a way he had found of driving some of the tiredness from his body. Also, the coming of morning helped. It meant the world around him was awake. He even welcomed the distant noise of the city, for with noise and light he seemed to be able to stave off sleep. The sleep which brought terrifying nightmares of Marie stalking him with a long kitchen knife. And always the leaden feet. Trying to run and finding it impossible, whilst all the time her heavy breathing and cackling laughter grew nearer and nearer.

He left the shower with the nonchalant air of a sleepwalker and absently towelled his body. Omitting to shave or clean his teeth, he padded through to the bedroom and began to dress in the same rumpled suit he had worn the day before. He was still tired but his mind was running at full speed. Today was the day after all. The day the Hercules left Alaska. The day the Red Cross unwittingly fronted an eighteen-million-dollar fraud. A week from now it would all be over. The thought somehow consoled him, for he believed that once the transaction was complete and he could leave Switzerland, his life would change and the nightmares would be a thing of the past.

He lit a cigarette and spent a few moments emitting a racking cough which turned to a dull hurt deep within his chest. He grimaced, waited for the pain to subside then went down the stairs to his study.

The room was depressingly bare with the exception of a second-hand desk and chair, next to which a number of office files were piled neatly on the floor. Furnishings, von Klaus had long ago decided, were an expensive luxury which served no useful purpose. True, he had a collection of paintings, most of which were carefully stored in the cellar, but he had never considered them as a part of the household. They were simply an investment. Money which made more money.

He sat at his desk and opened the Iranian file. The latest correspondence had been the coded telex from Lisa requesting the Iranians lay on a sea passage for the three aircrew members of the Hercules. The route given was from Chah Bahar in southern Iran to Djibouti. He withdrew the telex, along with his reply, which confirmed all was in order and that the crew would be further advised upon their arrival in Chah Bahar and laid both documents to one side.

The next sheet was headed MILANO: For Action 21 November. And that was today. Item one was to obtain confirmation on the exact terms of the letter of credit from the Italian bank. He had, of course, received the details from Rashid Suliman but that meant nothing. From bitter experience he knew what happened if someone forgot to cross a 't' or dot an 'i'. The bank would refuse to honour the payment. He would telephone Lisa later in the morning. She could check into it.

Item number two was the release of the eighteen million US dollars. Naturally the two million dollar payment to Suliman would make a large hole in the net profit, but as he had dispensed with the blackmail threat, at least it was only two millions.

Item three was the commission due to Chance Fitzgerald. A minimum of one million had, of course, been over-generous. But as he had no intention of paying it the matter seemed of little consequence; what did, however, was the execution of the plan. The continued prosperity of his affairs was foremost in his mind when he thought of the swarthy Arab. Now there was an interesting man. A man with a desire to be rich. A man with a desire to be a Westerner. A man who spoke excellent English but who was still an Arab. And a man with such a mind would be very useful. Especially when one viewed their cheap regard of life. Not that Suliman would take on the role of assassin without reason, von Klaus was pretty sure of that. For money he would, but as he was already receiving two millions it was unthinkable to offer him any more. But what if he thought that Chance Fitzgerald was an untrustworthy and unscrupulous mercenary who might just – at some later date when his soldier's pay had run out – inform the Iranian authorities that Rashid Suliman had duped them and was now living an exotic life, with their money, somewhere in Europe? Indeed, Fitzgerald, a cruel-hearted opportunist, would be just the type to sell another man's soul for thirty pieces of silver.

Von Klaus looked down the sheet of paper to item four. It was a pencilled notation regarding payment to the three aircrew. He laughed out loud. Nothing was a figure he liked most of all.

In London, Lisa Wendell-Holmes was sitting at the window watching the rain pounding the shiny tarmac street below. But for all the damp dreariness the dark sky was unleashing, she was happy. It was the same warm protective happiness she had felt as a child. The cold, wet autumn days had been fun, even though they had confined her to games in the house where fires blazed warmly and dark shadows spilled from beeswaxed furniture. Even Monty the dog and Tabitha the cat had joined in the fun, while her mother had bustled from room to room cleaning and polishing. Sometimes on those dark, wet days, and after the work was done and lunch out of the way, she would sit her daughter on her knee and tell her stories of her childhood, of a very different upbringing in the army garrisons of India; of many servants; of the house with the wide verandah screened with wire mesh and how the monkeys would come down from the hills at breakfast time and cling to that same wire mesh, chattering impatiently to be fed; of dusty bazaars filled with brightly clothed merchants and blind beggars with deformed limbs and mysterious snake charmers. And the settings were just as exotic as the characters which filled them: Lucknow, Simla, Quetta, Lahore, Calcutta. And always there was a mention of the big white ship which brought them home.

Lisa smiled at the memory and glanced across the ugly sprawl of Victorian houses. At last she seemed to understand that it was nothing to do with the place. The cold, wet, bleak day could still hold as much promise as the magical land of her mother's childhood. If you were happy. She looked across at the telephone and willed it to ring. She needed to hear his voice to reassure her that this was not some silly, girlish mistake. It remained silent. She gave it ten more seconds, counting silently under her breath. It rang on ten, making her jump with surprise. She ran across the room and picked it up and only then realised it was the doorbell.

It was the postman with a special delivery. She signed for it and closed the door. It was only then that she looked down at the damp envelope in her hand and saw it was addressed to Chance Fitzgerald and not her. She had a strong desire to open it. No, she couldn't do that. It was his mail. Instead she laid it on the dining-table and went through to the kitchen to make some fresh coffee. When he telephoned she would tell him, and he no doubt would ask her to open it and read out the contents. But what if he didn't phone? What if he had been delayed? Had an accident! What if the message was something to do with the flight itself? At least if she opened it she would know how urgent it was; know if she needed to try and trace him.

She went back to the lounge and tore open the envelope. The message was brief. Brief and cruel and full of lies and hurt and deceit. She stared at the words until they became a blur. No, she told herself, it was not true. It was just not true.

Her hands were shaking as she forced her eyes to read the words again: 'Chance, darling, forgive me for not contacting you sooner, but have been away on business. I will be in London tomorrow (Friday) and will drop by your apartment. You will have my answer then! After Jersey, what do you think? Love you, Maxine.'

Tears were rolling down her cheeks when the telephone started ringing. She didn't answer it.

Konrad Zwicky was suffering from a hangover. And if that was not enough, Mariella's landlord had given him only seven more days at the house in the Grande Rue. Following his sister's death it had been one disaster after another. The house, which he had thought was hers, had turned out to be rented. As for the money he had found, hidden in various drawers, it had only just covered the funeral expenses with a few thousand francs left over to keep him in eating money. His bout of self-pity had quickly turned to anger when he realised that Mariella must have spent every penny she ever made on clothes. Her wardrobes were packed with expensive dresses, fur coats and more scanty underwear than one woman could wear in a lifetime. Other than that, he had counted 270 pairs of shoes, some still in their original boxes and never worn.

He slumped down in an easy chair in the sitting-room and took his wallet from his pocket, removing the piece of paper Mr Fitzgerald had given him in Zurich. The first item on the list was already done:

Plan route Milan to Geneva on the following lines: Shortest and fastest road to a point on Lake Maggiore. Estimated time for this journey?

Check rental of fast boat to carry two passengers to nearest drop-off point in Switzerland. Where will this be? How long will boat journey take?

Finally, a car will be needed from Swiss drop-off point to nearest airport. Also check times for flights to Geneva. Once again give estimated times of journeys.

The next request had been more difficult. In fact without Mariella it had proved to be impossible: 'Check out any details no matter how insignificant, concerning the meeting between the Arab – Rashid Suliman – and Otto von Klaus. This is most urgent.'

Konrad looked at the list with renewed interest. Apart from the forty-five thousand francs Mr Fitzgerald still owed him, the fast boat up Lake Maggiore sounded interesting. He could make a fat little commission from some unscrupulous Italian boat owner on that one. He stuffed the list back into his wallet and went through to the kitchen to make a few investigative phone calls. It was strange that Mr Fitzgerald had not called him the previous day about the date and time they should meet in Milan. Strange! No, it was downright typical of rich people, always treating the less well off with disdain.

He picked up the phone and started dialling the number of a friend in Zurich. As his finger engaged the third digit he realised something was wrong. He pressed the receiver to his ear and clicked the lever a number of times. It was dead. Lifeless. He put it down and tried again. Nothing changed. It was only then that he realised he had been cut off. Searching through a pile of unopened letters on the kitchen table, he eventually found what he was looking for. A bill from the telephone company. The amount was for 4,300 Swiss francs and the pay-by date was marked as 19 November. Two days earlier. He swore violently when he realised he had sat by the telephone the previous day for practically ten hours waiting for Mr Fitzgerald to call, and all the time the phone had been dead.

Picking up his coat he rushed out of the house. He had to find a public telephone and call Mr Fitzgerald in London.

Six miles down, Skagway became Juneau, and Juneau Telegraph Creek. Further still, and blanketed by the arctic freeze of a Canadian night, were such exotic place names as Ominea Mountains, Dawson Creek, Peace River, Buffalo Narrows, Opasquia and Weagamow Lake.

Light years above, Ursa Major and the zigzagging Cassiopeia, the red supergiant Betelgeuse and Orion's belt pointing south to the brightest star in the sky – Sirius.

But for once the magic was lost on Chance Fitzgerald. He was thinking of Lisa. Trying to picture her face. Up until the

189

very last moment, minutes before take-off, he had tried to reach her, but the telephone had remained unanswered. Now he was worrying. His mind inevitably drifted back to the disastrous marriage to Maxine and his resolve to stay away from future involvement. But he hadn't reckoned with Lisa. With that deep, mysterious force which had taken over his life. The selfsame force which had made up his mind on the flight to Anchorage. He would ask her to marry him. Sure he might not be the best catch in the world, and he didn't know why one man was not as good as another. Even the million dollars he was making from the deal would not impress Lisa, he felt certain of that. He also recognised the need to mend his ways. This sort of game was all over. As Guy had said, they were too old to be fighting wars. Wars were for fit young men with lightning-fast reactions. Even flying airplanes was a kind of war. A childlike escape from reality. A distancing of man and woman. No, when this was over he would leave the stage. He loved the sky and the close-ranked camaraderie of flying men, but he loved Lisa more. Besides, what good did it do to scheme and fight for a place in the world if the place was empty and lonely when you got there?

He turned his head. In the dim glow of the instrument lights he could make out the sleeping form of Guy on the bunk at the back of the flight deck. Pedro, ever the workaholic, was back in the cargo bay aft of bulkhead 245, checking off an inventory of spare parts. His eyes went to the right seat and the immobile figure of Hiram P. Gaylord III. The man from Vacherie, Louisiana, sat quite still, his face in the shadows having taken on a granite ruggedness. A quality of strength and dependability while the eyes were full of too many air miles to make him anything other than an aviator.

Fitzgerald flipped his intercom switch. 'Ever get the feeling you were too old for this kind of business?'

Gaylord's eyes remained transfixed on the starry sky. 'Every other day,' he drawled.

'So why are you still here?'.

'I guess the same reason as you. Once upon a time there was a young kid who got shipped off to a war. He somehow

190

learned to become blasé about gunfire, killing people and watching men die being the staple diet. Of course the war had its rewards like the Air Force giving him an Air Medal for every twenty-five hours of combat flying . . . The problems came after the war. The kid had grown up too fast, and I guess he kinda liked being a hero; so he went off and found another battle. And when that was through, another and another.'

'And if you could go back . . . would you change it?'

'Hell, yes . . . you know there was a girl in Vacherie where I was raised . . . I always knew I was going to marry her and maybe set myself up in the real estate business . . . three or four kids and a pile of respectability . . .'

'And then the war came.'

'Yeah,' Hiram said sadly. 'Then the war came.'

'So what happened to the girl?'

'Oh she's still there. I went back a few years after the war. She'd married my best friend. After that I saw no reason to hang around . . . still I'm going back some day.' He laughed. 'Huck Finn's getting a mite old . . . even so I'll miss the sights.' He waved a hand towards the heavens.

Fitzgerald followed the hand. He picked out Orion, while further north lay Aldebaran and the star cluster called the Seven Sisters. And he knew he was saying goodbye.

In Jersey, Maxine Audley was late leaving the house for no other reason than oversleeping. The Greek holiday had taken more out of her than she had realised. Then there was the unpacking. And sorting out her wardrobe for the following day. And telephoning her private investigator in London, before sending the telegram. Lastly, she had phoned the local air-taxi company and chartered a jet.

She was climbing into her red Ferrari when the postman arrived, apologising for his lateness and explaining that early morning fog had delayed the mail plane. She thanked him and took the letters to the house. It was as she was sorting through them that she noticed the one addressed to Alice. What was more, she recognised the handwriting. Chance Fitzgerald. She smarted at that. But it was the sort of low trick that he would get up to. No doubt trying to

191

poison the child's mind against her mother. She slipped the letter into her handbag and returned to the car.

Jersey airport was relatively quiet as though girding its loins for the onslaught of pre-Christmas passengers which began around mid-December. Maxine went into the terminal and turned right. The executive lounge of VIP Air was through a doorway to the side of the police office. It was one of those luxurious suites furnished in pale blues and dove greys and had the usual amount of sparkling glass and chrome and rubber plants. Behind a sweep of counter a number of uniformed girls keyed a hidden bank of computers. Maxine swept forward with the air of a minor royal.

'Good morning, Miss Audley . . . I chartered one of your jets to take me to Gatwick.' Her tone of voice was as imperious as her bearing.

The pretty dark-haired girl looked up and smiled and felt a twinge of envy. The pastel mink and matching Cossack hat and glitter of emerald ear-rings were quite enough to signal a wealthy tax exile.

'Good morning, Miss Audley. Please take a seat; I'll arrange for someone to escort you out to the aircraft.'

Maxine gave the girl a tight little smile and strolled across the lounge. It was how she imagined travel had been many years ago. Opulent, luxurious, stylish. Something out of reach of the despicable working-class. She sank gracefully into a low chair and took the letter from her handbag. She was intrigued to see what lies Fitzgerald had spun.

My darling Alice,

I thought it about time I wrote to you again, especiall as I was in Jersey recently. And especially as I didn't find the time to come and see you.

Of course I realise you may always find it difficult to understand why your mother and I were divorced all those years ago, and that my continual absence may seem to distance us. But always remember you hold a special place in my heart. And even if I'm missing your growing-up years, I hope we'll find more time to be together when you finish your schooldays.

Your grandfather told me about your horse, Long Shot, and that you had been winning lots of rosettes at the local gymkhanas. That made me very proud. I was always fond of horses when I was a boy; beautiful creatures. Nothing like people who can at times be very selfish I'm afraid.

I'm going to Canada now on business, and from there to Africa and Italy. I'll send you a Christmas present when my travels are over.

Well, my precious girl, as I have a plane to catch I suppose I should end now. Remember if you should ever wish to come and see me just write to the above address. Take care of Long Shot and remember that animals need just as much affection as people, perhaps even more.

Lots of love,
Daddy.

Maxine Audley was still seething as she strapped herself into her seat on board the Citation jet and heard the engines whine into life. People can be very selfish, indeed. A veiled attack on her if ever she heard one. Selfish! She would show Chance Fitzgerald who was selfish. She had him by the balls now, and when she was finished he would rue the day he had set eyes on her.

Rashid Suliman found his unlikely companion on the Olympic flight from Tehran to Athens to be an Hungarian who introduced himself as Lajos Verkerdi. His occupation, engineer. To Rashid, who had not slept since his visit to Mount Damavand, the man was obviously lying. It was nothing tangible. Nothing he could put his finger on. But more of the way of the Bedouin who can smell water in a dry dusty desert. A kind of sixth sense. No, if this man was an engineer, then he Rashid Suliman, was Allah himself.

It was, of course, Fazlollah Mahallati up to his tricks. Having failed to confirm whatever suspicions he had, he was now using one of the SAVAKs — the Iranian Secret Police — lackeys, to accompany him on the first leg of his journey. And after that! A changeover at Athens, with a new pair of eyes to follow him to Egypt and eventually on to Khartoum. Of course it was clever. A Hungarian or a Russian national. The last type of person to be suspected of working for the Iranian government. Clever, yes. Perhaps too clever. Too subtle. Being on his guard and having pushed the thought of sleep to the back of his mind, Suliman now listened to the engineer engage in the kind of small talk that travellers sometimes do.

'You have been to Hungary?' Lajos asked.

Rashid, whose eyes had been admiring the full and rounded hips of a dark-haired flight attendant, shook his head. 'No, never.'

Lajos sighed. 'You should go, my friend. Wine and gypsy violins and pretty girls. Plenty of romantic fun if you get my meaning.'

'It is not the Arab way,' Rashid said coolly. 'Also I think it sounds strange for Hungary. It is Iron Curtain, is it not?'

Lajos laughed. 'We call Hungary the jolliest cellblock in the Soviet concentration camp. After the revolution of fifty-six, Khrushchev called ours "a goulash Communism", but it is more. We are a small West trapped within a large East.' Lajos's voice took on a deep and emotional patriotism. 'But one day, my friend . . . one day we will again have our Eger.'

The flight attendant came then with drinks. Rashid took tea in accordance with his faith, and Lajos, three miniatures of vodka. The Arab noticed the labels on the bottles. Stolichnaya. He permitted himself a brief smile. A vodka bottled in Russia rather than the better known proprietary brands. Strange for a man who voiced his dislike of communism.

Lajos's round peasant face was lined in a smile. 'A toast, my friend. *Extra Hungariam non est vita, si est vita, non est ita* . . . which roughly translated means: outside Hungary, no life you'll find. And if you do, it's not our kind.' He threw back his vodka in one practised movement.

Rashid sipped his tea thoughtfully. 'You mentioned that one day you would again have your Eger . . . I do not understand this.'

The Hungarian poured out the second vodka. 'A town in my country. In 1552, two thousand of our people, women

194

fighting alongside their menfolk, won a famous victory against 120,000 Turkish invaders . . . perhaps one day we will do it again against the clodhopping Ivan Ivanovitch.' He chuckled at the thought and tossed back the second vodka.

Rashid partially relaxed. He was certain he was wrong. No Russian agent would say the things this man was saying, not even in fun. No, it was his state of nerves. He was seeing shadows where none existed. Fazlollah had got him more rattled than he had realised. Even so, he would listen. Observe. He was after all something of a scholar. He had read widely. He knew more about Hungary than the man on his left could have even guessed.

The talk continued spasmodically throughout the flight, with Rashid listening and throwing in the odd disguised question in an attempt to draw the wrong answer. None came and by the descent into Athens Rashid was almost convinced that the man really was who he purported to be.

Lajos, slightly the worse for wear after countless vodkas, said, 'Have you heard the latest Lenin joke?'

'No, I would have thought it an unwise choice of subjects.'

The Hungarian smiled. 'Oh, but it's not. Even the Russians have a contest for the best Lenin joke . . . the winner gets thirty years in Siberia.' Lajos was still laughing as the plane touched down.

As the aircraft was taxiing in Rashid remarked, 'And from here, you go to Budapest?'

Lajos rolled his eyes. 'Sadly not . . . no, I go on to Cairo to consult with Egyptian engineers. There have been minor problems at the Aswan dam.'

The stark, palpitating fear which had gripped Rashid at the beginning of the flight was back. The Aswan dam had been a direct result of Soviet technology. Indeed the Egyptians still retained a small army of Soviet engineers to maintain the dam. What of Hungarians? Would they put an Hungarian engineer to work on such a project? Especially when they had enough engineers of their own! He didn't know, that was the short answer. What was more worrying was that he too was changing flights at Athens to travel to Cairo, before the final leg to Khartoum. He saw again Fazlollah's bearded face and cunning eyes.

'And you?' Lajos enquired. 'Where do you travel from here?'

'Also Cairo.'

The Hungarian grinned broadly. 'Good. That is good. We can travel together.'

It was as they were leaving the airliner that Rashid's mind settled on the religious issue. From his study of world history he knew that after World War Two, Stalinist communism put St Stephen into eclipse in Hungary. But not for the real Hungarian.

'Is it not Stephen who is the patron saint of your country?' he asked Lajos.

'That is correct . . . how did you know that?'

'Perhaps I read it somewhere. I also seem to remember there is an unusual name for Sunday . . . *Varsarnap*, I think.'

'Yes, that is so.'

'What exactly does it mean?'

Lajos looked puzzled. 'Mean? Just Sunday.'

'Ah, yes. It has no other significance then?'

'No.'

Rashid poked a finger under his eyepatch and scratched his empty socket. And that is the final proof, he thought. For any true Hungarian would know that *Varsarnap* meant market day, made so by King Stephen himself, so that all the shoppers could be herded into church when their commerce was done.

Lajos was looking at his watch. 'We have one and a half hours before the Cairo flight,' he said. 'Perhaps we should get something to eat.'

'But we have eaten on the plane.'

Lajos laughed. 'Another matter I forgot to mention. We Hungarians are big eaters.'

The terminal was packed. A sea of milling faces with that airport mixture of happy, sad, lost, confused and annoyed expressions. Against the hubbub of voices was the ever present stream of multi-lingual flight announcements. For Rashid, it was a moment of decision. The briefcase he was carrying contained the plastic explosive in the false compartment. The timer and detonator were kept separately in the airline bag slung over his shoulder.

To take such things through an airport security check was not a problem. Firstly, the briefcase would travel through the X-ray conveyor machine, the PE appearing to be a part of the moulding of the case itself. The detonator was slightly more difficult. The first action was to transfer it to your key-ring. When you walked through the gate-shaped personnel check a red light and/or bleeper was activated, indicating you were carrying metallic substance. As the security men moved in you laughed and produced the keys from your pocket. The detonator being no more than an inch long would appear, at first glance, to be another key, or at least one of the ornamental nick-nacks people attach to key-rings. Security officials never checked that closely anyway. The Israelis perhaps, but this was Greece. As for the timer, that was nothing more than a travelling alarm clock. It would go through the X-ray check without question, except Rashid Suliman was not taking the explosives through security.

Telling Lajos he would meet him in the restaurant, he went quickly to the toilets and locked himself in a cubicle. Transferring the contents of his briefcase to the airline bag he wired up the detonator and timer to the PE and checking his watch, set the timer to activate in ten minutes. His final action was to press the green button on the top of the Braun quartz clock. The orange secondhand began its silent sweep of the analogue dial.

With steady hands he closed the briefcase, hid the airline shoulder bag at the back of the cistern and hurried back into the terminal. He reached the restaurant with six minutes and fifteen seconds to run and panicked momentarily when he realised he could not see the Hungarian. He scoured the tables, feeling the impatience rise within him. He looked at his watch. Five minutes and thirty seconds. Perhaps there was another restaurant. Or a coffee shop. Fool. Fool. Why had he not checked that first?

He was about to turn and hurry away when a large hand dropped on his shoulder.

'You are all right, my friend?' the Hungarian enquired. 'You look hot.'

Rashid, who could feel the sweat collecting on his forehead, managed a weak smile. 'A brief attack of my malaria that is all. I have just taken one of my tablets in the washroom. It will help.' He followed the Hungarian to a table by a glass partition.

Lajos seated himself and picked up the menu. He frowned. 'Not much better than what they served on the plane,' he said. 'Perhaps we should not bother.'

'Something I think,' Rashid said quickly. 'Something light. I feel a little hungry now.'

'And the fever?'

'It helps to eat something . . . I always find that.' Rashid looked at his watch again. Two minutes and eighteen seconds.

'There is something wrong?' Lajos asked.

'Wrong? No, there is nothing wrong. I was making sure we have the time to eat before the flight leaves.'

'Always time for that. Especially if they have *paprikas csirke galuskaval*.'

'What is that?'

'Paprika chicken with dumplings.'

Rashid suddenly put his hand to his shoulder. He looked all around, his face showing concern. 'My shoulder bag,' he explained. 'I must have left it in the toilets. Please, you will excuse me.' He stood up to leave.

'What of your order?' Lajos said.

'Fish would be nice. Perhaps you could order for me.' He placed his briefcase on the chair. 'I will leave my case with you for a moment. That is all right?'

The Hungarian smiled. 'It is not a problem,' he said, and went back to studying the menu.

Rashid Suliman reached the toilets on the far side of the terminal with twenty-five seconds to spare. He locked himself inside the same cubicle which was thankfully unoccupied and sat down on the toilet seat to wait for the explosion. He felt no regrets that innocent people would be killed. In fact it was the perfect way to get rid of one of Fazlollah Mahallati's shadows. This way no blame could be attached to himself. No suspicion. Especially as Fazlollah's man would be one of many and as the press would lay the blame at the feet of the PLO or the Islamic Jihad or any one of many similar organisations.

Five seconds . . . four . . . three . . . he lifted his hands to his ears and silently counted to zero. Nothing. No sound. Just the pulse beating rapidly against his finger tips. He counted another five seconds. Still nothing. Now he was worried, concerned the timing device had failed or that the detonator was useless. His fingers were coming away from his ears when the flat echo of the explosion slammed through the building. The cubicle and the toilet on which he was sitting seemed to lift in slow motion, shake itself violently and then return to the floor. White dust floated down from the ceiling in a miniature snowstorm. And then silence. But only for a moment. In the very next instant, the air was filled with screaming, sobbing voices and the smell of smoke. Rashid stood up and dusted himself off. In the Arab way of things life was cheap. A few infidel lives to protect his future, that was all it had been. And had not Allah himself said, 'We will sternly punish the unbelievers and pay them back for the worst of their misdeeds. Thus shall the enemies of Allah be rewarded. They shall abide in Hell for ever, because they have denied our relevations.'

Suliman collected his shoulder bag and strolled casually out of the toilet. He would be one more horrified onlooker. And as for the Hercules, his soldier's wiles would find another way of blowing it out of the sky.

In London, Lisa Wendell-Holmes had spent a number of traumatic hours being plagued by suspicion and doubt. She had repeatedly told herself that the special delivery was not what it appeared to be. She also regretted not answering the telephone. That way, at least, there would have been reassurance. Now there was only an empty desolate silence. A silence in which to brood and feel the pain of anguish gnawing at her insides.

The doorbell rang at three o'clock. Lisa dabbed her eyes hurriedly with a small lace handkerchief and went to answer it.

Opening the door, she was confronted by a beautiful woman. Her eyes were large and deep brown in colour. They were set in a flawless skin which had the texture and colour of gold. The pastel mink and matching cossack hat completed the exquisite picture. The woman looked surprised.

'I'm sorry,' she started. 'Is this the right apartment . . . I'm looking for a Mr Fitzgerald. Chance Fitzgerald.'

'Yes,' Lisa replied. 'Please come in.'

'Thank you. I'm Maxine Audley by the way.' She held out a beautifully manicured hand with long blood-red fingernails.

'Lisa. Lisa Wendell-Holmes.'

Maxine swept into the room, carefully taking in her new surroundings. The lounge was plain, sparsely furnished. Pictures of aircraft hung from the white walls and book-shelves were filled to overflowing. A white china vase with faded red roses was the only concession in a predominantly male room. A telegram was on the mantelshelf, propped up against a carriage clock. It had been opened, as she had hoped it might. And that, she thought spitefully, would account for the woman's red puffy eyes. She had been crying.

Maxine smiled quickly to herself, then turning round said, 'Is Chance here?'

'No . . . he's away flying.'

'Flying!' Maxine echoed with feigned surprise. 'But he is back later. Today?'

Lisa said guardedly, 'No, I'm afraid he won't be back for some time.'

Maxine, fully aware of Chance's movements from Mr Woodley's report, sighed deeply. 'I don't believe it. Not again.' She moved towards a chair by the dining-table, reaching out to steady herself. 'Do you mind if I sit down. It's been a long and tiring day.'

'I'm sorry, please do.' Lisa moved across and sat on the other side of the table. How did she tell a strange woman what seemed to be happening? 'You are Chance's ex-wife, aren't you?'

Maxine looked up. 'Yes, forgive me . . . have we met before?'

'No, it's not that. Just that he's mentioned you.'

'I don't follow,' Maxine replied.

'May I ask you a personal question?'

'Of course.'

'Did Chance . . . did he come to see you in Jersey last month?'

'Yes. Why do you ask?'

'Because . . . because, I've been living with him for some time.' The tears pricked at her eyes even as she spoke.

'Living with him . . . with Chance?' Maxine looked dumbfounded. 'Oh, my dear, I'm so sorry.' The conciliatory tone changed to one of quiet anger. 'I should have realised it was all lies . . . even that damned letter this morning.'

'Letter!'

'He asked me to come back. For the sake of our daughter, of course. Said that it was a moral responsibility; to make a go of it . . . the . . . the bastard.' She sank her face into her hands. 'I'm sorry,' she added, composing herself, 'I shouldn't have said that. It's just that after last month, when he came to Jersey . . . I feel used.'

She stood up and paced angrily across the room. Lisa followed, her brow wrinkled in concern. This woman was nothing like Chance had said. She seemed kind and understanding, concerned about the welfare of her daughter. And what had she meant by 'used'? A searing flame of jealousy ran through her body. She moved towards Maxine who was standing by the window and noticed the tears running unchecked down her cheeks. Oh my God, she thought, what is happening? She had been around long enough to know bitches. She could tell them a mile away. Sometimes they were sweet and coy; sometimes they would protest their innocence so much they would become sickening. And sometimes their eyes told you everything you wanted to know. But Maxine seemed nothing like that. Take away the trappings of wealth and she was nothing more than a weak and vulnerable woman. Lisa moved up to her shoulder and put an arm around her.

Maxine half-turned and gave a small tearful laugh. 'I'm sorry to make a fool of myself, Lisa . . . you don't mind if I call you Lisa?'

'No, of course not.'

'It's just that . . .' she faltered. 'Could I have a glass of water please?'

'Would you rather a cup of tea?'

Maxine sniffed and dabbed her eyes. 'If it's not too much trouble.'

They sat opposite each other at the kitchen table. Maxine had removed her coat and hat. The emerald green jersey dress with the high neckline showed off her slim figure, whilst the wide black patent-leather belt highlighted the tiniest of waists.

'How do you feel now?' Lisa asked.

'Better. Confused . . . but better.'

'Would it help if you told me what happened?'

'Happened!' Maxine said in a faraway voice. 'The same thing that always happens it seems. I met his mother once; Chance's mother that is. She was an American. I remember hating her because she had nothing good to say about her son. She said he was like his father . . . always running away.'

'His father! But he was killed in the war, wasn't he?'

Maxine smiled sadly. 'No, he didn't come back that was all.' She gazed reflectively out of the kitchen window; at the grey sky. The rain had stopped now, and the clouds were breaking up bringing a promise of fair weather. 'She even told me that his grandfather was a pilot in the Royal Flying Corps in the First World War. The story went that when the last shots had been fired he landed his plane in some tiny French meadow, got out and walked away. Apparently, they found his helmet and his uniform jacket lying in the grass, not far from the machine. He was never seen again. Like father, like son, she said to me. But of course I didn't believe her. Chance was different, I felt sure of that. Nice and kind . . . with the looks of a young god . . .' the words choked in her throat.

Lisa was feeling stronger now. Somehow the other woman's misfortune and weakness made her so. Strong enough to push her own anguish aside. But then she had faced anguish before. And loneliness. Going back would not be as difficult as she had first thought. Besides, she felt a strong compassion for the woman across the table, as though she wanted to take her in her arms like a small child and rock her gently to sleep.

'And when he came to Jersey; it was to ask you to go back to him?'

Maxine sipped her tea. Her hand was shaking as she placed the cup back in the saucer. 'Not at first, no. There was a party at the house.' She looked up and her voice strengthened for a moment. 'I'd lost an ear-ring in my bedroom and was looking for it when he came in . . . one thing led to another, I'm afraid,' she lowered her eyes shamefully. 'Weak and stupid I know . . .'

'No, Maxine, not stupid.'

'Oh yes, Lisa, stupid. How could I have been fooled by that glib tongue again? After all the years of knowing him . . . and then there was Alice, our daughter. I even told her he was coming back . . . and now? Now I find he's up to his old tricks . . . and there's you, of course.' She bit her lip and offered up a sad smile. 'I wouldn't dream of standing in your way, Lisa. Anyway, it's possible things could work out better for you than they have for me.'

Lisa said, 'You know, that is one of the nicest and most unselfish things I've heard. No, Maxine, you won't be standing in my way. I managed without him before and I can do so again.'

'So, what will you do now? Do you live in London?'

'No, Switzerland. And I'll be going back tomorrow.'

The telephone rang in the other room. Both women started.

Lisa said, 'That will be Chance; from Alaska . . . he said he'd call.'

Maxine, sensing a weakening of Lisa's resolve said, 'Please don't say I'm here, whatever you do . . . I think I've had enough for one day.' She took a handkerchief from her handbag and dabbed gently at her eyes.

The telephone continued ringing.

'No, damn it. I've had enough for one day too. Would you like a drink? A real drink.'

'Yes, I think I would.'

'There's nothing in the house. Why don't we go into town?'

Maxine considered the question. Perhaps it would be safer if they did. That way she could plant a few more seeds of doubt. It would also keep Lisa away from the telephone should the bastard Fitzgerald try to contact her again.

'Why not,' she smiled. 'Why not indeed?'

22 November

North Atlantic

SATURDAY 0600 HOURS

NEWFOUNDLAND IS THE MOST easterly part of the North American continent and thrusts into the bleak North Atlantic ocean far from the nation's industrial heartland. Its significance to air travel as a stepping stone on the long and often hazardous route across the North Atlantic came to an end in the early 1960s, when the long-range jet airliners superseded the shorter range propeller-driven aircraft.

For aviators also, it was the end of an era. The departure of the seat-of-the-pants flyers. Those larger-than-life characters who had successfully prevailed over God's Little Acre of sky. Now, however, was the time of the jet jockeys. The clinical technicians. The computer minders. Men who spoke easily about quadratic equations and calculus; of machmeters and compressibility and 'coffin corner'. White collar workers who wore the wings of aviators. Imposters who, within a few short generations, would have relegated romance back to an MGM lot. Imposters who had about as much natural flying ability as the dodo or the penguin.

Fitzgerald, Stanton, Gaylord and Pedro were definitely of the old school. Men who bent the rules just for the hell of it. Their technical stop at Gander to refuel had been a nostalgic reminder of their youth. They had been weaned on the cold desolation of Gander, Goose, Frobisher, Sondrestromfjord, Narssarssuaq and Reykjavik, and a thousand other far-flung outposts where sub-zero temperatures and white-outs had been transformed to the strength-sapping heat of the tropics. Between them, they shared more than a century of skies and storms, and mistresses which ordinary people referred to as airplanes, except ordinary people did not understand that those vast unlovely hulks of aluminium had a heart and a soul. Real aviators did.

Now, as the Lockheed Hercules – November Five Nine Lima – levelled off at twenty-five thousand feet, the four ageing crew members were feeling the effects of tiredness. It was day three since their departure from London, and in that time they had had no more than twelve hours sleep. Coupled with jet lag, which affects crews as much as passengers, they viewed the coming week with trepidation. Fatigue was a dangerous companion on any flight deck. It was the prelude to disaster.

Gaylord, who was flying left seat on the leg to Athens, turned to the rest of the crew. 'Not that I particularly object to being elected as captain of this flying garbage container, but unless someone pushes a cup of coffee into my hand within the next sixty seconds I might have to refer my complaint to the airline management.'

Fitzgerald, who was working through a pile of Red Cross logistics paperwork on the three seats at the back of the flight deck, came forward as Pedro went across to the galley to fix the coffee. He slipped into the flight engineer's seat, which was central to and slightly aft of the two pilots' seats.

'How's it going?' he said lightly.

'Apart from the catering . . . fine. Where's Guy?'

'Back in the cargo bay, he's fixed up a hammock.'

'Sleeping . . . again!'

'Too many four-ringers up here he said.'

'Could be right.'

Fitzgerald's eyes did a quick sweep of the instruments. 'Everything seems to be working OK . . . one good sign.'

'Yeah, except that lot frightens me.' He pointed down to the two inertial navigation systems (INS) which were basically complex computers which told, amongst other things, the exact position over the earth's surface at any moment in time. 'I mean, have you seen the accuracy figures for that box of tricks? A matter of yards error at most when we reach the other side of the ocean.'

Fitzgerald smiled. 'So, what's wrong with that?'

'Wrong? Everything. I preferred the guys they sat in the back and called navigators. No guarantees with them; more fun. I remember one telling me on a flight from Goose to Prestwick at the backend of the war, that the 'E' on the compass didn't stand for east . . . he said it meant Europe. Mind you, he did his best ever on that trip. We came out at Manchester.'

'Close,' replied Fitzgerald, 'almost the same ballpark. Anyway, I'm just reworking the final checklist. Anything you want to throw at me?'

'Nope. Other than the registration. Why are we still on the US number? I thought we were re-registering under some South American flag.'

'No good reason, other than as we are now working for the Red Cross I thought it would appear more legitimate than skulking round on a banana republic registration. Also, and as we're so above board we stay out of the limelight. I mean, how many planes are there on the US register? Too many to start checking right. The fact that Relief Air is a Panamanian registered company doesn't mean a thing . . . unless someone starts digging. And even if they did, by the time they caught up with us it would all be over. Plane delivered or crashed, depending which side of the fence you happen to be standing on at the time.'

Pedro passed the coffee out. 'I'm impressed,' Gaylord remarked. 'Must be the easiest payday I ever did attend.'

Fitzgerald laughed. 'After a lifetime of getting it wrong, I'm inclined to agree. Anything else?'

'Pedro reckons we should take on full fuel at Athens.'

'Any particular reason? It's not that we need a great deal on the run down to Khartoum.'

'Cost. He figures the prices in the Sudan will be about double what we have to come up with in Greece. And considering that this lady holds nearly 63,000 pounds of turning and burning fluid, could save a few dollars.'

Fitzgerald was leaving the seat when the flight engineer tapped him on the shoulder. 'The fuel on the Khartoum—

Iran sector,' he wheezed, 'should be OK if we shut down one engine in cruise. Flying on three at two hundred and forty knots will give you a possible reserve at Chah Bahar of thirty minutes.' He pushed a grubby piece of paper into Fitzgerald's hand. 'The calculations are there.'

'Which engine do we shut down?'

'Either three or four. Hydraulics come off one and two.'

Fitzgerald patted him on the shoulder and handed the paper to Gaylord. 'Our answer to the fuel problem on the Iran run. According to these you'll arrive with thirty minutes' gas remaining.'

'Working on the assumption that we find the field first time you mean.'

'True, true . . . and if you don't you'll have thirty minutes to make your peace with God.'

'The one thing I've always liked about you, Chance. Always got an answer.'

'Ah, yes. The electric chat of the Irish.'

It was two hours later, when the first hint of daylight was creeping into the flight deck, that Hiram's raised voice shattered the tranquillity of the crew compartment. 'Chance we've got a mayday on the emergency frequency.'

Fitzgerald, who had been struggling to keep his mind on the paperwork, and away from the fact that he had once again failed to contact Lisa during their brief stop at Gander, picked up a headset and went forward.

'What is it?' he asked.

'Young kid ferrying a single engine ship . . . got problems . . . reckons he'll be ditching any moment now.'

'Low on gas?'

'No . . . engine missing badly . . . he told me it's his first solo crossing . . . sounds real scared.'

Fitzgerald rubbed the left side of his face with the palm of his hand. Damn. This was definitely not to plan. Responding to a mayday call would attract the attention they had been seeking to avoid. 'Position . . . where is he?'

Gaylord looked down at the chart neatly folded on his knee. 'He figures approximately fifty-two degrees thirty minutes north and thirty-three degrees west.' He marked the position on the chart and handed it to Fitzgerald. 'About a hundred miles north of us.'

Fitzgerald sent Pedro aft to get Stanton. Standing behind the flight engineer's seat squinting out into the bright high altitude sunlight, he knew there was a decision to be made. He mused on the moments in his life which had bordered on near starvation. Of hitching rides around the world looking for work. Of the privation and loneliness and mental torment. And now! Now he had found his fortune. But more than that, he had found the woman to share it with. With one proviso. And that was he keep a low profile. Stay out of the firing line. And what about the aviator? the little voice within asked. What about the kid who's just about to ditch in perhaps the worst place of all? How long will he survive in the waters of the North Atlantic? And whichever way you want to view it, he is one of you. One of that special breed. A flyer.

When the full crew compliment were on the flight deck he put the question. 'OK gentlemen, this is the situation. We have a ferry pilot out there about to ditch. Now, we can either keep going and assume that somone else will respond to the mayday, or we can go and take a look see ourselves. Bear in mind however that once we commit ourselves to searching for him we have become high profile. That is, we will have to make out an extensive written report once we reach Athens. Not that that might appear much on the surface, but bearing in mind what our operation really is, and that we are all known in certain quarters, it could . . . and I emphasise could . . . blow this deal wide open.'

There was an air of perceptible tension as each man came face to face with the rigid code of the mercenary. No lame ducks. No passengers. And the injured are left behind . . . after you have put a bullet through their brain.

Stanton was first to voice his opinion. 'I say we forget it. I mean, what are the odds that the chap will even pull off a successful ditching. Usually they dig their nose in and go straight to the bottom.'

'And what if he doesn't,' Gaylord replied. 'What if the plane floats long enough for him to get out?'

'Then he climbs into his bloody dinghy old boy and paddles away.'

Fitzgerald, sensing the animosity in Stanton's voice interrupted the conversation. 'We'll debate it later. Right now we vote. Those against?'

At that very moment it was twelve-thirty in Geneva. Lisa Wendell-Holmes had taken a taxi from the airport directly to Otto von Klaus's house. Now she was sitting in the high-ceilinged, dark panelled living-room withering under a barrage of insults from her employer.

'You say you have not had contact with Chance Fitzgerald since Thursday morning when he left London?'

'Yes.'

'Yes,' he snapped angrily. 'Yes. Is that all you can say? Did I tell you to become . . . to become involved with this man? No. I told you to watch his every move. To report everything he did back to me. And now!' He lifted his fat hands above his head in exasperation. 'Now you threaten the entire operation. Yesterday I tried to contact you in London over this letter of credit matter to Milan. Now what do I do? Today is Saturday and the bank is closed. Which means I have to wait until Monday. And when will Fitzgerald arrive in Italy?'

'He said provisionally on Wednesday. I had arranged to meet him there.'

'And what if there is something wrong with the plans? What if he has been delayed? Have you thought of that?'

Lisa felt her own anger rising now. Damn it, she was not a child. And she resented her employer's tone of voice. Besides which, she had been through a very traumatic period. It had been a day which had culminated in Maxine staying the night at the apartment and blurting out the final earth-shattering truth. And that was the moment when the brave face she had been wearing had given way to an uncontrollable flood of tears and the admission that she had missed her period ten days earlier. It was something that never happened. She never missed. Never.

She may have been a rich girl with all the possessions that other women yearn for, but to Lisa she had also been a human being. That Chance should have deceived *her* was one thing; but to have gone out of his way to destroy another woman's life – and possibly her daughter's too – was something else. Of course she had tried to console Maxine; to convince her that she should have an abortion. Maxine had clung to her in desperation and in a sobbing voice said: 'But I'm a Catholic, Lisa. I could never do that . . . never.'

Now, reliving the moment, her nails dug deep into the palms of her hands as she clenched her fists in a fierce anger. God, that rotten bastard Fitzgerald. That unspeakable rotten bastard. She would kill him.

'Well,' von Klaus snapped, 'what if there has been a delay?'

'Don't worry Otto, I will find out.'

Von Klaus sighed audibly and went across the room to a drinks cabinet and poured himself a large whisky. Perhaps he should not be so hard on the girl, he thought. Perhaps her disastrous love tryst with Fitzgerald could even work to his advantage. He poured a second tumbler of whisky and took it over to her.

'Here,' he said, 'drink this.'

'What is it?'

'Whisky.'

She felt like saying she didn't much care for it, and especially not neat, but she knew the futility of arguing with the German. His word was law. She glanced up at his unshaven face and bloodshot eyes and realised she despised the man almost as much as Fitzgerald. Still, that was not important at this moment in time. What was, however, was that she must look out for herself, in the way she had decided before Chance Fitzgerald had entered her life. She took a sip of the whisky and nearly choked as the unfamiliar harshness caught in the back of her throat.

'Lovely,' she croaked. 'Have you had lunch by the way?'

'Lunch? No.'

She stood up. 'In that case, I'll make you something.'

'I do not care to eat,' he said.

'Perhaps you don't,' she replied, the old confidence returning to her voice. 'But have you looked at yourself in the mirror lately. I leave you for a few weeks and you start to fall apart.' She clicked her tongue as a mother might to an errant child. 'Also, Otto, I am very sorry for the mistakes I have made ... I can assure you they will not happen again.'

'Yes, well, that is forgotten. Come, I will show you to the kitchen.'

Otto led the way, his mind mulling over what he had to put to her. It was difficult.

She was searching through the cupboards when he said, 'You will have to go to Milan, of course. The money you understand. You must be there when Fitzgerald collects it.'

She froze for a moment, then turned slowly towards him. 'I'd rather not see him again, Otto ... isn't there some other way?'

Von Klaus took a Turkish cigarette from the gold case and lit it. He suppressed a cough. 'I am afraid not, Lisa. But I will arrange that Rashid Suliman also comes to Milan. He will act as your bodyguard.'

'Suliman? The Arab you mean?'

'Yes.'

'But isn't he going back with the airplane from Khartoum?'

'It is not necessary,' von Klaus replied dismissively. 'Besides I am worried about Fitzgerald. If he will let down a woman, then why not a man. And eighteen million dollars is a great deal of money to trust to someone like that, don't you agree?'

Lisa's eyes hardened. 'Oh yes, I agree all right.'

'So you will go?'

'Yes, Otto. As you rightly say, your money is not safe with such a man.' She gave him a brief smile and turned back to the cupboards.

Von Klaus sat back in his chair and drew heavily on his cigarette. His eyes, as if for the first time since her arrival, suddenly noticed the change in his secretary. The hair was beautifully coiffeured. And the tight blue woollen dress she was wearing was something quite daring; outlining her small jutting breasts and shapely hips. It was also shorter than anything he had ever seen her wear before, so that

212

when she now reached up into the cupboard it rode high above her knees. He felt the old familiar desire stirring in his loins. It seemed a long time since he had had a woman.

At two hundred feet above the Atlantic the air was dangerously turbulent. Rain squalls lashed the windshield of the Hercules with a sound of rising and falling thunder. A heavy sea was running, with black oily waves sending armadas of white horses racing eastwards.

Fitzgerald was conducting operations from the flight engineer's seat, having despatched Pedro aft to prepare for a life-raft drop. His eyes turned towards Stanton who had taken over the left seat from Gaylord. 'What do you reckon, Guy?'

Stanton, wrestling with the controls, said with a heavy irony, 'What do I reckon? I reckon you're bloody crazy . . . that's just for starters of course. I mean, old boy, why bother to run an undercover operation at all. Why not simply hand out a press release to the London *Times*?'

'What about the kid?' Fitzgerald persisted in the same level voice. 'Do you think he could have made it in this?'

'If he landed along the swell and didn't try running into wind, maybe . . . but even then it's bloody rough.' Stanton punched his stopwatch and banked the aircraft through ninety degrees. The second leg of the square search pattern.

Fitzgerald adjusted the mike on his headset and turned to Gaylord. 'Anything from Gander?'

'Nothing on HF. Too much static; I'm trying for a VHF relay . . . sure to pick up one of those high flying jet jockeys before too long.'

The Hercules rocked violently through the malevolent storm. Fitzgerald tightened his seat harness until it dug painfully into his waist and shoulders. 'Pedro, you there . . . Chance.'

'Fives. Go.'

'How's it looking?'

'Four rafts ready to inflate . . . confirm we're de-pressurised?'

'That's affirmative.'

'OK. Once you spot him I'll need a hand down here . . . Hiram can be the link man.'

'I'll keep you posted.' He turned back to Stanton.

'Anything?'

'Negative . . . how long do you want to keep this up?'

'Hadn't thought about it . . . we'll review the situation in thirty minutes.'

'Thirty minutes!' Stanton grunted. 'Do you realise how long he'll last in that water if he's not wearing the right gear . . . five minutes at the most. After that, the hands will be completely useless as will the arms and legs . . . the core temperature of the trunk will be all that's keeping him technically alive . . . and that won't last very much longer.'

'I get the message, Guy . . . let's drop down to a hundred feet.'

'A hundred feet . . . have you seen the size of that swell?'

'Indeed I have, and if memory serves the size of a man's head bobbing around in that lot is one hell of a lot smaller.'

Stanton grimaced and eased the Hercules down towards the angry sea. The tension was building with each passing second. Now it wasn't just looking for a downed aviator. Now it was flying a search pattern almost at the level of the crests of the waves in blinding rain and sick-making turbulence. One mistake and they were all dead.

Stanton, visibly sweating, wound on a handful of nose-up trim. Hiccup factor they called that. Should your hands be separated from the controls for any reason the theory was that the airplane would go up.

Gaylord broke the tension, if only temporarily, when he said, 'Now I know what Lyleburn must have felt . . . he was a kid I went to school with; got himself swept away in a particularly bad stretch of the Mississippi. Yessir, he must have felt the same dread that's knotted behind the third button of my shirt at this very moment.'

'And you want to go back?' Fitzgerald joked.

'Sure. As long as you don't fool with it, it's quite safe . . . besides you see some nice sights from the river.'

Stanton eased the Hercules gingerly through another ninety degrees and reset the stopwatch. Fitzgerald saw his lips silently moving and knew the Englishman was singing.

214

It was one of his trademarks when the going got rough. And always hymns.

'What is it today, Guy?'

'What's that?'

'The hymn . . . what is it?'

Stanton began singing in a tuneless voice: 'All things bright and beautiful, all creatures great and small . . . all things bright and beautiful the Lord God made them all . . .'

Gaylord raised a hand for silence and started a brief conversation on one of the VHF frequencies. When he was through he flipped the intercom. 'Message relayed through a Pan Am Clipper. He's talking to Gander right now.'

The search continued and the tension returned with a vengeance when a severe patch of wave spray smashed into the windshield. No one spoke, but they were all thinking the same thing. That it was the first impact! That they had flown into the sea.

It was fifteen minutes later that Gaylord saw it. And even then he wasn't sure. 'Right ten . . . up ahead . . . down a little . . . hold it . . . there . . . d'you see it . . . Goddam it, it's a flare . . . a flare . . . Goddam the kid's made it.'

Fitzgerald leaned forward in his inertia reel harness, staring out into the sea smoke, taking a small area of sea at a time. Then he had it. A red flare diluted by the water vapour hanging in the air. Diluted so that now it was almost pink in colour.

'Ahead,' called Gaylord, '. . . 300 yards . . . 200 . . . 100 . . .'

Fitzgerald said, 'One hundred feet, Guy, east to west . . . got it?'

'Got it.'

'Hiram you're link man . . . we'll drop a couple of rafts on the first run . . . let us know the score.'

Fitzgerald left the flight deck and staggered aft to the cargo bay, the aircraft pitching and rolling like a ship in a heavy sea. Pedro had four eight-man life-rafts ready and was wearing his harness. Fitzgerald plugged in his headset to the long extension lead the Chinaman was holding out.

'Reading me OK?' Pedro gave a thumbs up. 'Inflate two . . . what do you want me to do?'

Pedro grabbed the side of the fuselage for support. The

turbulence was increasing. 'Harness . . . get that on unless you want to end up in the water.'

'Then what?'

'When I've lowered ramp . . . we take a walk . . . red light on at five seconds . . . green at zero . . . on green let your life-raft go . . . OK?'

Fitzgerald said, 'Is that all?'

Pedro laughed. It was a reaction which was steeped in the roots of some distant past. His forebears had been Hakas, the true sea people of China. A people happy in adversity. A laughing race of mariners who had faced the dangers of the sea since the beginning of time. To Pedro, the air was simply another ocean. He shuffled away towards the rear of the cargo bay.

Fitzgerald cupped his hands around the boom mike. 'Hiram . . . Chance. OK for the ramp?'

'Whenever you want.'

The top door and lower ramp of the Hercules opened on a mind-chilling vision of a backward running sea and the thunderous roar of slipstream and engine noise. Fitzgerald tugged the nylon harness one last time to make sure it was secure, then edged his raft back towards the ramp. Pedro was already there. A black silhouette against the morning light, and beyond him, a too-close sea pitching violently. Is that all, Fitzgerald said to himself, remembering the remark he had made to Pedro. Is that all! Mother Mary. One slip, one failure of the frail harness, and he was food for the fish.

Gaylord's voice crackled through the intercom. 'Commencing run in . . . now . . . one hundred feet . . . speed one thirty . . . fifteen seconds . . .'

Fitzgerald eased his unwilling legs further out on to the ramp. The wet arctic air stinging his face.

'. . . eight . . . seven . . . six . . . red light on . . . three . . . two . . . green light GO.'

There was a split second of two bright orange life-rafts tumbling back in the slipstream and a glimpse of a small white upturned face, before the sea smoke swallowed up the scene.

Fitzgerald and Pedro clambered back to the safer confines of the cargo hold, each massaging their arms and bodies to generate warmth, as the Hercules began a gentle climbing turn. The intercom crackled. 'Chance . . . Hiram . . . stand-by . . . may have to try that again, over.'

'Not close enough you mean?'

'Roger . . . about fifty yards too late.'

Above the thunder of rain, engines and slipstream, Fitzgerald yelled, 'We've only got two rafts left . . . Tell Guy to try and slow it up on the next run.'

There was a short pause filled with crackly carrier wave. 'Says he's back on speed as far as he can go, over.'

'Get him to drop down to fifty feet then.'

'He says you're a lunatic.'

Fitzgerald made no reply but stared bleakly out of the rear opening of the aircraft. He eased himself back out on to the ramp, back into the shrieking wind and freezing rain. A matter of feet below the waves were being torn into ragged streaks of foam. He thought of the young pilot down there. How long would he survive in such a sea? Perhaps Stanton was right. Perhaps they should have ignored the mayday and run strictly to plan. Pedro, who had moved back to inflate the last pair of rafts, called him on the intercom. He went back on rocky legs and collected one, walking it inch by inch to the very edge of the ramp.

'Running in now,' Gaylord called. 'Ready back there?'

'Ready.'

'. . . eight . . . seven . . . six . . . red light on . . . three . . . two . . . green light GO.'

Again, two rafts spilled end over end into the ocean and even though he was half blinded by the numbing spray and rain Fitzgerald still caught a glimpse of the aviator's face. White. Upturned. Then the Hercules was climbing and turning at take-off power.

Fitzgerald staggered back into the cargo hold and sank to his knees with exhaustion. 'How does it look?' he called over the intercom.

'We're turning back . . . standby . . . standby.' Gaylord again. The power reduced on the four Allison engines and the aircraft dipped down towards the raging sea. 'OK . . . we see him now . . . right on target.'

'Is he in one?' Fitzgerald shouted excitedly.

'No . . . not moving . . . just supported by his life vest . . .'

'The rafts . . . what about the rafts?'

'Drifting away now . . . I guess he's dead, Chance . . . Sorry . . . Do you want to abort . . . over.'

Fitzgerald was silent. His face full of sadness. He climbed slowly to his feet. 'Hiram . . . Chance . . . One last run . . . low and slow.'

For the last time, Fitzgerald went out on the ramp. Standing there feet apart, he joined his hands. 'Not much, kid, but it's the best I can offer . . . The Lord is my shepherd; I shall not want. He maketh me to lie down in green pastures; he leadeth me beside the still waters. He restoreth my soul: he leadeth me in the paths of righteousness for his name's sake . . .'

The Hercules, at one hundred and thirty knots and one hundred feet, commenced its run in. There was a break in the clouds then, and the only sunlight to be seen that day in a thousand square miles of north Atlantic, beamed down on to the breaking waves. Stanton dipped a wing in salute as the Hercules crossed the body of the young aviator for the last time. Fitzgerald made the sign of the cross and went back to the cargo hold.

'Hiram . . . Chance, over.'

'Go.'

'Roger . . . we'll abort now . . . thanks.'

The four Allisons screamed in unison and the Hercules soared up through the clouds towards the distant sunshine.

It was early evening when Rashid Suliman arrived in Khartoum. His unplanned execution of the Hungarian at Athens airport had been the reason for the twenty-four-hour delay. The briefcase of plastic explosive having killed nine people and injured thirty-five more. It had also destroyed a large area of the airport terminal. The police and army had sealed off the area to check for further devices. Rashid had been annoyed. He knew there were no other bombs. But then he could hardly tell anyone. So it was, that along with a few hundred other stranded passengers he had had to remain overnight in Athens.

Now, today, he was nearing the end of his quest. The

road was growing shorter. Even the haboob which had seemed to threaten the safe landing of the Boeing jet had not worried him. Inshallah, he would get to his destination when he was meant to; not sooner and not later.

The broken-down Datsun taxi bumped on over the poorly surfaced roads, the driver blasting his horn at the oncoming glimmer of headlights in the thick sand haze. Rashid's nose picked out the new smells, those which were subtly threaded through the more apparent ones of sand and gasoline and exhaust fumes. There was spice from a nearby suq and tea perhaps. Then a meal of dura being prepared, and as the taxi careered recklessly around a corner, from beyond a high villa wall the unmistakable scent of the tamarind tree. He breathed deeply and enjoyed the sensation. The hustle and bustle of a predominantly Arab town. The blind and deformed beggars, maimed at birth to provide an income for their fathers. The sly-faced merchants who bartered in the suqs; their wares being anything from spices and tea and sugar to plastic shoes and a vast inventory of goods from the World Aid programme which, through the intricate web of officialdom, had been sold off by corrupt government officials, only to be resold at five times their value by the wily storekeepers.

Rashid the scholar smiled at the iniquitous history of the Sudan. Was it not Major-General 'Chinese' Gordon who had been slain by the Mahdi's followers, ending the reign of the Egyptian khedive? And was it not also that Lord Kitchener – sent by the British to avenge Gordon's death – who defeated the Sudanese forces at the Battle of Omdurman in 1898, so starting the era of the Anglo–Egyptian Condominium, which ruled until the Sudan gained independence in 1956? And was it not now that the wheel had turned full circle? Once again Sudan was two countries, the north and the south. The south of the Zandes, the Nuers, the Lotukas and the Dinkas – the black Africans. The north, men of lighter skin and flowing white jellabahs, which spoke of an Arabic and Islamic heritage. Two countries bound by the common thread of the Nile. Little more.

Rashid pushed the thoughts aside and turned to the

soldier within him – the way to down the Hercules now he was without the bomb! This indeed was a problem as his knowledge of aircraft was more or less that of the layman. But then wasn't he looking with the eyes of a blind man? Could it be that the answer lay in something other than the airplane? In the crew themselves perhaps!

The taxi braked to a screeching halt outside the Khartoum Hilton and Rashid stepped out. A black Sudanese with the tribal marks of the Nuers materialised out of the shadows and collected his baggage. Rashid haggled with the taxi driver, settled on what he considered a fair price and watched the car rejoin the skirmish between vehicles and pedestrians.

'Yes,' he said to himself quietly, 'perhaps in the crew themselves!'

He knew one man in Khartoum, a rogue by the name of Ali Abdul Rashaida. An untrustworthy and dangerous man, but a man who might nevertheless have the answer to his problem.

It was pitch-black night as Hercules, November Five Nine Lima, began its slow descent over Paxos in the Ionian Sea. Hiram Gaylord was asleep on the rear bunk and Fitzgerald had taken over as co-pilot.

Stanton adjusted the auto-pilot. 'How long's it been since Gander? Seems like a week.'

Fitzgerald checked his watch against the flight log on his knees. 'Just over the ten hours. Say ten and a half on landing.'

'What did we plan for?'

'Nine.'

'The chap in the water took up that long did he?'

'More or less.'

'One of your less wise decisions, commander,' Stanton added with a hint of bitterness in his voice.

'As it turned out, yes. On the other hand we could have saved the kid's life.'

'And what of our lives? Who gave you the right to play God with those?'

Fitzgerald stared bleakly out into the darkness. Imperial

bloody echoes, he thought. Typical of the arrogant English. Still, no point in rocking the boat now. 'You're right, Guy . . . and from now on we'll play it by the book.' He turned to Pedro, who was dozing in the engineer's seat. 'Any coffee going, man of many talents?'

Pedro clasped his hands together in Oriental fashion and lowered his head ever so slightly. 'Black or standard NATO?'

'Yes, why not. All the trimmings as Hiram would say. The milk and sugar might take the taste away . . . and give one to the "colonel" in the back there. Tell him we'll be landing in twenty-five minutes.'

Fitzgerald's eyes returned to the black night. He took a strange comfort from the postural numbness which had distanced the feeling between body and legs. That and the dull edge of some related pain, and the gritty eyes, and the body sweat, and the stubby chin. And the noise. Always the noise. The whines, the whistles, the faint rumblings. Engines, propellers, pressurisation system, carrier wave static from the radios. The constant bombardment on the inner ear, the brain, the mind; so that the end of any long-haul flight entered the danger zone. The zone which embraced the most exacting and dangerous aspect of flight, the landing. The pilots, of course, would openly laugh off any suggestion of danger. Privately they would entertain other viewpoints. Those who did not were the accidents waiting to happen. The vain, foolish men, who laid presumptuous claims to immortality. And immortality, as any wise man knows, is the preserve of gods.

Gaylord, coffee in hand, drifted up and stood behind Fitzgerald's seat. 'Still lost?' he drawled.

Chance nodded and affected his bog-Irish accent. 'That we are, sir. Took a wrong turn at the Bay of Biscay; about the time the good Lord switched off the light . . . and I never could do this sort of thing in the dark.'

'So you wouldn't know exactly where we are at this moment in time?'

Fitzgerald pointed down to the right. 'The legendary Gulf of Patras . . . but not being a Catholic you wouldn't have heard of that would you?'

'No . . . but I get the feeling you're going to tell me.'

'Scene of a famous battle. The last between the great oared vessels of the sixteenth century. The Christian fleet, paid for in part by the Papacy, defeated the Moslem . . . the Ottoman fleet. According to the history books it was the first victory by the Christians in such a battle.'

'Sounds interesting.'

'Oh, it was that all right. The entire area is a haunting ground of sea battles and romantic figures. Helen and Paris . . . Antony and Cleopatra. Perhaps when I retire I'll buy a villa down there; a small olive grove as a hobby, and a few glasses nightly at the local taverna with Spyros and his pals.'

'An Ionian Irishman!' Gaylord laughed. 'Sounds lethal.'

'Only on Saturday nights, Hiram old son . . . but then the "crack" wouldn't be up to Dublin and the select at Ryan's pub, would it?' He reached down for the checklist. They were nearing the Athens terminal area. 'One last word, gentlemen, and on a more serious note. If you could make out your wills tonight. Usual procedure. As from tomorrow the water gets decidedly hotter.'

No one spoke. It was one of those frozen moments in time. A stillness descended on them all. Private thoughts. Life and death. Heroism and cowardice. The love of a good woman.

For Hiram Gaylord, it was a moment to reflect on a boyhood not unlike Huckleberry Finn's. A moment to remember Lyleburn, and fishing poles above a dappled creek, and fighting a nest of mud dauber wasps, and poking at a dead snake. And then the war, and travel, and another war. It was the second one, in Korea, when Pedro had pulled him from a blazing P–51 and saved his life. After that there had been other wars which had had the effect of cementing their friendship. They were now like brothers. Inseparable. But Hiram still dreamed of the wide and majestic Mississippi where the paddle steamers had once ruled, and Lyleburn . . . and the fishing poles.

Pedro's thoughts were less romantic. He was an engineer who loved all things mechanical. His ageing mother he loved in a dutiful way. Then there was his one true friend –

Hiram. It had been his Chinese half which had settled on the custom of his people. If you save a man's life, you are responsible for him forever. So it had been that Pedro had watched over the man from Vacherie.

Guy Stanton felt fear and anger. The anger was directed at the irresponsibility of the Irishman. At risking their lives in a futile bid to save a downed pilot in the Atlantic. He had known the impossibility of such a mission all along. Had spent a period of his life ferrying aircraft across the North Atlantic. Had seen them launching out of Goose and Gander. Knew they lost anywhere up to a dozen guys a year. Also knew the survival rate was practically zero. His fear was of returning to the desert lands which had spawned a kind of shell shock. Fear of letting the team down. Fear of being killed. Fear of being buried in some alien earth. Fear of not seeing his wife again. It was something he could not fully understand, and to his dismay he found that his hands were already shaking.

For Chance Fitzgerald it was Lisa. Nothing else seemed important.

It was one hour earlier in Switzerland. Exactly quarter past nine. Von Klaus was in his study when the phone rang. He stubbed out his cigarette and answered it. There were several clicks against the hissing background noise which came and went like an erratic tide.

'Hello . . . hello . . . is that you, Otto?'

Von Klaus pushed the instrument closer to his ear, at the same time cupping his free hand over the other one. 'Yes, it is, Otto . . . speak up please. The line is very bad.'

'It is Rashid . . . Rashid Suliman.'

Von Klaus's spirit lifted. 'Rashid. It is good to hear from you. Where are you?'

'Khartoum . . . I am staying at the Hilton . . . I am calling to check the arrival time of the machinery we discussed.'

Otto picked up the piece of paper from his desk. Lisa was back. Neatly typed memos. All the precise details he needed. She had, through a series of telephone calls, tracked down every last item of information. Even to transmitting a message to Athens air traffic control for

Captain Fitzgerald to contact a Geneva telephone number prior to his departure for Khartoum.

'The machinery is arriving in Athens this evening, according to our latest information. My secretary assures me it will be with you tomorrow. She will telephone you in the morning to confirm the time . . . There are no problems from your side I hope.'

The tide hissed loudly distorting Suliman's answer.

'I did not hear, Rashid. What did you say?'

'I said there are no problems. And everything is well at your end?'

'Yes, but there is something you should know.'

'I am listening.'

The German carefully outlined his doubts about Fitzgerald's integrity, which he stated were a direct result of an in-depth investigation by certain members of his staff. Not that the lack of integrity would harm the deal in any way of course, but could cause severe problems later on. And then only for Rashid Suliman.

There was a nervous silence which seemed to last for too long. Otto said: 'You are still there, Rashid?'

The voice sounded thoughtful. 'Yes, I am still here . . . you are sure of this . . . this information?'

'The only reason I tell you.'

'Yes, I see. I will think of this tonight. We will speak again tomorrow.'

'Tomorrow yes . . . goodnight, Rashid.' Von Klaus put down the phone and reached for a cigarette. Good. It was very good. He had planted a seed of doubt in the Arab's mind.

He lit the cigarette and was coughing violently when Lisa came into the room.

'I'm ready,' she said brightly.

He looked up, his face a deep red from the coughing fit.

'Take off the coat,' he ordered.

'My coat!' she said with surprise. 'But I thought we were going out.'

Otto indicated a blue box tied neatly with a large red ribbon. It was lying on the floor at the centre of the ill-furnished room. Then, settling back in his chair he picked up an unfinished glass of whisky and watched. She removed the grey tweed coat to reveal a stunning black evening-dress, sequinned bodice and flowing chiffon skirt. Her shoulders and arms were quite bare. His eyes moved lower to the seamed black stockings, and he wondered if they were like those Marie used to wear, the ones with the black suspenders which dramatised the white flesh of the thighs. He felt his pulse racing at the very thought.

She was opening the box now. Kneeling on the carpet and lifting the lid.

'Otto,' she cried, lifting out the full length silver fox fur. 'Otto! What is this?' He made no reply as she pressed it to her cheek, eyes wide with disbelief. Then she slipped it on and hugged herself as a child might. 'Thank you, Otto,' she said a little breathlessly. 'But it's far too lovely. I can't accept a present from you like this . . .'

He finished his whisky and banged his glass down on the desk, then looked at his watch. 'Come, we are late. I promised you the finest dinner in Geneva after all.' He noticed the questioning look in her eyes. 'I bought it this afternoon, while you were checking up on the details of the airplane.'

'But it's far too expensive.'

'Expensive, rubbish, Lisa. I am a rich man. I have now all but retired. I have also realised how invaluable you have been to my company. This then is a small gift.'

'It's hardly small . . .' she started.

He waved her words away with an impatient gesture. 'If you have a problem,' he said stridently, 'it is that like all women you talk too much at the wrong time.'

It was on the drive into town that Lisa finally harnessed her exuberance. She had earned the coat after all. Three years of low salaries were testament to that. Even so, this wasn't the Otto she had known all that time. A man who owned a mansion and was too mean to furnish it was hardly the type to throw his money away on expensive fur coats. Her brow was furrowed in concern as she contemplated the reason for such a dramatic change.

23 November

Khartoum, Sudan

SUNDAY 0920 HOURS

ALI ABDUL RASHAIDA had an unlikely guard. He was an ancient Zande man from Yambio on the Zaire border. His black face was gnarled and bright with sweat, and his neck was creased with the concentric circles of age. His back however was ramrod straight, and his chest carried the memories of World War Two when he had fought for the British in numerous campaigns. Apart from the medals pinned to the dark shirt he wore a khaki bush hat, the kind favoured by Australian soldiers. He snapped smartly to attention when Rashid Suliman gave his name, then ushered him wordlessly across the small dusty courtyard.

The house itself was a plain two-storey structure surrounded by a high stone wall. Within the garden a number of tamarind trees struggled for survival in the dry cracked earth. Peering down on the scene from the north end of the graded dirt street, was the sandstone coloured minaret of the central mosque.

Ali Abdul waved his guest to a chair. The room was large and contained a quality collection of art, which ranged from Greek crosses and Roman statues to Chinese porcelains and Japanese Katana swords. The air-conditioning system wasn't working, so that the room was hot and dry, the taste of sand in every breath.

Ali Abdul, dressed in a traditional jellabah and turban of sparkling white, said, 'Welcome to my humble home, Rashid. Please, you will take tea?'

226

'Shukran, Ali Abdul.'

Rashid watched as the wiry little man with the crafty animal eyes moved to an open door and shouted to a close-at-hand servant. He returned, his sandals slapping loudly on the marble floor, and settled into a chair at the ornate ottoman desk he used when dealing with his business affairs.

'It has been many months,' he said. 'You are still travelling?'

'Sometimes I think too much . . . and you?'

Ali Abdul nodded. 'Everywhere in a hurry. A Western philosophy which is difficult in this land of ours. And if we do not learn to hurry we will be left behind.'

'This is true,' Rashid commented gravely. 'But what of the camels?' It was a reference to the nomadic Rashaidas who had emigrated from Saudi Arabia some two hundred years earlier, bringing with them the reputation for breeding fine riding camels, which were periodically convoyed to Egypt to be sold.

Ali Abdul pulled his jellabah with him as he turned in his seat. 'The camels,' he said sadly, 'are no more. Khartoum, like Cairo, has too many people and is very much modernised. The camels do not make the price any more. Now it is the Datsun camels.' He laughed at the small joke. 'But Allah is good. Today there is business to be done. Tomorrow . . . bukra . . . Inshallah.' He lifted his hands. Question answered. Now it was Suliman's turn.

A young Arab boy appeared with a tray. He had dark curly hair and shiny eyes as black as coals. He laid the tray on a low table, poured the tea and handed a glass to the guest and his master, salaamed, and disappeared as silently as he had come. The two men took up the glasses of the hot sweet liquid and drank, their conversation drifting languidly on against the still heat of morning and the faint sound of car horns from the distant street. It was perhaps half an hour later that the reason for the meeting was finally approached. Ali Abdul was laughing.

'It is not a problem, my friend; I will send you six young Nuba girls dressed only in beads, their bodies glistening with oil.'

Rashid poked a finger under his eyepatch and scratched the irritation that had once been an eye. 'Six girls . . . six! I think the bull is not as young as he once was. But then my heart is strong.'

'It is not your heart you should be worrying about.' Both men rocked back in their seats with laughter.

Rashid eventually adopted a serious countenance and said, 'Business, Ali Abdul. A pity to spoil the morning so, but there it is. I have a small problem. In fact three small problems. Shall we call them enemies. Men who need to be silenced.'

Ali Abdul hunched forward across his desk, ears pricked. 'And when has that ever been a problem, my friend? A knife, a bullet. It is too simple.'

'Not quite,' Rashid replied guardedly. He thought for a moment, choosing his words carefully. To say too much to this man could be dangerous. 'These men will be travelling together with no other people present . . . and three against one could present, shall we say, unfavourable odds.'

'Travelling together, you say. In a car perhaps?'

'Perhaps.'

'A bomb,' Ali Abdul said simply.

Rashid jerked upright in his chair. Surely his ears were deceiving him. 'A bomb!' he said in astonishment. 'But where would one find such a thing in Khartoum?'

The merchant tapped the side of his nose knowingly. 'When is it for?'

'Straightaway.'

Ali Abdul put a hand to his chin and stroked his neatly clipped beard. 'Straightaway, you say. Straightaway.' His eyes met Rashid's. 'It will cost much you understand?'

'Naturally. What sort of bomb can you get?'

'Dynamite.'

'It will need a timing and detonating device . . . this is possible?'

Ali Abdul smiled. He was thinking of his contacts at the Chevron oil company. They used dynamite in their exploration work. How it worked he was unsure. But for money he would find out. He clasped his hands together.

'All things are possible. I will contact you later in the day. This will be satisfactory?'

'Yes.'

'Good.' Ali Abdul stood up. 'Now I must leave; much has to be done.'

Rashid was sitting in the back of a yellow Datsun taxi as it bumped its way down the dusty unmade road. He was smiling to himself. A bomb! It was perfect. Even so, he was aware that Ali Abdul would exact a very high price for so rich a prize. The taxi lurched around the corner by the acacia-shaded gas station as Rashid concentrated his mind on the other problem. The one offered by his good friend Otto von Klaus. The problem called Fitzgerald. He would kill him in Milan, he decided, once the money had been safely collected from the bank. The way? A gun. Ali Abdul could throw one in on the dynamite deal.

In Athens, Chance Fitzgerald was controlling his anger. It was only now on his departure that the Greek in the flight clearance office had handed him the message. The one he should have received the previous evening. The urgent message from Geneva. The one signed Lisa. The Greek had made a half-apology, saying that the bombing of the terminal two days earlier had caused a great deal of disruption. Fitzgerald waved the apology aside and rushed to find a telephone. It took a number of minutes for the collect call to be put through, then he heard her voice. Clear and firm. As though she was in the next room.

'Lisa . . . Lisa, it's Chance. I just got the message. Where have you been? I've been trying to contact you.'

There was a breathless silence. She had been taken aback by the sound of his voice, by the soft magic of the faded Irish accent.

'I . . . I had to come to Geneva,' she said hesitantly. 'Some urgent matters to arrange with Otto.'

'Never mind,' he answered, feeling happier than he had for days. 'It's lovely to hear your voice . . . you can't believe how lovely.'

Lisa stood at Otto's desk in the empty study and fought back the tears which pricked at her eyes. Damn what was happening to her. He was a bastard. Hadn't he double-crossed her? Played fast and loose with her affections! Destroyed Maxine; made her pregnant. And yet, here he was talking in that beautiful soft voice. Full of charm; so much charm. She could picture his handsome face, his blond hair falling across those impossibly blue eyes. She gripped the edge of the desk as a wave of dizziness swept over her. Damn the man, damn him, damn him. Why had she ever become involved? And why did it hurt so much inside?

His voice was there again, cajoling her out of her silence.

'Lisa . . . you still there?'

'Yes, Chance, I'm still here.'

'You are all right aren't you . . . there's nothing wrong?'

'No . . . nothing wrong. Where are you? Where are you speaking from?'

'Athens. The airport. Just about to leave for Khartoum.'

'Good. I will tell Otto. He'll be relieved. What time will you be arriving in Khartoum? I have to call the owner with the details.'

'About five and a half hours from now.'

Lisa made a note. 'I've booked four rooms at the Khartoum Hilton, they're in your name.'

'Pity you're not with me.'

She ignored the remark. 'When do you think you'll be arriving in Milan?'

'Don't know exactly. I'll call you from Khartoum . . . give you all the details then.'

'When will that be?'

'Hopefully this evening . . . latest tomorrow.'

'I'll speak to you then,' she said, aware of an edge of iciness which had crept into her voice.

'Lisa.'

'Yes.'

'I miss you.'

Even without Otto's instructions to act normally when he called, she felt she would have said it anyway. 'I miss you too, Chance.'

Fitzgerald, hearing the line go dead, returned the phone to its hook on the wall, and turned to the first-floor window. He was concerned at the reserve he had sensed in her voice. She had sounded like a stranger. He looked out of the window, which framed a car-park and dark cypress and silvery olive and an arching blue sky. The reason came to him suddenly. Otto von Klaus had been in the room while she had been talking. And she did have a certain shyness after all. He smiled with a sense of relief, pushed his hands into his pockets and went to find the rest of the crew.

Everything, it seemed, was back on course. Back the way he had planned it. Even the lengthy written report on the mayday situation in mid-Atlantic seemed destined to take longer than normal to be relayed to the Canadian and American authorities. The bombing of Athens airport, however savage, barbaric and cowardly, had given them a short breathing space, should anyone start asking questions.

There was one dark cloud on the horizon, however. His failure to contact Konrad Zwicky, whose contact number in Geneva was apparently out of order, which left him with a great deal more work to do once he reached Milan.

It was an hour later in Geneva when Otto von Klaus put the phone down. In spite of the dark, snowy day he was in high good humour. It was not so much the conversation he had just had with Rashid Suliman, as the long blissful sleep. Lisa, who had agreed to stay at the house, and who was sleeping in one of the guest rooms, had somehow had the effect of warding off the evil spirits. His sleep had for once been totally free of nightmares. So much so that he had slept through until eleven that morning. He had only woken then because Lisa had brought him a tray with coffee and croissants and the morning paper. She had drawn the curtains before leaving the room and he had breakfasted in leisurely fashion before taking a bath. Shaving, he had noticed a faint glow of colour in his cheeks. After that he had dressed in light grey trousers, white shirt and pale yellow sweater, and gone down to the study. The details from Fitzgerald had been typed out and were waiting on his desk. He had phoned Rashid Suliman in Khartoum and passed on the estimated time of arrival of

231

the Hercules and had in turn been told that Fitzgerald would be taken care of in Milan. From Suliman's cryptic usage of the English language he had put that down to a killing.

Finally, he had confirmed with the Arab the expiry date and time of the letter of credit – Thursday 27 November, 3.45 p.m. Italian time – which meant that the Italian bank would receive the telexed confirmation from Suliman minutes prior to the deadline. The Hercules would take off a few minutes before the same deadline. It was a mirror image of what Rashid Suliman's masters had intended.

Now, phone call complete, he was logging the details carefully in his diary. Of course there was one small obstacle left. Lisa. He would have no problem in convincing her to keep Fitzgerald on the Italian side until Suliman arrived on the scene. Similarly, he would have no problem in getting her to take charge of the money during the first phase of his plan. But the killing! That was something else. Certainly she hated the man. But did she hate him enough to want him dead?

High above the steep cliffs of the Acropolis and the columns of the Parthenon, the Hercules climbed on course for the Sudan.

Fitzgerald, standing behind the co-pilot's seat looked down on a brief moment of history from his own life. In Athens twenty years earlier he had nightstopped, with a bunch of fellow mercs, on their way from Saudi Arabia to England. It had been a night of bawdy fun taking over a nightclub, thirty of them, spending money like it was going out of fashion at midnight. The club owners had naturally been very accommodating. At some time during that night, he and six other pilots had ended up in a brothel, sitting around a large circular table playing cards. Their guide for the evening – a man by the unforgettable name of Polychronis Chintilas – had been out combing the city. He eventually arrived back with every free hooker from the Athens streets.

The wild night had continued with too much wine and too many women, so that by the time of the dawn boarding on to the ancient DC–6 airliner at the airport everyone was glad to find a seat in which to sleep. The sleep, however, became secondary when it was found that one of the party was missing. A guy called Joe Mitchell.

He was found later that morning by the Greek police, in a dirty back alley, with a knife in his back. His pockets had been emptied of the two years' wages he had been carrying.

Fitzgerald and two others stayed behind for a few days looking for Polychronis. As Mitchell had been seen with the fat Greek in the early hours it seemed more than likely that the Greek would know what happened – like which of his friends had put the knife in! The few days eventually passed and the Greek wasn't found. Chance and his friends returned to England on a regular airline flight, split up at London airport, and went their separate ways. Twenty years. Twenty long years, when he had been a young man setting out on some ultimate adventure. An adventure which had somehow never ended; dragging him from one country to the next. Keeping him away from the steady round of family life and a nine-to-five routine. And now, when he sometimes yearned for it, it was too late. In lots of ways too late. He hoped and prayed that Lisa would keep him tied down long enough for the flying bug to be erased . . . if it ever could.

He looked back at the receding city which filled the bowl of stony hills. He didn't like the place. Not since Joe Mitchell. And last night, in the bar of the hotel he had found himself checking faces, looking for the fat Greek – Polychronis Chintilas.

Stanton who had just switched on the auto-pilot, noticed the bitter look on Fitzgerald's face. 'You OK, Chance?'

He turned and the easy smile was back in an instant. 'OK, sure. And why wouldn't I be?'

'You tell me. You look pretty cut up about something.'

'Friend of mine lives back there that's all. Joe Mitchell. Hot shot fighter jockey. Age twenty-four . . . the only problem is, he doesn't get any older.' He turned to the flight engineer. 'Coffee all round Pedro. I'm buying.'

Gaylord spoke for the first time since the after take-off

checks had been completed. 'Think we may need something a mite stronger than that when we reach Khartoum.' He waved a copy of the *Herald Tribune*. 'Latest news on the American arms to Iran for hostages, is that the President and his team diverted some twenty million dollars profit to the Contra rebels in Nicaragua . . . weren't you flying for them, Chance?'

Fitzgerald who had been only half-listening, said: 'Contras! What about them?'

'Weren't you just down that way flying for them?'

'Yes.'

'Bump into any CIA guys?'

'No more than usual.'

'You'd better read that then.' He passed the newspaper. 'They're calling it Irangate back home . . . we sure as hell picked a good time to be working for the wrong team.'

Fitzgerald took the paper and began reading. An icy chill ran down his spine long before he had finished. Their operation could be construed as a carbon copy of what was now threatening the American presidency. Except they didn't have the excuse that they were doing it in the interests of hostages.

Sure the Red Cross subterfuge was watertight, but only up to the departure of the Hercules from Khartoum. After that, there was going to be a lot of luck needed to complete the operation in the way they had planned. And the faked 'crash' of a mercy flight was going to bring newspaper men running to the scene, which meant the attendant publicity could rapidly reach the wrong eyes and ears. American intelligence was thick on the ground in Nicaragua and Chance Fitzgerald had been a known quantity. So what was a mercenary pilot doing flying for the Red Cross in the Sudan? A guy who had quit being straight-arrow after Vietnam. A guy who had been killing people for the past twenty years. Killing machines don't turn John Wayne; not in real life at least. He handed the paper back to Gaylord and took the cup of coffee from Pedro. Three pairs of eyes were watching him.

He shrugged. The enigmatic smile was back. 'Two observations, gentlemen. Number one: last night I mentioned the water getting hot after Athens. Delete hot. That now reads scalding. Number two: no one lives forever; but in the event you have a private little pact with your maker to the contrary, I've just doubled your pay cheques.'

Stanton was the only one who didn't smile at the remark. He turned back to the instruments and felt his hands begin to twitch. In his last days of flying combat he had become very superstitious, methodically checking and double-checking that fate didn't trick him into a flight at the wrong time. He was searching his mind now. Looking for the flaw which would doom the mission. All he could think of was that things happen in threes. And if that was true, the first had been responding to the mayday in mid-Atlantic, which, as they were all aware, had rendered them high profile. The second was the political time-bomb which had exploded in Washington over the arms to Iran cover-up. The third?

He removed his headset and unfastened his lap strap. 'Chance, do you want to take over for a while . . . going to the toilet.'

Fitzgerald, noticing the sheen of sweat on the English-man's forehead, said, 'You feeling OK?'

Stanton laughed nervously. 'Fine, old boy . . . probably something I ate.' He left the flight deck on rubbery legs and locking himself in the toilet was violently sick.

It was mid-afternoon in Tehran and Fazlollah Mahallati was seized with panic. He was at the mosque, where afternoon sunlight penetrated the arches of the high windows, illuminating the white stone with a rosy tinge. He glanced sideways at Saddam Assad and repeated the words he had just spoken. 'But I know not this man Lajos Verkerdi.'

'The Russian,' Assad prompted.

Fazlollah felt a chill run through his body. The Russian! One of those seekers of a different kind of freedom. He had been the engineer who had sought political asylum. He had even married an Iranian girl. Of course the freedom and the wife had a price. Verkerdi, being something of a linguist, had been put on courier work. His last job being to follow

Rashid Suliman to Cairo from where a new man would take over.

The voices went on matter-of-factly, hushed whispers amidst those seeking Allah's forgiveness.

An explosion at Athens airport. What of Rashid Suliman? What had happened to him? Uninjured, apparently. Now believed to be safely in Khartoum.

Believed?

There had been a lengthy silence, lest the recording angels be distracted from their work, then Saddam had asked the inevitable question: 'How trustworthy is Rashid Suliman?'

Fazlollah pondered the question. A tall, wide question indeed, for in its answer lay his future. 'He was a good soldier,' he offered warily. 'A fine, brave soldier . . . now, however, I am unsure.'

'Unsure!' the voice echoed, as if levelling an accusation. As if saying: 'But have you not assured us he was worthy of the role we entrusted to him. The sole authorisation to deal for arms. Also, there is a great deal of money at stake.'

Fazlollah had countered with, 'Do we not have a man in Khartoum?'

The voice, strained and quiet had said, 'We do. Not an altogether trustworthy servant of Islam, but one who will find out what we need to know.'

'And you will be contacting him?'

There was a thoughtful silence. 'No. Perhaps it is better that you do. I will send a messenger with the necessary details. However, the man's name is Ali Abdul Rashaida.'

Fazlollah made a mental note. 'And that is all?'

'For now, I think. For now.' Assad's yellowish smile showed under his drooping moustache. It was a smile the head of the secret police had perfected. A trick of the lips to draw the victim's gaze away from the dark cruel eyes. 'Except . . . remember the barsman of the old days!'

Fazlollah remained long after Assad had gone. Fearful for his future. The barsman was to do with sacrifice. It was when the holy man recited with a loud prayer several sacrificial formulas. The twigs from his barsman-bundle were spread out on the ground when a sacrifice was offered. Of course the killing would not be in the traditional way with a mace. A gun was far easier. Or a bomb concealed in the trunk of a car! As for the burial, that would be the eternal damnation. No clear flowing springs. No reclining on couches lined with thick brocades, reaching for the hanging fruit. No bashful virgins whom neither man nor djinn would have touched before. Instead there would await an eternity of hell fire.

He went out of the mosque into the street. The first drops of rain were spitting from a leaden sky. It was that time of year. He walked on oblivious to the weather, his thoughts far away. Picturing a burial which would bring him no peace. A burial where the exposed corpse was left for the dogs and birds of prey. Parasites which would feed off his flesh.

In Khartoum, Ali Abdul Rashaida arrived back at his house late in the afternoon. The wind was gusting strongly out of the north, the lifted sand obliterating the sun, rasping across the windows with the sound of vermin scratching beneath the floorboards. To the Arab, however, it could have been a bright clear sunny day. He was in excellent spirits.

He opened the green canvas sack and looked once more at the explosives. He smiled when he thought of Simon, the Nuer, who wore his tribal scars under a hard hat. Simon worked for Chevron and had risen to the position of roustabout foreman. But for all his apparent education he was still a product of the Bilad as Sudan – the land of the blacks. A simple man. Like their neighbours of the south, the Dinka tribe, who would rather till a field by hand than use ox and plough. Yes, they were all simple, which left the Arabs of the north a free hand in the business of buying and selling. After thousands of years in the market place they were good at what they did. Too good for the simple black.

So it had been that Ali Abdul had beaten the Nuer foreman down to a price of fifty dollars American. They liked that; more so than being paid in Sudanese pounds. Like the ox, possessing American dollars carried respect and status.

He picked up the telephone and dialled the number for the Hilton. It took a few minutes before he was speaking with Rashid Suliman. 'You are well, Rashid?'

'Fine, Ali Abdul . . . and you?'

'A tiring day, nothing more.'

'And the goods! You have them?'

Ali Abdul's voice dropped slightly, finding a note of regret. 'Not yet, my friend. It is perhaps more difficult than I first imagined.'

'Difficult?' There was an edge to Suliman's voice.

'Yes, but do not worry. I will do everything within my power to find what you need.'

'How long will this take?'

'One day, two, three . . . a question only the Lord of the two Easts can truthfully answer, Rashid.'

'No more than three, Ali Abdul. I must have it by Wednesday night.'

The merchant smiled to himself. 'Wednesday night, Rashid. I will try. I will surely try. However, you understand the price may be very high. Such things are not easy to buy. And the people I am dealing with, sensing my urgency, will only make it more difficult to bargain for the fair price.'

'I understand.'

'Good. I will phone you again.'

'One other request, Ali Abdul.'

'Your servant.'

'I will need a gun . . . a handgun.'

'Not so difficult . . . it will be done.'

'Shukran, Ali Abdul.'

'Afwan, my friend.'

The merchant replaced the telephone and grinned. Fifty dollars American had suddenly grown. Two thousand perhaps! And a gun. Ah, life was good and Allah was kind. He reached down into the sack and pulled out a stick of dynamite. What Simon the Nuer tribesman had called gelignite. He tossed it up and down. He was totally unafraid. And why not? Had not Simon said that without the detonator it was quite harmless. And had he not also said you could throw it about, cut it open with a knife, and even set fire to it, and still it would be safe.

What the Nuer with the tribal scars and the hard hat had failed to mention – through his own ignorance of explosives – was that such treatment only applied to clean and new gelignite; and only then was it safe if you knew exactly what you were doing. What Ali Abdul was now tossing up and down was anything but new and clean. It was old. Old and sweaty. And the sweat was none other than nitro. The gelignite was highly unstable. Quite deadly. The Arab, tired of the game, opened the sack and made to throw the stick of gelignite back amongst the others. His hand was arcing back when the telephone jangled noisily. He turned and placed the explosive carefully on a side table, and picked up the ancient black receiver. The conversation was short, but from the slowly changing expression on Ali Abdul's face it was fruitful. When it was concluded he stood up and paced slowly through the large room of many treasures.

This was surely a miracle, he thought. A call from Iran. A request to seek out a man by the name of Rashid Suliman. A request to watch over the man and report anything out of the ordinary. And the ordinary had been: he will be departing Khartoum on Thursday in a C–130 aircraft. Times and names had also been passed. Ali Abdul had frowned and said it would be a difficult task, especially as there was so little time, and as Khartoum was such a big and crowded place.

Now, standing amidst his collection of Chinese porcelains and Roman statues which looked down from the tops of ornate plinths, he realised the price of the explosives could well be any figure he wished to make it. He clapped his hands loudly, to summon the boy. Now was the time to take tea. And after that he would arrange a small gift for Rashid Suliman. He had, after all, promised his friend six young girls dressed only in beads, their bodies glistening with oil.

The Hercules was drifting down the early night sky. The crew were silent. A kind of reverence, as though the very air was steeped in the history of the places they had overflown. Pompey's pillar in Alexandria; Cairo and the tomb-mosque of Kuait Bey in the City of the Dead; Giza with its legendary Sphinx and Great Pyramid. Then on to Abydos and the Hypostyle Hall of the Temple of Seti. Still high above the Blue Nile, Karnak; the Obelisk of queen Hatshepsut at the Temple of Amun and the statue of Rameses II and his wife. To the west of Karnak, the immortal Thebes and the Colossi of Memnon.

Now Upper Egypt had changed to the Sudan. Ahead lay Khartoum where the Blue and White Niles began. Fitzgerald, who was in the left seat, copied down the latest weather from Khartoum air traffic control. The wind out of the north at twenty-five gusting thirty-five. Visibility dropping by the minute. He turned to Gaylord.

'What do you think? They're giving a visibility of six hundred metres in dust haze.'

The old aviator tightened his seat harness. 'Sure as hell sounds like a pretty way of saying sandstorm.'

Fitzgerald smiled and flicked off the auto-pilot. He needed time to renew his love affair with the airplane. To get used to the feel of her controls before shooting a minimum approach. The altimeter slipped silently through ten thousand feet and the glimmer of stars disappeared one by one.

'Some goddam dust haze,' Gaylord murmured. 'Almost as high as the goddam moon.'

'Not going to do a lot for the paintwork either,' added Fitzgerald. He looked back at the flight engineer. 'What about the engines . . . will they hold up in this?'

The inscrutable eyes glimmered in the semi-darkness. 'Factory recommends not more than half an hour.'

Fitzgerald looked thoughtful as he turned back to the instruments and checked the time. 'OK, Hiram, let's go for the pre-landing checks.'

Gaylord picked up the check list and started the mechanical procedure of running through some thirty-seven items.

The tension started as the turbulence in the lower levels reached up and clawed at the aircraft. The muted voices continued their prayer-like patter. From the seats at the rear of the flight deck, Stanton, who had maintained the pretence of an upset stomach watched with the eyes of a horrified onlooker, staring at the dull glow of instrument lights and the three dark shapes hunched forward in their seats like three of the four horsemen of the Apocalypse. Three dark cloaked figures, with fleshless skulls, riding the equivalent of eighteen thousand screaming horses down an angry sky. The engine note changed as Fitzgerald banked the aircraft sharply round. They were south of the field now. Ten miles from touchdown. He took up a heading of three six zero. The altimeter was holding two thousand feet. Waiting for the glideslope needle. Fighting the unseen turbulence which tried to deflect them from their path.

'Three greens confirmed,' Fitzgerald called. Wheels down and locked.

'Roger, and you've got flaps at fifty per cent . . . let me know when you want the rest.'

The Irishman nodded and sought a more comfortable position in his seat. 'OK, Hiram. 140 knots approach . . . 120 at the fence . . . call me the lights.'

Gaylord's eyes fixed on the windshield. Unblinking. Waiting for the first sign of ground contact.

The sweat, the first sign of increased heart rate and wide open adrenal glands, started to run down Fitzgerald's neck. An uncomfortable chill seemed to settle on his body. When had he last flown an approach down to practically zero feet? Not this week that was for sure. And instrument flying was a skill you could only hone by practice! There was one of those moments, a disconnected space in time, when he remembered another pilot. An ageing pelican from what could have been another lifetime. But an Irishman at that. Leo Concannon had been one for the blarney all right. Like asking him why he was named Leo; not the least bit Irish. He would say: 'Ah well, I was named for one of the Popes.' The non-pontifical smile would follow. But then put Leo into an airplane and you had a bird. And if there was ever a problem he resolved it with one stock answer: 'Well, I'll give you a little tip,' he would say with a wink, and down would go his voice to an ear-tickling whisper. 'Tell her she's the sweetest colleen you've ever known and that you'd never leave her for another woman . . . she'll look after you then.'

I hope you were telling the truth, Leo boy, because if not I could be joining you a lot sooner than I'd planned.

Seven hundred feet flickered past. Speed – 140. Fitzgerald fought to keep the ILS needles locked together. The only way. Keep the needles in the perfect cross and hope there's a runway at the end of it.

Four hundred feet. Rough. Bloody rough. Eyes pricking with gritty pain. He could almost feel the desert reaching up to smash into the flight deck.

'Anything?' he asked quietly. Too quietly, it seemed. Hiram had not heard. What the aviating doctors would refer to as Presbyacusis, deteriorating auditory acuity associated with growing old.

Fitzgerald eased the boom mike closer to his lips. 'How's it looking?' Louder this time.

Gaylord's eyes remained transfixed on the windshield, his face wreathed in sweat. He said, in that laconic way he sometimes used, 'As black as ten foot up a bear's ass . . . but don't worry, you'll be the first to know.'

Fitzgerald dredged up a smile. Thank you for that, he thought. A moment of humour. A moment off the hook.

Two hundred and fifty feet. Speed checked, OK. On the glide . . . on the localiser. Now left . . . come on, sweetheart, we're on the same team remember. Steady . . . hold it. The aircraft began shaking violently. Fitzgerald's grip tightened, whiteness showing in his knuckles.

One hundred and fifty feet. Pedro's hand covered the power levers, preparing to go to take-off power when overshoot was called. Fitzgerald caught the movement in his peripheral vision. Ignored it. There would be no overshoot. The surface wind was increasing, picking up more sand, reducing the visibility even further. The aircraft rocked below one hundred feet. Fitzgerald felt his feet straining to lift off the rudder pedals, trying to avoid the image of earth which was building in his mind. The image which would become reality in the last fleeting micro-second. The too late micro-second. Now the sweat was running towards his eyes. The final trick. Because that was all he had. Vision. Vision to watch, believe, and fly what the instruments were telling him. The eye. The supreme soloist

242

in the sensory orchestra. The eye. Capable of creating order out of chaos. Blinded by sweat it would be useless.

Sixty feet. Please God there are no high masts. Please God the earth is flat and the runway is where I believe it to be.

Fifty feet. No one was breathing any more. No eyes were blinking. No lips were smiling. It was a frozen moment in four men's minds. The tension had reached breaking point when Gaylord's voice shattered what had become an eerie silence.

'Right five . . . lights . . . lights.'

Fitzgerald kicked viciously at the right rudder pedal. Only way near the ground. Flat turn. He saw them then. A handful of flickering runway lights, showing orange through the lifted gauze of sand.

'Flaps one hundred.' His right hand reached out. 'And my throttles.' The Hercules hit hard. Fitzgerald didn't give a damn. They were down. Leo wouldn't have minded the rough landing anyway. He had always said they couldn't be good all the time. It was like playing the percentages between luck and judgement . . . up and down like a whore's drawers. He smiled at some distant memory as his right hand brought the power levers into reverse and the Hercules slowed to a near stop.

They were sitting drinking black coffee. The passenger lounge was empty but Michel Sigel, the Red Cross representative, obviously had enough pull for that not to be a problem. As he had already explained, the catering staff had been trying to leave for the past hour ever since the weather had effectively closed the airport for the night. He had persuaded them to stay at least until the Hercules had diverted to some other airport.

Fitzgerald and the rest of the crew were now sitting in hard uncomfortable chairs, staring with bleary eyes into their coffee cups, trying at the same time to adjust to the bright neon lighting. Other than that, their bodies sagged with the weariness which comes with burning up an excess of mental energy. Fitzgerald took a sip of his coffee and wished he still smoked. He needed a cigarette now.

Something to calm the nerves. Untie the knots. He pulled his feet back under the chair. There was a scraping sound of sand on concrete.

'A bad night,' Sigel was saying. 'The sand gets everywhere. Still you are here and that is good.'

Fitzgerald said, 'Indeed, but you'll have to excuse the state we appear to be in . . . it's been a long week, and I'm thinking we all need a hot bath and bed.'

Sigel lit a French cigarette. 'So,' he said. 'A hotel. You have made arrangements?'

'The Hilton.' Fitzgerald replied.

'Ah, that is good. I will drive you there . . . when you are ready of course.' He took a card from his wallet and passed it to Fitzgerald. 'My home and office number. Perhaps you will telephone me in the morning; when you are rested. We can then discuss the relief programme.'

Fitzgerald took the card and slipped it into his shirt pocket, his eyes doing a quick sweep of the rest of the crew. Their eyes showed nothing except fatigue. 'Thank you, Michel. What time will be convenient? Eight o'clock!'

'Eight o'clock will be fine.' He pushed his chair back and stood up. 'Of course, I don't think we will be doing much this week. The weather man tells me that this sandstorm can last for many days. Not as bad, but enough to make our missions impossible I think.'

It registered in Fitzgerald's mind as they were walking through the empty terminal. Not doing much this week. That's what the Frenchman had said. And Otto's instructions clearly stated that they needed to depart this Thursday coming. Something to do with the expiry date on the letter of credit with the Iranians. Even though the Iranian representative Rashid Suliman should already be here and ready to depart with the aircraft, if the weather remained anything like as bad there could be a problem.

He was still deep in thought when they arrived at the Khartoum Hilton.

'Seemed a nice enough guy,' Hiram remarked, as they stood at the receptionist's desk filling out registration forms.

'Who?' Fitzgerald said. 'Michel?'

'Yeah. Pity we're not going to be doing much to help.'

Fitzgerald looked casually over his shoulder. A few Arabs and a few Europeans were milling around the lobby. He turned to Stanton and changed the subject. 'How are you feeling, Guy?'

'In the pink, old boy,' he lied. 'Good night's sleep and I'll be as good as new.'

'Hope so. If not, they're sure to have a house doctor.'

Stanton's body stiffened. 'No doctor,' he said emphatically. 'I'll be perfectly all right in the morning.'

Fitzgerald collected his key, dismissing Stanton's shortness as fatigue. 'Seems we're all on the third floor,' he said, 'but if any of you are planning a party, count me out. I'm sleeping.'

Gaylord laughed. 'You wouldn't have said that twenty years ago.'

'And there's the sadness, Hiram. The spirit is willing as they say, but the flesh fell asleep the moment we stepped off that flight deck.'

'See you at breakfast then.'

'Make it eight-thirty to nine. I've got to talk to Michel first.'

The room was like any other hotel room around the world, except for the fine sand which had sifted through unseen cracks, the buzzing rattle of a poorly maintained air-conditioning system, and the mosquito net festooned over the bed. Fitzgerald hoisted his bags on to the stand alongside the built-in wardrobe, kicked off his shoes and went through to the bathroom to run a warm bath. He paused for a moment to inspect his face in the mirror. The tiredness added ten years to his age, the grime and sweat combining to accentuate the lines which ran down from his nose, the forehead wrinkles, the sun spokes around his eyes and the tramlines around his neck. He turned on a tap and splashed cold water on his face.

The knock on the door was so soft that at first he mistook it for another door further down the corridor. At the third attempt he took a white hand-towel from the chromium-plated rail and drying his face, went to check.

The man was an Arab, but dressed in a Westernised style

of grey slacks and white short-sleeved shirt. His face was very dark, almost brutal in appearance and he wore a black eye-patch over his right eye.

'Good evening, Mr Fitzgerald?' The voice was accentless.

'Chance Fitzgerald, yes.'

The Arab held out a hand. 'I am Rashid Suliman, Mr Fitzgerald.'

Fitzgerald ushered him into the room and closed the door. 'Take a seat, Mr Suliman.'

The Arab went to the circular table by the window, where the sound of blowing sand on glass was reminiscent of light rainfall. Fitzgerald joined him.

Suliman said, 'Everything is well with the airplane?'

'No problems . . . yet.'

'Yet?'

Fitzgerald explained his meeting with Michel Sigel from the Red Cross and how the weather could keep them grounded.

Suliman's face became stern. 'Weather or not, Mr Fitzgerald, the flight must leave Khartoum at 1640 hours on Thursday the 27th. This Thursday. That time, as I'm sure you know, corresponds with 1540 hours in Milan.'

'Any particular reason? What if the weather picks up before then?'

The Arab's face remained impassive. 'There are many reasons. Not least of which, I have arranged with our bank in Milan to pay out the money at that time. You, of course, will be there to collect it on behalf of Mr von Klaus.' He scratched the socket beneath the eye patch and continued. 'Then there is Chah Bahar. How long is the flight from here?'

'Round about eleven hours.'

'Good, that puts the aircraft's arrival time after midnight, as I thought it might be. The defences in the Chah Bahar sector have been warned, you understand. They will be expecting the plane. However it is imperative that the captain use the call-sign "Qadr One". This way he will not be shot down.'

'Qadr?'

'From the Koran. The night of Qadr . . . of Glory.'

'Ah yes, appropriate. And you have a frequency for the radio at Chah Bahar?'

Suliman took a neatly folded piece of paper from his pocket. 'It is all there, including details of the ship which will transport the crew to a point near Djibouti.'

Fitzgerald took it and ran across the closely typed details. 'Good, very good.' He stretched in his chair and suppressed a yawn. 'You'll be wanting to look at the machine I take it?'

'Yes, perhaps tomorrow if that is convenient.'

Fitzgerald thought for a moment. 'I'll be out at the airport from about ten in the morning. However, the Red Cross will be there as well.'

Suliman stood up. 'That is not a problem, Mr Fitzgerald. I will be inconspicuous. One of many Arabs intrigued by the arrival of the new aircraft.'

When the Arab had gone Fitzgerald started unpacking. A cold man, and that was for sure, he thought. Cold and precise. Like a German. Like Otto von Klaus. It had been as though he was reading from a carefully prepared script. And Arabs didn't do that. Arabs talked about anything and everything for a long time before they even reached the heart of the matter. He pushed the nagging thoughts from his mind and picked up the telephone. He would try once again to contact Konrad Zwicky in Geneva. After that he would call Lisa.

Rashid Suliman was smiling as he returned to his room on the second floor. It had been a successful day. Almost too successful. And after the hard work come the many pleasures, he thought, entering his room. Ali Abdul had been good to his word. The note had said: 'Perhaps they are better in pairs!'

He looked now at the two young girls. Tall with closely cropped hair and forehead scars. Skin as black as the night and glistening with fragrant oil. They were dressed only in prettily coloured beads and copper coils on ankles and wrists, and each had a large star-shaped scar around her navel — the result of some tribal adolescent beauty ceremony. They smiled, showing brilliant white teeth, then moved forward and with practised hands began to undress the Iranian.

247

* * *

In Geneva it was a clear and crisp night. There was no wind
and the snow, caught in hedges and trees and lying evenly
on rooftops, glistened in the moonlight. Konrad Zwicky
moved slowly towards the back of the house, the only
sound the creaking of his footsteps in the frozen snow. He
had arrived twenty minutes earlier to watch the house for
movement expecting a long cold vigil until the lights finally
went out and the occupant went to bed. As it happened the
occupant, Otto van Klaus had walked out of the house with
a woman minutes earlier. They had climbed into a silver-
coloured Mercedes and driven off in the direction of the
town. Now, following a quick check at the front of the
building from which he had deduced there were no burglar
alarms, he was going around the back to force an entry.

A number of factors had eventually overcome his
lassitude, not least of which was the forty-five thousand
Swiss francs Fitzgerald owed him. As there had been no
reply from the London number he had only one other
course of action. To try and find out when Fitzgerald would
be in Milan. As Fitzgerald was working with von Klaus it
seemed logical to assume he would find some clue at the
German's house.

The entry was made through the kitchen window. Willy
Storck had told him about that. People always open them
for ventilation when they are cooking, he had said, usually
forgetting to close them afterwards. Otto van Klaus, it
seemed, was no different. A top window was open in
welcome.

From the comfortable warmth of the kitchen Zwicky,
with the aid of a pencil flashlight, moved through into a
corridor. The first door led to a poorly furnished sitting-
room. He moved stealthily across to a sideboard and
checked the drawers. They were empty. He picked up the
whisky bottle on a drinks tray on the top of the sideboard,
found a glass, and poured himself a drink. The fiery liquid
revived his flagging spirits and he continued looking
around the room. There seemed nothing of importance –
not even a television, he noticed.

He moved back to the corridor and went to the next

room. The thin beam of light swept quickly around the walls. Completely empty . . . then the beam stopped on the solitary writing bureau against the wall on the left side of the room. There was also a chair. On the floor, numerous office files were piled high in neat columns. He went over to the desk, put down his glass and settled into the worn leather seat. Working his way systematically through the drawers at either side of the knee hole, he found accounts, legal papers, title deeds to the house, and sheets of inventories clipped together. That was all. He checked the top of the desk as an afterthought. There was a circular leather-bound container full of pens, a number of letters from local trades people – most of which were unpaid bills, and a pocket diary. He picked it up and started from the back. It was a habit of his. In the same way he always read newspapers from the back to the front. As it transpired, it was a lucky habit. He found what he was looking for almost straightaway.

The information was written in a small neat hand. 'Chance Fitzgerald. Palace Hotel – Milano. Single room. Two nights 26/27 November – confirmed. Address: Piazza della Repubblica 20, Milano.'

He turned another two pages and came to the name Rashid Suliman. Against the name was the wording: 'Commission – Two million US dollars.'

Konrad let out a low whistle. Two million dollars! Jesus and here was he thinking that forty-five thousand francs was a big payday. He read on down the page. 'Suliman – has arranged disposal of aircraft in Khartoum. Plastic explosive. Very clever idea.'

Konrad felt his pulse began to race. Disposal of aircraft! Plastic explosive! What was this? Then the next line: 'Suliman – to Milano. To dispose of Fitzgerald.'

He put the diary down, unable to comprehend what he was reading. It seemed that disposal of the aircraft meant using explosives. So what of Mr Fitzgerald? What did that mean? Kill! Whatever it was he must get to Milan. To the Palace Hotel. Perhaps the information was worth money. He picked the diary up and flicked through a few more pages, stopping inadvertently on Wednesday 1 October. His eyes had just picked out his sister's name with the notation '9 p.m.' written alongside, when the telephone by his left elbow rang. He leapt with surprise, knocking the glass of whisky from the top of the desk.

He reached out to the phone, willing it to stop. It rang again. And again. Afraid of the noise, he rushed from the room. It was only when he had reached the front door and was about to let himself out that he remembered the whisky glass. He ran back into the room, wiped some of the spilt whisky from the desk top with his jacket sleeve, picked up the glass from the carpet and bolted. The phone was still ringing as he hurried down the snow-covered drive. Only then did he realise he was still carrying the whisky glass. He swore and threw it into the bushes.

24 November

Khartoum, Sudan
MONDAY 0700 HOURS

FROM GUY STANTON'S bedroom window the early daylight limned the edges of distant buildings. He watched for a time. Through the night he had listened to snatches of Arab music caught on the wind, imagining the men who would listen to such sounds. Dark faces, half concealed under corded headclothes. Black Bedouin robes thrown back to expose a cartridge belt, a pistol, a sheathed curved dagger. He had lost a crew to those sort of people. Watched a barbaric torture of hands being thrust into white hot coals; heard the pitiful screams; smelled the roasting human flesh. A secondary air-strike had saved him. Given him the time to escape, to run for the helicopter gun-ship which was coming in for survivors. He had been lying on the floor of the Huey feeling the wind and clatter come in through the open doors. Against the burgeoning glare of white sun he had caught a last glimpse of the burned-out shell of the Hercules. Fat Albert, as his young American co-pilot had called it.

Then they were running down the wadi at zero feet, the Huey's waist gunners strafing the entire area. Against the stench of cordite Stanton could still smell the burning flesh. It had been his last war. There had been no frustrated hatred and desire for revenge when it was all over. Just a promise to himself that he would never go back. Never, never, never.

* * *

The coffee shop was hot and dusty. The air-conditioning system had failed. Even so, Fitzgerald found a smile. Past Suez you expected it. That was the secret. Never get rattled by the Inshallah bukra and malesh philosophy — Tomorrow God willing and never mind was the code of fatalism by which the Arab lived and died.

He was drinking his coffee and considering when he would next attempt to contact Lisa and Konrad, when Michel Sigel arrived.

'Nice of you to invite me round for breakfast,' he said in that broken French-English way.

'Not too early for you, I hope.'

Michel shrugged his shoulders. 'No, it is as you said earlier on the telephone. The world starts with the light . . . not like Europe, I think.'

'Not quite, Michel. A million miles removed in fact.'

'Ah, so you have also noticed.'

They laughed. Fitzgerald studied the man. Curly black hair, streaked with grey. A pleasant lived-in face. Thick horn-rimmed glasses which framed peaceful grey eyes and faded khaki trousers and bush shirt. He felt sorry he was using the man for anything but the right reasons.

'So how long have you been in the Sudan?' he asked.

'A lot of years. Sometimes I go back to Paris for six months, but then I somehow miss the . . . how you say . . . primitiveness . . . and I come running back. And always it seems the wheel turns a full circle and the people are once again in need of food . . . I think sometimes they are like children. Unable to care for themselves.'

'And you believe this is the way to help them?'

'No, this is no more than how you say, plugging a hole in a guilty conscience. You understand what I mean?'

Fitzgerald nodded. 'And the real answer?'

Michel paused in that French way to give effect to his answer. 'A thousand years,' he said resignedly. 'Evolution. The same way that we learned; with gradual slowness . . . How do you make a Dinka farmer understand the modern concept of agriculture? How do you give him the computer and expect him to understand? I am afraid there is no answer, Chance, my friend. Some people say education;

but by the time we have covered a thousand years of teaching and brought these people to the present day, where are we? I tell you where we are. We are five thousand years away. What you see in these lands is what you will always see. The pages of our very own past.'

'So why do it? Why give your life to a cause which is futile?'

'It is all I know, plugging the holes. Some men are engineers, some like you are pilots. I, I am a man who plugs the holes in third worlds.'

Fitzgerald swilled the coffee around his cup. 'Speaking of plugging holes, which areas will my crew be operating in?'

'To the south-east at first. There is a new wave of Ethiopians coming in . . . the Soviet-backed regime in their country you understand.'

'And rebels? I heard there was some trouble in the south. Marxist element taking pot-shots at aircraft.'

Sigel took a cigarette from a half-empty packet and lit it with a battered Zippo. 'There has been nothing heard recently I think. But that may be because they have no more of the missiles.'

Fitzgerald lifted his eyes to the ceiling. Missiles. That was all they needed. The perfect undercover arms deal shot down by a bloody terrorist missile. 'Any radar cover here or down at Juba?'

Sigel laughed. 'The telephones work if there is an R in the month they say. There are power black-outs every other day on average and the Kawahlas — five hundred kilometres west of here — move north and south with the sparse rains, breeding their camels as they have always done. Radar? . . . No, I think they have more important things to worry over first. Although I understand your thinking. If we give our help freely we should be afforded a certain amount of protection.'

A waiter appeared then and they ordered eggs and toast and fresh coffee. Beyond the window the sand was lifting in a thick choking fog.

'One matter,' Michel said. 'Is it possible for me to ride in the Hercules? I have never done so before.'

'Sure it is,' Fitzgerald replied, 'although Captain Stanton

does like the first run to be crew only; sort of a shake-down flight. But once he's satisfied as to the safety of the operation he'll probably offer you a permanent slot as loadmaster.'

'But what of you? You will be flying also?'

'Not straightaway. I have to go back to Europe on business.'

'Ah, I see. But you will be back?'

Suddenly Fitzgerald felt physically sick. Tired of the lie which had somehow become his life. 'Sure I will, Michel . . . and what would ever keep me away.'

In Geneva, Lisa Wendell-Holmes had finally summoned up the courage to go to the airport. She should have checked before, of course. The previous Friday when she had arrived from London. But then she had been too hurt and confused to think clearly. Now, with a feeling of time running out, she was standing amidst the early morning bustle of arriving and departing passengers. She felt nervous. She had been raised in a very proper English way where crime was something you read about or watched at the local cinema. Now she was fighting her conscience. She fingered the key in her pocket and moved slowly down the main concourse of the terminal, telling herself to be strong.

The plan had arisen the previous month when Otto had telephoned her at the office saying he had fallen and hurt his arm and as he would be staying at home that day to rest, requested that she drove out to the house to clear some urgent paperwork. She had been shocked by his deathly grey appearance and packed him off to bed with a warm drink and a sleeping tablet. He had fallen asleep immediately. As she was leaving the room he started talking, the incoherent sentences gradually taking shape.

She already knew that Otto visited a prostitute in the Grande Rue every Wednesday night. Checking if he really had stabbed a man to death outside the woman's house was almost too bizarre to contemplate. It was however a chance to free herself from her Scrooge-like employer, to become independent for the rest of her life. The first blackmail letter had been written that night. Following that, there had been the seemingly insurmountable problem of engineering the collection of the money. She had finally thought it out on the flight to London to meet with Chance Fitzgerald. The airport left-luggage locker was a brilliant idea. What was even more brilliant was the posting of the second letter. A clever way to avoid suspicion. It had been the day she had taken Chance Fitzgerald to Heathrow airport to catch his flight to Jersey. She had watched him depart and had immediately caught a flight to Geneva. There she had rented a left-luggage locker, had a spare key cut, and posted the original with the demand for payment. Following that she had returned to London.

Now she was looking around nervously. The feeling of being watched was very strong. Would Otto have put a private detective on duty to watch for the pick-up? She moved into the row of lockers, taking the key from her pocket. Her hands were shaking as she slipped the key into the lock and pulled the door open. Surprise quickly changed to disappointment. The locker was empty. Even so she reached into the darkness, fingers probing the furthest corners. Nothing. Not a single penny. Disappointment washed over her as she pushed the door closed and walked away.

Leaving the airport, she attempted to console herself by thinking that Otto's ramblings had been nothing more than a bad dream. The dried blood on his clothes, however, had seemed to indicate otherwise. She climbed into her car and gripped the steering wheel with both hands. It didn't matter, she told herself. She would find another way to secure the financial independence she needed.

Rashid Suliman, dressed in a dirty white jellabah, pulled a dusty-smelling black robe over his strong shoulders and put the headcloth over his tangled hair. Satisfied with the transformation, he left the empty suq and made his way towards the airport. It was a long walk and his sandalled feet offered little protection against the sharp stones which littered the unmade path. It was unimportant, however. He was enjoying it. His last moments as an Arab. His last few days in the garb of the desert. He had even removed the eyepatch and walked with the aid of a twisted staff. He fancied he had taken on the appearance of a half-blind beggar. But for any man witnessing him appear out of the blowing sand, it would not be so. The one eye, as black as polished obsidian and the brutal ugly scar which had been the other, joined with the hooked nose and compressed lips to give a picture of cruelty. The face of Malek himself. One of the keepers of Hell journeying sure-footedly towards the unbelievers who would die at his hands.

Was it not just, he told himself. The cloistered Arab way had been his life for many years and had he not been devout in his faith? By the heaven with its starry highways, did he not deserve some of the spoils of his war? He walked on with a measured pace and was soon swallowed up by the swirling dust.

He arrived at the airport forty minutes later and slipped unnoticed past a sleepy-eyed guard. His sandals dragged over the sanded concrete, a rasping sound, lost in the urgent hiss of the warm desert wind. And then he saw it. The Hercules, the black shape growing in detail with every stride. The ramp was down and he stood and watched for a while as figures moved back and forth, assembling a large amount of loads on pallets near the aircraft. His eye finally found the man he sought. Fitzgerald. The man with the golden hair of the sun and the eyes the colour of the sky. He did not like the man, not so much for his white skin and unbelieving ways, more for what he was. A mercenary. A man who killed for money. A man who would indiscriminately bomb towns and villages, pillage and murder for a purse of gold. A man with no interest in political ideals. No belief in the cause for which he fought. He did, however, have the countenance of a professional soldier. It was that one isolated fact which put Rashid Suliman on his guard. Killing him might not be as easy as he had first imagined.

He emptied his mind and moved towards the Hercules. He was wearing the smile of the half-blind beggar again as Fitzgerald greeted him and ushered him into the dark confines of the cargo hold. For the Arab, the conducted tour would prove useful in the planned placing of the gelignite.

26 November

Khartoum, Sudan

WEDNESDAY 1700 HOURS

AGAINST THE LOW sun the crumbling pyramids lay black and silent in the evening light. Rashid Suliman stood in the lee of one of the ravaged monuments which covered the burial sites of kings and idly watched the sand swirling around the ruins of Merue.

He had arrived an hour earlier than Ali Abdul had suggested for no other reason than mistrust. Why this one and a half hour drive to the east of the city; to the former capital of the Kingdom of Kush? Ali Abdul had sounded sympathetic over the telephone. His contact, he had said, was a very frightened man. Afraid to enter the city with a sack of stolen explosives.

It was a threadbare excuse, but Suliman had had no option but to accept the merchant's terms. Now, dressed in his foul-smelling beggar's clothing, he waited. Waited and watched over the desolation which two thousand years earlier had been alive with bustling activity: plenipotentiary kings holding court, subjects gathering at the temple, a multitude of workers shaping the pyramids and scholars carving their history into stone tablets in the ancient and still untranslated Meroitic language.

His eye traversed the barren landscape, squinting as it passed the red disc of sun which was low on the horizon, while a light cooling wind dried the sweat on his body. He moved slowly away then, up the line of broken pyramids. The yellow sand, shaded pink in the setting sun, drifted in

257

gentle ridges between the scattering of rocks and boulders. His soldier's instinct was looking for something. He did not trust the merchant.

To the west of the pyramids the ground dropped away, sloping towards the distant outline of crooked palms and tamarisk which fringed the Nile. No village though. No Bedouin. No flickering pinpoints of camp fires. He went back to the place where he had been waiting earlier. This gave him the best view of the dirt road.

The white Toyota pick-up truck he had stolen from the airport stood no more than a hundred yards away. Of course he would not be able to return with it to Khartoum. That might prove dangerous. The weather had improved greatly with the passing of the afternoon and therefore he could be too easily spotted by a vigilant policeman. As it was, at the time he had taken the light truck, the lifted sand had provided an effective smokescreen into which he had escaped unnoticed. So it was that his fortunes continued forward. His visit to the airport had been nothing more than to witness the safe departure of the man Fitzgerald on the flight to Cairo and onwards to Italy. To Milan. With this done, he had waited patiently for the right opportunity to steal a car. It had taken many hours before the young Sudanese had stopped his pick-up truck near the main terminal and unloaded a heavy box from the back. The driver's door had been open, and the engine was still running. It was too easy. And now the good weather meant there could be no possible delay of the Hercules flight on the following day.

It was shortly after six when he saw the raised dust in the fading twilight. It was like the dust smoke of many Bedouins ghosting their way across a desert in search of water. He watched carefully, his eye unblinking, as the dust mingled with the racing noise of a car engine. The sound grew louder as the vehicle breasted a slight rise in the road. A saloon, white in colour. The only choice for the burning desert. There was a grating of gears as it slowed to a halt near the parked Toyota. Suliman stepped back against the side of the pyramid. The stone was still hot from the day.

Ali Abdul was alone. He came slowly from his car, his head moving nervously from side to side.

'Rashid,' he called softly.

Suliman remained silent. Still. The small Arab slowed his pace even more. He called again and this time Suliman replied.

'You are late, Ali Abdul.'

The merchant jumped with surprise, his eyes searching the gathering darkness. 'You are there, Rashid?'

'I am here, Ali Abdul.' He moved out from the pyramid.

Ali Abdul's face smiled with relief. 'You have been waiting long?'

'Not long . . . and how was your journey?'

'The road is not very good. The sand drifts across it and makes it difficult to find. Also I worry about robbers when the sun is going down.'

'And what of the gelignite, Ali Abdul? I mention it so quickly because I have a great deal of work before me on this night.'

The merchant lifted a calming hand. 'I have it; there is no problem. But first we must discuss the price. My contact had to run many risks, in fact he still does. He can still be found out. Therefore, as you will understand, his price is very high.'

Suliman studied the other man's face. He was an expert on faces. Had become so as a soldier. He could read fear and sorrow, and cowardice, and most easily of all, deceit. 'How high?' he questioned.

Ali Abdul said, 'Five thousand American dollars.'

'And there is also a detonator and a timer?'

'As you requested.'

'And the gun I asked for?'

'A Walther PPK with a white pearl inlaid handle. A very pretty gun . . . it is in my car.'

'And the asking price is five thousand dollars, this is so?'

Ali Abdul favoured Suliman with a crafty smile. 'Not exactly, Rashid. That price is what my friend requires for his part in this business transaction. I must also add some commission you understand.'

'And what is your price?'

'My price!' The merchant mulled it over in his mind. 'Shall we say a hundred thousand dollars?'

Suliman broke into laughter. 'A hundred thousand dollars . . . a hundred thousand! That is ridiculous. Where would I, a poor soldier of Islam, find such wealth?'

'I think easily, Rashid. In the same way I think your bomb is for the airplane which has just arrived from America.'

Suliman's laughter stopped and his face tightened. What words were these? What was he hearing? 'It seems, Ali Abdul, that you do a great deal of thinking . . . also perhaps that you attach too high a price to these thoughts.'

'Perhaps. But in this instance it is very difficult for me to lower the price.'

'Why so, when what you ask is so unreasonable?'

'Unreasonable? No, my friend, it is not that. You see, I know a man who will pay me that exact sum to find out what you are doing. A hundred thousand dollars if I mention that you are seeking to buy explosives to perhaps blow up an American airplane.'

Suliman's fists clenched at his sides. Guesswork! Bluff! He didn't know. What he did know, however, was the feeling of tension rising within his body. The same tension he had felt in the war zone under fire. The anger in his heart when one of his brothers had been blown limb from limb. He took a step forward. Ali Abdul's frail body tensed.

'And who would this man be? The man who offered so much.'

'One of your people . . . from Iran.'

Concern joined the other emotions which Suliman was experiencing. 'And his name?'

The merchant seemed uncertain. The dark figure before him was suddenly menacing. His right hand slipped unnoticed inside his cloak and gripped the pearl handle of the Walther. 'Fazlollah Mahallati,' he said with all the calmness he could muster.

Suliman's fists unclenched. So, Fazlollah had come this far. Tracked him almost to the final scene. A world away and yet he stood poised to steal the plunder. To wreck his plans of a new life in a new world.

The sudden movement surprised Rashid Suliman as much as it did Ali Abdul, for Suliman was no longer thinking rationally. A violent anger suffused his mind and body, galvanising him into action. Ali Abdul was no longer an enterprising merchant of Khartoum, but an extension of an enemy. An enemy who was seeking to destroy him. Ali Abdul let out a cry. A shrill, furious scream of anguish, as Suliman fell upon him. The Walther was in his hand for a fleeting second, no more. Suliman, after all, was the professional soldier, a trained killer of men. It was an occupation which was hard to forget. Something which had been forged into every fibre of his being. A training which, even after months of lying dormant, rushed expertly back to his willing hands.

'A grave mistake, my friend. My missing eye is the result of what an Iraqi did. That he failed to kill me was his greatest mistake because I then took a knife and chopped his heart out. Not that I stopped there . . . It cost the Iraqi dogs another hundred hearts. And it only stopped because I was recalled to Tehran. There it was decided I was too unfit to fight any more.' He pressed the barrel of the gun hard into Ali Abdul's neck. 'But you wouldn't say I was unfit would you?'

Ali Abdul was shaking, his breath coming in dry little gasps. 'A mistake, my friend. Forgive a foolish old man for his greed.'

Suliman eased the gun away from his neck. 'All things are possible, Ali Abdul. Did not Allah himself say so?' The merchant nodded furiously, although he could not remember exactly where in the Koran such words were written. 'So,' Suliman continued in a slightly less menacing voice, 'perhaps you will show me the gelignite.'

'In . . . in the car,' Ali Abdul stammered.

'The car! But you told me it was being delivered out here . . . at the old Kingdom of Kush.'

'I did, I know this. But the fool I was dealing with then changed his mind and brought it to my house this very afternoon . . . He needed the money.'

'Ah, the money,' Suliman said, following Ali Abdul across the rocky outcrop. 'And how much was that figure again?'

Ali Abdul made a small laughing sound. 'The price was a mere five hundred dollars.'

'But you said five thousand.'

'A mistake, my friend . . . a foolish slip of the tongue.'

'And the gelignite is new and clean?'

'It is the best,' the merchant said, eager to please. 'The best. Perhaps in the light of this unfortunate happening we should come to a new price. A fairer price.' He opened the door of his car.

'No sudden moves. Remember these hands have slain many men . . . one more is of little consequence.'

Ali Abdul, sweating with fear, withdrew the canvas bag very carefully from the passenger seat.

'On the ground,' Suliman ordered. 'Lay the bag on the ground and move away.' Ali Abdul did as he was bid.

Suliman quickly checked the contents in the dying light. Everything seemed in order. 'So,' he said at last, 'a fairer price. And what do you consider that to be?'

Ali Abdul, hands clasped before him, said, 'Shall we say nothing more than the five hundred dollars which I have to pay.'

'And what of your commission?'

'It is not important. Shall we say this is a favour for an old friend.'

'And what of Fazlollah Mahallati?'

'Pardon, I do not understand.'

'What is to stop you selling the information you now have. A hundred thousand dollars is, after all, a great deal of money.'

Ali Abdul stood rooted to the spot. A tight griping had seized his stomach muscles. 'My word,' he offered. 'You have my word.' His bowels moved; he needed to go to the toilet quickly.

Suliman brought the gun up to the aim; once more the soldier, the man with the training. During aiming process, marksman to hold his breath, thereby keeping torso and aiming hand steady. Trigger control in the fast rise method . . . first pressure on the rise . . . when pistol comes to a halt on target final pressure is applied.

Ali Abdul let out a strangled cry, twisting his body away

from the fast-rising gun. The Walther cracked, yellow flame tonguing from the barrel. The Arab's head jerked convulsively back and he fell to the ground. Suliman lifted the smoking barrel to his nose and sniffed. It was good. Pleasing. Something men of peace would not understand. He moved forward slowly, hearing the dreadful bubbling sound. He had been too high with his aim. The bullet, obviously soft nosed and extremely destructive, had removed the Arab's lower jaw. The black eyes, wild and pleading looked up at him. He spat and looked with fascination at the teeth of the upper jaw. Dark with blood, they hung like tiny daggers over the pulsating mess of flesh. The exposed windpipe gurgled a few moments longer, then the eyes rolled and fixed themselves on a distant heavenly star. Suliman reached down and touched the warm deformation of face.

'That, Ali Abdul Rashaida, merchant of Khartoum . . . that is a much fairer price.'

He lifted the body easily across the broad shoulders and picked his way through the boulder-strewn sand towards the river. Minutes later, the sound of water gurgling in the reeds, greeted him. He stumbled through a thick clump of trees, pausing to lean against the trunk of a small tamarisk. His laboured breathing gradually eased, then, inching carefully forward he pitched the body into the Nile. Clawing his way back through the tangle of branches he set off towards Ali Abdul's car. There was no reason to hurry, to take up the measured double time of the soldier but he did so all the same. There was always the chance that the single gunshot had been heard. He looked quickly up at the starry sky scoured of clouds by a wind which was now dying into a desert stillness. Another mistake, Fazlollah. Another foolish mistake. You were never a soldier, my friend. And that has been your loss. Hunting and killing men is more than just an idea and a few well-phrased words. Much, much more.

The canvas bag was still lying by the side of the car. He picked it up and tossed it across to the passenger seat. He was about to start the engine when curiosity made him double-check the contents. It was a mistake in one way. In another, it was a blessing from Allah himself. The gelignite was old. Unstable. Sweating with nitro. His hands were shaking as he laid it gently on the seat. His hand went back into the sack with as much trepidation as a man seeking truth in a nest of serpents. His fingers located two pencil-slim detonators. About an inch long. He lifted them out one at a time. The sweat was streaming from his face when he inspected the first one in the dim glow of the car's interior light. It was also old, something which should have been condemned a long time ago. Crystals had formed on the outside of the metal case. Rub those away and two or three fingers would go with it.

He moved his body and the detonator slipped betwen his fingers. His ugly face froze in fear as the sliver of metal bounced on the passenger seat and came to rest next to the sticks of gelignite. It was a long while before he removed the second detonator and all the while his tongue was running nervously over his dry, cracked lips. He sat for a moment eyeing the dangerous cargo. One sharp or sudden movement and the lot could explode.

He stepped gently out of the car. It was more than an hour's fast drive to Khartoum. With unstable explosives as his passenger, it could take all night. When he finally reached the city, he had to assemble the timing device and go to the airport to plant the bomb on the Hercules. Then there was the telex message to the bank in Milan and the last minute meeting with Captain Stanton, the meeting in which he would regretfully say he could not accompany them after all due to urgent business meetings in Europe. The workload was piling up and he was running out of time.

He climbed cautiously back into the car and arranged the gelignite and the detonators so that they could not roll around on the seat then with sweaty fingers turned the ignition key. The dirt road before him, pitted with holes and strewn with rocks was now a minefield. With one difference. He was carrying the mine.

Suddenly, he was terribly thirsty. The back of his throat parched. He opened the window as far as it would go and pushed his head out; sucking in the cooling breeze generated by the car's slow forward movement. It was whilst his eye was off the road that a wheel struck a rock. The car jolted. He let out a strangled cry, at the same time feeling fear squeeze tightly at his bowels. Bringing his head back into the car, he fixed his eye on the swathe of road cut by the yellow headlights.

And so he moved on into the night like the blind beggar. One step. Another. And another. His body ached, but he did not hesitate. The infinity of darkness and the unstable gelignite were but one more burden to be endured. He smiled and took comfort from the Koran. For there it was written: 'Every hardship is followed by ease.'

Konrad Zwicky had been in Milan since early morning. He had checked in at a cheap hotel on the Via Santo Spirito, from where he had telephoned the Palace Hotel, leaving an urgent message for Mr Fitzgerald to contact him on his arrival. It was six-thirty in the evening when Konrad's nerve finally gave out. He stubbed a half-smoked cigarette into an overflowing ashtray. He was going to the Piazza della Repubblica. To the Palace Hotel.

The snow, like elsewhere in that part of Europe, was early that year. It was falling heavily as, head down, he hurried across the Piazza Cavour and into the Via Manin. On his right, the trees of the Giardini Pubblici were drained of colour, black skeletons on a white desert. He glanced past the iron railings, remembering a similar park in Zurich. When he was a boy he had played there with his sister. The winter had always been the best time. Snowball fights, tobogganning, building the big snowmen. The thought that he would never again see her again brought on a fresh emptiness, a feeling of desolation. The hiatus in his mind suddenly pitched him back to another snow-covered scene. The grounds of Otto von Klaus's house in Geneva and the shrill ringing of the telephone which had driven him from the desk in the tall empty room. The last thing his eyes had focused on had been a diary with his sister's name. His sister's name! Marie. The same way she had written it on her suicide note. But as Konrad knew, his sister had always used her full name – Mariella. Always.

Coincidence! His vivid imagination playing tricks! Or had von Klaus somehow been responsible for her death?

One kilometre away in the sumptuous lobby of the Palace Hotel, Chance Fitzgerald had just completed filling in the hotel's registration form, when the desk clerk hurried across to him.

'*Scusi, Signor Fitzgerald?*'

'*Si.*'

'*Telefono, signor,*' he indicated with his hand towards a row of house phones. '*Numero quattro.*'

'*Grazie.*'

'*Prego.*'

Fitzgerald went over to the phone. 'Hello, Chance Fitzgerald.'

'Chance, Lisa.'

His spirits lifted immediately. 'Hello, my lovely girl, and if that isn't the most beautiful voice I've heard all day . . . where are you?'

'In Milan.'

He didn't understand. 'When will you be here?'

'That's why I'm calling, Chance . . . I won't.'

'Won't! Why? What's happening?'

Lisa was silent for a second or two. 'It's all over. I . . . I've decided not to get involved.'

He heard the words, but he didn't believe them. 'You must forgive a simple Irishman, my lovely girl, but I still don't follow. I'm feeling the effects of Sudan tummy, ringing in the ears and Alitalia's plastic food . . . couldn't we perhaps meet and talk about things?'

The harshness had left her voice when she said, 'Please don't say any more, Chance, it's hard enough. Just believe that I'm very sorry it's turned out this way.'

'Is there someone else . . . is that what you're trying to say?'

'No, of course not.'

'So why can't we talk?'

'It wouldn't help,' she said in a small voice. 'It really wouldn't do any good.'

He listened to her with a sinking heart. He realised he

266

had never told her he loved her. He felt it, but could somehow never say it. A mental block from a hundred years ago? Or what seemed like a hundred years. He didn't know, and that was the truth of it. And there was no way he could explain.

'Are you still there, Chance?'

'Can't get rid of me that easily.'

'You have the details for the bank and the afternoon banking hours?'

'Yes. I – '

'I'll meet you there at three thirty-five. Ten minutes before they close.'

'Lisa.'

'Yes.'

'I'd still like to know the reason.'

'Perhaps after tomorrow we can talk. Not now.'

Sensing the line was about to go dead, he said quickly, 'Where are you staying?'

There was hesitation, as though she wanted to tell him.

'I'll see you tomorrow, Chance . . . I'm sorry.'

He replaced the receiver, but didn't move. His eyes were fixed on the wall. All he could think was that it was a lie. She didn't mean what she had said. Couldn't. Perhaps she was in trouble! Perhaps someone was on to the deal! His imagination ran riot for a moment, picturing the shadowy figures of CIA agents who had been discreetly following every step of the operation. Now they could be holding her, waiting for the payout on the following day. Then they would seize him and the money, and everybody else involved. And what of the plane and the crew?

He rushed back to the desk and asked for a list of hotels in the city. The clerk gave him a booklet entitled *Un Ospite di Milano* – a guest in Milan. Opening it to the two pages of hotel listings, Fitzgerald looked with dismay. There had to be close on a hundred hotels, assuming, of course, she was staying in a hotel. And where did he start? Asking the clerk to take care of his luggage he went out through the revolving doors. The umbrella-carrying porter escorted him to a waiting taxi. It was driving slowly down the access road which runs from the hotel into the Piazza della

267

Repubblica as the figure of Konrad Zwicky, collar turned up against the falling snow, hurried past into the hotel.

In the bar of the Khartoum Hilton Guy Stanton was getting drunk. He had left the airport with the rest of the crew an hour earlier, having discussed the following day's 'food drop' with Michel Sigel of the Red Cross.

Feigning a return of his upset stomach he had put Hiram in charge and sat back in the hot dusty room, only half-listening to the loading details and route the Hercules would take to the Ethiopian border DZ.

Now, with Hiram and Pedro showering off the dust and sweat of the day before dinner, he had come straight to the bar. It was a vain attempt to silence the memories which sought to destroy him. He picked up the tumbler of whisky with shaking hands and forced it to his mouth. Some of it spilt and dribbled down his chin. He wiped it away quickly with the back of his hand, aware of the eyes of the pre-dinner drinkers upon him.

He looked across at the barman who was expertly working a cocktail shaker. He had spoken to the man a short while earlier, before the rush had started, and found out he was from Belgium. Working a one-year contract to make a little extra money. He stared glassily into the bottom of his whisky and reflected that things had to be bloody bad when you started to envy a Belgique barman. He finished the drink, spilling an equal amount to what passed his lips, and took a cigarette from a battered packet and lit it. He would have preferred a half corona but they were up in his room. And he didn't want to go there. The laid-out valise and flight bag would only remind him how close tomorrow was.

He shuddered. No, what he wanted was some hard drinking time. And this bar was becoming too noisy for comfort. It was time to move on. Weaving his way through the growing crowd he went out on to the hotel steps. The night was warm and cloudless. The smells belonged to any African town: dust and car exhausts and whenever a black was close, stale rancorous body odour.

He braced himself. It was a long way from the playing

fields of Eton. A long way from the room with the fold-down iron bed, where Faulkner major had sat and swapped the latest line in dirty books. A long way from the vocabulary of beaks, school dress, burrys and dames. A long way from the school chapel and those damned hymns. Even so, setting off down the street he began to sing.

'And did those feet in ancient times, walk upon England's mountains green . . . And was the holy lamb of God . . .' The quiet tuneless voice grew steadily in confidence, until a few streets further on it seemed to fill the African night.

At the same moment as old Etonian Stanton was singing his way unsteadily towards a fresh watering hole, Ali Abdul Rashaida's guard was looking at his watch. It was eight o'clock. He opened the tall metal gate and looked up the dusty stretch of road. His master had said he would return no later than this hour. No later. A furrow of concern deepened in the old man's forehead. His master had taken care of him and his family for many years now, providing them with a home and food and clothes. They had fared much better than others of the Zande tribe who had stayed in the south to farm.

Old memories filled his head. The stories his father had told him by the late-night fire. How, many years earlier the Zandes had been a highly developed military empire, one which had swept into the Sudan from the Congo basin. Once proud warriors, they were now part of a dying culture. Even the knowledge of their glorious tradition was fading. He remembered his last visit to Yambio in the far south, his pilgrimage to the tomb of King Gbudwe. It was surrounded by thick grass and vines; there was no path any more; no care for the greatest king they ever had. Like the spirit of the Zandes themselves, it was being swallowed up by the land they had once conquered and ruled.

He smiled with an old man's sadness and focused his gaze back to the graded dirt road. A battered yellow taxi rattled noisily past, pluming dust in its wake. A pie-dog ran after it, barking furiously. Across the street, high on a sand-stained building, a neon sign for Bata shoes flickered spasmodically. But still there was no sign of his master.

269

Now he was worried. He had seen the Arab from another land and sensed the aura of evil he carried with him. And that is where his master was now, conducting business with the one-eyed man. The ancient Zande warrior fingered the curved dagger at his belt. It had been many years since he had used the weapon, but his limbs were still strong and his eyes clear. And his master's instructions, on the course of action to be taken should he fail to return, were indelibly clear in his mind.

Otto von Klaus was frightened, like a landsman scared of the vast emptiness of sea. Except it was sky. Night sky. Dark. Threatening. Filled with dense snow clouds which buffeted the small airliner. He glanced nervously at his watch. Nine-fifteen p.m. They had been in the air for twenty minutes. Which meant another thirty-five minutes to Lugano. It wasn't important he told himself. The Swissair pilots up front were used to this kind of weather. They were good. The best. Even so, he secretly wished he had made the journey by road, or had at least taken an earlier flight during daylight. There was something safe about being able to see the white-capped mountains below.

A tired-eyed stewardess stopped by his seat and placed the whisky he had ordered on the small fold-down table. He looked up.

'The flight. It is on time?'

'Please?'

'We will be landing at Lugano at ten minutes to ten?'

'At twenty-one fifty, yes.' She moved on disinterestedly down the narrow aisleway.

Von Klaus sipped at the whisky and tried to concentrate his mind on the Lake Maggiore business. There was solace there, it seemed. Unknown. Unplanned. A seasonal stroke of luck. Not that it had appeared so initially.

At first it had had all the earmarks of a very difficult problem. Charter a fast boat from Locarno at the north end of the lake to Sesto Calende, at the Italian southern end. The distance, about sixty kilometres. What were the customs formalities? Did the Swiss and Italian customs officers have boats? How did you legally cross the border of water? His enquiries had led him to a telephone number of the Dogana Svizzera – the Swiss customs – at a place called Brissago. However, each call he had made remained unanswered. As for the Italian customs, his enquiries had drawn a complete blank.

The solace, the stroke of luck, had arrived in the name of Bruno Grimaldi. The name had been passed to Otto von Klaus by a crooked business acquaintance who spent a great deal of his leisure time yachting on Lac Léman, and who had many contacts in the boating world who were not averse to a bit of smuggling.

Over the telephone, the Locarno-based Grimaldi had sounded very much like the German's kind of man – easygoing, mature voice, full of innuendo. Otto's mention of his business acquaintance's name had been enough.

'Run down to Sesto and back the following day! No problem, Mr von Klaus.

'Customs? You check in at the small town of Brissago and clear southbound with the Swiss. Then you sail a few kilometres down the lake to Piaggio Valmaro and complete the Italian formalities.' Grimaldi had laughed when he added: 'Of course if you arrive between twelve and two, forget it. They enjoy their lunch you understand.'

Von Klaus had asked: 'What do you do in that situation?'

'You wait. Unless you have booked them that is. Or if you have something to hide you keep on going.'

'Booked them?'

'In the winter, Mr von Klaus. Not much traffic on the lake. You must telephone, perhaps the day before, to let them know you will be coming.'

'I see . . . and this is the only way?'

'No. I have a plane also.'

'A plane?'

'A single-engined Cessna. It is amphibious . . . I could therefore fly you from Locarno airport and put you down at the southern end of the lake . . . near Sesto.'

'What about the customs at Sesto Calende?'

Grimaldi had laughed. 'No customs, Mr von Klaus . . . what we call a scenic pleasure flight. I take you out of Locarno airport for a two-hour joyride around the Swiss

271

mountains . . . that we accidently stray south into Italy is down to my poor navigation.'

'It sounds risky . . . surely they can see you on the radar!'

'Radar does not see through mountains, Mr von Klaus. We stay low . . . as simple as that.'

'And you think this is easier than making a boat trip?'

'If you want to avoid the customs, yes. Also it is much quicker by air.'

Von Klaus had made no reply. His brain had been too busy for words. Eventually he had arranged to meet Bruno Grimaldi at Locarno airport on the Thursday morning at 10.00 a.m. They could discuss the matter more fully then.

Von Klaus finished his whisky, regretted it was not Kir Royale and looked again at his watch. Nine thirty-five. Fifteen minutes to go. He was half smiling at his apparently straightforward border crossing plans, when the airliner began its descent, jarring its way violently down the night sky. He reached for the sick bag in the seat pocket in front of him, cursing his weakness, or at least that of his stomach.

'I am a very rich and important man,' he told himself. 'Rich and important men are not sick in airplanes . . . and especially not in front of ordinary, poor people.'

His skin continued to prick hot and cold, while the taste of sickness rose in his throat. And for once, his credo that money had power over all things, failed him. His mouth went swiftly to the opening of the airsickness bag and remained there for the last minutes of the flight.

27 November

Khartoum, Sudan
THURSDAY 0307 HOURS

THE NIGHT WAS warm and airless when Rashid Suliman arrived back in Khartoum. He parked the car at the rear of the hotel and switched off the engine. He felt the energy drain from his body then and he muttered, 'Allah be praised.'

He rubbed his grimy, sweat-covered palms on the beggar's cloak in a futile effort to clean them. Vaguely, he was aware that this moment was nothing more than a brief respite from danger. He still had to construct the bomb; to carry it to the airport; to place it on the aircraft. But first his parched throat screamed out for water. He stepped from the car and was turning the key in the lock, when his sensitive nostrils picked out the smell.

It was harsh against the subtle blend of tamarind and flinty desert. Man smell. Black man. Stinking body odour, possibly caused by eating dog flesh – the result of which was an evil, lingering smell which tainted all it came into contact with. For an instant he stood there frozen. His mind was still considering the move to be made when the faint rustling footsteps and the sudden swish of air made him twist defensively to the side. Even so he was not quick enough. The heavy thud in his left shoulder felt nothing more than that at first. A stunning blow. The pain followed as he turned to face his assailant, and saw the knife plunging down for the second time. He turned his body and caught the knife arm in a typical commando move. A

273

quick, breaking action of the arm across his knee and the glinting weapon fell uselessly to the ground.

Fingers clawed at his throat. They were bony and strong. Very strong. Suliman struggled as they clamped around his windpipe. The excruciating pain in his shoulder; the tightening leaden hurt in his lungs, the dizziness . . . all were overcoming him. He summoned the last of his failing strength and delivered a stunning punch to the man's sternum. Given more freedom of movement, he would have fractured the rib cage. As it was, it proved enough to make the hands drop from his throat. That was all Suliman needed. He broke free, his right hand reaching down and scrabbling in the dirt.

Finding the knife, the unblinking eye locked in crazed fascination on his prey, he moved quickly forward. In desperation the old Zande warrior threw himself at the Arab, hands outstretched, reaching once again for the throat. The knife found his heart before his grasping fingers had secured a hold. He fell silently to the ground and rolled over. His left leg kicked once in spasm, then was still.

Suliman shut his eye briefly and forced his right hand to grasp his wounded left shoulder. The pain almost made him faint, but he continued to probe, seeking the extent of his injuries. It was not as bad as he had at first imagined. Even so, it would need stitches which meant a doctor and questions. He cursed violently and set about loading the body of the African into the trunk of the car.

'A worthy servant, Ali Abdul,' he croaked. 'Perhaps better than you deserved.'

Task completed and breathing shallowly on account of the expended effort, Suliman began to shuffle slowly towards the hotel. Captain Stanton, the Hercules pilot, could help him find a doctor.

The Duomo glistened white in the early morning sunshine. The freak snowstorms which had caused havoc in Milan and other areas of northern Italy had gone. Now the snow was melting and life was returning to the normal daily bustle which befits a centre of business and high fashion. It was a few minutes before nine o'clock when Chance

Fitzgerald made his way across the crowded piazza, the gargantuan Gothic cathedral towering over him. He looked tired and old, the result of an all-night search for Lisa. A fruitless search which had ended two hours earlier in a small café on the Corso Porta Vittoria. There, he had dozed fitfully over coffee and grappa, before setting off aimlessly through the bracing morning air. That he eventually arrived at the Piazza Duomo was purely accidental. He had rounded the corner of a street and there it was. The most beautiful cathedral he had ever seen. Even so, it seemed somehow out of place. Too magical, too breathtaking for its drab surroundings. He went there now to find the peace and stillness he knew existed. In such a place he might resolve some of his problems, or at least find the strength to continue.

The interior of the Duomo was simple, majestic and vast. Five great aisles stretched from the entrance to the altar. Enormous stone pillars dominated the nave and in the apse three large and intricate stained-glass windows shed a soft half-light into the area behind the altar. He moved slowly down the left transept past the gruesome statue of the flayed St Bartholomew, carrying his skin, genuflected and sank wearily into a hard wooden pew. His eyes settled on the altar and the figure of Christ on the cross, and the red light flickering like an eye from the suspended oil lamp.

Strange, he thought, how the Catholic conscience lasted from cradle to grave, blasted away the cobwebs of sin like a clean, strong wind in a dusty attic. He sank to his knees and started to pray. 'You didn't expect to see me again, did you?' Naturally, there was no answer, but Fitzgerald persisted. 'No, of course you didn't. Figured I'd gone across to the other side . . . what was it someone once said? As the shoemaker builds shoes, and the baker makes bread, so the sinner makes special efforts to sin every day . . . and I suppose I do qualify as something more than one of your usual run-of-the-mill transgressors.'

Fitzgerald shuddered at the cold dampness of centuries which seemed to penetrate his clothing. His eyes searched the gloom, his nostrils finding the faint incense which seemed to linger within the very stone. His gaze returned to the altar. 'And I suppose you'll be asking what I'm doing in your house ... about to confess ... ask forgiveness ... how about a deal instead? A deal that gives me back the woman I love. Ah, you say, but what could you possibly offer me in return? You remember when I was a kid? Sure you do. And you remember that I was quite devoted to you ... so what did I have then that was so important? An impressive line in prayers? No, I think not. Or did I come to your church more than was necessary! Once again, no more than most. Or was it the goodness! I think we can pass on that too. No, it was the soul. The soul you wanted. That one intangible asset of man that you lay claim to at birth. Not too impressive now of course. High mileage on all the wrong roads ... but it's all I have.'

It was some time later when he deposited a few thousand lire into a padlocked box and lit what used to be called a penny candle. That one was for Alice. Not for forgiveness or understanding, but that she might find the peace and happiness which had always eluded him. He watched the candle flame for a moment. It was one of perhaps a hundred more. A hundred quiet prayers to an unearthly and untouchable God.

With no one else to pray for, Fitzgerald went back to the outside world where pigeons wheeled in flight and crowded trams criss-crossed the piazza. 'What now, old son,' he said to himself. Finding no immediate answer, he shrugged and set off in the general direction of the Palace Hotel. It was a long walk, but there seemed no other way to kill the hours until the bank appointment.

As he crossed the street towards Milan's famous Galleria, he collided with Konrad Zwicky. Both men stepped back, eyes registering shocked belief.

Fitzgerald half-laughed, 'God save us, Konrad, and what would you be doing in this sacred place of Ambrogio?'

Zwicky, who had been up all night conducting a lonely vigil at the Palace, smiled tiredly. 'Ambrogio?'

'The patron saint of Milan.'

'Ah ...' His eyes flickered, as if trying to regain a train of thought. 'I have been looking for you, Mr Fitzgerald. I waited at your hotel for you.'

'The Palace?'

'Yes . . . I left a message for you yesterday. You did not get it, I think.'

'No, I've been out all night. But how did you know I would be staying there?'

'A long story, but first I have some information for you.'

Fitzgerald looked about him. 'Let's not talk here, too public. Have you eaten this morning?'

Konrad said sheepishly, 'Not for one day now. I have no money.'

Fitzgerald put an arm around the young man's shoulder and steered him into the Galleria.

They were seated in a café and had just ordered breakfast when Fitzgerald said, 'What happened to your phone in Geneva? I tried to contact you a number of times.'

'It was cut off. The bill was not paid and before I realised this I could not reach you in London.'

'No matter. So what news do you have?'

'I broke into Mr von Klaus's house,' Konrad announced.

'You what?'

'I had to find out when you would be here in Milan, and the only way seemed to be through Mr von Klaus . . . I did not want to phone and ask him for the information, you understand, so I broke in.'

'And you found out when I'd be arriving . . . a man after my own heart.'

'I'm sorry, I do not follow.'

'Not important, go on with your story.'

'Apart from your travel details I also found . . . in a small diary . . . some notes about the Arab called Rashid Suliman.'

'You have the diary?' Fitzgerald asked eagerly.

Konrad pointed to his head. 'No, it is all here. The first part said that Rashid Suliman was to be paid a commission of two million dollars.'

'Interesting . . . go on.'

'Then it said something like, Rashid Suliman has arranged for the disposal of the aircraft in Khartoum.'

'Disposal? Are you sure that was the word . . . not delivery from Khartoum?'

'No, I am sure. Disposal.' Konrad scratched his head. 'Ah

yes, and after that it said, plastic explosive a clever idea.'

Fitzgerald stiffened, his eyes widening. 'Explosive! Plastic explosive? You're sure that's what it said?'

Zwicky nodded eagerly. 'Yes, yes. And then after that it said. Rashid Suliman travelling to Milano to dispose of you.'

'Me?'

'To dispose of Fitzgerald it said.'

In that passing second Fitzgerald's face turned ashen. He immediately sensed that things had gone as wrong as they possibly could.

At that very moment Lisa Wendell-Holmes was lying in bed in her room on the fourth floor of the Palace Hotel. It had been a simple trick. One conceived by Otto. Register under an assumed name and pay off a desk clerk to inform her the moment Chance Fitzgerald arrived. The telephone call, inferring she was staying somewhere else, would put him at a disadvantage, while she, through the same bribed desk clerk, could keep a discreet eye on his movements. Otto had been adamant over that, positive that Fitzgerald was planning to double-cross him. Lisa's convictions on the other hand had waxed and waned with the day and night. And now she was away from Otto's powerful influence she was less sure.

Her mind was once again troubled by the chain of events which led her to this place. Her affair with Chance Fitzgerald, and the gentle love making. And the day Maxine Audley had arrived at the London apartment. The day everything had begun to crumble into a confused and disquieting series of mishaps.

Presently she felt her own hands touching her thighs and belly through the thin material of her nightdress. she could almost imagine it was his hands. Strong and powerful. Gently massaging, gently touching. She flushed and sat up abruptly. It was disgusting, she thought, to let her imagination run away with her like that. No matter how much her body ached for his, that was disgusting.

She swung her legs off the bed and went over to draw the

curtains. It was a bright morning, the sky cornflower blue and cloudless. She was making her way to the bathroom, mentally planning the day before her, when the telephone rang. It was Otto.

'Where are you?' she asked.

'Locarno.'

'Locarno! In Switzerland.'

'Of course, where else?'

'But why? I thought you were remaining in Geneva.'

'A small change in the plans, Lisa. I have chartered a plane . . . a float plane. I will be arriving at Sesto Calende early tomorrow morning . . . you know of the place.'

'Yes, at the southern end of Lake Maggiore.'

'So.'

'But why? You still haven't said.'

'You have a pen?'

'Yes.'

'Good. The plan is as follows. Rashid Suliman will arrive at Milan's Linate airport at four-thirty tomorrow morning. He will be on an Alitalia flight from Rome . . . you have that?'

'Yes.'

'You will rent a car and collect him. From there you will drive to a pre-arranged place in Milan to meet up with Fitzgerald . . . I suggest the place is the hotel where you are now staying. Rashid Suliman will then stay with Fitzgerald and you will bring the money to Sesto Calende . . . the small plane I have chartered will land on the lake shortly after seven, at first light. The pilot will taxi the aircraft to the end of one of the pontoons. You will watch to see which pontoon the plane comes in to. You then bring the money, board the plane and we leave.'

'What about Chance and Rashid Suliman?'

There was a pause and a sharp intake of breath. 'Do not worry about either of them. I have found out that Fitzgerald cheated badly his last employer. Not that this is any concern of mine you understand. But I am a businessman and I cannot afford to take chances. Furthermore, I have spoken with Rashid in Khartoum; he also expresses doubts about the' – he paused, searching for the right word

– 'about the integrity of Fitzgerald. When he arrives in Milan he may have some more information. It is therefore imperative that you work closely with him. You understand this?'

'Yes, Otto, I understand. There is one problem, however. Chance will have the money from this afternoon . . . when we collect it from the bank. What happens between then and the time I collect Mr Suliman from the airport?'

'A good question, but I have already thought of that. You both check in at the Palace Hotel together and deposit the money in the hotel safe under joint names. Then when you return with Rashid you can claim it back.'

'Stay here with him . . . tonight,' Lisa said shakily. 'Otto, I would rather not . . . I don't think I could face that.'

'I am not asking you to sleep with the man,' von Klaus barked. 'Just check in together and deposit the money . . . after that you can sit in the lobby . . . you do not have to speak to him if you do not wish. This is clear?'

'Yes, Otto.'

'Good. I will see you in the morning at Sesto Calende.'

She replaced the telephone and went back to the window and the warm sunlight. Her body was trembling. Damn you, Otto von Klaus, she thought. I will not whore for you or for anybody else.

A smile spread slowly across her face as the implication of the earlier part of the conversation sank in. Leave Chance Fitzgerald with Rashid Suliman and take the money to the lake. Which meant that she would be alone with the money. All eighteen million dollars worth.

In Khartoum it was Michel Sigel's 'every second day' – the day of power black-outs. The temperature was climbing rapidly through the eighties and the air was full of fat, white-bodied flies as Rashid Suliman left the Hilton with Guy Stanton.

'I trust the arm is feeling better,' Stanton said as they settled into the back seat of the taxi.

'Fine, Captain. It is not a problem. Of course without the painkillers I think it might be a different story.' He leaned forward and instructed the driver to go very slowly. 'My arm,' he said to Stanton by way of explanation. 'The jolting could open the wound.'

Stanton nodded sympathetically, not realising that the briefcase on the Arab's lap contained enough explosive to despatch the car and its occupants across an acre of city.

'You're absolutely sure you won't be coming on the flight now?' Stanton enquired.

Suliman feigned disappointment. The injury had proved useful as an excuse for staying behind to seek further medical care. As for his story, about being attacked and robbed in the hotel car-park, that brought no further questions. No one wanted the police making enquiries. Even the doctor, a fat old Egyptian, down on his luck, had been easy to bribe. Suliman said: 'No, just my final inspection this morning. Following your departure I will telephone my superiors and give them an estimated time of arrival in Chah Bahar.'

'Provided that the phones are working. The hotel manager seemed to think the power would be off for most of the day.'

'Not like your country, Captain . . . but what of the airport? Surely you need radio communication and therefore power to take off?'

Stanton's face was grim at the prospect of the pending flight. 'The airport has its own standby generator system, so we'll be away at the appointed time.'

The taxi jolted through a pot-hole. The Sudanese driver had quietly been increasing the speed to something in keeping with his profession. Suliman broke out in a cold sweat. The delicate construction of the bomb had once again shown him how very unstable the gelignite was. He reached forward and struck the driver on the shoulder. 'Slowly, you idiot,' he shouted in Arabic. 'Much more slowly.'

Stanton took a half corona from his shirt pocket and lit it. He puffed a cloud of blue smoke through the open window. 'And what do you think of the Hercules, Mr Suliman?'

The Arab's dark face, covered lightly in sweat, was fixed to the front, watching the road for more holes. He poked a finger under his eyepatch and scratched at the nagging itch.

'The aircraft,' he answered, in a flat, noncommital tone, 'will doubtless serve its intended purpose.'

They were silent for a short while, then Suliman added: 'You must forgive me if I appear to have something less than a soldier's liking for aircraft ... with you I think it is different. You after all are an airman.'

'Not so different,' Stanton replied.

'You tire of the game perhaps!'

'A perceptive answer, Mr Suliman; yes, I tire of the game.'

'And the reason for becoming involved in the first place?'

Stanton puffed on his cigar. 'I was in the Royal Air Force; when I left it seemed natural to continue. A way, one might argue, to escape the rigours and responsibilities of the real world.'

'But surely being the captain of a large aircraft carries a great deal of responsibility?'

'A different kind ... something like your battlefield, I shouldn't wonder.'

'Perhaps. And before your Air Force career, you were at an English public school?'

'Eton.'

'Ah, Eton. I only ask because I have observed you at the hotel. You seem to be the very epitome of a P.G. Wodehouse character. The archetypal English gentleman.'

'I imagine my father would disagree with you on that ... you've read Wodehouse then?'

'And Chaucer and Shakespeare, Dickens, Thackeray.' Suliman smiled with his lips. 'The worst kind of Arab, Captain ... one of the educated ones.'

The conversation continued spasmodically throughout the slow journey to the airport. By the time they arrived, Rashid Suliman had gained sufficient respect in the Englishman's eyes to put his final request.

'There is one favour I wish to ask of you, Captain?'

'Whatever I can do, Mr Suliman.'

'I am, you will understand, a Muslim. My faith, therefore, is of very great importance to me, and to this end I would wish for a few minutes alone inside the aircraft to pray. A blessing, shall we say. A prayer for Allah to watch over the long and arduous journey which lies ahead.'

Stanton smiled and thought: bloody Arabs and their never-ending prayers. 'Of course, Mr Suliman. Request granted. I'll be in the main terminal. Perhaps you will join me for coffee when your prayers are over.'

Suliman inclined his head in thanks. 'It is kind of you to offer, Captain, but perhaps it is wiser that we are not seen in each other's company . . . political repercussions, you understand.'

Both men smiled and shook hands, and under the burning glare of the sun went their separate ways.

Chance Fitzgerald sat in the cheap hotel room in the Via Santo Spirito waiting for the telephone to ring. He had come to Konrad's hotel for no other reason than it was closer than the Palace.

The hotel operator, a shrunken little man, who also served as desk clerk, porter and general factotum, had tried three times to put the Khartoum call through the International exchange. Three times they had been unable to complete the call. They were trying again.

Meanwhile, Fitzgerald had given Konrad a bundle of lire and told him to have an early lunch. He needed some time to himself.

From what Konrad had told him, it seemed certain that von Klaus and the Arab Suliman were conspiring to blow up the airplane. But why? They were getting paid after all. That very afternoon they were getting paid. And it couldn't be an insurance swindle. The aircraft was registered in the name of Relief Air and he had decided against any form of insurance for the simple reason of giving out information. And what of the Arab? He was obviously being paid two million dollars as a backhander. Nothing unusual about that; it was the way the Middle East worked. As for him coming to Milan as a one-man execution squad, Fitzgerald put that down to the greed of the German which had now seriously backfired. Which left the bomb on the aircraft. Why? It didn't make sense.

Then there was Lisa. A knife twisted inside him when he

thought of her. She would have known all along about the bomb and the two million backhander. She had been the spy in the camp from day one. And what was it Konrad had said over breakfast? 'Just before I broke into Mr von Klaus's house he left in his car with a pretty blonde lady.' The vague description he had added seemed to fit Lisa perfectly. So, she was living with her boss. Had been all along. 'You never could pick them, Chance old son, could you now?' he said with a soft irony.

It was as the faint echo of his own voice faded that he thought of his crew. Guy, Pedro and Hiram. The last real aviators the world had to offer. And if anything happened to them . . .! The words struck a discordant note somewhere deep within him. Because if anything happened to them, there was no one left. He was the last. He would be alone in an empty world full of the empty people he had never understood. His blue eyes glazed over in a thousand-yard stare as his mind reached back to his first kill in the skies of Vietnam.

In Tehran, Fazlollah Mahallati waited until the steel doors closed behind him and a second pair opened in front. Then he drove slowly into the vast compound. For the first time in his life the large fortress of the Gasr prison frightened him. He stepped out of the car and looked around. The enormous gates, the high walls and the guard towers. The strategically placed machine-gun nests. There seemed no way out. But he had to check.

The absence of any communication from Ali Abdul Rashaida in Khartoum had been a kind of warning. Something was wrong. Very wrong. Rashid had tricked him. How, he did not yet know. He would of course find out, except by then it might be too late. By then he could well be incarcerated inside the evil place he was now visiting. A prisoner awaiting execution.

He shivered at the thought and made his way to the chief guard's office. There he would locate the plans of the prison. Whatever the future, he would be prepared.

In Khartoum it was hot and windless. One more scorching

day when the runway became a shimmering silver sea and giant invisible thermals belched sickeningly skywards. Stanton joined the rest of the crew under the giant wing of the Hercules. He was feeling the pressure building up within him, scrambling his brain with a thousand unwanted thoughts. Knotting his muscles. Compressing his lips into a thin angry line. Destroying any love of flying he might still have possessed. He wiped the sweat from his forehead with an angry gesture and looked at the two figures in sweat-stained olive-green flying suits.

'Time check, Hiram.'

'1615 local.'

Stanton checked his instruction sheet. ' "Departure Khartoum 1440 GMT. Local times corresponding to this: Khartoum 1640 hours/Milano 1540 hours. Critical that accurate time check is kept. Arrange airborne time to within plus or minus 30 seconds." That's about it then.' He turned to the flight engineer. 'Load OK?'

Pedro, chest rattling noisily, coughed twice. 'The Red Cross consignment was more than we thought. Puts us overweight.'

'How much?'

'A ton.'

'A ton,' Stanton exploded. 'A bloody ton in this temperature.' He covered his eyes in exasperation. 'Why didn't you offload it?'

'We couldn't without arousing suspicion,' Pedro replied. 'According to the load sheet we are running on minimum fuel. As Mr Sigel had a copy of the load sheet documents from Chance, he therefore worked out we could take a maximum load . . . the ton overweight is the fuel we shouldn't be carrying.'

Stanton swore again and turned to Gaylord. 'What do you figure on take-off distance available, Hiram . . . enough to get this bitch off the ground?'

The American, ever calm under pressure, drawled, 'According to my reckoning it puts us between heaven and hell right about there.' He pointed to a spot at the far end of the runway.

Stanton's eyes followed the outstretched finger. His

stomach ached at the prospect of ending his life in this place. And with a dangerously overloaded aircraft the threat was very real. But then he could hardly start removing some of the pallets now; especially after what Pedro had just said. No, it had to appear to be a normal everyday airlift. He followed Gaylord into the stifling heat of the aircraft.

A few feet behind him, under the three seats at the rear of the flight deck a stopwatch ticked silently on. At 1710 local time; in forty-five minutes time it would active the detonator. The six sticks of gelignite would do the rest.

Two miles away, Rashid Suliman was once more praying to Allah. This time for power to be restored to the city. The coded telex message in his hand, ready for transmission to the Milanese bank, was at that moment more valuable than life itself. He looked at his watch. There was still time to get to the airport and stop the plane taking off. Still time to dismantle the time-bomb. Still time to rearrange the letter of credit. No. He had killed Ali Abdul. And that would mean Fazlollah would have guessed the truth . . . or at least a part of it. He swore at his own stupidity. A power failure was one eventuality he had not considered in his carefully worked out plans. Something so simple and yet something which was going to rob him of everything.

He paced impatiently up to the glass door of the bank. The street beyond was busy with traffic. His taxi was waiting to take him out to the airport to catch his airline flight to Cairo with a connection to Rome and Milan. He would have to go, of course. There was no way he could return to his own country. But without money in a new world!

Lights flickered on and the buzzing of the air-conditioning units greeted his ears in that most desperate of all moments. Allah had once again saved one of his sons.

At that same moment in Milan, Chance Fitzgerald was arriving at the Arab Bank in the Via Fulcorina. He had left Konrad Zwicky with an explicit set of instructions should he be able to get through to Khartoum by telephone.

Lisa was waiting on the pavement outside the bank. It was a cold afternoon and she was wearing the silver fox which Otto had bought for her. With the collar turned up against the biting wind. Chance had not at first recognised her. It wasn't until she called his name that he stopped.

He had promised himself he would stay in control of his emotions, even though she had cheated him. This then was nothing more than a routine business transaction. He felt his heart miss a beat.

'You're early,' was all he could think to say as their eyes met.

She gave him an embarrassed smile. He was still the most beautiful man she had ever known. An ageless Greek god who was turning her stomach to jelly. Taking away her breath.

'Yes . . . how are you?'

'Well enough, and you?'

His voice sounded bitter, she thought. Why should that be? I am the one who has been hurt. 'Fine . . . and everything went well with the flight to Khartoum?'

He wanted to say, 'You tell me, you bitch,' and 'What of this talk of a bomb on the aircraft.' But he couldn't. It was all second-hand information. Circumstantial. Words that Konrad had read in a diary in Geneva. Words which needed proof.

'Everything was OK when I left.'

'And you have the papers?'

'Papers?'

'To withdraw the money.'

'Yes.'

She glanced quickly at her watch. 'Shouldn't we be going in? They close in ten minutes.'

His face showed no emotion as he opened the door for her. Then she brushed past him and he caught the familiar fragrance of her perfume, and he knew nothing had changed. He wanted to tell her he loved her, but he still didn't know how.

The afternoon sunlight slanted harshly through the windows of the flight deck and caught the instrument panel. Squares of light jerked violently up and down and back and forth as the Hercules staggered through the bumpy air. The overweight aircraft had used every last inch of runway to become airborne, and now one minute later, and at less than five hundred feet, the crew were dry mouthed with fear as they collectively watched the instruments struggling to overcome a one-sided equation.

'Nice take-off,' Gaylord eventually said over the intercom. Stanton, face sheened with a light film of perspiration, and working hard at the controls, said grimly, 'We'll keep the pretty adjectives for later if you don't mind, old boy; right now we need to be thinking of getting rid of part of that bloody cargo. The extra weight's knocking hell out of the speed.'

'Just say the word.'

'We'll give it it ten minutes or so; need to be clear of any habitation.'

Back in the control tower of Khartoum airport, Michel Sigel – who had watched the departure of the Hercules – was preparing to leave. He had to arrange the following day's consignment of powdered milk. The telephone call, as he was half-way through the door, stopped him. The Arab controller called him back, holding out the phone.

'For you, Mr Sigel.'

For a few moments Sigel's pleasant face remained normal, as words were exchanged in hurried French. Then there was a hesitant pause in his speech and his face went deathly pale. He pushed the phone back at the Arab, his eyes full of confusion as though not fully comprehending the enormity of what he had just heard.

'We are still in radio contact with the Hercules?' he said quickly.

'Inshallah,' the Arab replied, then noticing the look of consternation on the other man's face, added, 'There is something wrong?'

'A bomb!' Sigel uttered in disbelief. 'I think there is a bomb on the aircraft.'

The Arab became alarmed. 'A bomb! That was the phone call?'

'Yes, yes,' Sigel was panicking now. 'We must try and get them back . . . they could be in great danger.'

The Arab had received his training in America and, being particularly good at his job, didn't move. He considered what his instructor had taught him. Big Red, the man with the unhurried Texas drawl who had possessed all the answers. 'When the shit hits the fan, panic first. Get that out of your system. Once it's passed, take matters one slow step at a time. No one, and I repeat, no one, wants a rattled controller . . . you read me "Khartoum"?'

The Arab, ready as he ever would be, picked up the handmike. 'November Five Nine Lima this is Khartoum, do you read, over.'

Gaylord picked up the transmission immediately. He turned to Stanton. 'Hear that, Guy, Khartoum trying to raise us.'

Stanton had heard. He now felt fear gnawing at his gut. Somebody had found out. They were being warned. Military interception would be next. Why the hell hadn't he stayed back in Norfolk? Even without money he could have survived. This way; in this stinking desert land, there wasn't a hope. Gaylord repeated the statement.

'Forget it,' Stanton snapped. 'Just bloody well forget it.'

'Why? What's the harm . . . might be some sort of message from the Iranian guy.'

'I don't give a damn. I don't want to talk to another controller until we're safely inside Iranian airspace.'

Gaylord shifted uncomfortably in his seat, then tightened his harness. It was a rough Mothah. Goddam rough. The Arab's voice filled his headset for the third time and he sensed the urgency. It was a remote, distant, niggling something. Something which belonged in his memory. Except the Arab controller's voice had prised it loose. Gaylord was positive something was wrong. He turned to Stanton who was fighting the turbulence and trying to gain more height.

'With respect, Guy, and I guess we've kicked around the world for a lot of years now, but you're just going to have to go to hell your own way . . . I'm going to find out what the man wants.'

'Touch that bloody radio and you're through,' Stanton yelled.

'At my age, pal, that's kinda what I had in mind.' He thumbed the mike button and called Khartoum.

There was a long carrier wave pause, the result of a transmit button being held down. A man searching for the right words.

'Five Nine Lima from Khartoum . . . be advised we have received unofficial report . . . that you have a bomb on board your aircraft . . . I say again . . . we have unofficial report of bomb on board your aircraft, over.'

There was a numbed silence on the flight deck as three men, who had distinctly heard the message through their headsets, sat in a state of shocked disbelief. Somewhere in those horror-filled moments Guy Stanton found his true self. It was not the bravado he had portrayed as a younger man. That had been a front. An illusion. A clever deceit he had learned from his schooldays, when a boy with an inferiority complex would be ragged unmercifully. Now he had found the steel he never knew existed.

Banking the Hercules in a long gentle turn, he said calmly, 'OK, I've got the radio . . . you get down below with Pedro and get rid of the cargo; we need to get down to something like safe landing weight. Let me know when you're in your safety harnesses and I'll lower the ramp.'

Hiram unstrapped himself and followed Pedro from the rocking flight deck. He paused long enough to pat Stanton on the shoulder. 'You manage OK?'

'The old team, Hiram . . . didn't we always say we were indestructible . . . now move your arse there's a good chap.'

Turning back to the controls he rolled the aircraft out on a heading for the airport. His watch said 1655 local time. They should be back on the ground by 1710, give or take a minute. He pressed the transmit button. 'Khartoum, this is Five Nine Lima.'

'Five Nine Lima, go ahead.'

'Roger, returning to you, estimating the field at one zero.'

'Understood Five Nine Lima. Be advised we have one jet

to roll in the next few minutes; after that, the crash trucks
will be standing by.'

'Thanks.'

'You are welcome, Captain. Allah be with you.'

Stanton blipped the transmit button twice in
acknowledgement and began to reduce power in preparation for the cargo drop. He was thinking of his wife Josey
and the green fields of England when he started to sing
Jerusalem.

In Milan, Chance and Lisa were once again outside the
bank with the large holdall in the Irishman's hand.
Eighteen million dollars in one-thousand-dollar bills.

Lisa, shivering in the cold wind, said, 'Otto has given me
new departure plans.'

'Which are?'

'The money is to be taken to Lake Maggiore.'

'The same idea I had in mind.'

'Yes, but Otto has arranged a plane. It will be waiting.'

'A plane!' Fitzgerald echoed in surprise.

'A float plane he said.'

'Whereabouts on the lake?'

'Sesto Calende.'

'And we're leaving now?'

'No . . . not now,' Lisa stumbled, trying to remember her
instructions from Otto. 'We are to leave Milan together at
five-thirty in the morning.'

Fitzgerald made no reply. He was studying her face,
trying to understand her reasons for cheating him. She
shuffled her feet and found the words she had known
would be difficult. 'In the meantime I will stay with you at
the Palace Hotel.'

Fitzgerald's eyes flashed angrily. 'He doesn't trust me
with the money, is that it?'

Lisa felt her face flush. 'No . . . it's . . .' her voice faltered.

'Let's get one thing straight, Miss Wendell-Holmes. I was
hired to do a job. And that job has been carried out to the
best of my ability. My brief was to get the money across the
border into Switzerland, to Geneva. Except now you tell
me that part of the deal has been changed. Fine, that's OK

with me . . . but as for you and I staying together until the morning, forget it. One, I don't like being mistrusted, and two, I don't want to be involved with von Klaus's mistress.'

'Mistress!' she shrieked. 'And just what is that supposed to mean?'

'It means that secretaries who live with their boss and wear expensive fur coats . . .' He didn't get any further. Her hand lashed out and caught him a stinging blow across the cheek. His eyes had lost none of their anger when he said, 'Don't worry about the money. I'll take care of it.'

'Yes, perhaps that's best; I don't particularly want to be with you either.'

'You have a car?'

'Yes.'

'OK, I'll meet you at the Cimitero Monumentale on the edge of the city at five a.m. It's about forty kilometres from there to Sesto Calende.'

'Why so early?'

'More snow is forecast. I have the feeling that the roads may be difficult.'

'Wouldn't it be easier to meet at the hotel?'

'No.'

'Why?'

'One, I won't be staying at that hotel, and two . . . just let's say I don't trust you.'

'Bastard.'

'I've been called worse,' he said quietly. He turned on his heel and walked quickly away down the street.

In the Hercules, Stanton was still singing. The airport was in sight now, the runway clear. Gaylord and Pedro were back on the flight deck, hurriedly fastening their seat harnesses. Stanton avoided their eyes, however. He didn't want to see fear. Not now. Not now he was convinced that everything was going to be all right. Three minutes to touch down. Three short minutes.

He called for the pre-landing checks. The aircraft jarred violently in the low level turbulence. His sweating palms slipped on the wheel. He wiped them one at a time on his trousers. The flight deck vibrated softly to the sound of the gear going down. He retrimmed slightly and was aware that the jolts from the turbulent air were now less abrupt. Less violent. A result of the speed falling back to 140 knots.

'Three greens you have ... gear down and locked,' Gaylord confirmed.

Stanton said: 'Roger, flaps fifty per cent.'

'On the way.'

The aircraft was on final approach, three miles out when Stanton, eyes fixed straight ahead, said, 'Hiram, Pedro, I want you off the flight deck now. Get down the back and hold on ... once the wheels hit, lower the ramp ... when you think you can make it, jump.'

There was a brief silence, then Gaylord replied, 'When I said go to hell your own way, it was just a figure of speech ... what I mean to say is I'd rather stay topside ... I'm sure that goes for Pedro too.'

'I don't give a damn, you sentimental bloody Yank, just do as you're told ... now move.' Two hands patted him on the shoulder and were gone.

Seven minutes away to the north, in a Boeing 727 of Egyptair, Rashid Suliman accepted the tea from the steward, swallowed another painkiller and consulted his watch. Nine and a half minutes past five. He smiled grimly to himself. It was almost all over. In thirty seconds the Hercules would be blown from the skies. The Koran even had a line for the misguided crew. A fitting epitaph. 'Are they waiting for the hour of doom to overtake them unawares?' It was a just way for unbelievers he decided. For would they not all eventually abide in hell, and drink of the scalding water which would tear their bowels apart?

He sat back in his seat and considered his next problem: smuggling the Walther PPK through the Italian customs at Rome airport. The Walther with the pretty pearl inlaid handle. The gun which would kill Fitzgerald.

The touchdown of the Hercules at Khartoum airport was perhaps the smoothest that Stanton had ever made. As the aircraft slowed, he felt the effect of the ramp being lowered. They had made it. They had struck lucky. And he was going home. To hell with the money. To hell with flying. He was going back to his wife.

From the control tower, Michel Sigel let out an old and tired breath and patted the Arab controller on the back. Out on the runway, fire trucks were following the slowing Hercules. He watched as the ramp lowered and two figures jumped and rolled across the tarmac. They were making sure, that was good.

What happened next was totally bizarre. The entire cockpit area of the aircraft suddenly disintegrated in slow motion. The hollow thump of explosion followed almost immediately. Then the machine slewed sharply from the runway. Through his tears he watched the flames consume the stricken hulk.

'Suliman, you bastard!' Fitzgerald exploded, letting the phone drop to the floor. 'You rotten heartless bastard.' When no more words came he sank wearily into a chair.

A confused Konrad Zwicky, who had heard some of the conversation, said: 'So it was the Arab!'

'That seems the way of things, Konrad. Yes, it was the Arab.'

'I am sorry. For the man who was killed I am sorry.'

'Yes, well you did your best, and I know two men who would thank you for that.'

'And now! What happens now?'

Fitzgerald looked up, and for the first time since he had known him Zwicky saw anger in the blue eyes. Not the flaming anger of the drunk looking for a fight. This was controlled. Below the surface. It was the kind of anger you avoided, if you possibly could.

'Now, Konrad! I'll tell you what happens now. The Arab is on a flight to Cairo. From there he'll keep heading north.' Fitzgerald climbed to his feet, went to the window and pulled back a curtain. It smelled of dust, much like the rest of the room. Beyond the window pane, the sky was darkening with heavy snow clouds. Below, the streets were practically deserted. He turned back to the room, his eyes fixing themselves on the holdall lying at the foot of the bed. 'You see he's coming for that . . . the money.'

'That is all money?'

Fitzgerald dredged up a tired smile. 'Eighteen million dollars, Konrad; one of those small fortunes men always dream about.'

'Small!' Konrad expostulated. 'I think not small. I think big. Very big.'

The Irishman made no reply. His eyes had gone back to the sky and the dark snow clouds. It was another unwanted memory which would remain forever. The return to the dingy hotel from the bank, and finding Konrad alone in that desolate room of broken-down furniture. The news that he had managed to pass the bomb warning to Khartoum airport. The rapid placing of another phone call. Getting through to air traffic control and hearing Hiram's voice . . . old and broken. And how the flight had turned back. How Stanton had played the bloody general; barking out orders in flawless English one minute, singing hymns the next. The landing, and Stanton still the bloody hero, ordering his crew to jump clear. The explosion. The fire. The death of an aviator. Sure he carried the imperial echoes in his sometimes overbearing voice. Sure he belonged to the silver spoon brigade. But for all that he had been the best. Then, after the explosion and the fire, how suspicions had turned to the Arab, Rashid Suliman. A quick check by Gaylord with the airline officials had confirmed the man with the eyepatch had caught the flight to Cairo.

Now feeling as low as he could ever remember, Fitzgerald went over to the holdall and emptied the contents on the bed. He counted out two hundred thousand dollars and handed it to Konrad Zwicky. 'There you are, son, enough money to set you up for life . . . if you use it wisely.'

Zwicky stared at it with disbelief. 'But what is all this, Mr Fitzgerald . . . this is too much.'

'That is what I paid the crew, Konrad. As you saved two of their lives I just put you on the payroll.'

Zwicky didn't move. 'But what of the Arab who is coming for the money . . . he is also coming to kill you. This is not so?'

'Perhaps.'

'But surely,' reasoned Zwicky, 'two pairs of eyes would

be better than one . . . I mean, how do you know when and where he will appear?'

Fitzgerald sat down wearily on the bed. He needed a few hours' sleep before he faced the remainder of the mission. And of course Zwicky was right, two pairs of eyes would be better than one, but he had no right to expect the young man to die for him. If he had been another merc, sure. But he was an untrained civilian. He wouldn't stand a chance.

'Because it's my job to know, Konrad,' he answered at last, 'and if it will put your mind at rest, von Klaus is coming in to Sesto Calende by float plane at first light tomorrow morning . . . the Arab, Rashid Suliman will no doubt be waiting.' He managed a weak smile. 'Now, take your money and go and live your life.'

He was half-way through the door when Fitzgerald called his name.

'Yes.'

'Good luck.'

The Swiss smiled and was gone. Fitzgerald lay back on the pillows and closed his eyes. And wished he was young. And back at the beginning.

28 November

Milan, Italy

FRIDAY 0530 HOURS

THE SNOW HAD returned in the night, bringing an arctic cold to the province of Lombardy. Chance Fitzgerald had arrived at the Cimitero Monumentale at four-thirty, half an hour earlier than the time he had agreed with Lisa. And now she was thirty minutes late. Thirty minutes he hadn't planned to spend in the bitterly cold night air. He looked around him, his eyes picking out the shapes of the tombs: macabre bronze depicting the grim reaper; then a pyramid; a bowing angel; and a life-sized kneeling soldier, hand frozen to his rifle. It was a folly. A huge glorious folly. Put up by the rich to honour their dead. It was also spine chillingly eerie.

It was some minutes later when car headlights scythed brightly across the high wrought-iron gate which formed the entrance to the cemetery. The engine died with the lights. Fitzgerald remained motionless, his ears pricked. A car door slammed, its sound muffled by the snow. There was no noise from a second door. But then if his hunch was right he had hardly expected it. The Arab was too smart. A trained soldier. He would know all the tricks. Still watching the entrance, Fitzgerald side-stepped towards the statue of the kneeling soldier. He had picked the spot purposely. Melodramatic perhaps. But then they were all soldiers of fortune in one way or another.

The flashlight was in his hand as she appeared at last, a dark shape moving slowly through the falling snow. And there was someone with her. He snicked the light on and off. The shapes came towards him. He transferred the flashlight to his pocket and felt his fingers close on the butt of the 9mm Llama pistol. It had been one of those last minute things. The owner of the sleazy little hotel where Konrad had been saying, quite happy to find the gun for a price. Fitzgerald took it slowly from his pocket.

They stopped about twenty feet away and he heard the distinct sound of a gun being cocked. 'Not a part of the plan, Miss Wendell-Holmes,' he said softly to himself, as she started to move forward.

Suddenly the Arab grabbed her and pulled her back on to him. Fitzgerald heard Lisa wince in pain. She said something he didn't catch before crying out again. He started to move forward when the Arab called out.

'Stand quite still, Mr Fitzgerald, and do exactly as I say.' Fitzgerald froze in his tracks. 'Now put the money on the ground and move ten paces back.'

'And if I don't?'

'I will kill the woman.'

'Chance,' Lisa cried, 'don't listen, take the money and get away.'

'Do not heed the woman, Fitzgerald,' Suliman shouted. 'Just obey my orders.'

'And then what? You'll let us go free . . . is that it?'

'If you wish.'

'The same sort of promise you made to my crew before you blew up the plane and killed one of them, is that it?'

There was a ringing silence. 'I do not understand what you are saying.'

'The Hercules returned to Khartoum; we found out that you'd planted a bomb on board, that's what I'm saying.'

Suliman said, 'I must congratulate you, Mr Fitzgerald, it appears you are a very thorough man. However, that is now of no importance. What is, is the money.'

'And Lisa . . . did she know of this?'

'No. She, like you and your crew were just simple pawns in the game . . . now the money, or the woman dies.'

Fitzgerald placed the bag on the ground and moved slowly back. His unblinking eyes watched Lisa move forward and pick it up. And all the time she was between him and the Arab. As she stepped slowly backwards Fitzgerald flung himself sideways, seeking cover behind the kneeling soldier. And then a gun started firing. Rapid shots. Bullets seemed to ricochet from everywhere, booming back and forth through the monuments. Fitzgerald lay absolutely motionless, as if he were dead. He was planning to make a move when Suliman's voice rang nervously out.

'I am leaving now, Fitzgerald. It would be unwise of you to try and follow . . . remember I still have the woman.'

'A warning before you leave, Suliman.'

There was a brief silence, for Fitzgerald had spoken in Farsi. Suliman, surprised to hear the familiar tongue so far from his homeland, called back in the same language: 'You are a man of many surprises, Fitzgerald . . . and what is this warning?'

'Harm one hair on her head and I will kill you.' There had been no anger in the voice. No emotion. It had been just a tired, resigned statement of fact. In that passing moment Rashid Suliman knew he had met his match.

Minutes later Lisa Windell-Holmes was driving at gunpoint towards Sesto Calende. Her tear-filled eyes were fixed on the snow-drifted road ahead. It was slippery. Dangerous. Suliman reached down and switched on the radio and found a station playing music; he grunted and turned it off just as quickly.

Lisa tried to ignore the man at her side. He had arrived at Milan's Linate airport wearing dark glasses and using a white stick. The disguise, he had told her, had been used in Rome to clear customs, to enable him to smuggle a large amount of dollars into the country. His reasoning, that the Italian officials took pity on disabled people, had been sound. There had been no customs search. The further use of the disguise at Milan airport was nothing more than a continuation. Customs at one airport would sometimes tip off their colleagues at other airports, asking them to watch out for certain individuals.

Except it had all been a lie. He had obviously smuggled a gun into the country. The same gun he had planned to kill Chance with. And then the discovery that Suliman had blown up the Hercules. Something that he must have planned with Otto von Klaus. And how she and Chance had both been used. She sniffled and bit her lip and realised she still loved him. Despite what Maxine had told her, she still loved him.

Suliman reached into his pocket and extracted two painkillers from a plastic bottle. The left shoulder was hurting again. He was feeling ill. His eye glanced quickly out at the swathe of snow and ice trapped in the car's lights. He shivered and for one of the few times in his life wished he was back in the burning desert.

They arrived at the small harbour at Sesto Calende a few minutes after seven o'clock. In the false dawn light the snow was turning to sleet, swirling coldly around the small boats lying at anchor in the grey waters. There was no sign of the float plane.

Suliman wiped condensation from the inside of the passenger window and peered aross the lake. They had parked at the end of the small pier near some large packing crates. With water on three sides and a clear view of the way they had driven in, the position offered the best lookout.

'You said just now that Otto would be here,' he said impatiently.

Lisa wound down her window, listening intenty for an aircraft engine. The visibility looked bad. She remembered Chance talking about the difficulties of trying to land in bad weather. 'That's what he told me . . . perhaps they cannot see to land.'

Suliman shivered as the icy morning air seeped into the car. 'Shut the window,' he ordered. 'It is too cold.'

Lisa raised a hand, gesturing for silence. Suliman quickly wound down his window and poked his head out moving it to and fro like a radar scanner searching for a blip of sound in the silence. The motion was a practised one, used at night in the battlefield to detect Iraqi commandos who would sneak into the Iranian lines, cut a throat or two, and silently return to their own side. His head stopped suddenly. He had it. A faint engine note, growing closer by the second. He looked up, there was nothing but dark wet snow clouds. They seemed to be touching the lake. Could the pilot make it in this?

As if in answer, the engine note changed suddenly. The pilot had throttled back. For a moment it seemed as if the engine had stopped. Suliman's eye registered a brief moment of concern. Then it was back. A low burbling sound. It came lower and lower. Suliman watched nervously. It was impossible. How could the pilot see? The engine sound drifted dangerously close and Suliman detected a faint whistling sound. Airflow he guessed. He saw the floats first. Going away from him. Away from the small boats at anchor. Then the red fuselage and the high wings came into view. The plane rocked down towards the water and with distance seemed to dissolve amidst the sleet and water smoke.

Lisa was half-way out the door when Suliman pulled her back. 'Wait,' he snapped harshly.

'Why . . . they've landed . . . Otto's instructions were to be waiting at the end of the pontoon . . .'

'We wait,' Suliman repeated, jabbing his captive unnecessarily in the side with the barrel of his Walther.

'We make sure it is Otto first. If it is not we drive away quickly . . . you understand?' Lisa nodded nervously.

The sound of the aircraft's engine drifted back to them. And then the plane itself emerged through the drifting curtain of sleet. The engine stopped and the machine coasted towards the end of the bobbing pontoon. The pilot's door opened and Suliman watched as a small figure climbed nimbly down on to the awash float. Then the pilot was on the pontoon tying up the aircraft. Suliman watched intently as the figure, no more than a hundred metres away, turned to the open door. He was talking to someone. The bulky figure of Otto von Klaus appeared next, climbing unsteadily down on to the aircraft's float. The plane rocked as the pilot helped the German up on to the pontoon.

'Good,' Suliman sighed with relief. 'Good. Now we go. You bring the money.' He climbed out of the car and waited for Lisa to retrieve the holdall from the rear seat. His left eye did a nervous sweep of the harbour. It was still deserted. He drew in his breath, sharp with excitement. He had done it. He had succeeded. He, Rashid Suliman, was at last a rich man. True, the Koran said 'The life to come holds a richer prize for you than this present one', but surely Allah would turn a blind eye to one of his beloved sons tasting the fruit a little earlier.

Otto von Klaus was nearing the end of the pontoon by this time. 'Quickly, Rashid,' he called. 'We must go quickly.'

'And what of her?' the Arab replied.

The overweight von Klaus, panting with the exertion of running down the pontoon, said, 'We take her with us.'

Before Lisa could give vent to her anger at such a betrayal, a thin voice rang out. 'Do not move, Mr von Klaus, or I will kill you.'

The German's face drained white with fear. His eyes turned to the packing crates. 'Who is that?'

'Konrad Zwicky, Mr von Klaus, and your next instruction is to tell the Arab to remain quite still. Should he fail to do so will mean that you die one second after he moves.'

Von Klaus, shaking with fright, turned to Suliman. 'Stay very still,' he pleaded. 'Very, very still.' His eyes went back to the packing crates. 'Tell me what you want?' he asked.

'The truth about my sister,' Zwicky said, watching the fat German from his hiding place.

'Your sister . . . I do not understand.'

Zwicky fingered the Browning automatic and felt the awesome sense of power it gave him. The previous evening in Milan, after Fitzgerald had paid him off and he was walking the streets a rich man, his thoughts had returned to his sister. He had found a second-hand gun shop and purchased the automatic for a mere three hundred dollars. Now he was set to avenge Mariella's death.

'My sister from the Grande Rue in Geneva, Mr von Klaus. The lady you visited regularly.'

Von Klaus tried desperately to fob Zwicky off. 'I think you are making a mistake. I do not know of your sister.'

'I think you are lying,' Zwicky said impatiently. 'I also think you killed her.'

'Killed her!'

'You thought she was blackmailing you for one million dollars . . . so you killed her . . .'

Von Klaus was panicking now. The man had obviously found out. His eyes darted from side to side. There was nowhere to hide. No means of escape. He looked towards Suliman. The Arab was edging his way slowly towards the back of the car. Nearer to the voice. He motioned with his head. Von Klaus understood. Keep talking.

He coughed and said, 'You keep saying "think" . . . you *think* I am lying . . . you *think* I killed your sister. And you are prepared to shoot me for that?' He gave a nervous laugh. 'As I told you, Mr Zwicky, I do not know your sister Marie.'

There was a tense silence followed by the sound of a gun being cocked. 'That was all I was waiting for, Mr von Klaus. You see I never told you her name. And even if I had I would have called her Mariella. She never shortened the name . . . so it seemed strange to me that she would sign a suicide note Marie and not Mariella . . . but you always called her Marie didn't you?'

'A mistake,' von Klaus pleaded in desperation. 'It was a mistake . . .'

Zwicky stepped quickly out into a small space between the crates. The pistol in his hand was already at the aim. He was too late by a fraction of a second. Suliman picked that exact moment to dive and roll across the path between the two men. As he rolled he fired. One shot. One perfect shot. Konrad Zwicky was flung back amidst the crates. The soft-nosed bullet struck one inch above the left eye, taking the top of his skull with it.

Suliman was on his feet instantly. He ran back to Lisa and pushed her roughly forward towards the trembling von Klaus. 'We had better move very quickly, the shots will bring people.'

'That they did, Suliman . . . that they did.'

Suliman felt his blood run ice cold as he spun towards the quiet commanding voice. Fitzgerald, who had appeared through the sleet totally unnoticed, now had everyone's attention. He stood motionless, his face a mask of controlled anger. The gun kicked at his side. Suliman reeled back under the onslaught of bullets, his body eventually toppling over the quay into the water.

Von Klaus had by now overcome some of his fear and using Lisa as a shield was slowly backing up the pontoon. In his hand was the Smith and Wesson he had threatened Marie with. The only difference being this time it was loaded.

'Stay there, Fitzgerald,' he yelled. 'Do not try and follow.'

Fitzgerald's eyes moved past the German. He was watching the pilot climbing up into the Cessna's cockpit. He had cast off. 'Looks like you'll be staying with me, von Klaus . . . your pilot's running out on you.'

The German turned as the propeller turned once then twice. The engine coughed and smoke belched from the exhaust. Then it died. Von Klaus screamed, 'Wait . . . wait.'

'There was no mention of guns, Mr von Klaus . . . you answer to the police yourself . . . it is nothing to do with me.' The pilot pulled his door shut and tried the starter again.

Von Klaus raised his gun and fired off three shots. The pilot slumped across the controls. 'Now, Fitzgerald, throw away your gun and get down here . . . hurry.' He pressed the smoking barrel of the Smith and Wesson against Lisa's temple, as if to emphasise his impatience.

Fitzgerald tossed the Llama into the water and moved down the pontoon. 'You'll never get away with it, von Klaus, people are gathering already . . . next it will be the police.' He looked into Lisa's tear-stained face then. Black mascara lined her cheeks. He gave her a little smile. 'You OK?' he said softly. She nodded, her eyes full of hope.

Von Klaus noticed for the first time a small knot of people gathering at the far end of the stone pier. 'You will do well to hurry then, because you are flying me out.'

'In that?'

'Yes . . . in that.'

'One problem . . . I don't fly seaplanes.'

The German waved the gun impatiently. 'Then you will have to learn quickly, Fitzgerald . . . now move.'

Having pulled the dead pilot down from the ten-foot-high

cockpit, Fitzgerald looked around the unfamiliar instrument panel, searching for switches and levers which would give him some idea how to fly the machine. There was a label on the co-pilot's side which read Cessna 185. A blind flying panel consisting of the usual airspeed indicator, artificial horizon, turn and slip, directional gyro, vertical speed indicator, altimeter. The straightforward set of engine instruments. Throttle, prop control, mixture. His eyes went back to the engine instruments; they were still indicating some residual temperature. Hot start! How the hell did you do a hot start on one of these toy airplanes? Prop control fully forward. Throttle half-way. Mixture lean. He engaged the starter. The prop clunked round once, twice, three times . . . nothing.

Von Klaus prodded him from the seat directly behind. 'Quickly,' he yelled. 'Quickly, the police . . .'

Fitzgerald looked out and saw two armed policemen running towards the pontoon. His hands went back to the controls. His eyes and brain locked in mental gymnastics. Then he saw it. Fuel boost pump. He pushed the throttle and mixture fully in and blipped the switch. Looking further across, a needle indicated fuel flow. He knocked off the pump, set the throttle at half and pulled the mixture to lean. Then he engaged the starter. The engine coughed, spluttered and belched grey smoke . . . and fired. He reduced the throttle and advanced the mixture simultaneously. The engine caught, its 300 horsepower settling down to a healthy burble.

The two policemen were less than fifty metres away, running down the pontoon, when Fitzgerald gunned the engine and sent the Cessna surging out into the lake.

Now he was faced with the second problem. Taking off from water. They were mushing along in a nose high attitude at forty miles per hour, water crashing over the windshield. He reduced power to get a clearer view. As far as he could tell in the driving sleet it was clear. As far as he could tell! That was a dangerous line for a pilot to adopt. It was an accident waiting to happen. He eased the throttle in, at the same time scouring his memory for some long-forgotten flying lore.

It came back in a jumble of words and phrases, a result of once doing a ten-hour conversion to float planes – except that had been twenty years ago. 'You don't have to take off into wind with a seaplane; you can take off any way you like – providing you've got enough water . . . If the lake is too small go round in circles to build up speed; when you think you've got enough straighten it up and take off . . . Glassy water take off, lift one float then the other . . . If you're tail heavy the plane will mush along in a nose high attitude . . . When you get to about forty mph pump the elevator back and forth to get the airplane on the step; after that, let speed increase to take-off speed.'

Fitzgerald's lips were compressed in a tight thin line as he advanced the throttle even further forward. Water was cascading over the windshield at an alarming rate as he glanced down at the airspeed indicator. Forty-five mph. Gingerly he began to pump the control column back and forth. Nothing happened. He reached out with his right hand and pushed the throttle all the way in. Then he began to pump again. The tail lifted and the speed began to increase. Fifty . . . sixty . . . seventy . . . seventy-five. At eighty he gently pulled back, trying to unstick the machine from the water. It didn't want to fly. He pulled again, harder this time. Nothing. He looked out of the windshield and through a split-second break in the crashing spray saw a shoreline looming up . . . Before that, however, were two small boats. He was heading straight for them. Out of desperation he finally rocked the elevator once more and pulled the control column hard back. The cockpit floor slanted sharply and the float plane leapt into the air clearing the masts of the two small boats by inches.

Fitzgerald gave a small sigh of relief. Now it was just an airplane. And as any aviator will tell you they all behave the same up there. He turned the plane on to a northerly course, levelling off at a hundred feet. He had to stay visual with the water until he had his bearings. To climb into cloud with high ground on either shoreline was nothing short of lethal.

'Where do you want to go?' he shouted back to the German.

'There's a small lake near to Lukmanier, I have a car waiting.'

'Where the hell's that?'

'The pilot had a map . . . he put it at the side of the seat.'

Fitzgerald found it, neatly stowed in a map pocket. It was a Hallwag motorists' map. Large scale. And the lake near Lukmanier was circled in blue ink. Sleet rattled against the airframe and the lake below disappeared. Fitzgerald reduced power and lowered the nose. Now they were flying blind. Low level blind. And shortly his northerly heading would run out of lake. The altimeter was wavering hopelessly between zero and fifty feet when the streaking white caps came back. Looking across to the left shoreline he saw a small town and the lake seeming to extend to the west. He quickly checked the map. Stresa. It had to be Stresa. He eased the plane a few degrees right. In about five minutes they would cross the Swiss border near Brissago.

Turning back to von Klaus, he said, 'I don't think we'll make this lake of yours.'

'We will make it . . . remember I have the gun.'

'The visibility is too bad, von Klaus, that's what I'm saying. And once we come off the lake we'll be flying between mountains.'

'So . . . so what is the problem?' von Klaus said in a strained voice. 'The other man Grimaldi could do it, why not you?'

'Local knowledge . . . the guy had probably been flying through those same mountains for twenty years.'

'But you have a map,' von Klaus argued.

'At two miles a minute in practically zero visibility maps are pretty useless . . . we'll have to put down on this lake.'

Von Klaus's face contorted in anger. 'You will keep flying,' he snarled. 'I will tell you when to put down.'

'Or you'll shoot me is that it!'

'No . . . her.'

Lisa who had been silent throughout the short flight said, 'Don't listen, Chance, he won't shoot.'

The German half turned in his seat and prodded her with the gun barrel. 'Silence.'

'Or perhaps he will . . . he did kill the woman in the Grande Rue after all.'

'A lie,' blazed von Klaus. 'The man was lying.'

'Why would he lie about such a thing?' Lisa chided. 'Wasn't she blackmailing you for a million dollars?'

Von Klaus ignored the words and turned his attention back to Fitzgerald. 'Where are we now?'

'About ten kilometres to the Swiss border.'

'Except it wasn't her at all,' Lisa was saying. 'I sent you the letters.'

Von Klaus turned and stared at her. His face was numb with terror and shock. 'You . . . you sent me the letters . . . you . . . not Marie!'

'After all the promises . . . the ones you made to Philip when he was alive . . . and then to me. You didn't think I intended to stay poor for the rest of my life . . . did you?'

'You . . .' repeated von Klaus, as the reality of what he had done to Marie sank in. 'You did that . . .'

He fell upon her, his fists beating savagely down. There was a muffled explosion from the gun before Fitzgerald, releasing the controls, had him by the neck. He was pulling him off Lisa when the plane banked viciously to the right, catapulting the German across the back of the co-pilot's seat. It snapped under his weight and his head crashed down on the door handle. The door flew open sufficiently to cause the aircraft to roll more violently to the right. Fitzgerald let the German go and grabbed the controls.

The waves were filling the windshield at an alarming rate as he pulled the aircraft out of the dive. Then the mountainous shoreline near Maccagno, reaching up into the low overcast sky, came rushing at them. The deafening roar of engine and slipstream filled the cabin as Fitzgerald hauled the machine hard to the left, back towards the centre of the lake.

The door of the airplane was still partially open as von Klaus reached back for support. Lisa, sensing her chance, lifted the holdall with the money and hurled it at the German's head. Von Klaus, sensing what was happening, twisted sideways. The holdall, weighing more than twenty kilos, crashed down and lodged for a moment in the open doorway.

Von Klaus flung his arm out in desperation as the bag slipped further into the slipstream. He was holding it now. The fingers of his left hand clamped firmly around one of the leather handles.

For Fitzgerald, the open door was causing greater problems. The extra drag was constantly pulling the aircraft right. He needed both hands to keep the controls hard to the left . . . even then he sensed he was losing the battle. He reached out quickly with his right hand in a vain attempt to close the door, but the German was in the way. His upper body already stretching out into the sub-zero gale.

The bag was becoming too heavy for von Klaus, his frozen hand incapable of holding the leather handle any longer. He pushed himself further out of the door, intending to change hands. His clothes billowed for a moment in the icy slipstream, then he was gone.

Fitzgerald opened his storm window and tried to reach across to pull the door closed. 'Lisa . . .' She reached forward and pulled. The door buffeted for a moment, then closed. Fitzgerald slumped back in his seat and massaged his aching arm. Close . . . too close, he told himself. He turned towards Lisa, and patted the broken right seat.

'Come up here.' She gave a little smile and he noticed her face was grey. She struggled into the seat, leaning against him for support. 'You OK?'

'Yes,' she said. 'I'm fine now . . .'

Fitzgerald banked the Cessna back towards Italy. Back down the lake. Sleet was hammering at the fuselage and the visibility was no better, but suddenly he felt happy. It was all over.

Lisa said, 'I'm sorry about the money . . . I should have thrown something else at him.'

'It's all right, we'll make out.'

'We will?'

'How does a million sound?'

'A million?'

'The Cimitero Monumentale in Milan . . . I stashed my share in the tomb of the kneeling soldier.'

Lisa laughed, then coughed. Fitzgerald looked at her with concern. She was sweating. 'You feeling airsick?'

'A little.'

'I'll land soon, then you'll be OK.'

'Yes . . . then I'll be OK.'

He reached out and took her hand. 'It's nice to be back.'

'Do you mean that?'

'Of course, my precious girl, why do you ask?'

'Oh nothing,' she was thinking of Maxine, but that didn't matter now. She was with the man she loved. 'Chance.'

'Yes.'

'Would you kiss me.'

'Here and now?'

She nodded. 'Here and now.'

'We might crash,' he said lightly.

'You're too good a pilot for that.'

Wedging his knees beneath the control column to keep the aircraft straight and level, he placed his right arm behind her for support, and kissed her gently on the lips. They tasted of salt and were very cold. He pulled her face into the hollow of his shoulder and found the words he had never been able to say. 'I love you, Lisa . . . I love you, I love you, I love you.'

As he eased his face away, he realised something was wrong. Her eyes were closed. And she was quite still. He withdrew his right arm from behind her back and found his hand covered in blood. The shot. The one shot from von Klaus's gun. He laid her head gently back on the broken seat and with the practised fingers of a mercenary checked her pulse. She was dead. He reached down one last time and kissed her softly on the lips.

His face was dark and angry when he returned to the controls. But he was old enough and world weary enough to know that it would pass. And that was the greatest sadness of all.

EPILOGUE

ALICE FITZGERALD RECEIVED her inheritance from her father on Christmas Eve. Philippe Dupres the Jersey accountant had been given the task of setting up a trust to the value of nine hundred thousand US dollars. Alice would inherit the money on her twenty-first birthday.

Maxine Audley, aggrieved at the knowledge of her daughter's inheritance, ran away with a rich Argentinian polo player early in the new year, leaving her daughter to be raised by her parents. Her father cut her off without a penny.

Rashid Suliman's plans to be a rich man were still having far-reaching repercussions in February of the following year. On 22 February the *International Herald Tribune* ran the following story with the byline John Kifner:

> Tehran Radio identified on Friday the thirty-seven Iranian officials killed when two Iraqi warplanes shot down an Iranian civilian aircraft in south-western Iran on Thursday, Reuters reported from Tehran. The dead included Fazlollah Mahallati, representative of the nation's leader, Ayatollah Ruhollah Khomeini, in the Islamic Revolutionary Guards Corps and eight parliamentary deputies including Hassan Shah-Cheraghi, head of the Kayhan group of newspapers.
>
> Iraq denied downing the plane.

Pedro died in the spring, his lungs finally giving up the long and strenuous battle. Hiram P. Gaylord gave him a good send-off.

As for Hiram himself, he returned at last to his home town of Vacherie. There he met up with his old sweetheart. She had been a widow for five years. They now take walks by the vast and majestic Mississippi, remembering their childhood long ago. They plan to marry in the fall.

Lisa Wendell-Holmes was buried in a small Catholic cemetery in Stresa, Italy. It is the most beautiful of places and looks out on Lake Maggiore. The priest who officiated at the funeral was an ageing Irishman by the name of Michael Cavanagh. For his troubles he received one hundred thousand dollars for the mother church.

Chance Fitzgerald remains unchanged, a slight figure with blond hair and the most startling blue eyes. And his voice still has the most magical of sounds. After Lisa's death he returned to Nicaragua to fly a vintage DC3 for the Contra rebels. As the supply drop aircraft is unarmed his life expectancy can almost be measured in hours.